JASON ANSPACH

NICK COLE

KTF

PART I

SEASON 2

BOOK 6

GALAXY'S EDGE

ISBN: 978-1-949731-77-4

Edited by David Gatewood
Published by Galaxy's Edge Press

Cover Art: Tommaso Renieri
Cover Design: M.S. Corely
Formatting: Kevin G. Summers

Website: www.GalaxysEdge.us
Facebook: facebook.com/atgalaxysedge
Newsletter (get a free short story): www.InTheLegion.com

EXPLORE ALL PRODUCTS AT

GALAXYSEDGE.US

WHO'S WHO...

What follows is a summary of some of the characters found in this book, and their stories up to this point. More characters will appear in this volume but listing them up front would kind of spoil things. If you find yourself lost, consider joining one of the Galaxy's Edge fan groups listed at the end of the book. There is no shortage of fellow leejes who love talking about the story of Galaxy's Edge (and speculating and theorizing about what comes next).

Aeson Ford – See Aeson Keel.

Aeson Keel – See Wraith.

Andien Broxin – A Nether Ops operative who worked closely with Legion Dark Ops (*Kill Team*). Broxin's military career began as a Republic Marine (*Forget Nothing*). She was selected for an experimental Legion training program (*Forget Nothing II*). Presumed dead at the hands of the Cybar (*Message for the Dead*), Broxin was saved by a dissenting Cybar named Praxus and is currently working with him.

Archimedes – The head of a peculiar Savage mini-hulk that gathers lost star-farers and pits them against combat simulations. Archimedes made a deal with an ad hoc alliance composed of Prisma, Ravi, and members of Goth Sullus's elite strike force, allowing them to leave the ship if they would restore control to Archimedes. He awaits a final solution to a high-value scenario... one that requires the help of Wraith.

Bear – Dark Ops captain who oversees Kill Team Victory. No longer regularly involved in direct action due to injuries suffered in the Second Battle for Utopion (*Retribution*), he fills the role once held by Major Owens. Has been overseeing the potential role of Nether Ops in supplying chemical weapons on the planet Kima.

Bombassa – Senior NCO for Kill Team Victory. Former legionnaire who sided with Goth Sullus's Black Fleet (*Attack of Shadows*). Following Article Nineteen, was sent undercover as "Lashley" to determine Nilo's motivations and capabilities (*Takeover*).

Bubbles – A Malinois-like dog with peculiar telekinetic and psychic capabilities. Forms an extremely strong bond with his handlers but has an unfortunate record of seeing them killed in action. Last seen attempting to save Sergeant Major MakRaven.

Casper – Also known as Admiral Sulla, Casper Sullivan, and a host of other aliases. A friend of Tyrus Rechs and Reina who shared their experiences at the hands of the Savages and was given exceptionally long life (*Imperator*). Sulla was the mastermind behind the galaxy's war against the Savages, convincing Tyrus Rechs to found the Legion and bringing about the unification of the galaxy through the forming of the Republic (*Savage Wars* trilogy). Casper's thirst for a power that could fully defeat the enemies of humanity led him to study under Urmo and ultimately to his betrayal and murder of Tyrus Rechs as Goth Sullus (*Imperator, Galactic Outlaws*).

Crometheus – A Savage marine who lived in a simulation on the edge of madness (*Gods & Legionnaires*). Part of the Savage tribe known as the Uplifted, he was presumed deactivated. After recalling the truth of his past, he has fled the arcade that was his prison and is currently on the run from Maestro.

Crash – See KRS-88.

Cybar – A species of mechanical, non-biological life. Created by unknown causes in one of the Temples of the Ancients (*Legacies*). Discovered by the Republic and recovered by Kill Team Ice (*Legacies*, again). Given the planet Khan Saak (*Legionnaire*) as a home world, while also used to construct a doomsday fleet (*Message for the Dead*).

The Dark Wanderer – A mysterious and evil entity tied to whatever darkness is looming for the galaxy. Was killed by Ravi, thus accelerating the galaxy's eventual demise.

Death, Destroyer of Worlds – Psychopathic and homicidal Nubarian gunnery bot originally acquired by Tyrus Rechs (*Contracts & Terminations* series). Now the property of Aeson Keel.

Donal Makaffie – Eccentric, existential genius. The inventor of H8. An expert on many things Savage, he possesses an ability to intuitively comprehend what they're attempting. A member of Kill Team Ice and veteran of the Savage Wars.

G232 – Admin and protocol bot originally acquired by Tyrus Rechs (*Contracts & Terminations* series). Now the property of Aeson Keel.

Garret – A technical wizard and savant. Was a former slave of Lao Pak, "liberated" by Aeson Keel, and now serves as a crewmember on the *Indelible IV*.

Goth Sullus – See Casper.

Honey – An orange-skinned female Tennar who assisted Jack (*Takeover*) only to later double-cross him and acquire Savage technology. She was then captured by Keel, attempted to double-cross him as well, and was killed by Death, Destroyer of Worlds.

J-316 – A very old "missionary" bot meant to evangelize and/or proselytize humanoid species. Programmed in multiple faiths, J-316 has been receiving "new revelations" concerning the worship of Oba.

Jack – A Repub Navy spy who went independent following Article Nineteen. He was hired by Nilo to obtain Savage artifacts only to be double-crossed and left for dead by a Tennar Nether Ops agent known as Honey (*Takeover*). He remains in the employ of Mr. Nilo.

Kill Team Ice – A team of volunteers, formed by Tyrus Rechs and Admiral Sulla during the Savage Wars, taking from the best of the Legion. Its members agreed to remain in cryo-stasis until a military application arose that required their unique talents.

Kill Team Victory – Dark Ops kill team founded shortly after the Battle of Kublar.

Active team members: Bombassa, Pina, Neck, Nix, Nobes, "Toots," Wello.

KRS-88 – Psydon-era war bot (*Tin Man*). Was repurposed to serve as a bodyguard for the Maydoon family and was specifically tasked to protect Prisma (*Galactic Outlaws*). Was left destroyed on the planet Umnar by Reina.

Lana Romanov – Medic assigned to Carter's kill team (*Takeover*). Continued in employment with Black Leaf. Has worked with Jack previously for Andien Broxin and Praxus.

Lao Pak – Only Pirate King who sees how stupid Keel is. Not like Ravi. Ravi smart. But Keel? So stupid.

Leenah – Endurian "princess." Exceptionally skilled mechanic. Former MCR rebel. Keel's main squeeze. A surrogate mother to Prisma for a time. An improving pilot.

MakRaven – Legion sergeant major and a legend in his own time. Formerly the premiere donk fighter in the galaxy (*Turning Point*). Killed in action while calling in an artillery strike to save Zombie Squad and Masters (*Last Contact*).

Masters – Quite possibly the sexiest man in the galaxy. Definitely the best abs in the galaxy. Screenwriter. Heartthrob. Dark Ops legionnaire. Took a rain check on the last several hundred cuts by the donks. Currently waiting out the war in a cave once guarded by a monstrous cyber-Drusic.

Nilo – A genius-level intellect who controls a vast corporate empire. His shadowy past involves parents who were apparently lost to Gomarii slavers, though he believes his father is alive and trapped somewhere beyond galaxy's edge. He is desperately seeking as much Savage technology as possible, despite it being illegal to possess such artifacts.

Praxus – A member of the Cybar collective who dissented from the directives of MAGNUS and CRONUS. He was the lone Cybar to oppose aligning with those discovered beyond galaxy's edge. He accepted exile in order to save the life of Andien Broxin, whom he saw as the next evolutionary step for the Cybar—the perfect blend of machine and humanity.

Prisma Maydoon – Juvenile girl whose father, Kael Maydoon, was murdered by Goth Sullus. She hired Tyrus Rechs to seek her revenge (*Galactic Outlaws*) and was swept up in the rise of the Cybar and the fall of the Republic. Upon finishing her training, she found herself thrust into combat with the Dark Wanderer. Currently a guest on a mysterious starship well beyond galaxy's edge.

Ravi – One of the Ancients, left behind to help humanity resist the destruction coming from beyond galaxy's edge. His defense of Prisma may have hastened this apocalypse. Currently searching for a way to thwart the advance of an ancient evil.

Reina – A Savage prisoner who helped free Tyrus Rechs and Casper Sullivan (*Imperator*). She later disappeared, though she seems to have had some communication with Casper before the man became Goth Sullus (*Gods & Legionnaires*). Trained in what Goth Sullus called "the Crux," she has returned to the galaxy, revealing to Prisma Maydoon that she is her mother (*Legacies*).

Sarai – An incredibly advanced AI created by Nilo with the help of pre-existing Savage technology.

Skrizz – Wobanki smuggler who briefly co-piloted for Tyrus Rechs (*Galactic Outlaws*) before joining the crew of the *Indelible VI*. "Tamed" by Prisma, Skrizz sought the girl out on his own before turning to piracy. He was enticed by Donal Makaffie into resuming the hunt for Prisma, this time by leading Makaffie to Aeson Keel.

Surber – Nilo's right-hand man. A no-nonsense enigmatic human who seems more suited for the boardroom than the sort of violent situations Nilo and Black Leaf continually encounter (*Takeover*). His name was given to Wraith as the source behind the termination contracts (*Legacies*). It is unclear if he is the same individual.

Tyrus Rechs – The founder of the Legion (*Savage Wars* trilogy). Given immortality by Savages while their prisoner (*Imperator*), Rechs escaped and dedicated his life to destroying them. Rechs has lived multiple lives, primarily serving as a soldier on the galactic stage. When the House of Reason sought to assassinate him (*Legionnaire*, Epilogue), Rechs went underground, living a new life as a bounty hunter (*Contracts & Terminations* series, *Galactic Outlaws*). Plagued by a degenerating memory, Rechs was killed by Goth Sullus and Kill Team Ice.

Urmo – *sad Urmo noises* (*Imperator, Last Contact*)

Wild Man – A tortured soul and exceptional sniper. Savage Wars veteran and member of Kill Team Ice (*Savage Wars* trilogy).

Wraith – See *Aeson Keel.*

X – A Nether Ops department head whose machinations led to the wholesale slaughter of friend and foe alike. A man accustomed to playing all sides, he ultimately aligned with Goth Sullus and the Black Fleet's imperial takeover of the Republic. He was killed by the legionnaire Exo (*Retribution*). While deceased, his plans are still being carried out by a deep state network of operatives.

Zora—The bounty hunter daughter of former Dark Ops legionnaire Doc. She was brought in by Doc to help train Aeson Ford to better serve in deep cover. Hired by Nilo to convince Keel to work for his corporation, Black Leaf.

PROLOGUE

The great stones of the Temple of the Ancients spread apart with a grinding rumble. Ravi, now the last of the Ancients left in the galaxy, stepped outside to a place he had not been to in many millennia. Placed around the temple at fixed intervals were massive braziers hammered out of a soft metal that glowed amber from the fires burning inside. Great gouts of black smoke whirled upward as liquified fats fueled the flames.

A young priest—tasked with attending the braziers in a carefully timed ritual that involved a prayer at the death of a flame, a refuel, and a reignition, followed by another rote prayer—heard the noise of the stones. But the thick, choking smoke, carried by the hot wind, obscured the source of the sound, and so when Ravi stepped out of the temple opening and stood before the priest, the shock of such a thing happening—*finally happening*—caused the priest to freeze in fear.

Ravi looked at the young priest. She was a member of a blue-gray, bipedal species with a rounded back that made them look vaguely insect-like. Indeed, these creatures could curl into a tight ball for hibernation or to avoid danger. She had large, glossy black eyes and a broad, flat mouth with human-like teeth developed for grinding roots. Though it was impossible to tell male from female by sight alone, all the priests were female according to the traditions of this species the last time Ravi was here.

"Hello," Ravi said in the tongue of this rare species unknown to humanity.

The young priest had just finished the prayers of death and was in the process of refilling the brazier with a mix of liquified animal fats and a gelled wax produced by a meter-long insect native to the planet. Then the prayers of rebirth would begin and the priest would move to the next brazier. But at the sight of Ravi she stood frozen, letting the contents of the clay vessel overflow the brazier, run over the sides, and dribble down onto the great stones of the temple. To Ravi she looked like a garden statue, perpetually filling a reflecting pool.

Startled to action when the splash of the fuel washed over her toe-less feet and soaked her leathery sandals, the priest pulled up the hem of her red and white robes and, in the process, dropped the vessel altogether. It bounced and cracked on its way down the steps of the temple, spilling its remaining contents on the unsanctified ground below.

The unholy clatter fully and finally pulled the young priest into the moment. She immediately flung herself down, turning the three-by-three-meter stone that served as a platform into a place of spontaneous worship. Never in the young priest's wildest dreams did she imagine that this would happen in her lifetime—or if it did, that she would be the first to witness this arrival. There were others much more worthy of the honor.

But Ravi... was not a god. And being aware of that truth, he was unwilling to accept such worship. Again using the old tongue, the one he had last spoken with to a generation that had died out long, long ago, he said, "Arise. I am no god."

The young priest unrolled herself from the tight ball she had formed, allowing her underface to look up at Ravi. It seemed she wanted to argue this point, because only a god could emerge from the temple, and the being before her had done exactly that. But then... hadn't the young priest looked upon this god, and did she not still possess her sight? That certainly wasn't supposed to happen...

"You are the high priest?" Ravi asked.

The young priest again ducked her face down into her body, forming a partial ball. Her muffled voice answered in a stutter. "N-no, lord. I am only... a novice."

The words were different. Not the language Ravi had learned long ago. A natural evolution that Ravi was able to understand easily enough, although he would not feel comfortable attempting to speak it. He calculated the odds that the priestly caste could still understand the old tongue as over sixty percent, the high priest at eighty. They had comprehended his basic greetings, but any concepts more complex might hit a language barrier. Not that there was much that needed to be said. The time for words was at an end.

"Run and find your high priest," Ravi commanded. "And tell your masters: the Great Time has come at last."

The novice rose and fled down the steps at once, trembling and nearly falling headlong as she went. She returned minutes later with a second priest who was, to Ravi, indistinguishable from the first. One would have to possess the species' peculiar olfactory capabilities to even hope to determine the difference in age, sex, and position.

"He wears black," this new priest mumbled, observing Ravi's robes and turban and sensing the grave tidings. Like the novice, this new priest flung herself down in a half-balled prostrate pose of worship. Seeing the senior do this, the novice followed as well, despite having already been told not to.

"Stand up," Ravi said once again. "I am not a god. If I were, I might undo the Great Time and allow your kind to continue to live without such a coming catastrophe."

The new priest also seemed to wish to argue with Ravi about the nature of her deity. This civilization had watched and waited for centuries for the coming of just such a "god" as Ravi, although none of their ancestors had had any such mistaken beliefs about Ravi when he first came to them. Still, Ravi had found that these things sometimes happened when given enough time. One only needed to look at the pervasive belief in Oba.

And besides, this was hardly the first time Ravi had been offered worship by one of the galaxy's species.

The new priest—whether she was the high priest or not, Ravi didn't know—picked herself up from the temple steps, not without some reluctance mixed with fear and... irritation. Few priests of high status are ever humble enough to receive correction from their deities.

"You speak the old throat," the new priest said, somewhat haltingly as she attempted to speak to Ravi in that ancient language.

"Yes, but I can understand your present tongue. We must not tarry. The Great Alliance must form now. The time your ancestors awaited after my first coming is now upon you all."

"The... Elder of the First Order... better speaks the old throat," the new priest struggled to explain. "He comes now. A... feast? Will be prepared in your... honor. All that my lord most... loves... will be there to... consume."

Under different circumstances, such a remark might have caused a mirthful and even mischievous smile to push its way through Ravi's dark and perfectly clipped beard. What did these marvelous creatures imagine he loved? He certainly hadn't discussed such things all those centuries ago when he was last here. But now was not the time to find out; such things would never be discovered. For the end of all things in this galaxy was at hand.

And Ravi—who had remained, together with Urmo, when the rest of the Ancients fled—had himself become the instrument of that end.

He shook his head. There was no longer time to search out the champions necessary to even hope to oppose the great invading horde. The men of this age would have to be enough. Or they would fall to the coming Consumption.

It was inevitable, Ravi told himself. *None could stand before the Consumption. My people knew it. Urmo and I were fools. Fools of two different minds, but the same foolish purpose.*

But even as he thought these things, they struck him as false. He had long searched for the one who could stand by his side at the head of battle. So many had been close to being that man. Tyrus Rechs. Captain Keel. Even the young girl Prisma. But each had registered, according to Ravi's unfathomable and tightly calculating mind, some unfixable flaw. Each lacked some crucial element, pushing the odds overwhelmingly toward failure. And there would be no second attempts.

Despite all this, Ravi held on to a hope that the inevitable might not be final. And for good reason—he had stood in battle that day over one thousand years ago, among a colony of men who had established for themselves a planet for their people and faith. A colony that was denied the opportunity to grow into a Sinasia or Spilursa because the Dark Ones came to it first. But that planet, positioned in the path of that small, breakout band, was positioned to be the first of their conquest... however far it may have gone.

The covenants enforced by the Ancients and created at a time when the full destruction of the Dark Ones was possible, though not at all sure, had kept at bay most of the Dark Ones. But the vanguard was overlooked, and for ages had ravaged yet another galaxy. Not bound by the covenant, they returned to the galaxy of men shortly after humanity had discovered faster-than-light travel. And they ventured forth to wage war on the first inhabited planet in their path.

There, the Dark Ones were stopped.

Ravi had stood among men who looked just like he did now; in fact, his visage had been chosen to honor them for as long as he lived. They had stood and fought and died to the last man, woman, and child. But not before stopping the first breath of the terrible Consumption that would follow. They had once saved the galaxy, and no one but Ravi knew it.

The armies coming now—invited by Ravi's failure to uphold the covenants when he slew the Dark Wanderer— would be much, much larger. They would fall upon world after world and purge every planet of life. The odds were as near to certain as possible that the galaxy's most distant star systems were already being ravaged. Those contained only primitive and simple forms of life that had not yet achieved the ability to think and reason, but by no means would their primitive state spare them destruction.

This world, where Ravi's visit had made such an impression, marked the first line of defense among planets inhabited by a truly sentient and intelligent species. Although the human-dominated portions of the galaxy would see this planet as primitive and undeveloped, the peculiar species here would hold the distinction—and the curse—of being the first to attempt to hold off the invading horde.

They would be slaughtered completely, of that there was no doubt. Ravi would be left as the sole witness to their utter annihilation and extinction. There was nothing he could do about that but hold them in honor until his own time to be destroyed finally came. He had long ago decided that he would not leave this galaxy to rejoin his kin when the fateful hour finally came.

This species' extinction would come all the swifter, however, if the priest before him failed to move on from obsessing about feasts and ceremonies.

"I must... insist," the new priest managed to say in the old tongue. "There can be no... gathering of armies if... the proper rituals are not... completed. The sacrifices you... require..."

Ravi noticed a look of extreme discomfort on the face of the novice. This species now thought of him as a god, and evidently not a benign one. But then, given what Ravi had told their ancestors, it made perfect sense that he would be seen as a bringer of war, wrath, and ruin. And wasn't that foreboding news—that the end of these beings was at hand—exactly what he was bringing?

A calculation was made and set. Ravi would persuade these beings in the manner in which they were most apt to be swayed. There was no time for anything else.

"You will gather your armies as sworn by your ancestors!" he commanded.

Ravi's voice was not particularly loud, but it was firm and clear. And from the way the priests both dropped on their faces and curled into half-balls, one would think that the very Temple of the Ancients itself had shaken from the proclamation.

"Rise. Go now and without delay. Do not provoke my wrath."

Ravi saw at once that his calculation was accurate. The new priest stammered and managed an archaic word in the old tongue that irrevocably swore herself to a vow of absolute obedience. Then she rose, turned, and ran down the temple steps, shouting as she went.

A collection of other priests, already busy with sacrifices, fires, and prayer, had gathered at the base of the temple, though they did not dare to look up at Ravi and instead fixed their emotionless eyes on the priestly herald. They seemed unable to move, despite the priest's exhortations to gather the armies. After all, there were feasts and sacrifices to be had, and the braziers were not to be extinguished. Indeed, the novice Ravi had first encountered was slowly creeping back to resume her tending of the very same.

"These fires will not save your people," Ravi said, gesturing to the nearest bowl of oily flame. "Gather yourselves for war!"

The novice fled down the steps and joined the other priests in their flight to do as Ravi commanded.

It took a full week—ten local days—for the primitive armies of that primitive world to march to the great field that lay open to the south of the temple. It was a holy place that was looked upon with dread, as it was the place where the great and terrible battle at the end of time would take place. Anyone with the sense to see would know the trepidation, awe, and outright fear that the various kingdoms, tribes, and warriors felt upon seeing that great plain before them as they marched. For this was a planet accustomed to warfare, but never here. Never among the priests in the shadow of the temple.

Ravi had selected this spot long ago when parlaying with the ancestors of these beings. It was large enough for the meager planet's entire population of warriors and, according to his old calculations, would remain so for millennia. The vast gathering before him now, marked with tall pikes, spears, and all manner of archaic weapons, was a sight to behold. Here was a planetary army, come together as one to truly defend their home planet. With its people dispersed, the planet would be ravaged and overwhelmed with shocking speed. But while gathered together… they could at least withstand the onslaught for a bit longer. They could require an accounting. Make the Consumption pay a cost—even a small one.

And then… the last warrior of this grand army would perish in battle, dying as they stood against wickedness. A worthy death.

Standing against evil was always good. Always.

The armies waited anxiously in the field. Days passed… and then weeks. Ravi's calculations for the time of the Consumption's arrival altered again and again until he was forced to accept that there were circumstances impacting the odds that he simply did not know. He could no longer put off the demands for a feast in his honor, nor could he deny the accompanying sacrifices insisted upon by the warrior kings who had acceded to the holy direction of the priests and marched their armies with those of their enemies, under an order of internal peace. Now those warrior kings' officers were busy only with managing supply lines to wait for a war where none were to survive.

The end would be swift, fierce, and final. The least Ravi could allow them was their feasting.

But soon old rivalries, temporarily suspended by the order of universal peace, reemerged. Mortal foes bristled in the presence of one another, old grudges resurfaced, and the bloody battlefields of before seemed again more important than the promise of a great future war that had always felt so much like a myth...

The sun set behind the hills. Six standard hours of night would follow. The temperature would cool to 250°F before rising again the next morning. This was no place for humans. Most of the untouched planets in the galaxy weren't.

As the sun glowed, red and menacing, Ravi watched the hills. Behind him, waiting patiently, was a retinue of the most important priests and kings. They all wished to ask him the same question he asked himself: *Where are they? Why are they not here?*

Ravi had run the odds. Something unknowable had happened. The sun set, and Ravi was in the dark. Small *pops* sounded from the field as green phosphorescent spores, which had cooked throughout the day, shot into the air, oblivious that their line of vegetable progeny was nearly at a permanent end.

Or was it?

Ravi turned to those priests and kings. "Something has happened."

Nervous looks were exchanged, but none spoke.

"I must leave. Stay vigilant."

And with those words... Ravi disappeared from their midst.

01

Sergeant Robert "Sparky" Cathey blasted another series of bolts into the structure on the far side of the street to keep the heads on those Hools from popping back up to the window so they could shoot. "Changing packs!"

The worlds of the Sinasian Cluster had been sent a garrison, sometimes with and sometimes without the Legion. The garrison was there at the cluster's request; there had been a real concern that rogue House of Reason loyalists would target Sinasia once again for retribution. Much of their underground vitriol had been levied against the cluster for being the first to speak out against the Imperial Republic, swinging the galactic momentum in favor of the treasonous Legion and its Article Nineteen.

So when unauthorized ships pushed past the planetary defense forces and began landing hostiles, Repub Marine Sergeant Sparky wasn't caught completely off guard. They wouldn't have been on these exotic worlds if things getting violent hadn't been a possibility. But the particular hostiles attacking them... yeah. That was a surprise.

The wily marine NCO dropped against what remained of the stone wall he'd been shooting from to hide from the aliens dropping heavy doses of lead at them. While the hullbusters had been using the N-6 Delta variant, the Hools were using old-fashioned slug throwers chambered in seven-point-seven millimeter. The heavy, caseless slug throwers were a bona fide buy from the night markets that populated the fringe of the Sinasian Cluster—and a favorite of the lawless who liked to run in and around the sector.

"Covering!" Lance Corporal Wes Patterson shouted. He raised his SAB above the side of the wall and picked up where the sergeant left off. One Hool climbed above the window just enough to get raked by a wave of blaster bolts painting the building. The heavily charged bolts decimated the head and torso of the alien, blasting its poisonous, colorful spines into ash. It flung its weapon into the air as it tumbled back, prompting a squadmate to reach for the tumbling rifle in lieu of helping his friend. The suppressing fire continued to hose the side of the building the aliens were fighting from, despite the roof being gone after a protracted battle with the marines, and while the heavily armored alien caught his friend's blaster, he took more than his share of bolts as the lance corporal raked back in the other direction.

Sparky pulled his battle board from the front of his armor and tapped a preset on the device to prime a grenade. While the N-6 Delta was an improvement over the Charlie, he still longed to have his hands around an N-4 like he had in selection. "Make do, Marine," he muttered to himself. "Make do."

The grenade was set to airburst by traveling a certain distance and detonating once it had reached a spot well away from the shooter. Sparky's laser designator would target the offending area, where the grenade would commence its deadly work of pasting the entire gaggle of Hools into whatever afterlife the hulking shiny aliens believed in.

"One hundred!" Patterson shouted, letting everyone know he was down to the last hundred shots in the charge drum unless he lowered the bolt intensity and thus reduced each shot's killing potential, something no marine would think of doing.

Loading the grenade into the breach on the underslung launcher, Sparky replied, "Give me fifty of it and I'll burst them a cease-and-desist holo!"

"Send it!" Patterson laughed.

Sparky dropped his helmet's monocle over his eye, allowing him to see the infrared targeting beam. He dropped his rifle onto the support of the shattered windowsill, not bothering with the crunch the weighty weapon made on the glass where there should have been a window. With the structure serving as a stable shooting platform, the weapon's beam sighted the distance the round would have to travel in order to dump its payload into a room full of surprised Hools.

Angling the rifle until the weapon's arc matched the targeting beam directed at the other building, Sparky sent the round. A throaty *poot* sent the projectile spinning like a pop fly in seamball—a sport that Sparky followed closely. He had missed far too much of the season on account of this deployment, but some Legion general or other had shouted to the rafters that the outer territories had to be protected, and it was the marines of the Twelfth who got the duty. While most of Bravo Company had hooted and hollered about getting that sweet deployment money with the tax-free kicker, Sergeant Sparky grumbled during the entire workup out of a concern that he'd miss the Spilursa United season if anything did pop off. If there was one thing the universe should have been warned about, it was to not deprive Sergeant Sparky of his seam-ball. Because now all that anger was laser-focused, like the targeting beam, into sending this grenade into the quasi-room full of Hools.

The grenade detonated over his enemies' heads, sounding off with a percussive slam that blew out the few walls that had been defiant enough to remain standing. The metallic casing turned molten as it splintered into fragmentation that tore through the powerful and damage-resistant bodies the Hools were known for. Blood and feathery spines intermingled with black smoke and dust from the walls dislodged by the concussion.

"Gold One Actual to Gold One-One. Over," Sparky said into the net.

"This is One-One, go," Corporal Volson answered.

"Gold One-One, automatic rifleman will remain on station to provide overwatch as we move. Gold One-Two will provide alternate vantage for cover. Advance to target location to assess battle damage. How copy? Over."

"Solid copy, One Actual. Oscar Mike. One-One out," Volson confirmed.

"Gold One Actual, this is Gold One-Two. I copy your last. One-Two out."

Everyone is on the money even though we're all broke at the moment, Sparky thought.

He crept from his position behind the bit of wall remaining to him as cover and joined the lance corporal currently scanning the target area below them. If it weren't for the Marine Corps battle uniform, Sparky probably would have missed the kid, or mistaken him for a piece of lumber, on account of how absurdly skinny he was. And it sure wasn't for lack of eating. Patterson would dig into a ration pack and be done with the thing faster than a tyrannasquid could eat a beach full of swimmers—and then he'd beg, borrow, and trade for whatever he could get from everyone else's rations. And still the kid was so thin he looked like someone had bundled some sticks together.

"I'm going down there to confirm we have those animals good and pasted," Sparky said, slapping the marine on his shoulder armor. "Cover our six. PFC Daharen will watch yours so you don't get snuck up on."

"I'm fine with that," Patterson said with a grin.

"Slow that roll, knucklehead. The last clown that tried to shimmy into those silkies got a busted jaw and a one-way ticket out a window."

"What ever happened to that guy, Sarn't?" the lance corporal asked.

"Wasn't a guy, and how do you think we got you?" the sergeant growled in warning.

He climbed along the outsides of the stairway frame on what was left of the support struts, since there weren't stairs to walk on, until he reached the spot where the stairway landing's dense walls had left the structure un-touched by gunfire. With his feet finally under him, he tapped his way to the bottom floor, dropped to a knee, and slithered into what had only half an hour ago been a storefront loaded down with enough snacks, drinks, and convenience items to make the next hours bearable. Unfortunately, the Hools had shot up most of the floor try-ing to punt the marine squad into the hereafter.

As Sparky slid through the broken shop toward the exit, his monocle remained down, allowing him to track Volson moving toward the objective. In the corner of his eye, he caught a glimpse of PFC Daharen aiming out the door.

A Cassari, Daharen had had to endure the scorn and lust of a marine unit deprived of free time while getting ready for deployment. Front-line marines assigned to an expeditionary unit usually had the attitude of: *If you can do the job, the job is yours.* They didn't care what planet or species you came from so long as you could hump the same ruck as everyone else. But things sometimes got dicey with races like Tennar, and of course, the Cassari. Those species whose females were a staple at the pleasure houses on worlds like Nyamar. The ones who could get just about whatever they wanted with enough pheromones in the air rarely got the same shake that other marines got, even when they passed boot and MOS school with flying colors.

Daharen was, allegedly, repulsive for a Cassari, and of such a low caste that service to the marines in exchange for the signing bonus and subsequent pay grades was all her tribe would ever earn from her. She looked pretty good to most marines all the same.

She chin-checked Sparky as he passed, her eyes fixed on her assigned sector of fire and ready to pour hot violence into anyone not wearing hullbuster fatigues trying to enter their space. After an all-clear from Patterson on the floor above him, Sparky crept outside, across the blasted-out intersection, with his rifle in the patrol ready so as to better observe the street. Every time his boots crushed some piece of debris or bits of glass shard, he cringed at the thought of the noise giving him away, even though the unit was bathed in noise from fighting in the surrounding blocks.

Volson, along with the two hitters comprising his fire team, slithered along the wall of an adjoining building before meeting up with the sergeant.

"Didn't think you'd ever come down from that ivory tower," Volson said.

"No thanks to you," Sparky joked.

"Bro, who do you think took off the roof for you to lob that grenade in?"

As the four marines moved into the building where the Hools had holed up, Sparky took the lead, testing each foothold on the stairs as he climbed. He and his marines had fought hard enough to punch blaster bolts through the duracrete walls and into the stairwell on this side of the building. It hadn't seemed like the firefight had lasted that long, but the expansive pattern of score marks told a different story.

Arriving on the landing to the next floor, Sparky went to grab the door handle when Volson stopped him.

"Don't do that, brother man. Hools are known for their traps and generally deceptive nature, especially when they fight. You might wanna check that handle and the jamb before pulling on it."

"That bad, eh?"

"Think of it like this. Suppose you're a member of one of the most foul-tempered, rude, and generally dangerous species in the Galactic Republic. You going to take any chances with anyone giving you a fair shake?"

"You got a point. But note that me acknowledging that you're probably right about this does *not* warrant an 'I told you so' when I find a tripwire or a door handle covered in Hool venom," Sparky said, while pointing at an actual tripwire.

Volson maneuvered toward his NCO, pulling a set of pliers from his armor. "Allow me, sir."

Sparky chuckled and tossed the joke back using his best mock core-worlds voice. "You're too kind, my good man. You are allowed, sir."

After clipping the tripwire, Volson asked, "Did Big-Daddy Guns get back to you with regard to what these particular Hools are doing here?"

"Not a word," Sparky replied. "We clear on this door?"

His team leader nodded. "Clear."

Sparky moved through the portal. "Gold One Gizmo," he said over comms. "This is Gold One Actual. Status on eyes? Over."

The Gizmo, or special mechanics marine assigned to every squad leader, responded with a voice that would make a Marine Corps DI envious. "Eyes up, Gold One Actual. On station and in your HUD. Over."

"Do it. One Actual out," Sparky said, giving a solid affirm to the drone launch as he moved carefully down the hallway. One side of the passage was untouched, but the other side, which had once contained a row of apartments, was now blown open, leaving only empty doorframes standing.

Sparky approached the body of a Sinasian human with black, wraithlike lines radiating from a puncture wound in the neck. Her face was twisted in the kind of pain that only comes from the entire body rebelling against itself. Sparky had seen it before—the ugly result of Hool venom from spines they used in defense, or better yet, offense. The squad leader motioned to the fire team behind him in a hand signal that left no doubt to his fellow marines that they were close.

The sergeant switched sides of the hall so that he had line of sight into the holes in the passage. Of course this meant that anything in those apartments had line of sight on him, but with his N-6 already up and open for business, there was a good chance he'd at least get a burst off before he got punched into the hereafter.

Ragged shrapnel burns peppered the carpet a few feet ahead like a road sign telling the sergeant acting as point man he'd come to the right place. A sharp turn and Sparky was facing the apartment he'd just lacerated with his airburst grenade. Six dead Hools lay all around the floor, the stink of their blood joining the scent of spent explosive.

Sparky had just raised his rifle to check the pulse of the bodies, Marine Corps–style, when something bumped up against his boot. Behind him, Volson yelled, "Grenade!" and even before the word was out of his mouth, Sparky was already dropping the center of his body armor on the device. The weapon popped with an explosive thump that hit his chest rig like he was a seamball and a wobanki had the bat. Although the armor absorbed the explosion, Sparky had to press his fingers into his ears to stop his brain spilling from the holes due to the sudden rush of surviving a banger grenade to the chest. He rolled over and retched violently—and saw the advancing nightmare coming from farther down the hall.

Volson brought up his rifle and quickly sent bolt after bolt into the advancing Hool, but the creature held a ballistic shield that easily ablated the incoming fire. With his other hand, he held a heavy blaster done up in chrome.

The alien charged at Volson. Volcanic red bolts from the heavy blaster pistol sailed into Volson's armor, punching him onto the burned, carpeted floor with smoking dents littering his armor. Another bolt punched through PFC Galeone behind him, tearing through her face and out the other side of her neck when she tried to turn and cover. Last in the stack, the lance corporal that had just transferred into the squad was drilled in the chest, ragged dents in his armor matching those of his team leader. He, too, hit the floor.

The alien emitted a heavy growl as it marched down the hallway to the downed team. It pressed its heavily taloned foot against the lance corporal, studying his armor, which was different from the others.

"What do we have here?" the Hool cooed.

Unlike the marines' fatigue pants and combat sh rt covered with plate carrier and shin and arm guards, the lance corporal had full plates like those of a legionnaire. The Hool lifted the plate with his weapon, revealing synthprene underneath featuring a vaguely hexagonal pattern—as if this was armored too.

"Hey!" Sparky shouted to get the alien's attention. "You shouldn't have done that." He rose to his knees, displaying a wide blast pattern that spanned his entire plate carrier, ruining all the charge packs hanging there and burning anything not covered by the plates. "Now you're gonna..."

But Sparky's head was still spinning from the blast, and he was suddenly overcome by vertigo. As he lost his balance and fell back on the floor, the Hool's mocking laughter added insult to injury.

"You don't say?" said the Hool.

His chuckle was cut off abruptly as the lance corporal's hand shot upward and snatched the alien by the throat. Only hacking noises escaped the Hool's mouth as a grip as strong as that of any bot threatened to crush its windpipe. The Hool tried to stop the marine by venting a heavy blaster into the man's chest, only to have his weapon hand caught in another vise as the marine abandoned his medium machine gun. To the alien's surprise, razor-sharp talons tore through the marine's glove from within, biting into the Hool's flesh. Even more shocking was that the toxic alien's blood washed over the monstrous hands with no effect, something the insurgent had never seen in any other race.

Rising to a sitting position, the lance corporal launched the fighter down the hall to land near Sparky. The alien rolled into a crouch, its arrow-shaped head bearing fangs dripping with venom.

The armored marine got to his knees, popping the restraints on his arm guards. Spines tore through his synthprene undersuit, and the kid grabbed the fabric at the elbow and ripped the sleeves free to reveal arms corded in muscle and covered in the same dense spines as their attacker. While one hand went for the daxovere blade at his belt—a weapon carved from the tusk of a bullitar—the other hand vented the helmet and lifted it free.

"No," the insurgent growled.

The marine grinned. He was every bit as much a Hool as their attacker.

"Get him, D'ghar!" Sparky shouted.

The enemy Hool shot to his feet at an all-out run for the lance corporal Hool named D'ghar. Two steps into the rush, D'ghar slammed the fully enclosed helmet back in place and busted straight through the wall at his side. Plaster and lumber exploded as the hulking marine pushed through the obstacle with no more concern than he would a door.

The insurgent stopped in front of the hole, looking into the apartment beyond in ticking motions, his predatory senses struggling to find the marine. He sniffed the air, then recovered his blaster and led with the weapon into the space. He paid no attention to the two human figures huddling in one corner with a turned-over table as their only cover.

"Where did it go?" the insurgent snapped at the frightened humans.

The plaster of another wall exploded, showering him in chalky white debris as D'ghar's fist ejected claws to dig into the enemy Hool's shoulder. The hand then yanked the Hool violently through the wall, smashing the surface framing and blasting through pipes, spraying water onto his dead comrades in the next apartment over.

A churning growl escaped D'ghar as he glared down at the mighty Hool he'd just thrown to the floor like so much garbage. "C'mere, pup!"

He sank his horn knife into the insurgent's side, tearing through the alien's naturally armored hide and bypassing the ribs to rake the lungs beneath. The inhuman marine then lifted his enemy, knife still buried in his side, and whirled him into a wall with enough force to shatter the support beams and topple what was left of the roof on top of them.

The lance corporal rained blows into the head and neck of the creature until it went limp, and still he continued to hammer the enemy. A heavy growl turned into a roar as he pulled the huge knife free and stabbed it into his adversary's flesh over and over. Then, with a tremendous rip that sent gouts of blood splashing across the apartment, D'ghar ripped the Hool's head from its shoulders and held it aloft like a hunter proclaiming to his tribe that he was the predator all things feared.

Pulling his helmet from his skull, D'ghar waved the disembodied head and shouted, "Marines!"

Whoops and victory cries shouted from the marines in the surrounding buildings, who had witnessed this violent show through the wrecked outer walls.

"*That's* what's up!" someone shouted.

"Get some, Hullbuster!"

"Show 'em what time it is, D'gharie boy!"

D'ghar tossed the head, not even bothering to watch it roll over the ruined wall and into the street two stories below.

Then he knelt down and offered his gloved hand to his squad leader.

Sparky looked into the face of the marine who'd just saved his life. A face with three scars radiating from near his eye and a severe blaster burn to his skull. Lance Corporal Dugmagharrerra was one of only three Hools who served in the Twelfth MEU. And what everyone who'd met the Hool would attest to was that D'ghar was a straight-up hullbuster.

"Here's your helmet, Lance Corporal," Sparky said with deep respect. "Can you check on Volson and Galeone?"

The chug-chug-chug of D'ghar's growling exhale was silenced as he replaced his helmet. In equal parts terrifying predator and digital speaker grit, he said, "Yut."

Sparky lay back against the rubble, cycling through the platoon net until he found his RTO. "Gold One Actual to Gold One Romeo. Status on Gold ops, this sector? Over."

The comm transmission operator was in his ear, frantic now that he had the sergeant's attention. "Thank Oba we have you back on comms, One Actual. Gold Six has urgent traffic for you she just got from FLAGCOM on the RSS *Lawson*. You ready to receive? Over."

FLAGCOM was the identifier for the fleet commander on boats that gave the Twelfth their ride to the many systems they were sent to work on the Republic's behalf. If they were getting traffic directly, the level of suck had gone from puddle to pool.

Sparky flicked the comms. "Send it, big sister."

His HUD brought up an image of their lieutenant, Soddin. Once the live feed registered a secured link, she began. "Sergeant Sparky, I'm reading three casualties including you. You good, hullbuster?"

"I took a grenade to the chest but the armor took it, ma'am. Thank Oba for the new armor; with the old flak vests, I would have been done for."

He looked down the hallway at the others. Volson was getting his feet under him, while D'ghar was applying skinpacks to the downed Galeone. Her blood and teeth were spread along the hallway, but the Hool gave the sergeant a nod to indicate she'd make it.

"Volson and Galeone were hit, but Volson is ambulatory. Galeone is hurt pretty bad; we'll patch her up and get her to the corpsman."

"And Dugmagharrerra?"

"Ripping heads off, LT."

"Well, I hate to do this after you guys just went through the wringer, but we have intel from the locals that more Hools and Gomarii just landed south of our position and they're looking to take down a communications tower. The Old Man thinks they're trying to blind the populace to something. Your squad is the closest."

"Can you send us a shopping cart, ma'am? We need new plates, a swap on packs, plus a top-off on rats and splash," the sergeant said, running down their list of needs.

"On it, Sarn't. Prep Galeone for transpo. She can ride out in the cart. Three minutes, Marine. Don't let that tower get slagged. Soddin out."

Sparky steadied himself to pitch the bad news to the rest of his squad. He looked up to see D'ghar carrying Galeone down the stairs, and despite her injury she was protesting the entire way, meekly struggling in the Hool's grip. She might not have been as strong as D'ghar, but the fight in that marine was as good as any.

"All Gold One elements, this is One Actual. Fall in on my position and ready for resupply and re-task. Acknowledge and sign off by number. Over," Sparky said into the comms.

"You ever get the feeling we just out here banging our heads while the ones back on ship are all cozy with their feet up?" Volson asked.

"You really want some four-star looking over your shoulder when you throw your kicks on the desk?" Sparky countered.

Volson held his hands to the sides in surrender. "Message received, Sarn't."

Sparky pointed for the junior NCO to make his way back toward the street. With the departure of his senior-most team leader, the sergeant sifted through the Hool bodies for any intel they could use.

The first thing that struck him was the lack of commo on any of them. Since this weird slaver run on Sinasia had been effected, the Hools assisting the Gomarii in invading the Taresaw Islands had been coordinated and quick in their strike against community targets of opportunity. A water reclamation plant here, solar collection plates for backup power there. Gomarii weren't conquerors, and abductions were being reported, but the Hool insurgents were going after objectives that would turn everyday life on Nyamar into a daily struggle for essentials. Maybe the Hools just paid for passage and had their own agenda. Regardless, the Hool strike teams were either operating as independent cells after their missions were handed out, or they had another way to communicate. One that Sparky and his marines were all missing.

The commo thing needed looking into, but it wasn't the only mystery here. Their tribal brands were another. Working with D'ghar had helped Sparky learn a little about Hool culture, and he knew that the Hools marked themselves with ritual brands in a spot along the center of their backs that the feathered spines didn't cover. These brands were similar but not identical; they varied by bloodline. While everyone was technically from the same nation, their first loyalty was to their kin. Hools competed against each other in all things.

"So why am I looking at multiple families working together in the same room?" Sparky asked aloud.

When he got to D'ghar's now-headless adversary, he found one other item of interest: an oblong hexagonal pendant. It meant nothing to him, but you never knew what was useful intel and what wasn't. He spun the chain around his fist to wind it into his glove, then ran down the stairs to rejoin his crew. He arrived at the same time as a trio of combat sleds.

Doc Mahelona was a moktaar. He used his innate agility to quickly clamber out of the side hatch even before the vehicles came to a complete stop. He dropped a repulsor gurney at D'ghar's feet and motioned for the brutish marine to put down his teammate. "D'gharie. How many times I gotta tell you? No chewing on the humans, yeah?"

"Hungry," D'gharie said through his helmet's external speakers as he set Galeone on the litter. "Supply forgot to send the Hool rations again."

That was always a complicating factor when diverse species served in the same units. The logistics of getting everyone fed with chow they could actually digest hinged on a functioning AI and flexible logistical fulfillment. Most species didn't have nearly the omnivorous range of humans.

Doc leaned over the wounded hullbuster, all joking now aside as he examined her wounds. "Oh, li'l sistah. You got yerself messed up pretty good in there." He handed D'ghar a hydration pouch. "Hold this, braddah."

Sparky walked around the doc to kneel beside his marine. "She gonna make it, Doc?"

"Don't worry, Sarn't. I'll take good care of little sistah until we can get her high side on a med bird." Doc waved over another marine from his sled and the two of them carried Galeone into the waiting vehicle.

"You sure *you're* good?" said a voice behind Sparky. He turned to find himself facing Lieutenant Soddin, who put a hand on his shoulder. "You and Volson took it heavy in there."

"New armor, a sip of water, and top off our charge packs and we're good, LT."

"It's all in the sled," Soddin said. She knocked on the side of the open ramp, shouting to the drivers in front. "Spread the word. CAS-COLLECT and top off in two mikes. We have more stops to make."

Sparky was already shrugging out of his armor as the crew he'd referred to as "the shopping cart" dumped equipment cases into the street. The marines from Sparky's squad descended on the offerings like birds on breadcrumbs. New combat shirts, pants, armor, and in some cases, weapons were switched out with gear they'd been carrying throughout the skirmishes plaguing the town. When everyone was refreshed and reloaded, the lieutenant approached Sparky once more.

"We're out, Sergeant. You got this?"

"All day long and twice tomorrow, ma'am. Can we have a sled?"

"Sure, if you want to trade jobs and deal with the brass all day," Soddin said drily.

"Eh… I guess we don't need that sled after all."

D'ghar approached, clad in fresh armor that covered him from head to toe, protecting his fellow marines from his lethal spines. That was a requirement for him to serve as part of a marine expeditionary unit; if he didn't generally remain completely covered while on operations, he was at risk of dosing his fellow marines with the ever-present venom and contact poisons his species was famous for.

"Sergeant. That is bad magic," D'ghar said. He pointed at the amulet, which Sparky had dropped at his feet while he changed. He'd meant to hand it over to the LT. "We call it the Old Poison. Is okay for me to crush?"

"What does that mean, Lance Corporal?" Lieutenant Soddin asked.

"Show you." The Hool marine picked up the amulet, then gave a finger wag at a hunched-over moktaar private loading used gear into the combat sled. "Move ear," D'ghar said.

The private came over and looked at him, confused.

D'ghar reached to the junior marine's helmet, took hold of his headphone cup, and pulled the device from his ear. Then he held the amulet beside the moktaar's head.

The private paused as though hearing something he couldn't quite place.

"Whoa," Sparky said. "His pupils are way dilated. You good, hullbuster?"

"I am, Sergeant. I... think. I feel like... I dunno, braddah. I feel like I should be... hunting," the junior marine reported.

And then, without warning, he lunged at Sparky. But he'd barely taken a step before D'ghar, who seemed to be expecting this, slammed the poor private into the sled—hard. That seemed to jar the marine from whatever had possessed him to assault an NCO. D'ghar then wrapped the amulet in the foil wrapper from a used skinpack and handed it to an open-mouthed Lieutenant Soddin.

The private immediately shot to parade rest, his fangs and his anger disappearing at once. "I am *so* sorry, Sergeant Cathey. I don't know why I—I mean, I'm not sure what happened, ya-ya."

"Lance Corporal Dugmagharrerra?" said Soddin. "How did you know Private Skymak would be affected like that?"

"Seen it before on Ballerophon. Moktaar and Hools fighting over the planet when one of the gods spoke. Both tore the other apart." D'ghar related this reluctantly, as if revealing a family secret.

"Why aren't you affected?" Soddin asked. Beside her, Private Skymak was eyeing the foil packet warily. The moktaar corpsman clearly seemed to be wondering the same thing.

"The god commanded me to fight a demon. I won, but the demon made me pay for victory. It deafened me to all the gods." D'ghar lifted his helmet, showing the scars and blaster burn along his scalp.

Soddin held up the foil packet. "I don't know what all that means, but I have to report this to the Old Man. In the meantime, Sparky, I still need you to defend that tower."

"We're on it, LT."

"One-Two, this is One Actual, how we looking?" Sparky asked over the net.

Corporal Tripp, a hullbuster sniper, cursed into the radio. "Didn't you say we'd be facing a squad? This ain't a squad."

"We don't get to pick where the fight starts," Sparky replied.

"Only where we do the victory dance. Roger that, Sergeant. Stand by."

They'd set up a crossfire position to catch the Hools in a killing field of interlocking high-cycle suppressive shooting that had driven the enemies to cover. Those positions of cover were right where Tripp had wanted them to be—and the few Hools approaching the comm tower the hullbusters now lay in wait to defend were about to pay for poor tactical planning in a big way.

The tower was set up at the edge of a large industrial park. Sparky and his hullbusters had set up in the dark recesses of a warehouse whose open docking doors gave them a full view of every avenue of approach to the tower from their position in the overhead rafters. Two teams of two Hools each were now attempting to move through the park, using a stack of empty shipping containers as cover. Overhead, an observation bot triangulated the

Hools' positions and fed targeting data to marine snipers who couldn't see their targets but had the right tools to hit them all the same.

The explosive report of a large-caliber weapon echoed across the industrial park. In his optics, Sparky watched as the shot burned through the side of a shipping container and ventilated the skull of one Hool while tearing through the leg of the Hool next to him. The bolt finished its run by burning into the duracrete and sending rocky fragments showering over the enemy. They all ducked after the shot, prompting the second team of Hools to realize that their move toward the tower was not as stealthy as they had supposed. They answered in a decidedly Hool-like fashion by rising up and firing in the direction the sniper's shot came from.

Another boom sounded. The second shot zipped between the bars of the heavy equipment to tear through a Hool's throat and punch him out of sight.

"Damn, Tripp. Those shots were a little low," Sparky joked. "Send the viper."

"Sending," Tripp confirmed.

Patterson and Daharen appeared at the corner of the cargo containers that obscured the Hools from Sparky's direct line of sight, crouched and hidden in the smoke. Bright fireworks popped overhead, creating distracting shadows that only served to further hide the pair creeping toward the sheltering Hool that Tripp had put on his knees.

Patterson moved to flank, aiming his pistol even though it left him exposed to the Hool's direct line of sight. The snarling Hool aimed its weapon just as Patterson ducked back behind cover. Daharen then ventilated the alien and sent additional shots into the other three Tripp had hit, just to make sure they were dead.

"One-Two, have your element pull back to position three for cover. Over," Sparky called over comms.

"Good copy. One-Two out," Tripp acknowledged.

The overhead observation bot identified more Hools advancing on the tower, taking a different approach vector and not seeming to want an engagement with the hullbusters—at least not until they took out the comms tower first.

"There's your squad," Sparky told Tripp as he leveled a pair of shots toward them.

But those weren't the only Hools making a move. Right at that moment, two Hools with small, curved black axes and pistols dropped from a skylight onto the gantry behind Sparky and his team. Running and vaulting across the rigging, they went to engage D'ghar, who was pulling rear security. Next to him was Volson on the N-60 grenade launcher, which so far hadn't been needed, given the meager number of Hools who'd shown up to the fight.

D'ghar backed up, blasting toward the rigging with his rifle, seeking to take down not only the two Hools who'd dropped in uninvited but any other Hools who might be staging on the roof. Several of his shots punched through the first Hool, spraying its blood across the gantry. The second attacker took two shots in its chest as well, lost its balance, and went tumbling down to smash into the duracrete floor far below.

"Clear?" Volson called.

"Not clear!" D'ghar shouted. He fired up at the skylight.

Taking D'ghar's cue, Volson aimed his distancing laser toward the skylight and added a meter for good measure. Racking the slide on the N-60, he squeezed off a grenade to sail it through the shattered breach. It detonated exactly where he'd set it to, bending part of the ceiling and perforating it to let sunlight stream through in dust-encrusted lances. Multiple Hools fell through the structurally compromised roof, flailing all the way down to their sudden end.

"That's one way to clear a roof," Sparky mumbled to himself.

The observation bot showed more incoming from the docks. Things were about to get unpleasant unless they could get some close air. The marine NCO cycled through the comms channels, switching to the company net.

"Gold Zero-Six, this is Gold One Actual. We have additional echoes running up from the dock. Request fire support on my POS to the following grid. How copy? Over."

Instead of Lieutenant Soddin, it was the gunnery sergeant who replied. "One Actual, this is Gold Zero-Seven. Zero-Six is tango-uniform this time. Will be a hot minute before I can run that fox on your POS. Self-serve in effect until then. Zero-Seven out."

Sparky swore and jumped back into the net. "All grenade-capable troopers, lase and plot for indirect to the following grid and send the hate."

Sparky transmitted grid coordinates to his fellow hull-busters, targeting a Hool force that was running straight for them. It seemed that the Hools had now decided that clearing out the warehouse was a first step before moving to destroy the tower. The grenadier marines racked their slides and tapped the triggers.

An odd feeling hit Sparky in the gut. He pinged the Gunny again. "Gunny, what's wrong with Lieutenant Soddin?"

He didn't know why he even asked the question, but Gunny's abrupt silence after saying, "Sergeant..." spoke volumes in Sparky's mind.

"There's been a... Doc Mahelona attacked her. Damn near tore her throat out. We subdued him but then that other kelhorned moktaar started shooting."

Sparky swallowed. "Roger. Out."

He looked back to D'ghar, the bad feeling mounting. Volson stood next to the Hool, watching the roof opening with his N-60, ready to repeat his trick if the kelhorns tried to drop in uninvited again. Sparky half-expected to see the alien that had saved his life suddenly turn on his fel-low hullbusters, just like the two moktaar had.

Which... was crazy.

But none of it mattered. Because right then, a cylindrical flash streaked past outside, followed by a blinding flash that dimmed the midday light as an orbital missile struck the tower in a cataclysmic explosion that turned the entire structure into several tons of high-velocity frag. The blast force funneled through the warehouse doors and windows like a tidal wave, knocking the marines from their catwalk roosts and catapulting them into the open air twenty meters above the floor below.

D'ghar caught the side of the gantry with one hand while snatching Volson with the other. But Sparky was thrown clear and tumbled end over end before hitting a stack of wooden shipping crates, punching right through them, and landing hard on the floor among packs of salted, processed meats about to be shipped to local shops for sale.

He struggled for breath as he stared through the roof toward an azure sky more brilliant than any he could re-member. As he absently reached for his weapon, which was no longer there, he saw a speck moving in front of the sun and growing gradually larger as it descended. It was clearly an enormous craft, the size of a Republic super carrier if not larger, and in moments it was launching smaller craft like mummy-bees leaving the hive.

A squelch in his comms competed with the ringing in his ears, and the marine net picked up a staticky transmission.

"All Swamp Rat elements... This is... Gomarii slave ship entering... drop pods full of zhee fighters... Additional Hool forces... Collapse on following grid and prepare to repel..."

Sparky never heard the coordinates. The enemy ship obscured the sun, making it all the easier for him to fade to black.

131ST LEGION

02

**Kham Do City
Temporary Legion Command Post**

Chhun covered his head as falling debris from the ceiling rained onto his desk, tap-dancing across his datapad. He grabbed the towel someone had found for him and wiped away the plaster. These command tablets were notoriously sturdy—the benefits of purchasing from a legitimate supplier versus the old House of Reason bidders. This model was purported to even be able to take a minor blaster hit before cracking, though Chhun had never seen that claim tested.

His assistant, a humanoid bot that looked like a metallic skeleton stuffed into some skinny kid's Legion armor, brushed dust off its chassis. "I am compelled to note that you would not need to cover your head, General, if you would simply wear your helmet."

"One would think," Chhun said. "But human instincts and reactions being what they are, you still end up covering your head even if you've got a bucket on."

"Perhaps that could be addressed in training," the bot suggested. "I should also note that using this position as our outpost remains ill-advised. Should hostile forces continue with their rocket attacks, there is a distinct possibility this structure may be compromised. Helmet or no, that would likely prove fatal, thus making for a terrible OER."

"Noted," Chhun replied, with not one iota of concern about what his current *officer evaluation report* might say.

He passed his hands over his battle board, checking on troop positions and battle assessments. Since moving from their spot on the airfield to take the cities, the MCR had dug in deep to repel the leejes looking to take back the big population centers. Heavy fighting had been reported over the last few hours, with some unique equipment appearing on the scene. But what was really sticking in his mind was the news of aggressive Gomarii slaving runs on Utopion, Enduran, and most recently, inside the Sinasian Cluster... just to name a few places. Reports were early but all indications pointed to a coordinated attack.

Such a thing wasn't unheard of in the Republic. The Gomarii, traveling in their massive slave ships, would disappear among the stars and reemerge to take new slaves on unprotected worlds, visiting much like the Savages had done before. The Republic waged a brief war against them, but Article Nineteen revealed that to be a mere pressure campaign to bring the Gomarii under heel, so that their resources and proclivity for slavery could be best used for the House of Reason's purposes.

And now, with the House of Reason gone, it seemed that the blue-skinned aliens were back to their old tricks. Their timing couldn't have been worse—or better, depending on your perspective. Chhun was already feeling pressure to wrap things up on Kima so that his Legion could be ready for redeployment should the Gomarii keep the attacks up.

Another explosion hit near the front of the building. Chhun watched the external holos and saw the spray of shrapnel. The blast nearly toppled one of the impervisteel barriers. Leejes ducked for cover and rode out the wave of violence until it passed over them in a shroud of dust. The choking cloud gave the expensive Legion sensor nodes a run for their credits; particulates and heavy smoke could wreak havoc with the vision modes typical on anything with a lens, but Legion gear was anything but typical, and where the building's holocams failed to maintain visuals, the Legion kit picked up the slack. Seismic grid mapping and thermo-sensory nodes collected data while the Legion buckets collectively burst their data through the L-comm and into a collection hub that assembled a HUD overlay every bit as good as real life.

It was a rare fight indeed where the Legion was ever blind.

A legionnaire nodded in apology as he made his way through Chhun's makeshift command room, passing the general and the bot. Outside, a tank turret mounted on four robotic legs came from behind the barrier to bring its weapons to bear. A four-shot alternating barrage from the twin barrels on either side of the dusty cupola barked their deadly serenade into the street. The MCR rocket teams scattered, and a repulsor truck arrived. The vehicle had an old recoilless rifle mounted in the back and used it immediately on the mobile defensive turret, denting the tank's armor with the last of its rounds and sending it into a tipsy stumble.

But the tank steadied itself and punched a hole through the middle of the technical as it attempted to reverse its way out of the combat zone. A second shot polished off anything still living in or around the truck as the vehicle's power cell not only blew, it took with it a nearby backup generator attached to a three-story building that had been burning for hours now. The generator's detonation showered the flaming wreck and most of the street in steel and duracrete.

"That's one way to do it," Chhun said.

"Incoming traffic for you, General." The combat controller bot moved aside so the general could see the meter-and-a-half-long digital work board flashing an icon in one corner. "And may I remind you, it's not just for your own sake but also Legion SOP that you should—"

"Have my bucket on. Yeah, I know, Chaz. You're sounding like an old point I used to serve under." Chhun pushed past his mech-de-camp, pulled his bucket into place, and hit the receive tag on the official Legion communication.

"Go for Chhun."

"General Chhun, this is *Centurion* REPO passing along traffic from *Centurion* Actual. Are you in place to receive?"

The question set Chhun aback. *Are you in place to receive?* Lieutenant Apollo was asking if he was out of the line of fire so he could talk. That was the kind of forethought that had been missing from the officer corps during all those years leading up to Article Nineteen. Professionalism and legit care for the boots on the ground because there was an understanding that what happened down below affected the game in orbit. And while Chhun knew the *Centurion* intelligence officer was a real pro back before she was hot-seated to the position on the Legion's lead boat, it was still a welcome change to get an interaction like this.

"Send it, LT," Chhun said with enthusiasm.

"I'm afraid I have a mixed bag for you, General. Peregrine Company boarded the wrecked MCR landing pod stranded in orbit after we hit it. The rebels inside were waiting for them. Losses were minimal, but the enemy managed to hot-drop four heavy assault mechs to the ground. One used its boosters to angle for the nation of Geram on the continent opposite you, but the other three are landing on Kham Do, just outside of Grafen, a major population center tied to the rebellion."

Left unsaid was what would likely happen if the *Centurion* used its main guns to take the assault mechs out before they hit the ground. Lots of civilian lives were at stake.

"We'll handle the ones landing on Kham Do," Chhun decided. "Get Colonel Scholtes to rig some anti-air and hit the floaters up close. He's on station running Second Bat. Right now."

"Will do, sir," Apollo confirmed. "The last elements of Victory Company are spinning up to join you in Kham Do. Third Battalion, Third Forward Strike Regiment, is taking command of Fort Blake, with a small contingent of Venom Company remaining in reserve."

"Good," Chhun said. He brushed his hand across the digital board, bringing the satellite feeds onto Fort Blake. The target acquisition arrays locked onto a flotilla of Legion aircraft leaving the AO. "Where am I with the rest of the population centers?"

"The major cities are being hit hard by elements of First and Second Battalions, with Third coming in behind to do house-to-house interdiction of the MCR, sir. We have five of the nine cities in control. The lesser targets are being handled by First and Second Free Rifle Kimbrin militia regiments supported by Legion kill teams."

"I guess Kill Team Venom got those First Rifles to pull their heads out of the sand and get into the fight," Chhun said.

"Yes, sir."

"As long as they're not pointing guns at us, I'm good with it. Thanks for the update, REPO. Anything further?"

"Yes, sir. I have Master Sergeant Masters calling in for you."

Chhun hadn't heard anything on that operation since Sergeant Major MakRaven took Zombie Squad and went looking for the operator. And now it seemed they'd found him? *Alive.* That kid had more lives that an Ankalorian sand cat.

"Put him through."

The L-comm's chime was followed by an echo-filled broadcast that was nowhere near the quality of a bucket-cast transmission. "General, it's Masters."

"Don't give me that 'General' schtick, Masters! You're good?" Chhun practically cried out.

"I'm cut up pretty bad. The donks tried to do that thing where they carve their comms digits into you. Real romantic. I tried to tell 'em my heart belongs to the Legion, but they just wouldn't listen. Whatever happened to no means no?"

Masters was saying the right things—saying what was expected, perhaps—but the usual flippant humor sounded forced, as though it was expected and so a performance was being put on. Something was wrong.

"Some guys just won't take the hint," Chhun said. "You sure you're doing all right? I need a sitrep but I can call Mak for it."

"Cohen... Sergeant Major's dead."

The words hit Chhun like he'd tried to cross a busy Spilursan street at rush hour. Sergeant Major Julius MakRaven couldn't be dead. But then, how many things on this planet hadn't been the way they were supposed to be? There weren't supposed to be any zhee on planet, and yet they had taken Masters prisoner. The MCR shouldn't have been able to overrun an entire Republic military base or, at last check, have giant troop movers capable of fielding mechs. And yet they were, and they did. It all felt like an ongoing series of impossibilities that somehow happened anyway. And now... MakRaven.

"How?" Chhun managed to say.

"He went down like a leej, sir," Masters said, his voice cracking.

"You out?"

"No, sir. Venom Company had to rain some heavy down on us. Danger close. Caused a partial cave-in. But that's not why I'm calling. I need you to look at the images we're sending."

Chhun's bucket received a file transfer from Lieutenant Apollo's station aboard the Legion super-destroyer *Centurion*. He opened it to a series of images of a Drusic-looking humanoid threaded with cybernetics and seemingly crushed under an avalanche.

"Masters, what am I looking at?"

"That thing you see crushed? It was talkin' before Venom dropped a mountain on it," Masters said. "But it had some kind of shield technology embedded in its body that was pretty close to what we see on Repub starships. It was talking some craziness about how our Legion working dog was the bringer of darkness, and by following it, we'd unleash the apocalypse or something. Now toggle over to the link to the live feed."

The general brushed the stills aside and brought up the L-comm signal from the bucket of one of the rescue team leejes, call sign Trent. The view focused on Masters's face, and Chhun noted the gashes and skinpacks renting space all along the leej's head. He had been horrifically cut, almost assuredly by the blade of one of those wicked *kankari* knives. Chhun gave the operator points just for being upright and coherent. No doubt he was running on stims and hate, and either one would last only so long in his condition. If Venom Company wasn't already on the move to pull the team out, Chhun would have to get there himself and do it.

But the purpose wasn't to show Chhun Masters's condition. Staticky and erratic, the feed panned to what looked like a cave, with ultrabeams revealing rock and stalactites... and then more. Someone had erected a set of plastite slats to keep the moisture and temperature at bay. An indicator in the leej's display showed there was a twenty-degree difference between the area with the dead Drusic-looking thing and the space beyond the slats.

Trent moved forward, and his ultrabeams pushed through to the other side, illuminating another part of the cave in eerie shadows.

An enormous, comfortable-looking bed hung suspended by chains off to one side. Shelves of books—actual paper tomes—were stacked on countless bookshelves, a massive hoard that collectors across the galactic core would envy. There was also a cluttered workstation and a cutting board that had been used both for vegetables and—from what Chhun could tell—the dissection of humanoids.

Chhun raised his eyebrows. "I'm not seeing anything that would raise my alarm, other than the cyber Drusic."

"It's this, sir."

Masters walked back into the frame, past another set of slats, and into an area of smooth, polished stone, with signs affixed to the walls. He beckoned for Trent to direct his feed at a metallic door featuring an old-school hand-wheel. Beside the door was a sign that read: *High-energy transfer in progress. Equalize all systems before entering.* And above the door, carved into the metal of the frame itself, was another message:

"We secure this, the brightest of our past, to secure our future."

— Thomas Roman

Chhun switched his bucket's view to panoramic so he could take in the scene as though he were there himself. "Does that quote mean anything to you guys?" he asked. The name was unfamiliar.

"Not a thing, General," Trent answered.

Masters pointed at the door. "We tried to open it, but it ain't budging, short of a bunch of cutting torches we don't have."

Chhun frowned. "I'm going to loop in Admiral Deynolds and her senior intel officer, First Lieutenant Apollo. Hold on, Masters."

It took less than a minute for Chhun to bring in the admiral and her intel officer and bring them up to speed.

"First of all," she began, "it's good to have you back, Master Sergeant Masters."

"Thank you, ma'am. Did you get the info burst LS-339's team sent you?"

"Yes, and we just had our filtering AIs sift through the video and images you sent. We've picked up some concerns on multiple fronts. But let's deal with this situation first. The sign above the door has raised multiple alarms with the algos owing to the style of Standard it's written in."

"We thought it was weird, too," Masters agreed. "Most everything on the planet is written in Kimbrin. This looks like a weird dialect of Standard."

"Very astute. The system identifies this dialect as ESE—Earth Standard English. Or at least the type of Standard we have from the earliest remaining records."

Lieutenant Apollo chimed in. "At this point, the only place you'll find ESE is in a few history books and the occasional museum piece commemorating early hyperspace travel."

Chhun sifted through his board again, coming up with the data packet sent from the *Centurion*. "It's interesting, for sure, but probably of more interest to an archaeological team—once the planet is secured."

"Okay, but check this out," Masters continued. "There's some kind of comm relay in here." The holo-cam shifted to show a device so rudimentary, Chhun simply had to take the operator's word on what it was. "It's bursting like crazy in here, looks like an L-comm, but not something we receive or decrypt-in-burst."

"We were picking up faint signals of something similar to L-comm coming from the planet," said Lieutenant Apollo, "but couldn't pinpoint its source."

"I don't understand," Chhun said. "Is it an L-comm transmission or isn't it? It's a fairly unique communications protocol."

Apollo nodded. "They use the same kind of quantum encryption but in a slightly different way. It's kind of like the difference between hyperchess and Skittra—both strategy games are played with the same pieces on the same holo-table, but they're not the same game."

Masters pressed the conversation forward, despite seeming more and more fatigued. Perhaps he needed what was uncovered to matter and in a big way. The price paid certainly demanded such. "This is where we need the big AI brains working for us. We've got this one site, which the locals apparently thought was inhabited by some kind of witch or shaman, only it's a cybernetic Drusic who's guarding a door written in ancient Standard ESP or whatever, and oh, it's also bursting its very own L-comm, only it's not an L-comm, but it's also not a Black Fleet S-comm, because at least we could decode those kelhorns. What in the nine hells are we looking at here?"

"Savages," Apollo blurted out.

Admiral Deynolds raised a critical eyebrow. "Excuse me, Lieutenant?"

"I'm sorry, sir." The lieutenant blushed. "The AI has it flagged just because of the ESE inscription. But I, well, take this with a grain of salt, but—"

"The point, Lieutenant?" Deynolds pressed. "General Chhun is busy with a war right now. And so are we."

"Right. In my *personal* study of Savage history, this feels like it checks too many boxes to be a coincidence. Quantum-based comms, ESE inscription, and a cybernetically modified alien species. These are all things that share a commonality with what we know about the Savages. The only thing missing are the Savage marines and whatever tech this tribe devoted itself to."

"That's a sizeable missing piece of evidence." Deynolds said sternly, before softening. "I'll take it under advisement."

While everyone in the comms circle pondered what that meant for the operation, Chhun went at the problem head-on. "Masters, you said the vault was secure, correct?"

"It's secure against the limited tools we have on site, General. Gonna need something brought in."

Chhun nodded. "For now, hunker down. Once I have some troop strength, I'll send in Venom or Warlock to escort you out. If they can spare the engineers, I'll have them investigate the door. But you may be there for some time. The fighting is still going heavy in the cities."

"Copy that, sir. Not like we've got anywhere to go."

"Good. And, Masters... make sure you get back."

03

**Kill Team Victory
Kham Do City**

"You sure we're going the right way?" Nobes asked.

Kill Team Victory moved hastily through a mostly conquered but still deadly city. The battle for Kima was marching to an inevitable end and a Legion victory—yet it was often in the twilight of such engagements where things went sideways for a soldier. The losers had nothing left to lose, and the victors, eager for an end to the fighting, could let their minds drift ahead to the anticipated peace.

"Since when do I get lost?" Neck barked from behind the wheel.

Nix leaned forward from his place in the back of the sled. "Well, there was that place in Bahnner Row—you know, the one with the bluish beach sand?"

"Mok-Shiva," said Nobes, giving the remembered place its name.

Neck rolled his eyes. "Oh come on! I wasn't lost. I just smelled those cinnamon pastry things we had on Sudlow."

Nix brought the omni-mags away from his face. They were out of their helmets and doing their best *not* to look like a group of legionnaires speeding at night in an open-air sled through a war-torn city. The place was supposedly under friendly Kimbrin control, but thus far, there was no sign of anybody, friendly or otherwise. "On Mok-Shiva? A moktaar world? Really?"

Neck, however, wouldn't relent. "What, moktaar can't eat cinnamon? And we all know that if I'd been right, you'd've thanked me."

"Granted," said Nobes, "those Sudlow pastries were worth getting lost for. If they had actually been there."

"*Thank* you." Neck slapped the sled's steering wheel.

A great, rumbling explosive boom sounded in the distance, several kilometers away in a still-contested portion of the city.

"Oof," said Nix. "That sounded like a building coming down. Hope we lit the fuse..."

The MCR tactics on display so far had been straight-up guerrilla warfare. Which was expected and surmountable, but not without a cost of time and potentially Legion lives—armor can't do a whole lot for a guy when six stories come crashing down on top of him.

But the kill team had other business to attend to. They sped through the streets, looking like a rich Kimbrin security detail.

Kill Team Victory's current op order was to stop the MCR from deploying the dangerous bioweapon VBX-13, apparently a darling of the Nether Ops weapons R&D sections. The toxin was deployed within an aggressive acidic-based, nanite-cycled vapor capable of desiccating flesh and even eating through protection suits. And yet the compound had absolutely no effect on anyone wearing enclosed Legion armor. That last feature was by design, as when missiles of VBX were launched at the civilian populace, the insane hope of the MCR seemed to be that the galaxy at large would assume that the Legion, not the MCR, was behind it.

Crazy people had a way of seeing the world in a crazy way. Unfortunately, that rarely stopped them from acting on those crazy conclusions.

It's always the other guy who's nuts.

Kill Team Victory had spent the last two days identifying key locations around the city. One of those was the Nghi-Han Assembly United building, a parts and electronics fabricator—a target the team had just finished painting. Toots, their breaching expert, had coaxed in a feed showing what was *actually* going on inside. A very motivated crew of MCR regulars was assembling the last pieces of a launching mechanism for a dispersion missile.

Team Leader and First Sergeant Okimbo Bombassa spoke over the net. "*Centurion* REPO, this is Victory Seven. I have TIM-y on target location. We have confirmed Victor Bravo X-ray on station, and streets in a two-block radius are clear of civilian traffic. Turn on the ultrabeam, over."

"Victory Seven," Lieutenant Apollo came back. "I read you. Target Identifier Marking is set. Target compound confirmed on site. No civilian factors, over."

"Roger, *Centurion* REPO. Execute."

Several heartbeats went by as commands were relayed between *Centurion*'s intelligence officer and the fire control officer, and approval was secured from the skipper in charge of an open line to the ground forces commander. It was one thing to launch an orbital strike or an EMP over open terrain where civilians weren't likely to be in the mix; it was another matter entirely to fire an orbital weapon into the center of a city. That was the kind of event that could end careers or land elected officials in the galactic hot seat, or worse—out of office.

REPO called back over comms. "Victory Seven, this is *Centurion* REPO. Mind the flash."

A lance of brilliant light burned in from the sky and slammed into the center of the Nghi-Han building. The shimmering bolt, nearly as wide as a grav tanker is long, seared its way through the reinforced roofing and dug straight to the power plant on the factory's lowest level.

But that heavy orbital bolt was merely carving a path. It was the second weapon, now already flashing through the clouds on a collision course with the newly formed hole in the Nghi-Han Assembly United factory building, that did the real damage.

The missile went unimpeded directly to the power plant at the base of the multilevel building. The resulting explosion put an end to the factory—and every building so unfortunate as to be located within a hundred meters. Shock waves opened fissures in the streets, and windows were shattered several blocks away. A giant fireball bathed the entire district in an eerie orange glow, and behind it, a dark mushroom cloud blocked out the moon.

Neck lifted his HUD glasses—a wearable piece of tech that bounced his usual Legion heads-up display before his eyes. He wanted to look on the destruction without a filter. "Did the targeteer for real pick out an OBB strike and chase it with a Hell Bat missile?"

"Hell *Fury* missile," corrected Bear from over the kill team's private net. "Bigger than the Hell Bat. Used for taking out decks on enemy cruisers."

Neck shrugged his shoulders. "Oh, is that all?"

"Movement on Target Two!" Toots shouted into the comms. "They brought a heavy."

The new target building, which was directly adjacent to their current parking structure, coughed out two medium walking mechs that probably last saw action during the end of the Savage Wars—a pair of Decahedron

Dynamics DM-71 Magpies. Each one looked like an armored starfighter with outboard chain guns and rocket pods above the cockpit. The entire affair rode atop a set of robotic chicken legs that were surprisingly agile.

The two mechs broke into a trot, their impact-compensating foot actuators tearing bits of duracrete from the street as they went. As they passed by the parking structure, the leejes could hear the electric hum of their power drives pushing them down the block.

"Okay, I'm getting a little curious about the whole military surplus thing these guys have going on," Neck said. "I mean, how big was the war museum they must have robbed to get all this stuff?"

"I wonder if they'd sell us a muzzle-loader," Nobes said drily.

Bear arrived on the back of an all-terrain repulsor, pulling back from a separate observation point to help the half of Kill Team Victory who now found themselves closer than they'd like to be to a pair of wandering mechs. The legionnaires were finishing pulling several cases from the rear of the sled. Bear joined the daisy chain of his men and helped slide the cases to the stairwell. The door to the stairs opened onto a group of armed Kimbrin unfazed at being nose-to-bucket with legionnaires dressed in tactical casual—these were the guys who were allegedly in control of this section of the city previously won by the Legion, then won again when a group of zhee moved in from nowhere. Their bodies still cluttered the streets.

The Kimbrin took the cases and shut themselves in.

Bear called through L-comm to Bombassa's half of the team. "'Bassa, we're set down here. How's it up there?"

"Ready on your go, sir."

Bear scowled in the confines of his bucket. Bombassa hadn't been quite the same since coming back from his time observing Nilo while in deep cover with a mercenary unit. While the man had been a legionnaire, a shock trooper, and a legionnaire again, being out in the cold all by yourself, surrounded by allies who would turn to enemies the moment they learned the truth, was a whole different beast. How Ford managed as well as he did was impressive. But then, some of the guys who knew him before, like Chhun, were adamant that the Ford they'd first met was a completely different person from the man he was now.

And then there was the matter of Bombassa's face. They'd changed his appearance and his voice prior to his infiltration mission. They'd had to, as there was a high possibility of him being recognized by other Black Leaf mercs who had once been legionnaires. But sometimes changing the man on the outside also changes the man on the inside. Bombassa had always been a leej of few words. Now he was downright cryptic.

But Bear knew as well as anyone that for a man like Bombassa, the job was the therapy. Slipping through shadows and running the knife... that was where a leej worked through the things that broke other men.

And they were knee-deep in a session right now.

Bear placed another call, this one to Brit, the Republic Internal Security Team's cyber warfare specialist that Bear had now been working with for several months.

After a moment, a young woman with white frosted hair in tight braids appeared in his HUD.

"Status?" Bear asked.

"Zier and his crew are suited up and outside the structure, waiting on your go," she reported. "I have control of the target building security. Make sure your team goes quiet. Those Mids might have non-networked security, and they just deployed a couple of guys in the street to support the mechs."

"Do you have false security feeds that can dupe them for a few seconds on that door the mechs came out of?"

"Doing it now," Brit confirmed. "Thirty seconds and scoot."

Bear made a *C* with his hand to show his team they had thirty seconds until they were straight at the target. Then the giant legionnaire tapped his comm for the Kimbrin INSEC strike team leader. "Zier, it's Bear. Hit it."

Above, the Kimbrin who had taken aero-precision launchers and missiles from the back of the kill team's sled opened fire on the mechs. Twin explosions sent sparks and debris flying across the parking structure.

"Mechs are dead," Bear reported to Bombassa. "Get your team moving."

From his place in position by the second building thought to involve the biochemical weapons, Bombassa pinged his half of the team over L-comm. "We'll take it at an angle and do a fast stack into the space. Toots, what's the track on that door?"

The special operator had launched a small observation bot to peer into the building's vehicle entrance, and now he sent the feed into the team's HUDs. Highlight reticles pinged seven Kimbrin guards with body armor and rifles. But while they looked wary—they couldn't have failed to miss the tremendous explosion of the Nghi-Han building—their posture suggested they weren't expecting serious trouble.

Except for one. "All I'm saying is we should at least close the door," came his voice over the drone's audio. "Didn't you say this building could withstand an orbital strike?" The Kimbrin held a pipe, and smoky tendrils drifted from his mouth as he talked.

"Not *that* strike," replied another man. "Besides, this door takes a full ninety seconds to close and then another ninety to open when we want to bring the mechs back in."

"Keep waiting," Toots mumbled—the mechs wouldn't be returning.

"I think we can spare a hundred and eighty seconds," said the first Kimbrin.

"Execute," ordered Bombassa, cutting short any reply that might be coming.

The legionnaires pushed forward and six Kimbrin went down in a moment, each with a blaster bolt to the forehead. Only one remained standing, frozen in place.

"Your lucky day," said Toots. "You get to be the guy still alive to help us."

The Kimbrin's weapon had already been dropped at the sight of the Dark Ops hitters, all wearing civilian clothes over a set of Legion slicks and topped off with the recon variant of their armor. The rebel was quickly pushed to his knees and ener-chained. He looked up at the legionnaire with defiant eyes. "And if I don't cooperate?"

Bombassa moved in. "I don't need you to cooperate."

A sled carrying Bear and the other half of the team arrived and unloaded.

"We good to keep going?" Bear asked.

Understanding appeared on the Kimbrin prisoner's face. "You're bringing me along in case I have to open any biometrics your people can't slice."

"And 'cause it's easier than draggin' a corpse around," Bear responded. "But only so much. Remember that."

Nobes waited by the lift door. "This is the service elevator for deliveries. Brit has us clear up to the third floor."

"Run it," Bear said.

Brit put a call in to Bear just as the elevator doors parted. "Hey boss, I have a feed coming off your Kimbrin there. He's broadcasting—both video and audio."

Bear scowled. "Nix, get over here and re-scan this fool."

The NCO took the Kimbrin from Bear and slammed him against the duracrete wall to daze him. Leaning him back to make the alien off-balance, Nix took off one glove so he could brush his fingers across the Kimbrin's eyes. He then held out his hand to Bear so the kill team commander could see the contact lens on his fingertip.

Nix flicked the device away and ran his hands across the rebel's kit. When he got to the Kimbrin's belt, he used his ungloved hand to remove a small device tucked into a fold in the fabric. He tossed it to his superior.

Bear inspected the casing for some marking to indicate what it was. Tapping the surface brought up a screen, but he still didn't recognize it.

Brit answered his unspoken question over the net. "That's a CDX-121 broadcast module. High-gain and capable of burst transmission on a multi-channel frequency-hopping band that can be cipher-coded with some of the latest and greatest."

"Sounds expensive," Bear grunted.

"Oh yeah. Right now, you're probably holding half a million credits in your hand."

Neck whistled. "Guess that's why they had to save money usin' those surplus mechs."

04

"Harvester Actual, this is Victory Six," Bear called into the L-comm.

"Good to hear from you," Chhun responded. He sounded like he meant it, which probably also meant something else was brewing beyond finishing up their current objective. "What have you got?"

"We're moving on the Vai-Kasa secondary labs. Ran into a speed bump, so I'm calling it in."

Bear rolled in the center of the stack as the group chewed up the stairs, having abandoned the elevator after discovering the rebel's transmission of intel. Bent in a shooter's posture and moving into the second flight, he could only imagine the burn the rest of the team had going through their quads as they were about to clear the third flight. Guys like Nix and Neck were PT fiends, but Nobes had a few more miles on the repulsors—and unlike Bear, he didn't have bionics in his legs. Though there was a part of Bear that felt lesser for having that advantage.

Nix flashed a hand signal and the legionnaires' buckets lit up with an associated warning—booby trap ahead. Without asking for confirmation or permission, the leej pulled a kit from his belt and got to work. A laser had been expertly set into the seam of the stair welds just above the duracrete, and anyone other than a legionnaire probably would have tripped it. But the stocky leej in the front of the stack had been running his bucket on flash scan, looking for just such devices threaded across the stairs.

Bear had been responsible for watching the upper walls and ceilings. Typical MCR improvised explosives in a stairwell included hollowing out the brick and then placing a poster or fire extinguisher mount over the hole after they'd set the charge. Sometimes they magnetically locked a detonation brick to the underside of the stairs, though those were easy to spot.

Chhun responded amid gunfire and explosions on his side of the comm. "You still have my attention. Bear. Hit me."

Bear quickly brought the general up to speed on the situation with the captured Kimbrin, and transferred images of the CDX-21 transmitter through the L-comm.

Chhun studied the image. "What are you thinking?"

The burly legionnaire took the opportunity to lay his suspicions on the table. "So we have this Kimbrin carrying a piece of kit that's worth more than I'll make over the course of my career. We have a convoluted attempt to paint the Legion as genocidal invaders by using this poison that we're immune to—and all the invoices we pulled in say the House of Liberty requested its use. Plus, seems like every MCR cell we come across has access to military surplus that's been parked in someone's garage for the last fifty years. The zhee, I don't know, but put everything else together, and you *know* what I'm thinking."

Chhun frowned. "Hold tight. I want *Centurion* REPO to look at this device."

After a moment, Chhun had not only the *Centurion*'s intelligence officer but Admiral Deynolds herself on the line.

"Cobalt Data Technologies hyper-com exchange module, model twenty-one," reported Lieutenant Apollo after only the briefest of glances at the device. "Two thousand of that particular unit were made under government contract with the House of Reason a few years ago, with a follow-up order for twenty-five hundred more, but that was interrupted by the invasion of Goth Sullus and the subsequent declaration of Article Nineteen."

"Was this an open military contract?" Deynolds asked.

"Negative, Admiral. Records say it was the House of Reason Committee on Strategic Affairs."

Both Bear and Chhun groaned.

"I take it that department is previously known to you, General?" Deynolds asked.

Chhun nodded. "That committee was one of the oversight and back-channel funding groups tying the House of Reason to Nether Ops."

"Sounds like it's time to get the House of Liberty involved," Deynolds said. "Will I be taking that meeting, or would you like to join, General?"

"I have my hands full here, Admiral."

"Understood," Deynolds said. "Send me everything you have on this, and I'll run it straight to our favorite delegate. While this isn't a smoking gun, it is a blaster hole. We'll see what can be done with it."

Bear sent a ping to Brit. "How are we looking on the other side of this door?"

"Roving two-man patrol is hurrying by the door now. Passing from your west to east in three, two, one. They will be clear of the hall in thirty seconds as long as they don't stop."

"Thanks, Brit."

Bear sent a tasking to his men through their buckets, and the leejes poured through the door like they were on mag rails. Ahead of them was the principle batch coding lab to program the nanite-infused pathogen the MCR had planned to hit the city with.

"You have one guy on the machine just inside the door," Brit called into the comm. "You have two more looking like they're waiting for the loader to put the gas canisters on the grav cart. The guys by the loader are armed. I can't see all of the Kimbrin by the workstation, but he doesn't look like he's carrying."

"Ping on overlay," Bear said.

A batch of dots appeared on a wire-frame map in their buckets. Nix put his hand on the door and transitioned to his pistol. "I have the two on the loader."

"Secure batch operator," Nobes called after him.

"Hallway right secure," said Neck.

"Hallway left secure," Bear echoed.

Bear sent the order that launched Nix into the room. Two bolts out of the rushing legionnaire's pistol punched the two cart-loaders onto the floor. Nobes was hot on the heels of the junior kill team operator, and he cut to the side, straight into the back of the machine operator. He slammed the Kimbrin's head into the console and then with a grab and a spin, had the man's hands ener-chained behind his back.

"Target secure," said Nobes.

"Targets down. Room secure," Nix called back.

"Finalizing last canister processing, halting processing on remaining batch," Brit said over the net. "No movement suggesting that remaining personnel are aware of your presence."

Bear and Neck joined the others in the lab and shut the door behind him. Bear approached the captured lab tech and addressed him with the intimidating tone provided by his bucket's speakers.

"When is the pickup scheduled for this batch of poison?"

"I not say anything to you, Legionnaire," the man spat back in Republic Standard.

Bear looked at the other leejes. "Everyone's suit good?" When he got thumbs all around, he walked over to one of the unprocessed canisters.

The Kimbrin's expression went from pure hate to *how do I get out of here.*

"You can't open that!" he shouted. "It has not been processed. If you open, it will kill you, even in your armor."

"I got a strong immune system. But all I want is answers. When?" Bear hoisted the canister by its carry handle and dropped it roughly at the Kimbrin's feet.

The lab tech seemed as afraid of the raw show of power—Bear had just deadlifted what normally took dedicated loaders to move—as he was by the poison.

"We have drivers," the man said, suddenly more agreeable. "This batch promised to factory down road for load into rockets. Other lab processing short batches."

Bear pressed his luck. "What's a short batch?"

"Small vapor in dispersion can. Set off by remote."

"That's not good," Nobes said into the L-comm.

"They're putting those together in the other lab?" Bear asked.

"Yes. Other side of floor."

"Brit, give me a peep at the other lab," Bear requested.

A moment later, a window popped into the HUD showing four men working a similar station to the one they'd just liberated. The only difference was that instead of loading heavy, oblong canisters, the crew moved small discus-shaped items from a conveyor and onto another grav sled.

Bear stood menacingly over the captured technician. "More talk."

The Kimbrin looked from the menacing operator to the deadly canister at his feet and back again, then stammered his response. "First orders were to gas those with corrupt Republic. Kick you and Republic off world. Not same now. Now we have bigger problem. New orders, have gas ready when need it. This batch program for short dispersion, no affect Legion. No affect Kimbrin."

"What *does* it affect?" Bear growled.

"The zhee. They were supposed to *help* us. Instead they attack!"

"Nobes. Isolation hood and secure," Bear ordered, tilting his head toward the prisoner. "We'll call it in after we take down the lab on the other side. Let's get after it."

Kill Team Victory stacked outside the door to the next lab. With no other labs occupied on this floor—at least according to Brit—they were free to use more severe methods to take down the space.

"Cooked micro-bangers going out," Nobes said.

Nix hit the release for the lab door, freeing the assistant team sergeant to double-fist a set of micro-concussion grenades into the room. The bangers detonated before they hit the floor, flashing the occupants with a fury of sound and pressure that knocked them into lurching stumbles. While the bigger models packed enough punch to kill life-forms like the Kimbrin in a confined space, these micro-bangers were more "scream in your face" than "seamball bat to the teeth."

Switching roles from last time, Bear went in first, slamming the Kimbrin tech into his workstation while Neck dropped in behind and ventilated the armored rebels doing the loading.

The remaining tech fell to her knees and raised a hand in supplication. "Please, I won't struggle. I promise," she said in near-perfect Galactic Standard.

Nix moved past his team commander to secure the new prisoner. "We're startin' to collect 'em all. You got an extra pocket we can shove all these spikers into?"

"Secure her in the other room like her buddy," Nobes directed. His HUD showed that a patrol of Kimbrin had left from a higher floor and were likely to be among the labs in another ninety seconds.

A moment later Bombassa called out that his team was in position to greet the security element once they exited the doors. A brief firefight rose and then fell as the other Dark Ops leejes eliminated the patrol.

"All clear," Bombassa reported.

"Nice work. Keep it rollin'," Bear said. "Got a feelin' the Legion commander wants us to hurry up and finish this job so we can start a new one."

05

Chhun ducked under a fallen support pillar as the forward part of the ceiling came down. Chaz, his robotic assistant mech, slowed the fall of a giant hunk of falling debris and then gingerly tossed it aside. At times like this, Chhun thought about how nice it might be if the Legion stepped out with a bunch of these bots at their side. It never took him very long to consider how much he'd equally lick his chops if an opposing force did the same. Bot armies were impressive when used on those unprepared to meet them; their utter destruction was equally impressive when going up against a foe who was.

"Chaz," he said, "time to get this show on the road. How's that bank I saw across the street earlier?"

Chaz held out his hand to relay an augmented reality feed of the nearby structure to Chhun's bucket. "The bank was compromised sixteen minutes ago, after the MCR determined that this was our primary staging point. They used one of the heavy assault mechs to drop mortars on the position. The bank was destroyed in the shelling, sir."

"I'll take suggestions on a new home, in that case," Chhun said. He whisked through screens in his bucket until he came upon a series of schematics that caught his attention. A quick study and his plan ran out of his mouth as though he'd had it in his hip pocket all along. "Chaz, instruct all commands to withdraw from the city center. Have all companies execute a rolling withdrawal at these points and give the Kimbrin a way to get to those spots in the city. Have Arrow Company block the zhee from getting there first, though."

Whatever the former Legion commander saw, the bot did not. "General, won't that give the rebels control over the city center and a way to entrench themselves?"

"That's what I'm counting on. Once they're in the middle, we close the gaps and fall on top of them."

"Ah. A trap."

"I spent most of my career in the Legion with zero orbital support," Chhun said. "Gotta make up for lost time."

He scooped up his ruck and handed the enormous battle board to his assistant. The bot took it without question under one arm. "General, it would be prudent to tell me where we are going so that I may protect you from incoming fire as we move."

"Believe it or not, I've been ducking fire long before you came off the assembly line." Chhun pointed to the battle board. "I'm signed for that, so no scratches."

Chhun waited for a break in the action before making a run for it. There was an anomaly one of his men in the nearby underground tram tunnels had identified that warranted a closer look while not taking any of his shooters off their rifles. He'd taken over command of the 131st Legion precisely for the freedom to move through the battlefield as he saw necessary, or to even pick up a rifle and participate directly like Pappy or General Rex had done in the past. It was just easier not to tell Chaz about it ahead of time.

A few shots peppered the side of the building at the sight of a new legionnaire stepping outside. The MCR's roving packs of fighters had to this point only sporadically harassed the city center, attacking from the commercial hub just outside of it that contained most of the various businesses, banks, and corporate headquarters that dominated the skyline. Intel suggested the MCR saw those buildings as something the Republic was less likely to destroy. Plus, by working all around Kham Do's center, they forced the Legion to spread out and meet them street-to-street and door-to-door.

Chhun had a strong feeling that they would adjust and move these actions to the city center itself if the Legion pulled out and set up its HQ farther out. The only wrinkle to the plan, aside from them not taking the bait, was this contingent of zhee fighters that seemed to have arrived only to wage an indiscriminate war against both sides.

No one had been able to identify a plausible reason for that yet, and Chhun had the uneasy feeling that the natural and well-known zhee propensity for waging war "just because" was carrying too much weight in their analysis at the moment.

A new sound joined the chorus of blaster bolts, explosives, and other ordnance deeper in the city: the heavy strike of mechanized feet slamming into the duracrete at a trot. A thunderous howl of outgoing repeating blaster fire tore apart a building just down the street where over a dozen MCR rebels had emplaced an old N-50. The HK-PP's machine blaster's single barrel, which had been coughing out a drumbeat of chaos, fell silent.

The mech's pilot came online. "General Chhun, this is Prowl One. Got a path cleared for your road trip."

As Chhun raced from cover behind a mobile gun turret lighting up rebel fighters on the other side of the street, a squad of legionnaires fell in behind him. Several rounds skipped off the duracrete close by, and occasionally one legionnaire or another would answer with a shot of their own. But whereas the MCR were throwing bolts downrange any time they had an opening, the legionnaires tapping their triggers didn't waste a shot. If their weapon barked, they made sure it had plenty of bite.

Chhun headed down a set of stairs leading to a belowground tram station. Normally this would have been a two-way escalator, but with the city's fluctuating power grid, the AI running city operations had converted the mobile conveyance into stairs. At the bottom, the general found several civilians huddled behind a heavy wooden table at the far end of the platform. At the sight of Chhun and the leejes, a man in athletic shorts and a ratty jacket stained with soot got up from behind the table and pointed a gun at them. It was an honest-to-goodness slug thrower complete with a revolving cylinder holding the bullets.

"Ya'tan," Chhun said and then tilted his head toward a leej medic, who stepped forward.

"Ya'tan," the ragged man replied, echoing the word for medic in their language. He tried to hand the weapon to the leej, but the medic waved it off while sweeping around to look at the others cowering behind the table.

A sergeant following the medic *did* take the weapon, and Chhun imagined the sergeant would also be looking for Legion asses to chew for letting that slug thrower get this far behind lines.

"What's the story here?" Chhun asked a legionnaire moving to round up the Kimbrin civilians. "This tunnel was supposed to be empty."

"Yes, sir," the leej replied. Which, while not helpful, was probably all the legionnaire could offer in way of an answer. Chhun didn't hold it against the man.

The Legion sergeant who'd taken the weapon was at the general's side. "Just pinged the L-comm to see what the story is, sir. We handed over security of this tunnel to Kimbrin friendlies an hour ago. Looks like these spikers were on the nice list and allowed through, but I'll send some boys to link up and verify."

"Let's get some observation bots sweeping this tram as well," Chhun ordered. "I want to know if our maps don't match up with the reality of the underground—might be that our Kimbrin guards were doing their job, and these got past them another way. Get me a full assessment of these people and why they didn't get to the city shelter at the other end of the tram line."

"Right away, General." The sergeant went to conduct his business.

A ping from Second Battalion promised a situational update. Colonel Peter Scholtes had been tearing from one city to the next, routing out heavy MCR emplacements and knocking their infrastructure back into the Stone Age. With every city taken, members of Third Battalion swept in behind and chased the MCR back to their holes to kill them where they slept. Chhun decided to get the report directly, but first it was time to notify Chaz to call off his hunt. These tunnels would do fine for a new mobile HQ. It was just too bad his moment of peace and quiet without the bot would come to an end.

He made the call and stepped over to an unoccupied space by the wall, allowed to move unmolested by the legionnaires and thanks to the absence of Chaz. Back when he was Legion commander, he'd have had leejes falling over themselves to ask if he needed help. They weren't being sycophantic; they were simply trying to show respect to someone they thought had the mettle, discpline, and moral compass it must take to rise to the post of number one legionnaire. So when no one jumped in to "help," he breathed a sigh of relief. It was gratifying to be just a general once more.

"Pete, it's Cohen. Hit me with some numbers," Chhun called into the L-comm.

"Good to hear from you, boss. Sounds like you guys are taking it heavy in Kham Do. We have seven of the nine major population centers on planet liberated. Third Batt is mopping cleanup with members of the local militia we already vetted. *Centurion* and the strike force just dropped Second and Third Battalion, Fifth Marines, to establish security zones throughout the cities and help reestablish planetary control for handoff to the Kimbrin Defense Force. We hit some lag here in Grafen, nation of Geram, though. MCR dropped some mechs into the mix and the damned things got through our anti-air. We'll pound 'em flat, but the price might be higher than desired."

"Make 'em pay, Pete. Check back with me in two."

"Roger, out," Scholtes said.

Chhun toggled to another channel. "Riggs, it's Chhun. Give me the numbers."

The first-person view that came up in his HUD was a blur of motion as blow after blow smashed through a Kimbrin combat helmet and then into the face beyond. The alien's face came apart like hamburger before Major Carden, call sign Riggs, pulled his fist from the helmet to allow a wet gurgle to escape what was once someone's jaw.

"Sorry about that, sir. Bunch of the KPDF decided to switch sides midway through our dealing with the locals. This one thought it would get him extra points if he brought his new bosses my scalp."

The loyalty of the Kimbrin Planetary Defense Force had been an ongoing problem. It seemed only the Yawds could be fully trusted.

"Looks like you're no longer on speaking terms," said Chhun.

Riggs laughed. "*He* ain't. I got your message from Colonel Blaine to leave avenues of approach for the Kimbrin to run the street. We were doing just that until the locals decided they didn't like us anymore. I got Bantam Company on the other side of the city getting hit something fierce with two heavy mechs that showed up, supported by a bunch of baby ones. My guys are good, though. Small batch of wounded, but that's all."

Chhun was glad for that. The Legion had suffered enough losses already. Actual Legion casualties were few, but every one of those men meant everything to someone out there. Chhun knew that as well as anyone—he'd had to notify more families than he could count after the war.

"Good idea to push us into the sewers," Riggs continued.

"Tram tunnels, not sewers. I also need you to check out the survivor shelters at your end. If they're still intact, I have some more to send you."

"Roger that, General. Riggs out."

As Chaz relayed Chhun's orders, the rest of the Legion platoon from the siege above started to make their way into the belowground tram station. Chhun called over someone whose stripes marked him as a platoon sergeant. "Hey, Leej."

"Sir. LS-364. What can I do you for?" The man's armor was dusty and scraped, and he sported a single blaster burn on the upper part of his chest plate. His name populated in Chhun's HUD as Sergeant First Class Nathan Gioconda, call sign Gio. The leej had been one of the many pulled off of Herbeer after Kill Team Victory discovered it was being used to hold political—and Legion—prisoners.

Chhun finished looking the man up and down. "Your LT still on this side of the grave?"

"Oh yes, sir. Lieutenant is up there with the RTO setting a trap for the Mids in case they come back for their weapons or their dead. You got something I can handle, General?"

"I do. If you have a leej who's handy on the sparks, I'd like to get some power to this tram so we can either use it or move it out of the way. I want it to be at the next station in twenty minutes."

"I'm tracin', sir," Gio said. He turned away from the task force commander and bellowed, "First Platoon, round up these civvies and get 'em all loaded on the train! And someone find me Clipper. I want this train hoppin' and poppin' five minutes ago."

Bear was eager from the moment Chhun pinged him on the L-comm. "General. Is this the part where you tell me you have another mission?"

"Negative, Bear," Chhun said into the comm. "At least not yet. Wanted to fill you in. We found Masters. He's alive and secure, awaiting exfiltration once we can spare some engineers to dig him out."

"That sounds bad and good. How is he?"

"He's been through a lot. And we lost Sergeant Major MakRaven getting to him."

Bear's voice dropped to almost a growl. "No. The big smaj? You sure?"

"Yeah. He held off a group of donks so the rest of the team could get into a cave for cover. Which is the other reason for this call. There are a lot of threads being spun on Kima and they're all starting to come together. I need to hear what you've been able to pull on the biochem situation."

Bear frowned. "It's not good. We managed to get the chem formula up to the *Centurion* so the geeks can pull it apart. This isn't like the first batch. Techs on the ground here say that it was all Dark Ops and Legion kill teams that put through the order for it. They're talkin' about Nether Ops, but don't know it."

"Most people see leej armor, they think legionnaire," Chhun said. "Nether Ops still hasn't had its day in the news cycle. House of Liberty will get to them."

"Yeah, well, that's not the worst of it. From the sound of it, these donks are s'posed to be here at the *behest* of Nether Ops. But it ain't exactly lookin' like the zhee are executing the plan. More like they're tryin' to take the whole planet for themselves."

"They're gonna have to pray real hard to the four bloody gods to get enough warriors for that. Zhee are complicating actions, but we're rollin' 'em, same as always."

"Ooah," Bear said and then paused. His eyes went to the side as he checked his HUD. "Got a priority comin' in from 'Bassa. Can I patch him in?"

"Do it," said Chhun.

"Go for Bear," the big man rumbled.

"We have a situation here," Bombassa said. "We were set up to ambush any rebels who came to investigate the station going dark. Sure enough, a whole group of Kimbrin in technicals rolled up. But before we could deal with them, they got shot to pieces from an adjoining alley."

"Did you see what hit them?" Chhun asked.

"General. Sorry, sir. I didn't see you there." If Bombassa was surprised, his voice didn't show it. The man was invariably dry and unflappable. "No sir, we didn't get eyes on. We spun up some bots, but it looks like they took off down the tram tunnel down the block. We caught some motion, but it was too far away in the feed to get a good look."

"Wait. They went into the tunnels?" Bear asked. "Isn't that where you are, sir? I just caught the FRAGO."

Chhun nodded. "Get me whatever info you can about what just happened, I need it yesterday."

"We'll work it, sir," Bear said. "'Bassa, you got someone to spare for a sneak?"

"I'll send the obs-bots down after them," Bombassa answered. "I'll hit you when it's set. Bombassa out."

"Hang tight if you can, General," Bear said. "I have something else for you."

The big legionnaire looked away and shouted, "Nobes! Get our prisoners ready to bounce on the quick. Have the carts in both labs rigged to blow if anyone but us tries to move them."

"Working it," the NCO shouted on the move.

Bear jumped back into the L-comm to focus again on Chhun. "General, I need a strike package prepped for my location."

Chhun was more than ready to make it happen. "Roger that, Captain. Hold position until I can get target confirm."

"Roger, sir. I read, hold position until TID."

The L-comm flashed a priority warning indicator in Bear's bucket that Bombassa was trying to reach him again. "Roger that, sir, looping in my first shirt. Go for Bear."

"Didn't take long for the bots to zip down and see what looks like a company-sized element of donks is pushing through those tram tunnels. They took out the peeper pretty fast too. They're dressed in black fatigues with plate carriers and blaster rifles and splitting into two elements. One force is pushing toward you, General. The other is heading down Yakato-Berra Boulevard right at us."

"First Sergeant," Bear began, "lie low until you're in the thick, then hit 'em. That's why you took one of those un-piloted antique mechs from the vehicle bay. How copy?"

Bombassa's voice was crisp despite the dire circum-stances. "Good copy. Going hot. Bombassa out."

"Looks like we're all going to be busy for the next few," Chhun said. "Call me back when you're ready for that O-strike, Captain. Chhun out."

06

"Okay, everybody." Brit clapped her hands, addressing the team who had called the filthy operations house their home for far too long a time. "Primary objective is complete and we're not sticking around to see what happens next."

The techs seemed to be waiting for this order, already aware that Kill Team Victory's securing of the final chemical warehouse marked the end of their needing to be hunkered down deep inside a city at war. Already the explosions and fighting were growing uncomfortably near.

"Anything bigger than that case stays," Brit said to one of the techs. "Prime the det-bricks and the thermos. This place is going nuclear."

As the techs moved around the dockside safe house piling up data cards, storage cubes, and feather chips while prepping their burner grenades, Brit deactivated her own workstation and readied it to join the immolation. One way or another, they would leave the place a scalded ruin. The only question was how far they could get toward friendly lines before the MCR noticed.

Gunshots sounded again, loud enough and close enough that Brit and every other tech on site instinctively ducked for cover. A volley of return blaster fire erupted from the roof as the security detail stationed there engaged what Brit hoped was a passing and *small* Kimbrin patrol.

"That's it, c'mon!" she shouted, ushering the techs out of the room and ready to toss the burner grenades onto the digital kindling.

One of the techs moved to the sturdy compound window and lifted up a slatted shade, forgoing the automated controls. "Zhee!"

Brit cursed herself for not seeing any indication that a zhee presence on Kima was even a possibility. None of the intel going into this invasion included the warring species anywhere in the picture, and even if playing a game of what-if, who would have guessed that the zhee who showed up to attack Kham Do and other cities on the planet would be so organized, equipped, and murderously sophisticated?

"Escape hatch just got breached," cried Dolphus, a burly human tech.

The "escape hatch" was actually the building's front entrance, which faced the water.

"Hallway turrets are up!" Dolphus yelled across the room.

Brit switched to the feed for the AI-driven defense guns. Hopefully they would be able to keep intruders on their haunches until Brit could burn it all, which was the entire point of bringing the heavy weapons in the first place.

The turrets began barking their automated fire, which could only mean that the zhee had already made their way into the compounds. Brit was starting to feel overwhelmed. How had these zhee evaded their sentries and how could they already be inside?

"Gun number one is down!" Dolphus shouted. "Any chance of getting that kill team of yours in here?"

"Working on it," Brit said. She had already switched to the kill team freq, intending to give a very different sitrep and request than the one she knew her techs would want to hear. But it was the only thing to do now. Zhee could be heard stomping on the roof, moving past dead security guards. They broke in windows and tossed bangers inside. Gunfire increased. The second turret whined away, trying to hold back a flood.

"Papa Bear, it's Brit. We're being overrun. Someone knew to hit us here and they sent the donks. Do not come for us. I say again. Do not come for us. We are lights out. Do not come. It was good working with you, Big Brother. Brit out."

She sent the message as a recording, knowing that if she spoke to Bear in person, he'd only try her resolve and tell her to sit tight. That wasn't a viable option. She had to burn the intel and take a page out of the Legion playbook by taking as many of the zhee with them as she could.

"They're climbing all over the roof," Dolphus shouted, his panic rising. "They're going to get in through the upper offices and come at us from above!"

"We planned for this scenario," Brit reminded the man. "No one's pulling us out in time. So we draw them farther in, keep them advancing, and *then* we light it up."

"Sket," a member of the team said, and then everyone seemed to mentally switch gears, abandoning any hope for survival. Weapons training kicked in, the kind that, once upon a time, had seemed so unlikely to ever be needed that they wouldn't have paid attention had it not been for the Dark Ops instructors making sure they learned the appropriate lessons inside and out.

An ear-shattering explosion rocked the building, and plaster and bits of support struts rained down as the ceiling opened up. But the zhee coming from above, eager to take out a Repub INSEC team, weren't expecting the reception they got. A deluge of fire and frag tore them to bits.

Brit turned to Dolphus. "Here we go."

"Sket..."

She primed the submachine blaster from her case. "Don't worry. If we do this right, you won't feel a thing."

Bombassa could see the towering flames of the INSEC building flare up into the night sky even from his vantage point far away while engaging with half of the zhee element that had emerged from the tram tunnels.

He would find out later that Brit and the rest of the team had been inside when it all went up. But now the chaos of the pitched firefight between his half of a kill team and too many zhee for comfort was all the information he needed or could process. The great equalizers in the fight were the heavy chain guns on the Magpie's chassis that chewed up the zhee fighters, who dove for any cover they could find. The legionnaires had powered down and positioned the mech so it would appear as though it had been knocked out of an earlier fight. But when the zhee got close, the war machine kicked up to its feet and went full metal Legion on the advancing warriors.

As Bombassa and his men opened up an ambush, the mech added its own firepower as it crashed through the first wave of advancing donks like a bullitar. Zhee were punted, slammed, and crushed beneath the thirty-five-ton mech as it charged into the center of the enemy line. They fired hand blasters at it and were rewarded for their efforts with nothing more than the heavy ping of small-caliber munitions bouncing off an armored vehicle.

Bombassa identified a zhee attempting to set up and fire an anti-vehicle rocket launcher. The donk had only managed to aim vaguely at the armored beast's chicken legs before well-placed shots from the first sergeant's rifle brought the zhee down.

The rout of the first wave of zhee gave Kill Team Victory time to move from their positions to fall back toward the lab building, seeking to set up a second ambush site for the zhee to stumble into. The operators used bounding overwatch as Toots backed the mech down the street and past a parking garage toward the designated structure.

That was when their luck ran out.

A shower of shattered glass and a hail of blaster bolts poured out onto the street, followed by a massive wave of donks who themselves had been lying in ambush.

"What the hell is this?" Toots called, swinging his mech around to put concentrated fire on the zhee.

While donks never shied away from sending their warriors to die in droves, usually it was part of a series of successive waves meant to overrun the opposition and bring about a slaughter worthy of their gods. And usually they just got dead for the trouble. But to send a wave in to get dusted just to *lure* the legionnaires into an ambush of their own... that was next-level thinking that none of the team had experienced from the alien warmongers before.

This group of zhee was organized. They coordinated their fire, focusing it on the coupling holding together the mech's knee joint. And as the mech spun to respond to the attacking squad, a second group appeared from the building across from the first, sending rocket-propelled grenades into the back armor where the machine's slider jets and communications hubs were housed.

The embattled mech pilot struggled to keep the machine upright. The machine now had a flutter in its step due to the attack on its knee, and the rocket attack had shut down the power core for the boosters while it ran a functions check.

"No wonder this model was discontinued," Toots grumbled. The sensor suite was showing multiple heat signatures in the surrounding buildings, and the legionnaire doused them with the arm-mounted chain guns. He checked his systems readouts. "Boosters might be offline, but the leg jets work just fine!"

In a sudden burst of speed and violence, the mech rocketed into the air and landed in a gaping hole in a building created by a poorly aimed RPG. He further studied his readouts. Outside, Bombassa and the legionnaires on foot were doing everything they could to keep the ambushers' heads down while watching for the eventual run from behind as more zhee surged from the tram station and out onto the street.

"Forecast is improving," the mech driver shouted. "We've got some Samurai model HK-PPs coming to check in on us!"

More fire came in heavy from the zhee, who seemed to sense that they weren't far from taking down the mech and then having the exposed legionnaires all to themselves.

"Mind if I play through?" came a voice over the L-comm.

Toots checked his rear screen. A *significantly* more modern mech had entered the battlescape, proudly painted with a Legion crest lest there be any doubt about whose side it was on. The Samurai program had been revitalized and reinvigorated under Chhun as Legion commander, and though their use was for now still limited to the special troops battalion—it was considered a trial run—their firepower and adaptability, when commanded by an experienced pilot, were worthy of an entire Legion squad.

But the old Magpie mech wasn't going to cede its spot in line. It came in behind the donks that had ambushed it only moments before. The *thump-thump-thump* of its outboard cannons began to tear apart both the donks and their would-be cover.

And then the Samurai mech called for its turn to play. It was a gangly thing, like a hunchbacked human with skinny arms—except it was coated in heavy armor and guns. Using the rail-gun launcher known as the SID-4, it dumped violence at six hundred rounds per minute, thundering out at nearly ten kilometers per second. The street turned into a hurricane of scrap, flak, and heavy debris, punching tickets for the donks to go see how their four gods liked the ambush so far.

Toots switched on the L-comm and signaled Bombassa. "Toots for 'Bassa. Marking remaining forces trying to angle on you from the building flanks."

"Solid copy," Bombassa responded. That was about as close as things had ever gotten. "Before you head over, drop a rocket on my indicator if you have any left."

Toots followed the blinking blip as it transformed into a reticle on his HUD. "Out of rockets," he told himself, "but there are a couple of MBLs..."

The micro-ballistic launcher system had originally been designed for fighting mech-to-mech. The guided missile could deliver a devastating warhead that would punch through most armor during the heyday of the Magpie's use. It was more of an annoyance to modern armored vehicles, but more than a match for a building where the contractors said they used all the best materials but maybe not so much. Which was precisely where Bombassa had instructed him to send the ordnance.

The Magpie jumped onto the street and began a limping trot down the avenue. A quick juke to the side and the mech changed course, crushing its way over street debris and the dead bodies of countless zhee who shouldn't even be on this side of the planet. A flash of the MBL sent a single plume of smoke racing from the launcher over its shoulder. Toots guided the weapon in a high arc that had it almost vertical when it made its descent. It changed course at the last moment, racing down the stairs for the tramway to the astonished faces of the fighters staging along the cover it provided. The street for nearly ten meters around the entrance mushroomed, throwing smoke and duracrete in all directions as the missile pounded home.

As the dust settled, it was Pina who made the call on Bombassa's behalf. "Yeah. That got 'em."

The Magpie and supporting Samurai mech moved triumphantly down the street, finding nothing but dead zhee.

"All right, Dark Ops," the Samurai driver said over L-comm. "I have orders from Harvester Actual to escort you and your team out of the AO. He wants you to report to him ASAP and get your kill team set for a follow-on mission."

Bear's voice responded. "Roger that, Prowler. Just talking to the general myself a moment ago. Have your crew line up with us and move out. I have confirmation from *Centurion* they're going to turn this block into a glass-topped parking lot when we're done."

07

The PLE-1J journalist bot waited patiently for its cue as the last throes of a battle between the Legion and whoever stood in its way worked toward a final, fatal end.

Actually, that was a good line. The bot stored it for later use.

The cue came from an embedded holocam that now floated before the journalist bot, framing it in front of an underground tramway entrance bustling with legionnaires and Kimbrin civilians.

"Thanks," the bot said, then allowed a brief pause for each holonews affiliate to insert the name of the local anchor who would appear to be throwing the segment to the foreign war correspondent. "I'm here outside the entrance to the tramway tunnels in the center of Kham Do City where we see Republic legionnaires working to restore order to this major metropolis. I don't know if you can see it, but that plume rising behind me used to be the First Republic Bank building in the heart of downtown. It was toppled by an aerial bombardment from the Legion's main battleship, the *Centurion.*"

Pausing for the network stations to get in their responses, the media stand-in bot used the spare cycles to check the status of its upload algos. On the other side of the broadcast, the stations could overly any reporter they wanted over the image of the bot—usually one who would reflect the local flavor and ethnicity—making it seem as if their own reporter was on the ground, up close with the troops and enduring the danger in order to witness and report the liberation firsthand.

"As you can see behind me, legionnaires are funneling civilians into their base of operations so they can be transported to the defense shelters deeper underground." Even as it spoke, the bot had to step to one side to get out of the path of a Legion main battle tank. The bot worked that into its update. "Troop operations come before the Republic's right to up-to-date battlefield coverage, I guess. The main battle tank, or MBT, is a staple of large Legion operations, and is particularly needed here on Kima now that the Mid-Core Rebellion has fielded a variety of bipedal mechs."

The bot paused again as the view panned to follow the Legion main battle tank, which stopped beside the crater that used to be First Republic Bank. Blaster bolts rained onto the vehicle from the closest buildings still standing, but its energy shield soaked up the damage, held it, and crackled as the power absorption built to a crescendo. Then it released it all at once, creating an energy wave that turned the dust in the air into a cloud of smoke that danced along the electric shimmer of the tank's energy field until the vehicle disappeared under the cloud's cover.

Here the algorithms recognized a choice. Some of the local editors would want to watch this unprompted tank battle, forgoing any further reporting in favor of the dramatic booms and rattles of small weapons fire. The cams would keep recording, but the PLE-1J had no reason to sit and watch. It continued on with its original story, serving those who were more inclined to air a story invoking humanoid sympathies, such as war refugees often did.

"Well, it seemed the Legion has matters well in hand," said the bot. "Let's go to our drone feeds over the improvised airfield in the river district where refugees are—"

The bot was cut off as it was dragged roughly away from its broadcast by a barbarian-sized legionnaire and pressed up against a combat sled just outside the tramway entrance. A media bot such as itself had limited defenses, mostly armor, but none whatsoever against the Legion combat knife that was shoved into the underside of the machine's CPU housing.

With a quick twist of the blade, the media bot signed off, permanently.

Bear examined the destroyed journalist bot at his feet and shook his head. He might take some flak for his choice in how to shut the bot down, but there was no way it had been granted approval to record and report on what was happening. And if it had... someone had screwed up.

The big legionnaire snapped to get Nobes's attention. "Get *Centurion* REPO to reach out to these news stations and tell them that running a media bot is cool, up until the point where they start taking pictures of combat zones and compromising Legion operations."

Chhun eyed the destroyed bot and then stepped gingerly over it on his way to grabbing Bear by the wrist and pulling him into a hug. "Good to have you back."

Bear, who was too strong to be pulled anywhere he didn't want to be, gave the back of Chhun's armor a colossal slap that rivaled the battlefield explosions. "Thanks, sir. Good to be back. What's doing?"

Chhun motioned him over to a gargantuan data board. "Got a change of mission for you."

Bear smiled and gave a grunt. "We knew that was comin'. Already have a pool goin' to see where we land."

"It's not going to go quite the way you were imagining it." Chhun removed the captain's bars from Bear's armor and attached a subdued oak leaf in their place. Then he swung his arm in a vicious elbow strike against the man's plate. "This op has a dress code."

The other men from Kill Team Victory saw what was going on, and they approached one by one, each one shaking *Major* Bear's hand and slamming the rank home as if their strike was the one that cemented it there. Chhun nodded after each hit to recognize the time-honored tradition. The hit on the rank reminded the newly christened leader that these people were his responsibility and the pain for their loss would be severe. And the handshake indicated respect. There should always be respect.

Bombassa approached last. He merely patted the rank and hugged the titanic legionnaire. Then he leaned close and said, "Get back to work, sir."

Chhun addressed Bombassa. "First Sergeant, get your team kitted up and ready for new orders. Gotta throw you back into the dirt."

"Yes, General."

Chhun then turned back to Bear. "*Major*, you are now the top Dark Ops leej for the sector. This was Major Owens's seat; you won't diminish it. Coordinate the Dark Ops teams and find me some answers. I want to know what the zhee are doing here, why they're fighting everybody they come across, and why all of a sudden they're using tactics that Legion SOG teams could only get one out of a hundred donks to execute. Kill Team Victory's job is going to be to secure Masters and assess his location while awaiting further orders. The place where Masters is holed up may have some connection to these other mysteries, and it may not. Either way, I want eyes I can trust taking a closer look and reporting back."

"Roger that, sir," Bear answered. "Sir, who's going to run my team until we find a new set of bars for them?"

"Trust me when I say that I know how you feel in asking that question, Major. I'll tell you what was once told to me, and was told to Captain Ford before that: it's no longer your concern. 'Bassa can run them until we figure it out. You get me that intel, Bear. Something is off here and I need you to find out what it is."

"Of course, General. I'm on it."

KEEL

08

The *Indelible VI* circled over a clearing on a small forest moon that Makaffie's homing device promised would lead to Prisma. Or, at the very least, would lead to the scout ship that Prisma and her mother, the enigmatic Reina, had taken from the Savage reclaimer. Captain Aeson Keel kept his attention split between his ships' advanced sensors and his direct visual on the ground below. Those sensors had found the beacon and identified a ship, but were coming up empty in a conical sweep for humanoid life.

Keel tilted the *Six* so that those inside the cockpit could likewise see down to the ship on the landing site below. Turning to Makaffie, who sat in the back seats with the Wild Man, the smuggler asked, "This the one?"

The odd, scrawny little operator craned his neck to peer through the cockpit's side viewport, looking like a strung-out star turtle stretching from its shell. Then he switched his attention to the cockpit dash and began to cycle through the external holos.

Keel slapped his hand away. "Stop fiddling."

Makaffie withdrew. "Just wanted a closer look is all." He sat back in his seat abruptly and heaved a shrug. "Looks like the one. But let's ask the Wild Man for a second opinion. Wild Man? Does that, or does that not, look like the ship that one Prisma Maydoon and her most useful war bot brought to the now-atomized Savage hulk? And does it, or does it not, *also* look like the very same ship that Prisma, together with her war bot *and* her mother, left with?"

"Yeah," mumbled the Wild Man. His voice permanently raspy and dry.

Leenah plotted a course from the navigator's chair. "We've got room to set down next to it." Her voice was tempered with anticipation. This was as close as they'd gotten to finding Prisma since they'd just missed her at En Shakar and again aboard the Savage reclaimer.

Keel inspected the proposed landing zone. "Yeah, that looks good."

The ship began its descent, and Keel thumbed toward the cockpit exit, looking at Makaffie and the Wild Man. "You two go get jocked up and ready to go. If you find Skrizz, see if he'll help you secure the LZ. I'm gonna check on Garret and then I'll be right behind you."

The code slicer was sleeping off his injuries under the influence of a carefully selected pain cocktail administered in the *Six*'s newly restocked med bay. He'd probably be surprised to wake up and realize he'd missed not only the resolution of the Savage ordeal, but also the capture of several Nether Ops agents trying to flee in an escape pod. Those zealots had used suicide capsules to avoid being of any use, but they still brought joy to Death, Destroyer of Worlds, who had been delighted to be tasked with dumping them out of the airlock.

More had happened as well—most importantly, a division between Keel and Nilo that had led to their party splitting into two groups and going their separate ways. Keel was bound and determined to find Prisma, no matter what. Makaffie stayed with him—he owed him that much—and Wild Man went where Makaffie went. But Nilo felt that going on some fool errand to find Earth was somehow the most pressing thing in the galaxy. He was accompanied by Jack and Zora, as well as by Andien Broxin and her peculiar associate, Praxus.

Broxin had pushed hard for Keel and his team to come along... but the smuggler wouldn't have it.

"A member of my crew has gone missing," Keel told her. "You know how I feel about that."

"I do. And... for what it's worth... I'm sorry. I still thought I could change things from the inside back then." That's what Andien told Keel at their parting, when minds were made up and all that was left to do was get going. "But before this is all over... we're going to need one another. We're all going to need each other. Find Prisma, by all means, but then... don't disappear. We're going to need you."

Keel had managed a chuckle at those words, but found they'd stayed with him. He was no Tyrus Rechs, but maybe something about him having that legendary armor made people look to him as though he were. Or maybe...

Maybe what had been, and who Aeson Ford truly was—though few people knew it, and even Keel himself only barely qualified among that number—maybe that was somehow a factor. No matter how hard he tried not to... he wondered.

In the cockpit, Makaffie stood, and the much bigger Wild Man followed suit, more slowly, and with a ponderous stretch. They were following Keel's orders. Makaffie saluted. "Yes sir, Sergeant Fast."

When the cockpit was reduced to just Keel and his navigator, Leenah folded her arms and raised an eyebrow.

"There's zero chance I'm staying on board this ship and waiting while Prisma might be out there somewhere."

Keel gave a half smile. "I didn't ask you to." He settled the *Indelible VI* down for a soft, almost undetectable landing. "Besides. I thought you and Garret put in place the kind of security defense systems that don't need someone staying behind."

As Leenah nodded, her pink, hair-like tendrils swept in front of her face. She brushed them back in that way that Keel loved but never mentioned. "Short of an army of war bots equipped with cutting torches, nobody's forcing their way on board the *Six* once we lock her up."

"And if that army shows up?"

"Garret has it so the ship will take off rather than allow itself to be breached."

Keel frowned. "He's not actually trusting that crazy AI, is he?"

"That 'crazy AI' isn't here anymore. There is no AI, just like you like. But the ship has some automated programming and sophisticated algorithms that will get almost as close."

Keel vented coolants and cycled through the landing sequence while his sensors and exterior defense weapons watched for threats. "Good."

"And I'm coming with you," Leenah said, again preemptively trying to overcome any effort the captain might take to leave her behind. "The ship is safe. And as for me, I don't want to be safe if being safe means not being able to help Prisma."

Keel smiled ruefully. "You know I won't try to stop you... I just have a bad feeling now that you've said that."

Garret surprised Keel and Leenah by already being up and on his feet when they entered the med bay. The young code slicer was looking around the room as though he wasn't exactly sure where he was.

Leenah held out her arm and walked toward him. "Are you sure you should be up right now?"

"Yeah," Garret said, his voice slightly singsong and his eyes still dilated from the recovery cocktail he'd been served through an autoinjector. He staggered a bit and then had to lean back against the exam table where he'd been strapped in. "Maybe... maybe a little woozy."

Leenah helped him lay back on the table. She stroked his hair. "It's nice to see you on your feet, but maybe a little too soon, hmm?"

"Yeah... a little."

"You gave us all quite a scare."

"I feel like I died."

Keel was leaning against the bay's frame with his arms crossed. "Glad you didn't, kid. In fact, if it wasn't for you, it's us who might've bought it."

"Oh," Garret said weakly, distantly, "that was nothing. You've done so much more for us... I was just trying to think of what you would do if you were me. The real problem was..."

Garret sat bolt upright, yelped, "Oh no!" and then was overcome with dizziness again and had to be laid back down by Leenah.

"Kid... take it easy." Keel was by the code slicer's side now, checking the bio readings displayed around him.

Things looked all right. Just the lingering effects of the drugs. There was a stim they could inject that would negate the cocktail, but Keel wanted the healing drugs to run their full cycle.

"We're not on the *Battle Phoenix*," Garret said.

Keel gave a slight shake of his head. "Not for a while now."

The kid sat up again, blinking away his dizziness and waving away Leenah's attempts to settle him back down. "There's something really important there. Like... *really important*. Did either of you bring a data cube with you? Did G232 explain?"

"No," Keel said, looking at Leenah. They both were at a loss over what Garret was after. "All the bots said was that they still had some more work to do to get the *Phoenix* back up and running. We left them to take care of that. Your buddy Nilo along with Jack and Zora are off looking for the end of rainbows."

"Garret, we think we've found Prisma," Leenah added.

The code slicer's eyes widened. "Oh! That's good. But also... we really need to get that data cube. See, when the *Phoenix* was attacked, I had to work with Lyra—that's Tyrus Rechs's old AI; I think he was in love with her or something—and anyway—"

"He was in love with an AI?" Keel said.

"Probably. But the point is, Lyra helped me shut down the *Phoenix* to keep the AI from taking over, and to keep her from being completely annihilated, I had her jump into a data cube at the last second. She did, but I think part of the AI jumped in after her and I took a look at it—just a cursory look because I had to bring you the armor—but I'm worried that this AI might belong to... well, I don't think it's actually his fault, but it makes sense because he probably used Savage tech to advance her as far as he did and you can't really trust Savage tech, and so if there really are Savages out there, then maybe she's working for them and that's why she tried to stop what we were doing, but I won't know until I can take a good look at the cube, and of course the lights were out when I had the chance, plus I had to deliver the armor and—"

"Kid!" Keel shouted, cutting off the flow of words. "Save the story for another time or tell it on the way if you think you're up to scouting around a bit."

Leenah looked at Keel disapprovingly. "Garret is in no shape to leave this room."

But the code slicer hopped off the bed, steadied himself, and said, "No! No, I'm good. I want to come. Especially if we might find Prisma. And look! I'm not even dizzy right now." He spun around in a circle. "See? Didn't pass out or anything. I can keep up. And if I can't, I'll just turn around. But this is important. We need to stay together, and I really should tell you the whole story."

"Fine by me," Keel said. "But let's get going. Makaffie said the LZ was secure a while ago and they're out there waiting."

Garret smiled and hurried after Keel, ducking his head low to hide his embarrassment as he rushed past Leenah, who still didn't approve of him getting out of bed yet.

As they moved toward the exterior ramp, Keel passed his workbench, stopped, went back to it, and grabbed a blaster he kept in one of the drawers. Nothing heavy-duty like his Intec x6, just a small, concealed job that could rip off a dozen medium-powered shots, lethal at close range. He handed it to Garret. "Time you start carrying, kid. Take it everywhere."

Garret stared in wonder as Keel fastened the weapon's holster around his waist and then gave him a quick tutorial. "No safety exactly, but you have to grip it exactly like this or it won't fire. See?" Garret nodded eagerly, and Keel continued. "This controls the bolt power. Don't touch it. It's where it needs to be. This releases your charge pack. You've got two more in your belt. Don't lose them and keep the empties. Cheaper to refill than buy new. To aim it, look down that tube, and wherever the blue line is, that's where the bolt will go as long as you're within fifteen meters. Longer than that, just duck and let me handle things. Got it?"

Garret nodded and then practiced putting the weapon into his holster and pulling it back out again until Keel was satisfied.

"Good enough for now, kid. We can work on it when we have more time. Let's go." Keel started to turn, but he could see there was something else on the code slicer's mind. "You got a question?"

"Is it a... *loud* gun?"

Keel stared at the kid for a second. "No."

And then the three of them went down the ramp to join the others.

09

It was Captain Keel himself who inspected the archaic scout jumper, exploring the small ship with his blaster drawn. He reemerged to find Makaffie and the Wild Man pulling security while Leenah and Garret waited anxiously for his report.

"What did you find?" Leenah asked.

"Not much. But I'm pretty sure it was Prisma's ship." Keel held up two strands of dark hair. "I found these inside a stasis pod. These old ships were meant for jumps that could last a while."

Leenah took the strands and held them close to her chest before shoving them in her coverall pockets like jewels.

Keel called out to Makaffie. "Think you coulda found a more conspicuous spot for that tracker?"

The skinny man shrugged. "I doubt it, and it doesn't matter. They didn't find it. And that's the important thing, Sergeant Fast. You see, most people in the galaxy don't think like us. They get into their sleds or ships with the assumption that there's nothing to be found. They don't even look. They never look. And so, why would a teenage girl look?"

"A war bot might," Keel countered. "Or her mother."

"Well, if you ask me, the bot wasn't all that thrilled about Prisma leaving in the first place. So it wasn't going to do a scan unless ordered to. The girl wasn't going to give that kind of order because it wouldn't occur to her. And as for the mother—oh, the mother!—well now, there is a type who *also* wouldn't think of looking. Not because she couldn't imagine it, but because she wouldn't have seen how *we* would dare to do something like that to *her*. She made it clear who had the power right away, and of course, when the blaster is to your head, you go right along with it. But then, she clearly underestimated our underhanded nature, didn't she?"

Makaffie pounded the Wild Man's armor at the chest, which was eye level with the smaller man, who gave his peculiar, tittering laugh.

Wild Man nodded but didn't join in the laughter. "Captain Fast..."

"Call me Captain Keel if you've got to use a title," Keel said. "Otherwise, Keel is fine. Wraith for formal occasions."

The Wild Man nodded and seemed to be slowly storing away this new piece of intel, as though he'd missed the sarcasm entirely. He licked his lips. "Captain Keel... when do you think we'll get back to killin' Savages?"

Keel cocked an eyebrow. "I dunno, pal. Not sure there's too many around, if I'm being honest. Those reclaimers might be the last Savages left around."

Makaffie looked at the Wild Man with concern, however. "We need to talk," he mumbled.

"I'm fine," the big man growled. Then, to Keel: "Nilo said there would be more."

Keel circled around as though looking for Savages to reveal themselves. "Yeah, well... not here."

The Wild Man opened his mouth and then seemed to reconsider.

Makaffie watched him for a moment. "For now, Wild Man, we're going to go ahead and find out what we can about Prisma. We told the good Sergeant Fast here that we'd do just that. Here comes Skrizz. If there are any tracks to be found, I'll bet a Lizzaar's bankroll the wobanki discovered them."

Skrizz emerged silently from a copse of trees atop a rocky bank that led down to a small but swift-moving stream. The wobanki moved casually, almost effortlessly, and yet covered the ground between the distant body of water and the humans alarmingly fast. There was something awe-inspiring in the way the large catman moved with equal parts grace and speed.

"Please tell me you found something," Leenah said, and then grew visibly excited as Skrizz yammered that he had. Leenah took a step forward, pensively, as though afraid she was getting too close to a truth that might hurt. But she had to ask. "Prisma? You found her tracks?"

"Nachu Prizz-mah," Skrizz clarified; he'd neither seen nor scented anything left by the girl or her mother. Nevertheless, the warrior was sure he'd found the direction they'd headed. A thing he explained in two simple words, spoken in Standard. "Warr botch."

"You're talkin' about Crash," said Keel.

Skrizz nodded an affirmative and led the team to a set of tracks that cut through the round riverbed stones and the silt that sat between them. Whatever they were, they'd been made by something large and heavy.

"That's the war bot all right," Keel declared. He turned to Leenah. "Good bet they didn't have it fly here by itself."

Leenah looked around, examining the tracks and well past them. "I just wish we could see Prisma's footprints, too. Just to be sure."

"Not likely with how many stones are here, but maybe somewhere farther down. Don't get your hopes up, though. Looks like a rain fell between now and whenever these tracks were made. It's just that Crash is too heavy to get his hidden so fast."

They set off, following the bot's imprints as best they could. Leenah walked protectively alongside Garret, though he was keeping up fine so far—the *Six*'s new med bay had proven itself more than capable of handling the kid's injuries. Keel brought up the rear, while the Wild Man and Makaffie staggered themselves behind Skrizz, who led the expedition and periodically stopped to sniff the air before bolting ahead and circling back to where he began as he ranged and roamed.

"How long ago do you think these tracks were made?" Makaffie asked the wobanki.

Skrizz gave a precise date but yammered it in a tone that meant something less than absolute certainty—an educated guess.

"That fits the timetable," Makaffie proclaimed. "We might just catch up to her yet. Although it's the girl's mother I'm most worried about."

Leenah bit her lip and asked a question that must have been on her mind for some time. "Tell me about her. Prisma's mother."

"Oh," Makaffie said, clearly not expecting the question. "Well, she, uh, I mean she was... well, that doesn't matter. But she, uh... I don't trust her."

"I gathered that much. I'm trying to picture this woman. I've known Prisma as an orphan for so long that her parents are an empty space in my mind. What did she look like?"

"She was beautiful. Almost too pretty, like you felt you shouldn't look at her or you'd stare."

"Prisma is going to grow up to be a beautiful woman," Leenah said. "That's not surprising to hear."

"Yeah. Well, I suppose they looked pretty well alike. Mouth was the same. Hair, too. Different eyes, but otherwise... Hey, forget what I said about her and being worried. I'm sure, I'm sure she's fine. It's her mother. I ought to be worried that we're just guessing wrong and these tracks belong to some other war bot who traveled to this world—though if so, it couldn't have been that long ago, given the nature of this planet."

"What do you mean, 'nature of this planet'?" Leenah asked as she looked up at the foliage—thin green leaves made golden by the sun radiating down through them. That filtered yellow sunlight cast the babbling stream at their side in a mottled mix of shadows and bright, reflective light that penetrated the clear water all the way down to its rocky bed.

Makaffie ignored the question. "It's a pretty world, isn't it?"

"Beautiful. I'm surprised there aren't any settlements. It isn't that far from the mid-core."

"Well, we just happened to have come at the right time. The beautiful season. See, this planet gets a spring that would burn most humanoids to death. But that melts the winter. Then, as it floats back away from the scorching sun, there's a period where things get real nice. And everything gets busy growing and looking like you see it now. Then..." Makaffie snapped his fingers. "Forty or fifty years of the nastiest, most unpredictable winter you can think of. One that always ends in a deep freeze at the farthest point. Then another thaw which is so catastrophic, the landscape is completely rearranged. That kind of thing does all sorts of damage to a housing market."

Leenah took another lingering look at the trees and the brook. "Hard to believe."

"Believe it," Keel said. "This is the kind of place that if it gets any visitors, it's just gonna be adventure travelers stopping in for a weekend. Still, I wouldn't put it past some enterprising land speculator to dump a few would-be colonists from the edge out this way. Credits to bring them to the land of plenty and then more credits to pull them out as things go to hell."

"Now there's a cynical take," said Makaffie, who paused to refill his canteen from the stream. "What do you think, Wild Man?"

"I don't know."

"Of course you don't. I should have been clearer, as I knew you didn't have any particular interest or opinion regarding speculative land investments. My mind was going back to what Skrizz said. What do you think about that? About the tracks. You're a tracker. We spent a lot of time stalking Savages together, and you did even more of that work in your prehistory, as I recall. So I'd like another expert opinion, since I have it at my disposal."

Makaffie had been watching the Wild Man during his windy speech, and noticed the slight, involuntary twitch of the big man's eye upon hearing the word "Savage." Just as telling was how the big man attempted to hide the reaction once he'd let it out.

"Seems about right," the Wild Man said.

Makaffie kept his eyes on the Wild Man, even while addressing Keel. "How about you, Sergeant Fast? Is there a divergent opinion to be had on the matter? Maybe something rattling around in that shooter's brain of yours?"

"You looking for a reason to turn around or something?" Keel asked, somewhat gruffly. The little man could be, sometimes, exceptionally annoying.

"Not at all. I'm just... thinking."

They went on in silence for the next few kilometers, settling into a steady rhythm of hiking. Of course, it was Makaffie who attempted to strike up a new conversation after enough time had passed. He fell back to Captain Keel upon seeing that the man had pushed to the middle of the troop to praise Garret on keeping up so well.

"Sergeant Fast. Do you know what this reminds me of? Think back now." Makaffie smiled at the sudden glare that Keel leveled at him; he'd been warned to give up the little games about their supposed shared past. "It reminds me of the time when we, and by 'we,' I mean you of course, and me, and let's see... I think Carter was there but Wild Man was recovering from a gunshot he'd taken aboard some Savage hulk or another, so he had to sit this one out. Walker was with us most likely. Also Albritton. I liked him, but I only remember that because I specifically recall he had his head cut off by a Savvie on the next op. There were eight of us in total. I can't for the life of me remember who the others were." Makaffie snapped his fingers softly, trying to recall the names. "No General on that bounce. Maybe Raff? I guess it doesn't matter. The point is, we were on this world, which was a whole lot like the world we're currently traversing, if you swap out the trees for that black grass that wouldn't burn for anything. And no water. Just those acid pools so we had to keep our buckets on nonstop to keep the fumes out. Nasty world, but otherwise, not too different from this one. And we were walking between those pools tracking down that model of Savage war bot... not the TC-50s if you remember those, but the ones that came just before it."

"I don't remember any of it and I don't care," Keel said.

"Well now, I didn't forget that you don't care. I remember you saying not to tell you about all that any longer. You were quite clear about your lack of caring. So please don't think you're crazy or misremembering. You very specifically told me that this kind of recollecting jammed your cosmic *chi*. But the thing about that is, people say they don't wanna talk about it or don't wanna hear it—whatever *it* is in these theoretical cases—until one day they *do* care. And on that day, they thank you for bringing it up. Only, they never tell you about their change of heart. Humans are odd that way. So, some brave soul, not fearing the harsh that comes with never learning and always offending, has to go ahead and venture forth to find out if today is the day. I told myself before we started talkin', maybe Captain Keel will care about all this today. Maybe he'll want to talk about that life. But clearly, you don't."

"No. I don't."

"Which I now know and understand. I guess I'll let our story end right there with us moving through the acid pools and hunting the war bots."

"Good."

They walked together in silence for several meters.

"I don't understand why you don't want to know these things about yourself, Ford."

Keel set his jaw, but wasn't angry. "Everything you're offering me, it's just... facts. Someone tells you that you visited this world and went to that sector back when you were a little kid. Okay. Fine. What good does it do you? You don't remember it. Can't learn from it. You're just taking someone's word for it."

"Well, that's a pessimistic view of things."

"I don't need someone telling me about all the bad things that might've happened in my past."

"Who says they're all bad?"

"You remember a happy ride with this Kill Team Ice, Makaffie?"

The scrawny man looked down. "Yes."

"And what happened after that. Except for you and your pal up ahead? They're all dead now, right?"

"Well, I suppose things always go bad when you give them enough time. Nature of life and the galaxy."

Keel gave a nod. "The past hasn't done a great job of earning a place in the future. So why not leave it there."

10

The war bot's tracks disappeared just before a fantastic Temple of the Ancients that sat in a clearing beyond a swift bend in the stream that had been carved out in the aftermath of the planet's last long winter. Skrizz couldn't find any further sign of Crash or the others on either side of the banks or around the temple. The wobanki yammered to Keel that it was possible that Crash and the others had begun moving through the river itself, but that seemed unlikely.

Keel waited for Garret to reach the rest of the group. The kid was falling behind just a bit, and had developed a slight limp, probably from a blister or some other such discomfort of the kind that always comes to feet and boots unaccustomed to long marches.

"Holdin' up all right, kid?" Keel asked.

Garret nodded and gave a breathy, "Yeah. I'll be okay."

"Good. Listen... Crash didn't have any repulsor capabilities, did he? Because from the looks of things, this is where his trail ends and Skrizz and I don't see him around anywhere."

Garret giggled at a joke Keel didn't know he'd made. The kid grew thoughtful, and then excited. "He doesn't—none of that model do—but really it wouldn't be too hard to do it if you want me to. I'd have to alter his chassis and custom-cast new armor plating, which would be an up-grade anyway so that's probably good since we know we can trust Crash. Power supply would be a problem because I'm guessing you'd still want his weapon system to function at the same level... probably a bare minimum, which you couldn't do if you made the power array supply the energy for repulsors. I could do a switch, but then it's a choice between repulsors or weapons, and really you want both to function together, so I'd have to install a secondary system which would be no problem since we're recasting the armor and getting a new chassis. In fact, if we do that, you could end up with *more* offensive firepower because the repulsors' power supply would be able to divert to a nearby weapons arrays I could add. Now that I think of it, with your new armor, I can see a lot of potential, things I didn't think were possible but seem obvious now, so if we find Crash and—"

"Young man," Makaffie said, interrupting the code slicer who, as usual, was completely oblivious to the looks of patient amusement all around him—especially on Keel and Leenah. "I believe our mutual friend the captain was simply making an offhand, if you will, remark about how it might be possible for these tracks, so clearly identified by our wobanki friend, to suddenly no longer be identifiable."

Garret blushed. "Oh. Sorry. Yeah... no. Crash doesn't have repulsors. Sorry."

Leenah was quick to encourage the code slicer. "I think your ideas for Crash are good ones." She looked to Keel. "Don't you?"

"Oh... yeah," Keel agreed. "Once we find him. Let's... uh, let's get all that done."

Garret brightened. "Okay, great!" All traces of embarrassment were gone in the face of this exciting news.

"We should look around," said the Wild Man. "Maybe they swept their tracks once they got to this clearing."

The group wandered the clearing, searching. Makaffie waded to the other side of the river, searching with Skrizz, then returned.

"No sign of the war bot anywhere on that side." He hitched a thumb behind him to the young woods that had grown up by the stream. "And they certainly couldn't have gone in there. So where are they?"

By *there*, Makaffie meant the Temple of the Ancients.

Keel examined the temple's face. "I dunno."

"You know something about Prisma that we don't?" Makaffie asked.

Keel frowned. "I mean… she's… different. Got some… thing about her. But no. Take a look at that patch of real estate at the temple base, though." Keel pointed.

The temple had a wide assortment of tender new growth coming up from its cracks and crevices. The thin plants were stretching in the waning sunlight, in a hurry to establish themselves and complete the lifespan needed to leave behind the long-slumbering seeds that could survive the coming long and dark winter. But there was one spot amid this life where every sprout had been brushed away completely—as though someone had swept clean an entrance that consisted of the stones themselves.

"I stand corrected," Makaffie said. He turned to the Wild Man. "Nice to have Sergeant Fast back, isn't it? So it seems that *someone* was able to get this thing open. Incidentally, my credits are on the girl's mother. That is, if there are any takers. No? All right. Just asking."

If anyone was reconsidering the option to wager, the chance passed the moment a strong, military voice shouted for everyone to, "Freeze!"

A legionnaire wearing the shiny armor so proudly introduced by the House of Reason emerged from the woods behind the temple. Except this armor didn't look nearly as flimsy as the sort that was rolled out when Keel was last an active-duty legionnaire. More such soldiers quickly bounded from their points of ambush, weapons up and repeating the order.

Keel shot first. A searing blaster bolt crumpled the bucket of the shiny legionnaire who had first voiced the command; the man dropped straight down mid-stride, his body failing. As the man fell, Keel grabbed Leenah tightly around the waist and kicked his armor's enhanced jump jets into action. He feebly reached for Garret with his free hand, but the kid was too far away... and then Keel and Leenah were rocketing up to the top of the temple. The man known as Wraith shot two more of the shiny legionnaires on the way up and another upon landing at the temple's apex.

The force below was not an overwhelming one, but the odds were stacked against Keel and his small crew. There were at least twenty soldiers, not including those he'd already killed. If there was any good news about this trap in the middle of nowhere that they'd somehow sprung, it was that these troopers apparently wanted them alive. They weren't being theatrical when demanding that Keel and his company freeze, show their hands, or whatever other crowd control orders were shouted. That was made clear when, a split-second after he jumped, a flurry of incoming stun bolts pounded the ground where Keel had stood. Garret, Makaffie, and the Wild Man were quickly dropped, but they weren't dead—just paralyzed. Their eye movements showed they were still alert.

So. Whoever these shiny legionnaires were—and Keel assumed at once they were Nether—they had orders to capture. Even to the point that they were willing to soak up four killed in action. How long that would last was anyone's guess, but as Keel shoved Leenah down to take cover atop the temple, he noted that they were still sending stun bolts up after him.

The initial chaos lasted all of ten or fifteen seconds, but that could feel like a lifetime in the middle of a firefight. With Leenah lying low and protected from any ground fire, Keel did his dance of death. He exchanged fire with shiny legionnaires who were hanging back at the wood line to get a better angle, dropping a pair before they fell back to the trees.

Spinning back around, he saw two teams below him moving to take the stunned members of his crew. But the Wild Man, it seemed, was too large and too stubborn to be kept down by a mere pair of stun bolts. He stretched out for his long rifle, found it, chambered a twenty-millimeter round, and hip-fired at one of the advancing leejes. The gunshot dug out a cavernous hole in the abdomen of the man that sent his comrades diving, horrified, for cover.

But that was not the only team in action, and another concentration of stun bolts put the big sniper down for good.

Meanwhile, more legionnaires attempted to encircle a snarling Skrizz. The wobanki lunged, decapitated a legionnaire, helmet and all, and then leapt and bounded into the woods as blaster fire—no longer set to stun—chased him.

Keel was forced down as more fire—again, no longer on stun—concentrated on his position. He popped back up in time to see the shiny leejes ener-chaining the rest of his crew. He prepared to open fire again, but halted at the sound of a greatly amplified voice speaking from behind a Legion bucket.

"Don't do it, Captain Ford!"

Hearing his name used by these people—his real name—gave him pause. And these legionnaires, for lack of a better word, could have killed his people now if they'd wanted to. At least the ones in ener-chains. Instead they held their weapons at the ready, tense, but evidently listening to whatever orders were coming from their commander.

"You're listening to reason," the amplified, helmeted voice said. It was impossible for Keel to pinpoint its source; the words echoed and reverberated their way up the temple until they sounded like they came from all directions. "Even if it's just the voice of reason inside your own mind."

"What do you want?" Keel shouted back.

"For now? I want to talk. There are questions I believe only you can answer. I want answers, Ford."

"You picked about the worst way to get me talking, if that's the case."

A wry chuckle came in response. This man, the leader it seemed, sounded genuinely amused. "That may be. But I have your attention now, Captain. And you must admit that you're at least partially responsible for our... introduction. One who knows how Captain Ford, a.k.a. Wraith, a.k.a. Captain Keel, operates, knows he'd best come shooting or not come at all."

"Aeson, what's going on?" Leenah asked in a hissed whisper. She raised her eyes up over the edge of the temple in an attempt to see Garret.

"Stay down," Keel warned.

"The others..."

"They're all right. For now."

The voice of what had to be a Nether Ops commander rose to cut its way into their whispered conversation. "Nothing to say in reply? But you have such a sharp tongue... I'm disappointed, Ford."

"Just waiting for you to get to the point," Keel shot back.

More chuckles.

Leenah whispered, "Why are legionnaires shooting at us? Why are they even here?"

"They're not legionnaires," Keel answered. "And they're trying to keep us distracted."

Indeed, the voice emanating from below continued to talk as troops entered the woods, presumably in pursuit of Skrizz. But nothing the man said was relevant or leading to any particular point; he made no demands, gave no hint of what he wished to speak about, despite his earlier statement. It was all a stream of loosely connected buzzwords and phrases designed to catch Keel's attention, keep him listening and wondering. He gave the names of friends, units, places he'd been stationed. A few classified codenames that had been dug up from his time in Dark Ops. There were guesses, too. Names of people Keel remembered from the 131st Legion but didn't personally know. Same with the names of smugglers that Keel had worked in the same circle with, but without a relationship. All said with the same knowing implication as the names that *did* hit close to home—like Legion Commander Chhun, Lao Pak, Exo, Masters. But nothing recent. No Jack or Zora.

The man was droning on about Exo and how it was "too bad the way that all went down. My files suggest he was a good man. A good legionnaire. Men like him never should have been driven out to begin with. Don't you think, Captain Ford?"

That was the first time in a long while that Keel had been given an opportunity to speak, and it coincided with three legionnaires reaching the top of the temple, the long meandering speech intended as a diversion to allow them to arrive without detection.

Keel was ready for them, however.

Three rapid shots from the hand cannon were followed by the clatter of armor tumbling against stone as the dead bodies fell from top to bottom with a final, muffled *whump*.

The remaining legionnaires down below shifted uncomfortably.

"Nice trick," Keel called down.

Again the shiny legionnaires shifted, seemingly unsure what to do. Or maybe they knew what they *wanted* to do but were prevented from doing it.

"Glad you liked it," the voice called back up. "I thought I might catch the Wraith napping. But don't laugh... don't laugh. It wasn't *that* long ago that Venema managed to do it when we sent him after you. Who's to say it couldn't happen twice?"

Nothing that voice was saying was without calculation. The man had been trying to distract Keel before. Now he was most likely attempting to intrigue him. Whatever the case, Keel didn't want to stay around any longer than necessary. And he had a few tricks of his own that might catch these kelhorns unaware.

"Leenah, tell me you can get the *Six* over here. I could use its guns in the fight."

"Bringing it isn't the problem... it's what those cannons might do to Garret."

"I'd rather risk that than watch the kid get executed right in front of us. This peace won't last long. Get it here as fast as you can."

"You remember Venema, don't you?" the voice below called out.

"Not really. The scumsacks all start to blend together," Keel answered. He would have liked to leave it at that, but with a plan in action, it was his turn to try to distract the other side of the field. "You said you wanted to talk, so let's talk. And I mean more than just dropping a few names and hoping I recognize one or two of them. What do you want to know? Or do you want to just keep sending up your boys to get dusted a few at a time? Either way works for me."

"I want to know, Captain Ford, if *you* know just how many AP launchers my boys have with them? Did you know it's enough to bring down even the fabled *Indelible VI* if you decide to bring it our way? Don't think I don't have peepers watching that freighter, my boy. And don't think I'm bluffing about the aero-precision launchers, either. Pop your head up and take a count."

Keel had seen some in the chaos already, spotting at least two bouncing on the backs of leejes. The *Six* could handle that much, but if too many more were nearby...

"Better call it off for now," he whispered to Leenah. "Just push it in orbit and keep it someplace safe. We'll see how this goes."

Leenah worked the control panel on her datapad as she nodded in agreement.

Keel slowly stood. "All right. Let's talk about—"

A blaster bolt from one of the legionnaires below struck the temple just before him, exploding into a shower of sparks but leaving no mark on the impermeable stone. Below, another legionnaire grabbed the offending trooper's weapon and forced it down.

"That man acted alone!" the voice called out, almost in a panic. It sounded to Keel like he was struggling. Was the leader also the man who had forced the rifle down? In that case...

Keel calmly sent a bullet into the commander's head before ducking back down to avoid being shot.

"Are you crazy?" Leenah hissed.

"Could be. Listen, they'll kill us once they get whatever it is they need. Best to bleed them while we can."

The voice was back. "You guessed wrong, Captain Ford. And while I understand your reaction, and might have accepted it had you shot the offender, I can't idly stand by and let my first sergeant get done like that. You just made my job a whole lot harder... I have no choice but to even things up."

Keel wanted to see what was happening, but he also felt he needed to stay low for a moment. His thoughts prompted the armor to advise him of a small observation bot embedded in the helmet. Whether it was something Garret had added or original tech, Keel didn't know and didn't care. He tossed it up and watched through his bucket HUD as his code slicer was roughly pulled to his feet and then forced down on his knees. It was clear that the kid hadn't fully regained his motor functions, and the forced movement must have been agonizing.

One of the legionnaires pulled his pistol and strode behind Garret. "I can appreciate your keeping low, Captain Ford. And here's your chance to get me after all. But know that your code slicer, who is in store for a great deal of pain, will be killed if you do." He waited. "Wise man."

The commander sent two tight-dialed blaster bolts into Garret—one in each calf muscle. The kid cried out in pain only to have his hair grabbed as his head was pulled back, forcing him to stare at the darkening sky as night fell. The pistol pushed hard against the code slicer's temple.

"Here's how I see it now," the commander announced. "You still have the upper hand, because you don't care how many of us down here die, whereas we... need you alive. You don't know it, but we damn near broke our necks and damn sure *did* break our jump drive just trying to get to this rock ahead of you. But understand one thing and understand it well: that advantage only applies to you and your Kill Team Ice boys. I don't need anyone else alive."

The Nether Ops commander pulled Garret to his feet, yanking him up by his hair. He pressed the barrel of his weapon so hard behind the code slicer's ear that it made him yelp, as though the operative were trying to push the weapon clear through the other side of the kid's skull. "That means the wobanki out there, that pretty little Endurian you've got with you, and this skinny little sket are gonna get dusted real soon if things don't take a more... *compliant* tone."

The man paused as if considering his own words. Maybe he just wanted to see if Keel had something to say. "Anyhow, you've got a choice. Tell me what I've been instructed to find out... or watch the kid get dusted here and now. I have no doubts you've figured that we're Nether, and right you are. Comprehend this: Nether Ops sent more than just this kill team. You've got at best two nights up there without food or water to watch your lady friend grow weak and cold—it gets *very* cold here at night—and then backup arrives and we settle in and you get colder and weaker the whole time. How well do you think you can protect her once we've got you ten to one? How about twenty to one? Is it worth watching what will happen, helpless to do a damn thing about it? Can you live with yourself? I know what I'd do, Captain Ford."

By now, the sun was setting in earnest, and despite the heat that had been baked into the massive temple stones, a chill was already settling in the air. The night *would* be cold—before being followed by a hot morning. Rapid temperature changes would make a prolonged siege with no food or water just as difficult as the Nether operative suggested. Keel knew it.

"Tell me what you want to know," Keel finally said.

"Everything you know about Kill Team Ice."

Keel scoffed to himself. Of all the things...

"You want to know about Kill Team Ice," Keel shouted back, "then you picked the wrong guy to be your information broker. Talk to the two you already have down there if you're so damn interested."

The barrel of his weapon still pressed against Garret's head, the commander looked over to where Makaffie and the Wild Man lay, still bound in ener-chains and breathing uncomfortably from the stun bolts. Something like a short laugh escaped his amplified bucket speakers and then he called back up to the temple zenith. "We already know what happened to those last members Goth Sullus scooped up. These two would already be dead except... orders. But you're gonna tell me how many others skipped out ahead of you, Captain Ford. Because one way or the other... we're gonna finish taking you boys out."

<h1 style="text-align:center">11</h1>

Night fell, and with it there were no further attempts by Nether Ops to dislodge Keel from his place at the pinnacle of the Temple of the Ancients. Garret and the others were still alive, or at least they were the last time Keel had seen them; they'd been taken away from the pyramid's base hours ago. The Nether Ops commander insisted that they were all fine—for now—and that Garret was even getting medical attention. Skrizz of course was still at large, and chasing a wobanki through a jungle was a fool's errand. And, as evidenced by the corpse of one blood-soaked and limp-bodied Nether Ops leej dragged by his buddies back into their makeshift barracks, a suicidal one.

Keel still wasn't talking, and the Nether Ops commander hadn't bothered to try to induce him otherwise for a long while. Which probably meant that the black-hearted soldier was simply waiting for a turning of the tide. He'd most likely been telling the truth about additional reinforcements. Keel had a hypercomm, but who could he call? Perhaps the Legion or Nilo... but even if they came, he doubted they would do so quickly enough to help. Keel would have to find some way out of this mess on his own. Maybe risk a run-in with the *Six*, just to see what happened. If he could catch these troopers off-guard, he was sure to cause enough chaos to at least get him and Leenah to safety. But leaving Garret… he wasn't willing to do that unless it was only a corpse they were leaving behind. And Leenah might have to be forced to do even that much.

The smuggler looked down at the Endurian "princess." The extreme dark of the night would have made her impossible to see, but the augmented vision of his bucket gave a picture of the woman through a mix of infrared, thermal, radar, and who knew what else to patch together something for his eyes and mind to understand. All seamlessly, as though the helmet's purpose was to give Keel the ability to truly see in the dark.

She was sleeping now, or at least pretending to. It had taken some convincing just to get her to lie down. Leenah had insisted that there was no way she could fall asleep given their situation, not to mention the worry over Garret and Skrizz. Only Keel's observation that she'd be better at facing what was coming next if she was well-rested rather than dragging from fatigue got her to finally give it a try.

"So when will your turn be?" she'd asked as Keel watched over the temple, using the sensors in his armor to stay alert. "Since getting rest is so crucial to our survival."

"Next watch."

"Sure. I'll just trust you to wake me up for that."

Keel only shrugged as Leenah laid her head down, both of them knowing that his promise to wake her for the next watch was a false one. Wraith wouldn't rest until all of this was finished. Only death could force him to shut his eyes early.

The bucket fed Keel information. Told him that she was, indeed, asleep. Gave her resting heart rate and declared it healthy for an Endurian female. If there was a restlessness in her dreams, she didn't show it. The thoughts of impending demise, of never finding Prisma, thoughts Keel knew she struggled with and worried over—because he knew her—seemed buried for now.

"I think it's time we revisit our options," the Nether Ops commander bellowed.

The amplified voice of the Nether Ops commander woke Leenah well before the end of that first watch Keel had meant to extend all the way through till morning. Her eyes opened, but in the permeating blackness she could hardly tell a difference. It was almost as bad as that terrible stretch stranded aboard the *Indelible VI.* She felt as though she'd been flung into another impossible situation.

This planet was without any moons to reflect the sun's light. A sparse, two-hundred-kilometer-wide asteroid belt helped a little in that regard, but only just enough to keep the planet's dark side from utterly freezing over during its stretch of summer months. Still, the chill was deep, and had already sucked out all the captured warmth in the temple stones. Leenah shivered and rubbed her arms, then attempted to get to her feet. Keel's steady hand checked her and guided her softly back down. She could barely make out his outline in the darkness, but knew his armor was capable of seeing much more than she was.

"Do you see them?" she whispered.

The Nether Ops commander went on. "You still have information that my superiors need. I still have orders to keep you alive. But time is of the essence, Captain Ford."

"Is Garret with him?" Leenah asked, the dread plain in her voice.

"No sign of him since they took him away," Keel said in a low voice, his natural voice, as though he'd lifted his bucket up to whisper to Leenah. What he didn't mention was that it looked like enemy reinforcements had already arrived. His bucket's thermals were now showing nonhuman heat signatures with the commander down below.

"You can't really be asleep up there?" the man said with a laugh.

"I can hear you." Keel didn't want to give Nether Ops any ideas that now might be a good time to test his alertness. There was only so much killing he could do before there'd be some kind of retaliation from the rank-and-file. Most likely deployed against his friends and their prisoners.

"Good. That's fine. I told you once already that it was all we could do to get here ahead of you, Captain Ford. Now, however, the rest of the cavalry has arrived—as they apparently used to say back on old Earth. Which in my mind makes for a good time to reevaluate our positions so that we may come to a better understanding of our respective... situations."

A powerful, intensely bright light sent a blazing white pillar straight up into the inky night sky, a beacon so strong it appeared solid. At the base of this blinding column, the light diffused along the ground, casting impossibly long shadows behind every stone and root. And it was in this glow that the Nether Ops commander strode forward, his armor dazzling in the brightness, cast alternately in impenetrable shadow or a painfully radiant shine.

Behind him stood two blue-skinned giants in full battle armor.

"If you're trying to impress me with your friends," grunted Keel, "you can do a lot better than Gomarii."

"I don't give a synth miner's pay whether you're impressed by me or not, Captain Ford. But I do need for you to understand the gravity of your situation. By midday, I'll have enough men here under my command to waltz to the top of the temple and drag you down ener-chained. Or maybe I decide to blow you off the top with the munitions these *friends of mine* brought with them. It'd be a shame for that pretty little thing by your side to be ripped into shreds of bone and flesh."

Keel readied his blaster in one hand, the hand cannon in the other. "Sounds like you're asking for the fight to start now. You won't last long, kelhorn."

"Against you? I know it. I venture not more than a minute from the time you get it in your head to really kill me to the time I breathe my last breath. And then someone in Nether Ops gets the promotion they've been after. We both understand that. Like I said, we're figuring out where everything stands. And you're realizing that if you do that... your friends all die. Including... this one."

The commander motioned with his arm, and one of the Gomarii pushed a raven-haired girl into the light. She looked up helplessly into the darkness where Keel stood atop the temple.

Keel stopped short. "Prisma."

12

Garret and the others had been taken to a small camp not far from the Temple of the Ancients. The concentrated, small-bore blaster wounds in Garret's hamstrings were meant to be painful... but also superficial. They had wanted him to suffer, but to still be able to move under his own power. Because despite what their commander had told Keel, the truth was they were under orders not to kill any of Keel's crew without approval.

Unless of course they attempted to escape, like the wobanki.

A medic in shining Legion armor cut away Garret's trousers and then roughly pulled away the scraps of cargo pants to examine his wounds. Everything the man did added to the pain the code slicer already felt, and yet all he could think about were the tools he kept in those pants pockets. He was glad he kept his most important tech and his most essential tools in his shirt and sleeve pockets.

The medic examined his wounds roughly, pinching them in a way that felt more sadistic than medical, then squeezed on a gooey sealant that disinfected the small holes in the legs. To Garret, the goo felt like having an icicle rammed into his flesh. As the medic applied skin-packs over the surface, he ordered his patient to "shut up," even though Garret hadn't said a word from the start and didn't intend to. Maybe he'd winced a little too loudly; he wasn't sure.

The medic used Garret's shoulder blades to push himself off the ground after the examination, exerting enough force to send the code slicer's face into the dirt. By the time Garret had pushed himself onto his elbows and rolled to one side, careful not to let the ground come in contact with his still-aching wounds, he found that Mr. Makaffie and Mr. Wild Man were both watching him. Both men were seated with arms ener-chained behind their backs, ankles likewise bound.

Garret's wrists were also ener-chained, but the Nether Ops legionnaires had let him have his hands in front of him. Captain Keel would have called that sloppy. Garret knew it was because they didn't see him as a threat. Which... was probably fair.

Makaffie and the Wild Man were still in their armor, although their weapons and gear—including helmets—had been taken somewhere else. There had been a heated argument between the soldiers about the big sniper's large and imposing long rifle. Everyone seemed to want to claim the spoil, and the discussion had gotten so loud and persistent that an NCO of some sort had had to come and put an end to it. As a result, all three prisoners knew *exactly* where their gear was stowed, just by tracking the source of the arguing voices.

"You okay, Garret?" Makaffie asked. He had been watching the kid undergo his treatments and spoke up the moment they were done.

A guard stationed over Makaffie kicked him in the small of the back. "Mute it."

"I'm fine," Garret answered, somehow thinking of the guard's warning as applying only to Makaffie. He might have added that he felt good enough to walk but figured that bit of information would probably be interpreted as him suggesting some kind of escape plan.

Makaffie's guard seemed annoyed that there was no one stationed near enough to Garret to administer the same sort of corrective kick he'd just given Makaffie. Yet the guard seemed unwilling to go over there and do it himself. So instead he struck the back of Makaffie's head with the butt of his blaster rifle, hard enough to deliver visions of stars but not so hard as to break the skin or knock the man out. Clearly, this soldier had found the line when it came to blunt-force trauma.

The scrawny operator rocked forward with the blow and grimaced, wishing he had a hand free—not to return harm for harm but merely so he could rub the back of his scalp. If it came to it, he would let the Wild Man handle any throttling that needed to happen. The look of murder in the eyes of his grizzly companion was clear enough.

The guard noticed the look as well. "Feel like getting up and trying it, big man?"

Wild Man, a professional killer, ground his teeth and stayed silent.

"That's what I thought," gloated the guard. "*All* of you mute it, or I start knocking out teeth."

That order was obeyed as the inky-black darkness of night fell over that distant world.

And though Garret knew his allies were only meters away from him, in that pitch-black night he felt completely alone.

Before the girl could speak whatever words she'd prepared to manipulate Keel into doing exactly what the Nether Ops commander wanted, Keel turned to Leenah and shared with her the information he'd gleaned from his armor. "That's not Prisma," he whispered.

To be sure, the girl looked exactly like Prisma. But the armor said otherwise, and it pointed out potential tells that supported its conclusion—such as a heat signature that, while it indicated a temperature level appropriate for a human female, was untrustworthy due to the unnatural and presumably artificial sources that generated the heat from beneath the dermal layer. Human beings were that temperature, but they didn't generate heat that way. This was a construct.

Keel had encountered something like this before. While rescuing his crew from the Cybar mothership built atop the *Deluvia*, he had been confronted by a perfect clone of Leenah. It was only circumstance and deduction that had allowed him to comfortably put the automaton down, despite his senses telling him that it was the genuine article. Here, too, his eyes told him that the girl standing before that beam of radiant light was Prisma. She looked *exactly* like she had that day on the Cybar ship.

"Captain Keel?" the not-Prisma called out into the darkness. "Where are you? They say they're going to kill me. I'm scared. They took Crash..."

"Prisma," Leenah said breathlessly, trying to get up.

Keel kept her down. "It's not her. You have to trust me."

The girl called again. "Is Leenah there? I need help."

For Leenah, not answering the girl—trusting the truth of what Keel told her—was the hardest thing she'd ever had to do. More difficult than any combat mission. In fact, she'd rather be facing down death in just such a mission right now rather than sitting here idly, hoping for… what? Her emotions were a confusing swirl, and all she knew for sure was just how much she loved Prisma and Keel and her life aboard the *Indelible VI.*

And that love was now tied to a hatred for Nether Ops, for all they were doing to her. She wanted to see these men and Gomarii dead for what they were attempting to do. To twist something so good and so pure… it was unconscionable. Blasphemous.

"All right, you got my attention," Keel called down. "What do you want?"

"Only the same thing I've wanted since the start of this standoff of ours," replied the Nether Ops commander. "Tell me about Kill Team Ice. Names of those who went out of service before or after you. Dates, if you know them. Suspected locations. *Anything* that comes into that killer's brain of yours. More men than you got out of that program early, Captain Ford. Most went into the Legion. Several are now dead. You'll tell me what you know so I can finally put an end to this hunting trip."

The commander paused as if considering something. His armor cast a mirror-bright shine onto the temple stones.

"And I want you to understand one more thing," he added. "No, not want. *Need.*"

He nodded, and one of the Gomarii left the circle and returned with another human girl. This one looked nothing like Prisma save for the color of her hair. She was haggard and tired, and wore the brown coveralls the slavers commonly outfitted their property in. Only, these shabby clothes were a size too large for the girl and hung loosely on her.

This new girl stood in the light with fear in her eyes. Her head would duck between her shoulders whenever one of the slavers moved an arm, already anticipating more of the abuse that came from those fists. Always expecting more.

"My job in the Nether," said the commander, "my *expertise*, as it were, is getting people like you to talk. A job that always has, and always will, boil down to *leverage*. An interrogator needs to find that thing that convinces the subject that talking—truthfully talking—is the best thing that could possibly happen in that moment. Better than living, better than dying. You'd be impressed by how many people have requested that I 'kill them now.' But only a novice kills a man who won't talk. The craftsman learns how to make that same man pour out his heart with no thought whatsoever of death.

"You can't rely on pain to get that kind of a transformation, Captain Ford. At least, not on pain alone. Administer too much and they'll tell you everything they can think of. Doesn't matter if it's the truth or not, so long as they believe it's something you want to hear. You'll get the truth somewhere in there to be sure, but the mind is so broken from all that suffering that you never quite get what you need. Just ramblings and pleas for mercy, and you spend more time trying to parse them through an AI than they're worth. That's the mistake of the less experienced men in my profession. They get the truth fast but don't know what to do with it, much less even believe it. In the end they may as well have just killed the subject and saved everyone the time and trouble."

The commander pulled out his pistol and inspected it.

"All that... that's just me talking about business. It's not what I needed you to know, exactly, Captain Ford. What

I need you to understand... is that I have all... the leverage... I need. I have it all right here with me. And if by some chance things get violent and your crew ends up dead and I end up dead and you end up captured—because there's no escaping this planet, Captain—you have to understand what happens then. Someone else who knows what I'm doing, not an amateur relying on pain and brute force or cheap psychological tricks... that person will take over. You'll be in a cell so dark and small that you won't roll over without a guard's help. And all the while they'll be gathering still more leverage. Mind you, I don't mean building a case, trying to get you to talk because of just how much we've saved up and can threaten to do to you. No, each new piece of leverage will be brought to you straightaway, the same as this girl here has been brought. You'll either play ball, or you'll pass. And each time you pass on whatever leverage we bring to you, it won't matter whether we were right or wrong about how much that person meant to you—because, sure, sometimes we may have followed an information broker's false lead and brought in someone you never actually even met. But either way... we don't hold on to our leverage forever."

The commander turned and shot the slave girl in the heart. The bolt tore through the child with an unholy force and left her lying on her back, only her naked feet still visible in the circle around the light spire. Then a Gomarii dragged the slave away into the darkness.

"You didn't know that child," the Nether Ops commander announced. "I know that. But... her blood is on your hands all the same."

Keel watched in the silence, stifling the urge to kill the man before him.

Not yet... not yet.

"Do you hear me, Captain Ford?" the commander called up to Keel. "Did you think it wouldn't end in blood? Of course it would. So it has started, and so it will end, Captain Ford! So. There's my first bit of leverage. Doesn't matter if you knew the girl or not. Her blood is on your hands. Whose will be next?"

The commander looked at the Prisma construct and tapped his index finger against the trigger guard. "This girl... Prisma Maydoon. She's important to you. You do know *her*. And you might be thinking that it's impossible that we have her. That there's some trick. A clone or an android. But come down and look. Know what you're doing before you do it. Hell, I'll even send her up. You can see her firsthand. And then you're either going to talk with me, dammit, or I'm going to go to your code slicer and put a bolt in his stomach. Then you'll get another choice: let him die in agony or start talking just to give him the mercy of a second bolt in the head."

Leenah was crying as the speech unfolded. She gripped Keel's leg tightly and uttered his name like some sorrow-drenched prayer. Keel wanted to see her face, to put his fingers through her soft, flowing tendrils. That was what Aeson Keel wanted. Wraith, however, could only pat her head and remind her to keep down and quiet.

"Send her up then," Keel said. "I need to be sure."

"I knew we could get somewhere if we could only be honest, Captain." The Nether Ops commander motioned to Prisma to move toward the temple. "I'm sending this girl up to you as a token of my trust. When she arrives and you've had your reunion, I expect you to start talking. We've gone over what happens if you refuse."

It was the initial offer and subsequent willingness to send Prisma up to him that settled whatever lingering doubt was in Keel's mind over the accuracy of his armor's reports. Because there was no good reason for this offer. The girl, if it really was Prisma, would be a better bargaining chip in Nether Ops' hands. All they would have to do was hurt her—not kill her, just hurt her—and it would be too much for Leenah. And then Keel would have to split time between watching for an attack and keeping the Endurian from rushing down the temple in a rash, half-crazed effort to save the girl.

But instead the commander had sent Prisma up. Unbidden. In fact he'd jumped at the opportunity.

This was not Prisma. This was a ploy to gain the upper hand.

The commander stepped away from the circle of light, leaving the two Gomarii, as Prisma took a step toward the temple. Not a faltering, doubtful step, but one of confidence.

Another tell.

Keel sent a tight burst from the slug-thrower into the girl's skull and felt a moment of dread as his optical overlays animated something that looked very much like blood spray. But the armor remained insistent that the target was not human... and that the attack had been a critical one. A moment later there was no doubt. Prisma pulled herself up from the prone position and sat upright as though being shot in the head by the uranium-depleted slugs was nothing at all.

The Nether Ops commander shouted. Keel fired at the girl again, this time with a powerful stun blast that radiated outward from its automaton target, delivering powerful neuro-damage to everyone in its bloom—certainly the two Gomarii and hopefully the Nether Ops commander. Screams of agony sounded in the moments before the rest of the troopers below sprang into action, emerging from hidden positions to execute whatever contingency orders had been in place should their ruse fail.

Which it just had.

Keel began shooting down the soldiers, one by one. He reminded Leenah to stay down and did the same himself, only popping upright for split seconds before dropping out of sight again and then using his jump jets to rocket across the surface so he could pop up elsewhere and deliver more unexpected death on demand.

"Leenah! Bring down the ship!"

"It's in orbit!" she called back. "It's gonna be awhile."

"Then get it to speed up!"

"You'd need a piloting AI for that. You didn't want one, remember?"

Keel deftly shot a Nether Ops legionnaire in the stomach, punching a round from the slug thrower through the armor and adding that much more shrapnel to the death wound. "Why can't it ever be easy?" he muttered.

Shots had been zipping up at him for a while, but now a grenade joined the incoming fire. The armor tracked it, and a burst from the hand cannon sent it off-course to explode away from danger.

Keel and Leenah had overstayed their welcome atop the Temple of the Ancients. He grabbed her arm and hoisted her to her feet.

"Where are we going?" she said.

"Downstairs to find Garret and then a way out."

All sides of the temple were taking fire, but not equally. Keel pulled Leenah over the edge with the fewest soldiers attacking. The temple was layered with stone blocks, creating a series of two-meter shelves each sitting two meters above the layer below it. Getting down was a matter of dropping down from one shelf to the next, then making quick lateral moves before repeating the process, preventing the still-organizing Nether Ops soldiers from getting clear shots.

They dropped down three levels before a barrage of blaster fire erupted straight at them and Keel had to turn his body to cover Leenah and absorb the hits with the armor. It hurt like the Nine Hells but wasn't nearly as bad as getting hit in standard Legion armor. It was even a modest improvement over getting shot in his old Wraith armor.

Yet he felt a distinct twinge of pain in his right calf and found himself limping as he grabbed hold of Leenah's waist, activated the jump jets, and rocketed them out of their attacker's sights. In the dark flight that arched him down to the temple's base, Keel sent bursts of fire directly on top of the heads of the three Nether Ops legionnaires who'd shot him. The men were dead by the time the pair landed.

The sound of running footsteps behind Keel was accompanied by a perimeter warning in his HUD: more humanoid life-forms were approaching. But as Keel spun around to take aim with his weapons, he heard the voices of his code slicer and Makaffie calling for him not to shoot.

So he didn't.

But neither did he lower his weapons. Because if these Nether Ops kelhorns could make a passing imitation of Prisma, why not do the same with these two?

He checked his HUD. The armor told him that these two were the genuine articles. Human beings.

Still, Keel's mind jumped with primal thoughts. Perhaps there was a guard behind the prisoners, urging them to get close to Keel by prodding them at gunpoint.

And a moment later, a figure in black did step forward. But it wasn't a guard.

It was Ravi.

"There is a sixty percent chance all of us will survive if you come with me right now and please do not make any jokes."

Keel was almost dumbfounded, but he managed to say, "Lead the way." And then... "Took you long enough."

13

Ravi came to the empty *Indelible VI* first. The ship, which had long been one of his anchors—a place he could return to at will no matter where it was in the galaxy—was moving empty through the orbit of a small world hemmed in by an asteroid belt. With no one on board, Ravi went down to the planet's surface, instinctively making his way straight for the temple of his people. There was nothing else of note on this world and Ravi could calculate no other reason for Captain Keel and the others to be here except in pursuit of Prisma. He would soon find whether the girl—or more likely the being who claimed to be her mother—had managed to make use of the temple. It was certainly within range of the Savage reclaimer, that horrible ship that had done its cruel work among the stars.

The temple was bathed in a black night much deeper than that of the faraway world he had just come from. And as Ravi took in his surroundings, he became aware that his coming was just in time.

Captain Keel was standing on top of the pyramid, speaking with someone who held out "Prisma Maydoon" as a captive. Ravi could see right away that this captive was not Prisma. He calculated an eighty-one-point-seven percent probability that Keel likewise did not believe the girl to be genuine. Indeed, the smuggler's body language was poised for immediate violence; Ravi had long ago learned to recognize when Captain Keel was ready to undertake one of his rash, death-inducing actions.

In a breath that took in much of the surrounding life, imprinting it on Ravi's mind, he sensed that Leenah was with Keel, though out of view from his place in the woods at the edge of the overgrown temple courtyard. He rejoiced over their reunion. Such glad things were to be appreciated, even if briefly and in the face of struggle. The goodnesses of life should always be acknowledged.

Ravi went searching for the others. He suspected that Garret was somewhere nearby since he had not been aboard the ship. He found the code slicer ener-chained and asleep, under the watch of a single guard, along with Makaffie and the Wild Man.

The guard was distracted; he regularly looked toward the spire of light that blazed before the temple. It seemed that all the other soldiers—Ravi had evaded several Nether Ops legionnaires and just as many Gomarii slavers—had been moved into position for whatever was meant to come to a head with the false Prisma. Perhaps the lone guard was feeling left out—or more likely he expected some eruption of violence and was watching for it.

Creeping about in the darkness, Ravi went first to the bound members of Kill Team Ice. He'd grown familiar with them from his time aboard the Savage reclaimer and believed that they could be trusted to assist in the escape. If for some reason, despite their capture, they were solidly a party to themselves, then it would be a simple matter to slip away from them.

The ancient one came around behind the two prisoners, who were still sitting with hands behind their backs, slumped forward in a torturous position. Ravi crept forward until his head was between the two men and breathed softly until he'd drawn their attention.

Makaffie started, but refrained from crying out. The Wild Man only blinked. His eyes were red from tears that had long ago dried, but left their cleansing trail down the grime of his face. Ravi gave a small nod, and received a fractional nod from each man in reply. It was enough.

He took the pommel of his sword and struck the ener-chains, deactivating them. The devices hung blacked out and loose around their wrists and ankles.

The guard kept his vigil on the spire of light. As Ravi slipped through the shadows and over to Garret, the Wild Man crept up behind the guard and stood at his full height, almost engulfing the shiny-armored legionnaire. Whether the Wild Man was too fast, or the leej's sensors too slow, the soldier was wrenched backward, the helmet pulled away from the head to expose throat and lower jaw. Wild Man slammed a massive fist into the man's Adam's apple. With a gurgling, pathetically quiet cry, the guard groped for his attacker's face, forgetting his training in that animal moment. The Wild Man gave up a few strands of his long hair—ripped from his head—in order to better take the guard's combat knife. He plunged the steel into the exposed throat, and with a quick flick of his wrist left the man to bleed out at his feet, though not before being liberated of his blaster rifle, which was passed to Makaffie.

The pair went to recover their gear, which they found unguarded amid the detritus of hastily eaten meal pouches and half-consumed cups of kaff. The Wild Man began to rummage through it all, but the sound of someone returning to the mobile awning brought him to his feet. A Gomarii slaver had returned, and seemed surprised not only to find a human prisoner free, but one tall enough to look eye-to-eye with. He also wasn't expecting the knife, still dripping red with the blood of its previous victim, which was driven into his thick blue neck.

As the last gouts of blood pumped out of the slaver, the confiscated weapons were recovered and systematically checked by the two men, who hurried back to Ravi.

Garret had slept through the entire bloody ordeal, though Ravi had disabled his ener-chains.

"R-Ravi?" the code slicer was asking, dumbfounded and rubbing his eyes as though expecting to realize he was dreaming.

"Yes, it is I. Tell me: are you and Keel and Leenah all that came down?"

"Mr. Skrizz came, too," Garret said. He explained Skrizz's escape into the trees and how the soldiers had grumbled loudly about their orders to break off the search for the wobanki in order to be on hand for something else.

"Yes, that something is happening right now. We must go."

Garret got up, limped off his wounds for a few steps, then nodded to say he was ready to move. "Are we going to go find Mr. Skrizz now?"

Ravi shook his head. "We will now have to rely on his penchant for looking after himself. Wobanki are particularly suited for self-preservation, and Skrizz in particular."

He led Garret and the others through the darkness, weaving a path that kept them out of sight of the various Nether Ops and Gomarii obstacles hiding along the way, their attention fixed on the spire and the temple.

They reached the courtyard just as the battle began to unfold following the replicant Prisma's demise. The streaking glow of blaster bolts lit up the battlescape in a soft, ambient light. Keel's jump jets appeared as streaking rockets. The Gomarii, needing more light to engage, activated portable illumination rods that chased away the shadows with a cold, clinical white light.

It was clear that the plan of those laying siege to Captain Keel had revolved around their false Prisma. Surely the painful neurological stun blast unleashed by the replicant was intended for those on top of the structure rather than those at its base. Keel's attack had confounded those plans, and the counterassault was stilted and confused as a result. Several teams fired haphazardly at the top of the pyramid, seemingly unaware that Keel had already left. It seemed that for the Nether Ops agents, the cost of the information they needed was finally too high to endure. They meant to kill the man now.

Ravi led his freed captives to find Keel, using the confusion to cover ground rapidly without needing to directly engage any of the Nether or Gomarii teams. It helped that their attention was entirely fixed on Wraith. In a very brief break from the fight, Ravi reunited with Keel and Leenah, and they agreed to follow him to escape.

Pockets of shiny-armored soldiers continued to move around the temple base, sporadic gun battles erupting and then quickly dying out as team after team realized they were no match for the former legionnaire named Wraith, who seemed to shoot better while on the move than he did while stationary. Soon Ravi's blade contributed its might to those enemies who came across his path. While most of the legionnaires attempted to engage the team at range, the Gomarii enjoyed feeling emotions up close, drinking in the pain, fear, and anguish, making them much more likely to seek out hand-to-hand combat. They routinely felt the cut of Ravi's spectral blade.

After Ravi took down two more such Gomarii, slashing his blade in an *X* and opening the slavers from their necks down to their pelvis with no regard for their battle armor, he led the team to the entrance of the Temple of the Ancients. To the attackers, this must have seemed a boon; their prey had trapped themselves between incoming blaster fire and a literal hard place that was infamously impregnable.

"This is our destination," Ravi calmly explained. "Please continue to shoot these people."

"Not like we've got any other choice!" Keel shouted between blasts. He sent alternating bursts of fire from his pistol and Intec that brought down a four-man squad, their dead bodies sprawled out as obstacles for whoever would next try to assault Keel and his team by maneuvering in that direction.

But with nowhere to run, all Keel could see was the inevitability of failure. "What kind of loony odds told you *this* was the best place to make a stand, Ravi? Leenah! Get the *Six* down here!"

The temple stones groaned as they opened, speaking just before Ravi. "Do not! Rather, send it to a safe location. Inside, all of you! We have our own way off this world."

14

"Let the bottom drop," Makaffie said as he marveled at the opening of the temple. It was a thing he'd only seen once before, at the hands of Goth Sullus. It was no less miraculous or magnificent now. And though there was a raging fight happening all around them, he didn't seem to think anything of asking the Wild Man his opinion on the matter. "What do you think of—"

Makaffie stopped as he looked around for his compatriot. Not seeing him, he called for Wraith.

"What's the problem?" Keel shouted as he split the smooth blue skull of a Gomarii who had been aiming a high-powered Krimm-Cycler game rifle at them.

"Wild Man! He's missing!"

Then, from a distance, came the thunderous crack of the big man's custom long rifle. The boom added some context to the sudden explosion of gore and carnage its twenty-millimeter round caused out among the shiny-armored legionnaires still pushing toward the temple.

"There's your answer," Keel said, while opportunistically dusting a few troops who had selected poor cover while diving from the sniper's view.

"Of course that crazy fool would set himself up somewhere to cover our escape," fumed Makaffie, mumbling to himself more than telling the others. He shouted, hoping to reach the Wild Man's ears, "Get back over here while you still can!"

The rifle answered with another crack that caused one of the slavers to explode into a gruesome outburst of blood and viscera so intense that Leenah turned away from the carnage. Her eyes were drawn back to the battlefield when Keel announced, "He's not covering for us; he's covering for Skrizz."

"All of you, inside the temple," Ravi ordered. "A swift decline in the odds of our universal survival occurs every instant you remain outside."

"You heard the turbaned one! Get in!" Keel called, and then gently pushed Leenah toward the darkness of the inner temple. But he stayed where he was, watching Skrizz move toward them, leaping and running before halting his progress entirely to sharply cut in a new direction and again accelerate. Ravi had been correct about the wobanki's uncanny sense of self-preservation.

Blaster bolts were zipping through the air with greater frequency, often terminating around the temple opening. The bolts made no mark on the temple stone, but they sent a light show of sparks to settle on Keel's shoulders.

"Makaffie!" Keel shouted. "Move!"

The scrawny operator didn't budge; he called for the Wild Man. Keel grabbed the Makaffie by his armor's drag handle and pulled him forcefully inside the temple. "C'mon already!"

"I can't leave him!"

"Then try giving him some suppressive fire instead of just calling out his name—but do it from the inside!"

Keel dropped back and fired from behind the temple's opening, using its thick stones as cover. He picked off the targets who attempted to move up, ignoring those who stayed in cover and provided suppressive fire.

Skrizz was a whirlwind of motion. He bounded over bewildered soldiers and Gomarii and used his powerful frame to knock some of these down while using others as a platform to launch himself from, flying several meters upward or in whatever other direction might best confound those trying to shoot him down. And whenever he saw an opportunely exposed head or neck, he was sure to reduce it to bloody ribbons as he powered on his way.

Through it all, the Wild Man's rifle barked its call of death, violently clearing a path for Skrizz with such horrific effectiveness that those shiny legionnaires who saw Skrizz coming moved in advance out of his way; they'd realized that any attempt to intercept was likely to result in a gruesome demise. The sound of the gun didn't fall silent until Skrizz reached the temple opening, his claws wet with blood while his face and the fur around his mouth were dark and matted with the same, though the latter was apparently from older kills in the forest, as this blood had long since dried. The wobanki fumbled with a blaster and charge pack he'd procured along the way, and settled in to join in the defensive fire. But a sudden blast of enemy fire singed his fur, and with a yowl of alarm he skittered back into the dark recesses of the open temple, out of the line of fire.

"Startin' to feel we're in trouble here, Ravi," Keel said before squeezing off a burst from his hand cannon. The return fire caused the smuggler to duck and roll back inside.

Ravi, however, was in no danger from the attacks. "Yes, it would seem they are quite determined to kill you, Captain Keel. I find myself wondering what you could possibly have done this time to induce such a fury."

"Nothing I remember... something to do with a unit called Kill Team Ice. Looks like you're not the only one with a mysterious past, pal."

Ravi cut down a Nether legionnaire who had decided to storm the opening by himself. Brave, but quickly fatal. The swordsman then turned to Keel and arched an eyebrow.

Keel kicked back out from cover and dropped a pair of Gomarii with his Intec. "What's that look, Ravi? Don't tell me you knew about all that."

"For now I will only tell you that you must fall back into the temple. They are nearly upon us and the Wild Man does not desire to join us. Each of his shots comes from a greater distance. He has been falling back while in support and has broken off entirely now that Skrizz is safely inside."

Makaffie's face came into the light provided by the temple's entrance. "Then we have to go out and get him!"

Ravi tilted his head at the man and then looked imploringly at Keel before steeling himself to cut down another advance; the numbers pressing in now were almost enough to force themselves past Ravi. Certainly at least some would breach the temple before he could seal it again.

"You heard him, Makaffie," Keel said as he gave the little man a hard shove in the chest that sent him back into the temple. "Your buddy is heading in the wrong direction on purpose. We laid down more than enough fire for him to catch up. Him wanting to sacrifice himself is one thing, us going out there to get him is another."

"You don't understand—you don't remember—he's sick. In the mind he gets sick, Sergeant Fast. He's gone off because he wants to go kill Savages. She got into his head again!"

"Now don't get crazy on me!" Keel ducked as a flurry of blaster bolts screamed their way into the temple, parting shadows and revealing the stones.

"They will be inside shortly," Ravi called. "Move back as far as you are able. I will do what I can once the doors are closed. Until then... it is up to you."

Keel pulled Makaffie back to the spot where his thermal overlays showed Skrizz, Leenah, and Garret covering deep inside the temple. While some light poured in from the artificial beacons outside the entrance, it wasn't enough to make the inner regions of the structure anything but utterly dark.

"Time for one more stand," Keel announced.

"I still have my blaster," Garret reported breathlessly. He was lying prone, watching the temple entrance.

Keel nodded despite knowing the kid could probably barely see it, if at all. "That's great, kid. Let's all just make sure we don't shoot one another in the back. Here they come."

Several waves of Nether Ops legionnaires and Gomarii came storming through the entrance. From their rear, the Nether Ops commander was shouting for "all teams" to "push up!" Whatever effects the false Prisma had leveled on him had evidently subsided.

Keel scanned for the man, very much hoping for an opportunity to put a bullet in his brain before Ravi had sealed them up safely inside the temple—although what they were supposed to do after that happened was still an unanswered question in the smuggler's mind. For now, the initial breachers needed to be contended with.

"Everybody, stay low!" Keel ordered as he quickly formulated a plan of destruction for those coming in with weapons blazing.

The blasts were focused well away from where the defenders had stationed themselves. Someone threw in a grenade, but it seemed that the floor itself engulfed it. The device made a small detonation with almost no sound accompanying the blast.

"I can hardly see a thing!" Leenah said.

"Ignore the bolts," Keel instructed. "Focus on the muzzle flashes coming from the right side. I'll take the left."

The attackers had split the room, with lead elements moving left and right into the darkness while a third group went up the center. Keel unleashed his hand cannon's wrath, sending copious fully automatic fire into those on his left. He mowed down the column of breachers before they could so much as turn their weapons toward him. The armor's aim assist did its job, and groupings of rounds went from one targeted head to the next with mystifying speed.

Return fire chased Keel from the middle and right of the breach. The operator's armor absorbed multiple shots, but they stung like mummy-bees, and he had to take a few stabilizing steps to avoid being knocked down. Leenah and the others took aim at the muzzle flashes on that side as instructed. Their accuracy wasn't on par with Keel's, but the additional blasters made up for it. Soon they were scrambling away from their position, avoiding incoming fire from the center column as Keel recalibrated and dropped still more enemy troops, this time a cluster of towering Gomarii—as evidenced only by their muzzle flashes and the readings of non-optical sensors. By this time, the temple had once again sealed itself to the outside galaxy, cutting off even the meager light that had penetrated its sanctum. Unfortunately, there still remained an alarming number of hostiles inside the place with Keel and his crew.

"Why not let the whole army in?" Keel mumbled to himself before saying loudly to Ravi, "We could use that sword of yours right about now!"

"Yes, I am helping. I am helping."

As Ravi spoke, the temple began to glow with a soft blue light made from an uncountable number of stars, all of them pinpoints in the cavernous blackness of the temple's interior. They cast a dusky hue over the stones that reflected on the bald domes of the Gomarii and sparkled brilliantly off the shiny armor of the legionnaires.

"All that's doing is making us easier to see!" Keel hollered.

"Please, for one time, simply be patient," Ravi said as he waved his hands, causing the stars to spin and grow and move in their courses.

With a sudden, swift movement of his right hand, Ravi sent a group of slavers to the other end of the galaxy, consigning them to instant atomization as they were cast into the middle of a great burning star. With similar transferals, he used the temple's powers to clear out the others, sending some to flash-freeze on worlds much too cold for them even to draw a final breath, while depositing others in the asteroid field near the planet where their corpses would be pulverized by the great rocks.

The swirling light show and sudden disappearance of the attackers left those inside the temple stunned; only Keel seemed to have the wherewithal to keep firing as his targets shouted in confusion at their loss of forces. Men fell from blaster bolts and then vanished before they could hit the ground. The Gomarii screamed in rage at their impending demise, dropping their weapons in exchange for an emotional overdose as a primal bloodlust befell them. One charged at Keel only to have Garret send a carefully aimed blaster bolt sizzling through the slaver's skull. The big brute halted abruptly, fell to both knees, and pitched forward, dead.

"I got one, Captain Keel! I got one!"

"I saw it, kid. Now let's get the rest."

But it was Ravi who did that, banishing all those who entered unbidden into the temple, sending them to certain death for their transgressions. Until... only the Nether Ops commander himself remained. The man had hidden himself in the shadows, aware that an insurmountable turning of the tide had started. He bided his time as his men vanished, searching for a way to still come out ahead.

And he was not without a plan.

15

Even as his men disappeared, the commander had found a target and aimed his weapon at her pink skull. Surely the loss of the Endurian would hurt Captain Ford the most. At any rate, harming her was far more likely than punching through that damned *magnificent* Savage armor.

"Looks like it's time once again to reassess our standings, Captain Ford."

The Nether Ops commander's voice grabbed the attention of the crew in that first moment of silence that came after the banishing of the shiny legionnaires and their malevolent blue-skinned allies.

There was a smug, self-satisfied smile on the man's helmetless face. His bucket had been tossed aside in preparation for this moment. There were times when being faceless was an advantage, and other times where it paid to make sure your opponents knew exactly what you were thinking and feeling. The commander was an older man, still strong but with thin white hair that gave no hints about how he might have looked as a young soldier. His smile lingered as the crew observed where his weapon was pointed. He could see that they all knew full well that the Endurian would be the price for the shedding of his own blood.

Keel repositioned his feet but didn't dare move his weapons, knowing that even the slightest hint of a threat could set off a fatal reaction that he was in no position to stop. He hadn't come this far just to see Leenah get shot by some career deep-state operative in a final act of malignancy.

"I told you already," Keel said. "I'm not the guy who can tell you about Kill Team Ice."

"Oh, I suppose that's true at this point. You know, I read your file, Ford."

"You've mentioned that."

The commander chuckled. "Most of what's there is just a copy of the Legion archive. You're more of a wraith than you realize. It was only an AI that even flagged you as a potential Ice member, believe it or not. File had nothing except those Legion records, some Dark Ops intel we stole... and a whole lot of speculation. Mostly, you're a mystery to us, Ford. Except for what little bits our other agents here and there send in."

"You're talking about Honey. The Tennar."

"Honey... Atumna... girl went by a lot of names. And it was never her name you remembered about her, anyway. I take it she's dead?"

"She's dead," Keel confirmed.

"She was good at what she did," the commander said, suddenly eulogizing this Nether Ops agent who'd only come up by chance. "As good at what she did as I am at what I do. Built a reputation as something of a preventive problem solver. She solved the problematic before they could become real problems. Among other things. Only, in her last mission—before yours became a mission of opportunity—the problem wasn't solved. It was only a partial success, and you know what happened after that. Though I suppose if that other member of your team didn't kill her, it was only a matter of time before you would have. You seem to have killed a lot of us, Captain Ford. Though you might not know it."

Keel risked turning himself to face the man head-on. He seemed to be in a talkative mood, so as long as they kept talking, perhaps he wouldn't mind. His weapons were still pointed away from the commander. "I was always satisfied when I did. What do you want?"

"An understanding, first. Men need to be agreed on some foundational things before progress can be made. I don't need your intel on Kill Team Ice. We've wiped out enough of you bastards to have relative assurance you won't be a problem. Checking on you for members outstanding was due diligence. My orders were to kill you once I drew a satisfactory conclusion about your knowledge on the subject. Technically, I'm supposed to do that now. Thing of it is... I've read your file—I know, I've mentioned that—and I know what I'm up against. If I pull my piece and try to punch through that helmet of yours, you'll put a hole where my eyes now sit. Before I even squeeze the trigger. It sounds like an impossibility, but... the file.

"So I can't kill you. And I'm left asking... how does this all shake out? How do I get out of this temple alive? Can't see a way that happens, if I'm being honest."

"Sure you can," Keel said, nodding at the pistol in the commander's hand, which was now trembling ever so slightly from being held in a shooter's aim for so long. "Put your gun down, turn around, and leave. Easy."

The commander gave a knowing grin. "Giving you a nice target for when you put a blaster bolt between my shoulder blades."

"Probably. Only now we've got ourselves to an understanding. Like you said."

Again the commander laughed. "We legionnaires have a saying: 'Always make them pay.' I used to say that when I was in the Legion. But the truth of it is... you *can't* always make them pay. Sometimes the debt they've built up is too high. Say your buddy gets blown up on some sket-filled rock out on the edge. You find the man who made the bomb, the man who placed it. You do them both and feel empty. So you do the wife and children and neighbors... anyone who saw it and could have stopped it. Doesn't help. How about the smugglers and the arms dealers? Not to mention the ruling class... and truth is, most of them *never* pay. And you'll never make them. They'll die old and fat and never facing the consequences for all the wrongs. And that first man? You dusted him so long ago he hardly even matters."

The Nether Ops commander drew in a breath and steadied his wavering arm. It was becoming a liability; he needed to be sure that his shot would do its work or he was as good as dead. "So I say... *make them hurt.* Every step of the way. Killing a man isn't making him pay, because once you're dead, it's all over. But to make a man live with the pain of his actions... that's a payment that never runs dry.

"You made choices, Captain Ford. Decisions that put you in direct opposition to something bigger, grander, and far better than your trite notions of freedom, liberty, or whatever else you want to call this pathetic excuse for an existence inside the Republic. Stiff-necked, unwilling to see the light at the end of the difficult path that hard men tried to lead you down. What's coming now is gonna be nothing but pain for people like you. Your civil wars and your Article Nineteen are mere sideshows. The real pain has been readying its arrival since before the Savage Wars ever ended. You can't stop it, and I can't find a way out of this temple. But I can die happy knowing the hurt I'm about to drop on you as you wait until what can't be stopped comes to fruition."

In that instant, the commander squeezed his trigger. But neither he nor his blaster bolt were in the temple any longer. Ravi had vanished him elsewhere.

The Nether Ops commander was less surprised by the sudden total blackout than he was by the fact that whereas he'd been standing on his feet, he was now lying on his side. A pressure-filled buzz sounded in his ears and vibrated along his sinuses.

He shifted to a kneeling position, then pressed down with his hands to push to his feet... only to windmill in horror as he found that the solid, cold ground where he put his hands—the ground he'd just been lying on—was now... gone. Entirely. In a panic, he felt the empty space, searching for the edge of whatever shelf he blindly knelt upon. With each shift of his feet or knee, with each motion, the shelf seemed to grow smaller until he felt as though his shins were balanced atop a thin horizontal beam.

"Help!" he called out in the darkness. A word he never used. The persistent, pressurized buzzing in his head was the only answer.

The pain of kneeling atop that bar turned to agony. He finally fell forward and slipped off over the edge, could feel himself falling. He screamed, and by the end of that scream, he slammed hard onto another surface. Still enmeshed in the darkness, he quickly realized that this one, too, seemed to crumble away whenever he moved. And so he lay there, perfectly still, sensing the trauma inside of him, though it brought no coughs of blood-tinged spittle. The shock of the fall had, however, opened his ears so that the buzzing now sounded like millions of voices taking up moans and screams of agony, anguish, hatred, and despair.

The Nether Ops commander lay on his perch, fearing what would happen if he moved but knowing that, eventually, his body would fail him and the pain would grow too great and he would roll or slip again over the side. To fall again and land again and add pain upon pain.

There, in the place reserved by that great army that marched, whose path he had worked to make easier, the commander suffered.

He added his own screaming voice to the multitude.

Ravi studied his friends in the silent moments between hearing the Nether Ops commander's last words and seeing his nascent blaster bolt disappear completely alongside the man. "We are secure for the moment."

It was Keel who said, "Glad you could take your time with that, Ravi. Maybe next go-round, you can cut it even closer."

"Surely, Captain Keel, you do not think I was merely testing my reflexes at an opportune moment. After all, that would be akin to waiting until the last possible second to make a jump to lightspeed with no less than five Republic corvettes in pursuit because you 'wanted to see how long you needed to dodge them before they gave up.'"

"You did that?" Garret asked Keel in awe, as he often was around the captain.

"I might have. That's not the point."

"It sounds like you," Leenah said.

"It was him," Ravi confirmed. "And there are considerably more such examples I could mention since I am being accused of risking your life for no other reason than—"

"Okay, okay," Keel said. "So what were you doing then?"

"I was listening. It seemed this agent may have been on the verge of providing useful information."

"And was any of it?"

"Perhaps. I will need to consider his words further once I have been filled in on what sorts of activities you have undertaken since we last traveled the stars together. I see already now that you have taken Tyrus Rechs's armor for yourself."

"What can I say? It fit."

"Yes, I think he would have appreciated your wearing it."

"You guys are old friends now?"

Ravi shrugged. "Not as such."

Leenah had been frozen in place while the Nether commander had held his aim at her, and was now working out the stiffness in her arms and legs. "Where did you send that kelhorn?"

"To his end. He is now seeing firsthand the terrible place reserved for those who have been seduced in exchange for their treachery. He goes to the evil that I have dedicated myself to stopping. It is a terrible place." Ravi swirled the galaxy around their heads with his hands. "We are going somewhere else."

Makaffie was watching the swirling cosmos with such an intensity that one would have thought he'd gone back to the time when he'd first formulated H8. "This... this is a stellar map. It's the whole galaxy, isn't it? This is... everything, man."

Ravi gave a quick nod. "This is how my people traveled among the stars. We had no need for such primitive things as starships and hyperdrives."

"Coulda fooled me the way you bummed your way across the galaxy in my ship," Keel said, bringing Leenah near while gazing at the stars. He tried to make out some clusters he could identify, but there were so, so many of them.

"Hoo, hoo, hoo," Ravi laughed. "I assure you I had other reasons for it. I enjoyed your company though, and I have missed our travels together. Now, allow me to navigate according to my own ways."

"Someday we need to have a talk and figure all this out," Keel muttered. "Good to have you back, Ravi."

The words didn't have the effect Keel thought they would. Ravi frowned. "You... might not say such a thing once this talk you mention has occurred."

"And on that note," Leenah said, "I'm guessing I need to send the *Six* back to the *Phoenix*?"

"Yes," said Ravi, businesslike again. "We would have to wait far too long for it to arrive where we are now going."

"Where *are* we going?" Keel asked, his annoyance at this still not having been addressed coming through in his question.

"To find Prisma."

16

"We shouldn't be here, babe. You know there's no kind of Savages here."

The Wild Man grunted in reply to this most beautiful of voices. The hike from the *Six* to the temple, following the wobanki, had been just another slog, albeit a pretty one, until she began speaking to him in earnest. Just to him. Always for his ears only.

He knew now that his wife was dead. There was a time where he thought that, maybe…

But now he knew. His wife, though her voice was vivacious and alive, was dead. And not just for a little while but for centuries. She had died before he ever left his home world. She was dead all during his mad pursuit of the Savages. Dead while he fought on New Vega. Dead while he served in the Legion and while he slept in suspended animation during his time with Kill Team Ice.

Dead every day since.

It was an odd thing, though he tried not to think about it that often. All that time fighting for her, and all that time she lay longer and longer in repose. Right from the start, he lost track of all dates and any sense of time beyond the movement of the sun on whatever planet he landed upon. And then one day he heard what year it was from some locals he was trying to defend from a Savage invasion—really, he was just there to kill Savages—and he realized it had been five years since she'd died, give or take a few standard months.

He didn't hear from her for almost a week after hearing that simple report of the date and time, so many centuries ago.

The Wild Man also remembered a thought, though not the occasion or context for that thought. He had realized after waking up for a mission that she'd been dead for more years than she'd ever lived. And then five times as long as she'd lived. And ten times. And on time marched, until it was nearer to a hundred times her lifespan since the day it happened.

Her life had been nothing when compared to all those ages after her heart stopped beating. The vast majority of her existence was as a corpse, a part of the great myriad of dead that most things were. The sum total of all life, erupting like a vapor before settling into nothing but the long, enduring grave.

So... even though she spoke to him during that hike to the temple, when the hope of finding Prisma was still strong, the Wild Man knew she was dead.

But also, there was the voice. Speaking to him. As alive and independent as she had ever been. Her voice outlived her body. Her voice wouldn't die. And the sound of it, so often singularly focused, had guided, comforted, and *saved* the Wild Man many times over. She had been the impetus to get back up, go farther, and always, "Do another one, babe."

How many times would he have died without her urging him to live? And so, if she was back now, just like she'd come back aboard that Savage hulk, which he thought must have been the cause of that long-due awakening...

then it must be important. Even if the message was the same, it must be important right now. About the Savages.

She was trying to save him. She was holding him accountable to do to the Savages what he had promised her he would.

The others could never understand that.

So when she spoke to the Wild Man as he marched toward the temple, all he could do at first was grunt. Because otherwise they'd know. Or at least Makaffie would. Captain Fast would have, once upon a time, but probably not now. Makaffie would have, though. He never failed to notice.

She didn't like when he grunted or made her wait for an answer. Even when she lived. She wanted to hear his voice. The little hints, like the grunt or a subtle wave of his hands, were either ignored or missed by her altogether. She would keep talking, repeating herself until he answered her. Or better yet, until he acted.

The only act that ever truly satisfied her was killing Savages.

"Did you hear me, babe? I said we shouldn't be here. We should be killin' Savages. *You* should be killin' Savages. And there's no Savages on this world. Never have been."

Wild Man wanted to tell her that this was just a stop on the way to once again killing his nemesis the Savage. Maybe this wasn't an ideal place to kill them, especially if none were on the planet, but what they were doing here would lead to finding more. She didn't understand how long it had been since he'd killed a Savage, apart from on that reclaimer. That had marked the end of a long drought. And this was just following up on what happened there. He wanted her to understand that this was only for a little while. She'd see.

But he couldn't say all that out loud and not bring Makaffie into things. So he grunted again, a little louder. He watched to see if his slim friend noticed; he didn't.

"We shouldn't be here, babe. Go somewhere else. Go find them. Do a Savage for me."

The Wild Man looked for a way to break off from the group. Not for long, just enough for him to explain things. He pretended to examine tracks that the wobanki had already followed and disregarded as belonging to something other than their quarry. It was obvious from looking at them that they were mere animal tracks, but maybe the others wouldn't see it quite so clearly. He picked out a track left by some sort of hooved creature and let out a deep-throated "Hmm" before walking off the path.

Makaffie immediately took note and hollered ahead to Skrizz about how it looked like the Wild Man, who was no mean tracker himself, had found something. Did the wobanki want to come back to take another look?

"S'nothin'," the Wild Man quickly said as he abandoned the tracks. He didn't want Skrizz to point out how these tracks weren't anything close to what they needed to follow, because that would only raise suspicion in Makaffie's mind. The little man was smart. It was a different kind of smarts, but it was still the sort that would question why such an obvious error had been made. And then... he wouldn't understand.

They didn't see her like he saw her. They couldn't see all the good.

The hike continued. She told him again and again how they didn't belong there. Urged him to leave and go find those Savages still alive and put them in the grave the same as they'd done to her and the baby.

Why should they live when she'd been dead for so long?

Finally, frustrated and on the verge of despair, the Wild Man mumbled, "Wait."

He hoped she'd understand what he meant. Needed her to see the delicacy of the situation. She'd never been good at that. Never one to see the big picture or the long gain.

She didn't reply.

But Makaffie did. "What's that?"

"Nothin'. Thinkin'."

"About Savages?"

The Wild Man's mind began whirring. He would now have to think as fast as Makaffie, which wasn't something he felt confident he could do. Give him his rifle and a target and put it a mile out and he wouldn't even feel his heart elevate. But this... this sort of thing didn't come easy to him. He slowed down and scooped some of the stream's water into his hands, then washed his hair with it. It was alarmingly cold for how hot the day had been.

"Yeah. About Savages. Just... tryin' to figure out how it's all connected. The admiral—I mean Sullus—he didn't say there'd be Savages. And after all that time, all those missions after the war... all of a sudden, that's all it's been for us."

Makaffie joined the Wild Man and stood facing the little river. "He said it was worse than the Savages. I didn't take that as a declaration that they wouldn't be involved. After all, he had to believe that whatever Savage construct still containing a working strand might have some living Savages nearby. But the big problem, well... I would've preferred a few more briefings on that before he sent us on into the galactic hinterland."

"I been thinking about that, too. And I think what he really wanted from us was to take care of the general."

"How long you been thinking like that?"

"Since it happened."

"I'd like to hear those thoughts."

The Wild Man shrugged. This wasn't a conversation he would have attempted to have if it weren't for her. But he felt that the surest way to keep Makaffie off her tracks was to be honest with him about other things. So far, it seemed to be working. Whatever suspicions Makaffie might have harbored in first bringing up Savages looked like they were fading now.

"Sullus was right about the Legion and the Republic. He was right about that. But how it all mattered because of the whole end of the world he was raving about, I always wondered if that wasn't something he whipped up just to make sure we dropped the general. Because he couldn't do it alone. And we both saw how the general wasn't interested in helping him; only wanted to kill him. So maybe the admiral knew that would happen."

"And woke up what remained of us to murder General Rex?"

"I think so sometimes... but then I think about everything he said about the Republic and the Legion. He was right. And the general... he let all that happen. I don't think the admiral was wrong about that. He was gone, learning his... power. But the general stayed. And he let it happen, Mak."

"Or," Makaffie said in a small voice, "it got to a point that he couldn't do anything about it anymore. Sometimes things just happen."

"Sometimes they do."

After that conversation, Makaffie felt comfortable enough to leave his friend's side and go talk with Sergeant Fast. Even so, the Wild Man had decided against going off to speak with her. That would still raise too much suspicion. But if he kept his marching pace just the right distance between Skrizz ahead and the others behind, they might not hear his voice, if he was quiet about it.

"Captain Fast is back," he said to her. "That's good. You know he doesn't love no Savages."

"Killin' Savages ain't his chief concern. You can see that as plain as I do. He got himself a pretty pink-skinned girl and he's doin' for her what you promised you'd do for me."

Wildman was confused. "How's that? You just said killin' Savages ain't his chief concern."

"It's not. But doin' what his girl needs done... that is. You know what I want you to do. You don't want to do it any longer?"

"You know I do."

Then...

"We shouldn't be here, babe. You know there ain't no Savages here."

His plan had been to sneak off sometime in the night. After his watch, so that nobody had to pull any extra duty. He would leave out a datapad explaining his every move so they wouldn't waste time looking for him. But then they reached the temple and the plan he'd formulated in the last legs of that long hike evaporated.

She wasn't happy he'd been captured. Not at all. He sat there with his head down, arms and ankles fastened with ener-chains.

But neither was she cruel. "Oh, baby. I tried to warn you..."

"I know," the Wild Man said back, his voice still carrying the scars of all the times he hadn't died. He was no longer concerned whether Makaffie could hear him. It hardly mattered now.

"Pray for a miracle, babe. Pray for just one more chance."

"I will," he croaked. He'd promised her his prayers many times when she was still alive, and many times since she'd died. It was a promise he rarely kept. It wasn't his way, even if he wanted it to be. Even if it was for her sake.

The miracle came anyway. Ravi arrived and removed those ener-chains. Wild Man needed no prompting to take action, which was fine because she didn't say so much as a word. The big sniper got up and killed the guard, then went about the business of getting everything he would need for what came next.

Nights on this planet were dark. But that darkness would only help him in his cause. As things grew more chaotic and the Gomarii slavers and imitation legionnaires activated light pylons in an attempt to find and destroy Captain Fast, the result was pockets of even greater darkness that he could slip into.

There was no final farewell to Makaffie. The Wild Man simply took a step in the opposite direction of his old friend as Ravi led him and the code slicer away. Makaffie would understand even if he didn't agree.

The Wild Man ran into a slaver somewhere in the dark. The Gomarii were one of the few species the Wild Man encountered who were bigger than him. Still, the sniper managed to put the slaver down with a swift strike from the butt of his rifle followed by stab after stab with his combat knife until he had to pull his wet and sticky hands away from the rage that kept them moving long after the alien was dead.

After that, things went easier. The darkness welcomed the Wild Man and its embrace felt somehow like it was coming from her. Except... she wasn't there. Or maybe she was but was choosing to stay silent. She did that sometimes. But why now?

She had always come and gone over the years. Sometimes because he asked her to. Other times on her own accord because of something he did. Gone until he called her back, which she liked the most. Sometimes coming back on her own.

He moved through the woods, avoiding the trail he'd taken with the others to reach the temple. He climbed a hill and turned back to assess the shooting he heard in the distance.

"They could use some help," he explained.

Silence.

He needed her to know why he was stopping, though. She couldn't believe that he was having second thoughts now. He would still kill the Savages. Checking on the team and sending some support wouldn't interfere with those plans. In fact, the more likely his friends' escape became, the less likely those shiny armored fascists would be to pursue a lone breakaway. If they knew about him at all.

Of course, if they didn't, they would. As soon as his rifle roared, they would.

The temple was lit up exceptionally well. Ravi had linked up with Captain Fast and the Endurian and was now leading the whole party around the pyramid. Skrizz was making his way back. The Wild Man unslung his rifle and made it boom in support, adding to the chaos from his impromptu overwatch position. The head of his target disappeared. He chambered another round.

"Don't mean nothin'," he told her. "Just cleanin' up a bit. I'll still get you a Savage, babe. I promise."

No answer.

He watched as the temple opened itself to Ravi and the others. He kept firing, taking care to clear a path for Skrizz and discourage any attempts from what remained of the hostile force to circle back and flush the sniper out.

"They opened the temple, babe," he said, savoring the smell of the smoke that rose from the barrel of his rifle. "Only time I ever saw that was with the admiral. Maybe... maybe if we go back, it'll bring us to some Savages."

No answer. Which was the same as her saying, "That ain't it, babe."

The Wild Man did what he could until the others had fallen back deep inside the temple and the stones began to close in on themselves. Through it all, he didn't remain in one position. He would fire, sprint farther away from the temple as he reloaded, turn, and repeat the process.

Finally he turned for good, leaving his friends to whatever fate was in store for them. Now was the time to focus earnestly on his own plan. He told her as much, but she still wouldn't answer.

"I'm sorry, darlin'," he huffed. He'd never been a strong runner. It was sheer willpower that kept him moving at top speed. "I should've... should've prayed, like you said. But... I was thinking. Workin' on the problem so I could...

do... what you wanted done. Your prayers... they were always enough for both of us."

He instinctively broke off from his improvised trail, sensing that at least some troops were following him. He lay in a hide until they arrived at where he had been and then shot them down with a pair of violent booms. He waited. It had just been the two of them. Perhaps they hadn't been stalking him but trying to regroup or get away altogether. Either way...

"Remember this ship?" he asked as he swapped his rifle for a personal defense blaster. "I rode in one of these for a long time early on."

He had arrived at the original LZ and now made his way to the scout jumper Prisma and her mother had left behind.

"Do you remember, darling?"

No answer. The silence was starting to bother him. Maybe he should have gone with the others. But the temple had to be closed by now. There would be no getting inside. And anyway... he really did have an idea of how he might find some Savages. That hadn't been a lie or wishful thinking. The ship, this old ship, would get him there.

He wished she would listen. She would be so excited.

But she wasn't talking.

"I'm sorry."

No answer.

There was an observation bot flittering above the LZ, its handlers all dead. Wild Man paid it no mind. He was pleased to see that the ramp came down just as easily as it had when they first arrived. He cleared the ship and did a quick sweep for trackers. Finding none, he closed up the ramp and hurried to the pilot's seat.

Sitting in the cockpit chair felt both familiar and un-settling. As though he were reliving some part of his life that had played out a long time before. His fingers remembered how to cycle the ship to life even though his mind would have stopped and stuttered with great difficulty if he had been asked to state each step in order. But the fingers, they remembered just fine.

The exploration ship was up and in the air, then through the atmosphere and calculating jump coordinates. If there were other ships nearby, its old sensors couldn't detect them.

"Almost out of here, darling," he said. "You'll see. I love you."

The jump computer in this old ship took much longer to plot its course than its modern counterparts did. The Wild Man had forgotten just how long those early hyperspace-capable ships took to find a safe jump route. But he had nothing but time if it meant making her happy again.

And then the stars elongated and the scout ship leapt into faster-than-light travel, accelerating the Wild Man as he began his hunt for whatever Savages still remained in the galaxy.

17

Transporting from the Temple of the Ancients to a sandy riverbank set before a great forest jungle was disorienting to the crew of the *Indelible VI*. That was putting things mildly. Only a moment before, they had been encased in a structure that had sat impenetrable for eons, staring up in wonder at a swirling miasma of stars. It was breathtaking, seeing the totality of the galaxy laid bare while Ravi navigated his way to wherever... this was. And when the crew thought of that moment later in life, if asked they would have told you that even during the shooting and the violence, the effect of that beautiful display hadn't been lost on them. Even Keel would have told you that.

None of them remembered the stony interior of that temple as being particularly hot or stifling, but it must have been so. Otherwise this uncomfortably cool breeze that stirred up the surface of the dark river wouldn't have felt so jarring. And yet... it wasn't the wind that set them on edge. An incredible sense of dread and danger weighed heavily on the hearts of all those who visited this planet.

"I don't like this place, Captain Keel," Garret said softly.

A deep and primal roar that sounded both colossal and prehistoric rose from somewhere deep within the jungle forest, its thick leaves and fronds creating an impenetrable shroud on the opposite side of the bank.

"I'm with you on that, kid," said Keel. "Ravi, where the hell are we?"

Before his navigator could answer, Keel's attention was drawn to Leenah, who had been studying something on the opposite shore. "Aeson, look at that."

"What?" Keel looked where she pointed.

A small creature with a flat face and beige fur was cautiously approaching the water's edge. It was followed by several of the same kind, many of which drank, pointing spotted black tails straight into the air as they sent their faces into the surface to draw in river water. Like the others, the first creature stuck its tail up as well and took a long drink. Then it sat down and looked suspiciously to the left and right, taking in its surroundings. It seemed not to even notice the other creatures crowding around it, though to Keel it seemed odd that they would all attempt to drink from virtually the same spot when there was so much open space along the bank.

"It's just a dumb animal," Keel said. "I dunno what—"

And then the smuggler saw what she must have been talking about. The creature moved to one side and occupied the same little piece of land as one of its neighbors. But instead of a collision or the two animals pressing in against one another, both animals seemed to fade and become less solid. Keel could see *through* the animals in the space where they overlapped.

Suddenly, one of them took off as though spooked, and it became solid again as soon as it left the shared space. It disappeared completely, like an apparition, before it reached the jungle foliage.

Now all eyes were on these strange animals. More came down and drank, always one at a time. Some stayed longer at the water's edge, and some were so skittish they didn't drink at all, turning around almost as soon as they arrived. They grew more transparent the closer they clustered together. Still, none of them seemed aware of the others. The last one to arrive at the river smelled the air by sticking its face straight up, then it began drinking—only to be caught in a white-pluming geyser that erupted from the water as something long and dark, with great ivory teeth, snapped its slim jaws around the animal and dragged it beneath the surface.

None of the other creatures reacted at all, though most everyone on the far shore observing—including Keel—jumped at the sudden violent attack of the river predator.

"What kind of creature is that?" Makaffie asked. "Not the fish... thing. I mean the furry ones. Are they... are they capable of casting some kind of holographic decoy of themselves to evade predators?"

"Wow," said Garret, immediately accepting this hypothesis as proven.

"An interesting hypothesis, but incorrect," Ravi said. "What you are witnessing is one single creature's life playing out. These are all the times the animal has visited this exact spot."

Gradually, all the other phantasmal iterations of the little animal faded into nothing, and the bank became empty again.

"What is this place?" Keel asked. He hadn't yet holstered his weapons, and nothing he'd seen so far made him think he should, but he put away the slug thrower in order to usher Leenah to stand just behind him.

Ravi smiled knowingly, but without humor. "A planet unlike any other in the galaxy. Should the time ever come when humanity maps the galaxy as my people once did, you will find that this planet sits in the exact galactic center, far beyond what you now call galaxy's edge. It is a point of union between realms. Between this world and the unseen realm, converging in the Quantum. All things that have happened on this planet are showing themselves, no longer held in check now that this world's keeper has perished."

Makaffie seemed to comprehend all of that mumbo-jumbo almost immediately. "I see what you're laying down, man. So that little critter... we just watched all the days of its lives unfold one after the other like a big cosmic tidal wave that churned it all together and spit it out on top of itself."

Ravi gave a curt nod. His eyes hadn't failed to monitor his surroundings since they'd arrived. "Precisely. We witnessed the creature's interaction with a particular anchor—this spot on the riverbed—at this exact time of day as many times as happened to it however long ago it lived. Were we standing elsewhere, the unfettered Quantum might have shown it doing some other ritual of life—or perhaps not shown us this being at all. In any case, you saw how its life ended. And so, we see it no longer."

Skrizz yammered uncomfortably.

"We still have to find Prisma," Leenah reminded him. "We can't run off now. And where would we even go?"

Skrizz gave a resigned hiss.

"So then, we can't be sure what's real and what's not," Makaffie observed. "Not a whole lot different from the ship we just left."

Keel gave a lopsided frown and crossed his arms. "Lucky us. How dangerous is this place, Ravi?"

"It can be fatal, to be certain. However, though you may die, the death may not be permanent. Depending on circumstances."

Keel uncrossed his arms. "Thanks for clearing that up, pal."

"Captain Keel, I do not wish to denigrate your intelligence—such as Lao Pak might—however, you must understand that the reality of this place is exceedingly difficult even to accept, let alone comprehend. Many humans who have come to this world succumbed to madness prior to suffering their final and permanent death."

Leenah's face soured at that news. "And Prisma's mother brought her *here*?"

Ravi closed his eyes for a moment and took in a full breath. Not in annoyance, but as one seeking focus. "Prisma is here... but... not in a state such as you hope for." He opened his eyes again; the sorrow they contained was unmistakable. "Nor in a form that will cause rejoicing. The way forward will be difficult, and the end more difficult still. But we must move. I will explain this place and its dangers as best I can as we travel. Please, stay alert. On Umnor, most everything is capable of killing."

They began to travel across the planet with Ravi as their guide. They were tired from the start. Their trek from the *Indelible VI* to the Temple of the Ancients hadn't been accompanied by any meaningful rest, and the fight that followed running afoul of Nether Ops had only exacerbated that fatigue. Everyone was a step or two slower than they might have been. Everyone except for Keel and Ravi, who both had to slow themselves in order to keep from getting too far ahead of the others.

And then there was Skrizz. The wobanki didn't seem tired and Keel wouldn't have believed him if he'd insisted otherwise. But the apex predator seemed unwilling to separate himself from the thickest group of humanoids, matching the pace of Leenah, Garret, and Makaffie.

Keel glanced at the catman over his shoulder as he strode beside Ravi. "Any idea what got into him?"

"Skrizz?"

"Yeah. First time I can remember being in a new place and he doesn't wander off."

The Ancient glanced back as if to assess the wobanki and then looked forward, pointing out a tangled root that snaked into the path, seeking to trip an unwary traveler. "I suspect Skrizz senses the chaos that has been unleashed on this world with the loss of its keeper, Urmo. Wobanki have a higher attunement to the unseen realm than all but the most gifted of humans. You must understand, Captain, that although you cannot see it, those capable can sense all the life on this world that ever was and ever will be... and all the death. Such can be quite unsettling."

"The little oddities we're seeing..." Keel said. "There's more—more that we *aren't* seeing. But he knows it's there?"

"Precisely. And you can imagine how sensing danger and death at the hand of predators and disasters, war and plague, may put Skrizz on edge. Imagine feeling as though a blaster were pointed at your head at all times."

"Don't have to imagine that feeling, Ravi."

"Hoo, hoo, hoo. But consider... there is no way to fight your way out of it here. Skrizz must only endure."

More examples of this "Quantum" bringing multiple instances of life to one physical anchor occurred as they traveled farther along the path that cut through the sparser jungle that sat on their side of the river. They saw simple migratory movements of small animals that seemed to span an unknown number of ages, sometimes witnessing the long adaptation of a species play out in only a few seconds as their path intersected some ancient migratory pattern or path to a nesting ground.

They traveled for two hours before encountering the first human.

It was a man wandering the jungle, searching for something. He spoke to someone or something, but his voice echoed and sounded distant, as if speaking across the cavernous expanse that was time itself.

"133, scout the hill. We'll camp here tonight."

"That voice..." Makaffie said, stopping in his tracks. He stepped off the path to look closer.

Ravi held out his hand. "Caution."

Keel went after the enigmatic man. "C'mon, Mak, stick to the path."

"Just gotta see if..."

The ghostly man turned, and both Makaffie and Keel recognized him.

"You know that face, don't you?" Makaffie asked, encouraged by the look of recognition he saw on Keel.

"Yeah."

"From Kill Team Ice?"

Keel's face soured. He shook his head. "No. Utopion. I shot him in the head."

"You... *what?*"

"Shot him. Goth Sullus, right? C'mon... he's dead and I'm not interested in trying to talk to his ghost or whatever the hell that is."

Ravi joined them. "He would not hear you. Or rather, he would have heard your voice distantly, then, if you knew how to speak across the Quantum. But whatever warning you might give, his path has already been fixed. Goth Sullus is dead. We must return to the path. Quickly."

They followed Ravi back to the game trail they'd been traversing.

"Why couldn't I see whoever he was speaking to?" Makaffie asked. He, more than anyone else, had become fascinated with the peculiar nature of their surroundings. It was an experience just like this one that he'd been pursuing, long ago, when he first developed the narcotic H8. Although with everything that had happened with the drug since then... he regretted ever experimenting with those lotus petals.

Ravi again closed his eyes and drew in a breath, taking his mind to whatever place held those answers. "It would seem... this man was communicating with a bot of some sort."

"Like over a comm link?" Makaffie asked.

"They were together. But you cannot see them together for the same reason that the stones, trees, and other natural elements are not constantly shifting before you. Not all that moves is life."

Garret hadn't been much interested in this world until the moment those words were spoken. He didn't like the conclusion that was implied. "So a bot is just the sum of its raw materials?"

Ravi nodded. "That is a good way of putting it... generally speaking."

"I don't believe it." The code slicer spoke softly but defiantly.

Makaffie looked around, watching a bird build all the nests of its life in the same nook in a tree. "This planet is starting to feel like a giant version of that Savage reclaimer."

"As well it might." Ravi pushed aside a hanging vine and held the path open for the others to pass him by. "I have given considerable thought to that vessel since first visiting. The reclaimers themselves, you know well, were not able to be killed in a conventional manner. This is because they existed like those on this world. Only... they had left Umnor."

"So you're saying they were here at some point?" Keel asked.

"If we search, I have no doubt we will find their physical forms in this place. Quite dead, now. It would seem the Savages knew of this world. Urmo... chose not to share this with me. But his ways were always his own."

"Are we going to get a cipher key for all the riddles you're speaking in?" Keel asked. "Because I can't escape the feeling that all this is important, but you're the only one who knows why. Well, maybe you and Makaffie."

Makaffie put his hand on his chest and bowed. "Thank you, Sergeant Fast."

"Perhaps I should have shared all up front with you, Captain," Ravi said. "But... time seemed limitless. Not like now. I wanted to be sure. Of both my doubts and convictions. You are right. There is much to be said. You of all people still alive deserve to know so much more than I have told you in all our time together. But now... we must continue after Prisma. Only when we have uncovered where she was can I consider where I last saw her."

Leenah's mouth fell open. "You mean you already know where she went after this? I thought you said she was here? If she went somewhere else, why aren't we going to that spot?"

Ravi looked sad. "Every step she took leading to that place is of vital importance. Only after they have been uncovered can we have any hope of finding her... and saving her."

18

The journey grew harder as the elevation increased. Ravi led them up something between a hill and a mountain. As they started their ascent, he warned them they were closing upon the place that would show Prisma... but it was the least stable part of the planet now that Urmo, the keeper of order on this world, was no longer living.

More apparitions came and went. Most emerged like phantoms out of the persistent mists that rose up the mountain, only to disappear just as quickly after playing out whatever event in the physical realm the Quantum chose to reveal. Most were peaceful and meaningless, unidentifiable travelers who had come to the world—and likely died here—traveling the same path at some point in centuries past.

But this was not always so. A man with a bloody face and wild, fear-fueled eyes ran toward them, screaming unintelligibly. Keel and the others instinctively moved to the edges of the path, looking for the cause of this man's horror and making a way for him to pass through. They watched as he stumbled and staggered, attempting to keep his momentum going forward in a mad scramble on hands and feet.

A large, saurian creature leapt from an elevated shelf above them and landed on the man's back. The man's scream cut into a gurgle as his back was broken and his ribs shattered. The last of his air was expelled, together with blood and other elements that ought to remain inside a man. At least his agony was short-lived. The creature, a bipedal reptile with the claws and teeth of a hunter, clamped his diamond-shaped jaw around the dying man's neck, nearly severing the head in one bite.

The creature then stood and let out the primitive roar they'd heard at the river when they first arrived. It was smaller than some had imagined, standing at "only" ten feet at the shoulder, but it was no less fearsome as a result. Snapping up pieces of its victim, it ripped meat away from bone and then tossed its head back to let the flesh slide down its gullet.

Yet as it gulped down the warm and dripping flesh, it seemed to notice the travelers—who stood frozen in shock at what they'd just witnessed. Slowly, the beast stepped off its kill and toward Keel and his crew, standing no more than four meters away. It turns its broad lizard head sideways and stared at them through one slitted, reptilian eye.

Ravi's sword flashed. "Ready yourselves…"

No sooner had the warning come than the creature shrieked and leapt at the crew, throwing its powerful legs in front of it so that forearms and feet alike had their black claws stretching to eviscerate whoever it reached first.

Keel's blaster bolts impacted in quick succession around the thing's throat and where he guessed its heart might be, but it was Ravi's flashing sword that ended the attack before any harm could be done. The great lizard fell dead at Keel's feet, its blood pooling around his boots.

The phantasm of the man killed by the monster faded from existence, dissipating as though it were a holotransmission slowly coming to an end. The creature, however, stayed corporeal.

Keel prodded its bulk with the toe of his boot. "Nasty kelhorn."

Makaffie squatted down to inspect the beast, then rose back up to address Ravi. "Let me venture a guess into the abnormality of this place. This thing exists primarily in the... Quantum, right? So it can move freely throughout time on this world. Hence why we witnessed it kill whoever that poor fool was and then were nearly its next victims, despite however much time passed between the events."

Leenah inclined her head toward Keel. "That make any sense to you?"

"Barely."

Ravi sheathed his sword. "You have the basics of it, yes. This creature was created by those capable of such things so that it might test those seeking to learn the ways of this place. One may battle it ten thousand times and be killed an equal number of times before finally discovering the way forward."

Makaffie pointed to the sword at Ravi's side. "And I suppose you... well, you made a shortcut for us with that cutter on your hip."

"Of a sort, yes."

Keel furrowed his brow, still trying to make sense of all this. "So if that thing had killed us, then what? We all bleed out and then get back up when the buzzer rings for the second round?"

Ravi gave a wan smile. "Had you been sufficiently attuned to this place... yes. But in your current state... no. You would have just died."

Keel shook his head in disbelief. "Nice place you brought us to."

"I would not have done so had it not been necessary in our effort to find Prisma. Thankfully we are near the conclusion of our trek."

They pushed upward. The mountains were engulfed in a deep and humid mist that felt as though it settled between the crew's body and clothes, creating a layer of sticky warmth that was inescapable. They watched for more creatures like the last but saw nothing.

And then a pair of glowing, yellow eyes penetrated the heavy mist. They belonged to a bot, a rather tall one, heading toward them down the path.

"Crash?" Garret said, in a quiet voice to himself, and then louder upon realizing that it really was the war bot turned servitor. "Crash!"

The code slicer ran ahead to greet KRS-88, but the bot didn't recognize him. Neither did it slow its pace or change direction. The two would have collided, but instead Crash become translucent the moment Garret shared the space where he stood. Then the bot disappeared completely.

"Ravi!" Garret called over his shoulder in excitement. "You see?"

"Oh, my," said Ravi. "I always would tell that noble machine it was not far from such things, and now..." The Ancient shook his head. "The odds of such a thing happening are... not high."

"Come on," Garret called as he started up the path, his eagerness overcoming his exhaustion. "Maybe we'll find more clues!"

Ravi held out a hand. "Garret, wait!"

But the code slicer was too excited to hear it. Or perhaps he simply couldn't hear it with the mists pressing in and obscuring and beckoning him to continue up, up, to the top of the mountain.

Keel took off after the kid like a shot, confident that he could overtake the runaway before he got himself into too much trouble. The mist seemed to thicken so that he couldn't see more than a meter in front of himself, but the armor gave a solid reading: Garret was just ahead, slowing as he reached the summit. As Keel ran, he could hear that echoing, far-off quality of human voices speaking through the expanses of time and possibility. Only this time it wasn't words, but a high-pitched shriek that would have been bloodcurdling were it not for the distinctive moan of deep agony that thickly tinged the cry.

That terrible wail was followed by another shout—this one from Garret. It was a cry of alarm, of distress and horror. Keel was upon the code slicer an instant later; he found him slumped on his hands, head down. With his blaster drawn, Keel looked at the plateau they'd reached and saw at once the reason for Garret's outburst... and the broken state he had collapsed into.

The smuggler gently patted the kid's narrow shoulders. "'S'all right, kid."

On the great field of delicate, silk-like grass there looked to be the aftermath of some great battle in the days of long ago, before blasters and explosions. A contest of swords and spears. Spread out before them were the dead of that army, most of them bristling with the shaft of the spear that killed them still protruding from their bodies.

All of them were Prisma.

"Don't let..." Garret tried to say, on the verge of sobbing but keeping his resolve. "Don't let... Miss Leenah come... come close. Don't let her see it, Captain Keel."

But before Keel could turn around and take action on the code slicer's sound advice, the Endurian arrived at the summit. She had jogged up after Keel along with the others and was now frozen in horror at the carnage laid out before her. It took her another instant to recognize *who* all the dead were. And when she did, she fell onto her knees and had her cry of sorrow—the piercing, soul-haunting shriek of a woman losing a child—cut off as what little remained in her stomach came back up.

"Hey, it's not her," Keel said, hoping at once the words were true and that they would be a comfort. He squatted down and rubbed her back, his weapon still ready as he surveyed the battlefield. As horrific as the scene was, Ravi had explained enough of how this infernal world worked for people with Prisma's... abilities.

Leenah rubbed her mouth with the back of her arm and nodded her head, accepting Keel's words. "How could her own mother do this to her?"

Ravi had uncharacteristically stepped away from this scene of emotional need; usually he was often the first to offer compassion. But he heard Leenah's question and answered it. "This is the way some would train their champions. I am happy to exclude myself from such company and it is not how I would have trained Prisma had things... gone differently. Had *she* been different and her heart not so fixed on vengeance. What you see here is Urmo's way." His fingertips gently caressed the butt of one of the spears that had run Prisma through and fastened her to the ground. "It would seem her mother emulated this training. She prepared Prisma for an altercation with Urmo himself... in preparation for a more difficult battle still."

The Ancient One looked down in shame.

The expression wasn't lost on Keel. But first things first. He shook his head and placed his hands on his hips. "So she fought this... Urmo, and he killed her. All these times."

Ravi looked up and pushed the sorrow away from his face. "Every time, it would seem, save the last. A final encounter that existed in this realm and the unseen together. I... sensed Urmo's passing. And when Prisma came to me with her mother afterward, I saw the proof that she had been the one to slay him."

Leenah was recovering her strength and was back on her feet, as was Garret. She couldn't stand to look at the carnage in the field, but mentally had accepted that despite all she saw before her, Prisma was alive. The more she thought of that, the less it surprised her. The girl was a fighter, a survivor. Only Keel himself seemed to have a stronger drive to keep living, one that, more and more, he'd expanded to include those around him. The man she'd first met would never have risked his own neck for Garret or Prisma or anyone else. And now here he was running headlong into the unknown for them. For all of them. She loved him for that.

Makaffie looked around with the dispassionate curiosity of an archeologist visiting a dig site. "So, have you found what you needed to in this unsorted mess, Ravi? Because if not, I do believe I see something of interest by that fire."

He pointed to a stone ring in the distance, hemmed in by stone benches. A small flame burned inside its confines. The ruined body of KRS-88 lay just beyond.

19

"He's in terrible shape." That was Garret's professional assessment of KRS-88, though the rest could see as much with their own eyes. The bot was battered and smashed as though it had been sent into the crushing depths of a gravity well.

"Can you fix him?" Keel asked. "He might have a record of exactly what happened here."

Garret shook his head slowly, which was not the expression the others expected. "I could make him *look* brand-new. Better, even. That's not the problem. The kind of catastrophic damage he's taken is so much worse than when the Cybar shot him to pieces. There might not be a Crash left inside all this armor."

Leenah put her hand on the code slicer's shoulder. "If anyone can do it, Garret, it's you."

The encouragement seemed to strengthen Garret's resolve. "I... I think it might not be so bad. Anyway, yeah. I'll try."

"It's gonna take one hell of an effort to drag him back down to the river," Keel said. Left unspoken were his doubts about whether KRS-88 could be repaired at all. Bots weren't invincible. Leenah was right, though: if there was anyone who could do it, it was the kid.

"We'll figure something out," Garret said, seemingly more and more ready for the challenge. "And then I'll figure out a way to get him back up and running again. Even if I have to start with an old, *old* backup, there may be a way to patch things together with the subspark…" He trailed off, suddenly aware that he was headed into a highly theoretical and genuinely frowned-upon theory of bot functionality. "I'll figure out a way. That's the thing about a bot: when they die, you always get a chance to bring them back." He got a faraway and watery look in his eyes. "Always a chance…"

Keel could sense long-buried pain behind those words, but now was not the time to draw it out.

"You will not need to transport him from this place," Ravi said. He had remained apart from the rest of the group, studying the surrounding area while they focused on the bot. He'd examined the fire, counted the stones, and paid especially close attention to the stone benches set up before the firepit. It all looked pretty mundane to Keel—excluding the slain instances of Prisma and the single ruined instance of Crash. Yet Ravi had lost interest in the former and had never had any interest at all in the latter.

"When the time comes for us to depart," the Ancient continued, "I will take Crash with us from this very place. Leaving a place is rarely difficult; I would have come to this exact spot directly had I known it was where Prisma's training took place. Regardless, now I know. Our purpose here is nearly finished."

Ravi circled the firepit and dragged his fingers across the smooth stone of the benches. "There is more to be seen in this place than the bloody training of our friend Prisma. Things that I must now attempt to draw out of the planet and into plain sight. Captain Keel, be alert for any dangers that may present themselves. I will not be able to act so quickly as the last time."

Keel had kept his blaster drawn the entire time, but now he drew his hand cannon as well.

Ravi nodded in approval and then closed his eyes, setting his face down as his arms went out to his sides. Gradually, and to the great relief of the *Six*'s crew, the battlefield was relieved of its dead as all the instances of the slain Prisma were sent back into the folds of existence.

But other scenes now began to take the place of Prisma's great and bloody trials, adding their context to the history of this terrible spot. Some that Ravi brought forth were banished just as quickly, as if he calculated their relevancy and found them wanting. These were often training, of the same sort that it seemed Prisma had undergone, though the faces of the men and women were unknown to those now watching. The creature Urmo was also seen regularly, pointed out by Ravi in all the separate forms he took. "Urmo would adapt his appearance and behavior according to the expectations of those he trained," he explained. But whatever mysteries the apparition of Urmo spoke to these men and women remained just that: a mystery.

And then Prisma returned, standing alive and before her mother as blaster bolts streamed near her. KRS-88 was unleashing its lethal arsenal at Reina, managing to wound her but unable to destroy her before the bot itself was destroyed.

"Oh... *wow,*" Garret mumbled to himself. This explained how Crash had become so damaged. The code slicer wondered what had triggered the war bot to take such a seemingly inexplicable action.

But Leenah's eyes were fixed on Reina. She searched for some clue or indication that she was in some way *deserving* of having Prisma as a daughter. Yet all that was on the woman's face was a snarl of hatred. Still, maybe it wasn't fair to blame her for that, seeing as Reina at that moment was fighting for her life against the war bot.

The encounter between bot and master was replaced by another conflict, a frightening flash as Urmo viciously lunged at Prisma using the same feathered spear they'd seen her myriad corpses gored by. But that battle, too, held little interest for Ravi. Even if it might have been of interest to Prisma's friends.

That moment faded and was replaced by yet another vision from the deep continuum that Umnor drew from. Urmo was there once more, but now he sat alone on a bench. He leaned against his spear and stared at the fire with dark, soulful eyes.

Ravi lowered his arms and opened his eyes. "This..."

A phantasm of Reina stepped onto the planet, replaying this moment in her past. She walked silently into the midst of the training grounds and then stopped to stand before Urmo. The little creature took no notice of her but continued to stare at the flames, which were reflected brightly in his glossy eyes.

Reina waited a moment and said, "I have come to share a word with you, Ancient One."

Urmo flitted his eyes contemptuously at the woman and grunted dismissively.

But Reina was not to be denied. "Is that any way to treat one such as myself?" She sat down on the opposite bench.

Urmo glowered at the woman. Clearly he did not wish for her presence, let alone for her to seat herself so near him.

"One such as yourself?" the little thing hissed, the very words an indictment. "And what is that, dabbler? You sail through the Quantum Palace inside a great ship not of your own making... but making plans, yes. Sowing seeds and setting stages. Seeking time. Time you seek. One such as yourself, dwelling on the surface of my people's ways. And because of this... you pretend to know the depth of such an ocean. You know nothing of the Crux."

Reina smiled gently. "Is that what you decided to call it this time, Ancient One? What your next champion needed to hear it named? I always wondered at that. Your appearance now is... interesting. Was that for your champion, too? Before he came to you, I knew him. Did you know that? Casper Sulla."

"Goth Sullus," came the hiss through Urmo's sharp little teeth.

"Of course. *Your* champions are always made into something new. I wonder if it would be the same with your turbaned counterpart... were he to ever stop searching."

Keel looked to Ravi, who only nodded in confirmation that the living memories were indeed speaking of him. Surely, thought Keel, *surely* this wasn't what Ravi actually looked like. It was almost... comical. And yet there was a sinister undertone about him, too. A thing of nightmares should all the things ever go all the wrong ways.

"And do you think," Reina began delicately, "that Goth Sullus will achieve your purposes as champion?"

Urmo snarled. "He will stop the Dark Ones and their coming Consumption. He will rule the galaxy."

"Rule the galaxy?" Reina raised an eyebrow. "That does not sound like the man I used to know."

"He does not know it himself yet." Urmo smiled, a vicious grin. "But it... is... there. Inside. Lurking. Such things are malleable and can be shaped into powerful weapons."

Reina arose and took a step away from the benches, and then stopped as though she thought better of it. She sat down again next to Urmo, and though he rattled his spear, he did not otherwise seek to prevent her from doing so.

When she spoke, it was in an almost seductive whisper. "He will fail. Just as *all* your champions have failed. You know the measure of a man. The best among them will grow corrupt, and in so becoming, they will destroy themselves. Ask me why I have not."

Urmo hissed again. "The whore of a Savage, whose time in the galaxy is no more than that of a still-suckling brat, would venture to tell me anything?"

Reina straightened and pulled back. But she maintained her regal air, unfazed by the verbal abuse. "Such insults are beneath those with confidence. I can only understand them coming from you, Ancient One, as an admission of fact. Goth Sullus will not succeed. The great power you've placed in his hands will consume, twist, and destroy him and his aims. As it has for all men. As it ever only can be."

Urmo didn't argue the point, which felt like an admission to Reina... and to those standing watch over these events that once took place.

Reina quickly moved off her bench and knelt before Urmo, suddenly petitioning him as if he were a king. "Consider this, Ancient One. There is one who has already mastered that which you revealed to Goth Sullus—just as

I have—but like me, he has done so in his own time and in his own way. He stands ready to stop the Dark Ones. Alone if he must, for his purpose is to rule the galaxy. The most high must be in the highest position."

Urmo snarled, but Reina seemed to have his interest. "You humans," he said. "Double-minded. Contradictory. Goth Sullus will be corrupted, but not... oh no... not *this* one."

The little creature let out a mocking laugh that sounded too large for its diminutive frame.

"He is no man," Reina persisted. "He is the Golden King. The Uplifted who rules all the Pantheon and abides in the Quantum Palace. He is humanity's master... and its future."

Urmo removed his hand from his spear and stroked the fur of his neck. "Strange that such a being exists. Would I not call such to be my champion?"

"The Golden King does not come when bidden." Reina sounded defensive now, her words hotter than they had been. "He comes only of his own accord. He has come here now... and it is to *your* great honor that he has deigned to do so."

A man, tall and great, with glowing golden skin, stepped toward the meeting. But to call him a man was only to draw a comparison. He was something more... a super man. A physical embodiment of what perfected man *could* look like. He stood next to Reina, who bowed reverently and then moved behind the Golden King. And though she was a tall woman, she seemed slight in the king's presence. And Urmo... he seemed almost miniature.

The Golden King swept aside a great black cloak with a gilded hem, revealing his fantastic, powered battle armor, a deep bronze that made his golden face shine all the more brightly. But the armor only lent added weight to an already imposing figure: naturally broad shoulders that appeared mountainous; a core that was like a tree, straight and tall; arms and legs that were bristling with latent power. This was a man who could rip the galaxy in half with his bare hands.

The crew of the *Indelible VI* watched with interest, watched in awe. Except for Makaffie, whose slight frame made him look sickly and inferior just by standing so near to the great, golden king.

"Not him," Makaffie muttered. "We... we killed him."

20

"What are you talking about, Makaffie?" Keel spoke quickly, trying to coax some information from the verbose and enigmatic soldier before the conversation between Urmo and the Golden King began. The powerful newcomer to the fire's glow seemed to be waiting for Urmo to speak first. He loomed over the little creature, but not with menace. More like... expectation. As though he anticipated some reaction that the fuzzy creature leaning on his spear had no interest in providing. Urmo stifled a yawn as he stared down at the massive boots that completed the king's impressive armor.

"He's a Savage. It was after New Vega." Makaffie let the words come tumbling out, forgoing his usual habit of letting each word come at its own pace. Like Keel, the man seemed to sense that the pregnant pause in the scene unfolding before them would soon end. "Just before we woke you up the first time to activate Kill Team Ice. That mission was your first since nearly buying the whole colony back on NV. See, the Savages—"

Makaffie had already silenced himself just as Ravi said, "Later."

There was a shifting in position by the Golden King. A moment later, he spoke.

"I do not come offering gifts or praise, Ancient One." The Savage king's voice was both powerful and beautiful. "Apart from the benefits my plans and purposes will provide to you... if you serve me as the rest of the galaxy soon will. But know this: whether you bend your knee or not, it is my destiny to check the Dark Ones and bring an end to their devastation. Even before it can truly begin."

An amused, almost crazed laugh erupted from Urmo, drawing a look of hatred from the king.

Urmo stopped almost as abruptly as he had begun. "The combined might of the Ancients was judged to be inferior to what comes. So much so that my people abandoned what they had built—"

The Golden King waved his hand dismissively. "Don't ask me to mourn a few primitive temples abandoned to cowardice."

Urmo ignored the disdain. "Coward, am I? And Ravi?" He laughed at the thought. "Many things. Not cowards. Ravi stood with a small planet's worth of men. Warriors. Champions, though frail. *His* sort of champion. Heh. But men capable of killing body and soul. Of cutting through this material world and into the Quantum. They stood against an insignificant band of the Dark Ones. Mere skirmishers broken off from the great and coming Consumption. You will still find their bones on that world. Ravi... nearly died for his choice in champions."

The mention of that world full of bones that lay parched on the final battlefield made Keel look at Ravi in surprise. Had he not found Ravi, that "program," on exactly such a planet? He added the question to the list of those needing discussion at some other time, though that list was growing long indeed.

"Do not speak of these things as if I were ignorant," warned the Savage king. "I have been to that world and learned its secrets. In your pride, you forget to say—perhaps do not wish to admit—that your counterpart and his 'frail' champions stopped that bloody and wild vanguard. How many of your champions went out to do the same and never came back?"

A look of wounded hate transformed Urmo's face. His sharp little teeth shone in the firelight and he tightened his grip on his spear. Those watching at a safe distance might have found the small creature almost comical, but the crew of the *Indelible VI*, though watching from across the long span of time, could sense the danger in that moment.

Reina put her hand on the back of the Golden King, afraid of what might happen next.

Seeing this, Urmo relaxed and let loose his cruel laugh once again. This great warrior king before him was not so great that his *queen* didn't fear his demise at Urmo's hands.

The Savage king turned and glowered at Reina, who quickly pulled her hand back from the folds of his mantle. He struck her with the back of his hand and she fell to her knees, bleeding from the mouth.

The king's rage turned at once on Urmo, restrained as it was to mere words. "I have a power that *far* exceeds yours! One that dwarfs even Ravi's." He snarled, and the beautiful golden face grew terrible to behold. "He is your superior in every way. Deny that truth to me if you dare. Do it."

The Golden King paused for the briefest of moments to give Urmo that chance, but the meager opportunity was only there for show; the king was clearly more interested in continuing his rant than he was in hearing any reply the little thing before him might give. "You sit here on this primitive world day after day sending victim after victim to their death in pursuit of a hopeless task. But *I* have grown great with knowledge. My understanding of all things has been made complete. From the moment I discovered the Quantum at a research station numbered eighty-eight, comprehension followed. What terrified your ancient brethren—a race worthless to the galaxy—I stand in defiance of. Even now, a race born of the Quantum, calling itself the Cybar, is in communication with the Dark Ones. The two groups seek a way to join together, now, as one, and forge a path into our galaxy that will not defy your covenants and safeguards. Fool."

Urmo shifted at hearing this, as if he was unaware.

"My servants, in monitoring and using this species, have discovered that in them is a way to thwart the Consumption that they seek to bring about. It is *not* inevitable, as you suppose. The Dark Ones can be imprisoned. Trapped. Forever. Under my rule."

Urmo stood and looked up at the great king, taking in the living testament to what man could become if only he shed himself and his humanity. A certain respect that had been lacking was now in the Ancient's voice when the little creature said, "Go and do it, then."

This address seemed to soothe the Savage king. His voice grew less hot and more measured. He shook his head and for the first time addressed Urmo as a creature bordering on an equal. "Urged by my sons, I once moved... prematurely. These sons, my generals, brought about a failure at the hands of the Legion that undid... everything. And all because of another failure by the one who birthed them."

He scowled at Reina, whose head was lowered and shrouded by her hair. She might not have seen the rebuke, but she could surely feel it in his words. She had recovered from the blow well enough to sit pliantly on her knees, hands clasped in her lap, lower lip fat and bruised, her brilliant white gown marred with her own blood.

"You know how much time must pass before the Dark Ones may enter this galaxy by the means of the covenant," the Savage king continued. "Much can happen in such a span. For much has happened since I left the Quantum Palace. Intrigues mount. Maestro serves me well, but serves himself first. And my queen, in seeking through her scheming to make permanent my power, instead brought about the greatest hindrance to my rule... one whom you have now trained to possess an even greater power than what was bestowed under her watch."

Urmo grunted. "Goth Sullus, my champion, would destroy you. Yes."

The snarling curl of the Golden King's lip showed what he thought of the Ancient's assessment, but he held his temper in check. Clearly, he needed something more than banter from Urmo. "And does Goth Sullus know... that I live?"

Urmo looked away. "No. He did not come to me seeking your end. He did not come to me thinking of you at all. Only the restoration of his Republic, the love of which I could not drive away. He came to stand against the Dark Wanderer and his Dark Ones. To prevent the Consumption. But first, he must unite the galaxy. A task he now knows can be done only through power. A power he now possesses. He is not afraid to use it."

It was at this point that the Savage king pressed his claims and made clear his purpose for being on Umnor.

"He will fail. Surely you know that by now. They will all fail. Men. But *I* will enslave the Dark Ones. Only I will not wait. I will not let entropy and intrigue unravel the plans I have put in place since withdrawing my presence from this galaxy. You will serve me. You will seek out the Dark Wanderer and slay him. Break the covenant. Let them come. And watch as I stop them before they have hardly set foot in our galaxy."

Whatever begrudging respect Urmo had shown for the Golden King before, it faded as his low chuckle grew into a thick, mocking laughter. "Men will fail, this one says. But no man can possess such great evil and not find himself possessed. You cannot enslave the Dark Ones. And you cannot destroy them. *You* are man. A man beset by self-deceit."

"I tell you, Ancient One, I am no *man!*" snapped the Savage king. The very word seemed to disgust him. "Men are Animals. I exist as the pinnacle of being. I live in a perfected state."

Urmo spoke from behind his arrow-tip teeth. "You are an old man whose great riches came at the expense of his fellows. A man whose fortune bred dreams of greatness beyond his nature and means. You Savages tell yourself you have evolved into something more than the dust you were born from. Does the truth change? You work tirelessly to scrub the galaxy of truth and surround yourself with lies of your own greatness. But... Golden King, the truth remains. Shall I speak it to you? Shall I speak of your Earthbound dreams of perfection among the stars?"

At the mention of Earth, the Savage king's knees nearly buckled. He steadied himself in an instant, standing proud and tall.

Urmo laughed maniacally and would not stop.

The Golden King whirled around and left, his cape billowing in his wake. "Come," he ordered Reina.

She arose but did not follow at once. Instead she scowled and addressed Urmo bitterly. "What my lord has spoken, he will do. And *you*. For your insolence, you will not live to see the day of the Dark One's defeat. I will come again, Ancient One. As a bringer of your death. Mark the words!"

Urmo went on laughing throughout her vitriolic oath and continued to laugh as they traveled out of the fire's light. Only then did he call out after them, "Run! Run from the truth, O great king!"

Laughter.

"Find your Earth!"

More laughter. The little creature was working himself into a mad, fevered raving.

"Surely your mastery of the Crux will reveal it at last. You *plan*!" The laughter was nothing short of insane now. "But you have no plan. You have spent so much time searching to destroy the last traces of truth only to find you could not destroy those who might discover it."

Urmo cackled all the louder at the retreating king.

"Perhaps another invasion of New Vega will reveal it? Run and find the truth which cripples you, O powerful king! Until you do, live in fear that someone will gaze upon the perfect face of the perfect being and speak the name *Thomas Roman*."

Urmo faded then, together with the fire, and this event, recalled from the Quantum by Ravi, came to an end.

The crew of the *Indelible VI* looked at Ravi, puzzled. But the Ancient continued its business, first peering across the mists of the place and then moving to KRS-88 as though he were ready to transport the bot. Kneeling by the war machine's side, he looked up to address Makaffie.

"You fought this Savage once?"

"Not exactly… more like we fought his armies. They were a different sort of Savage. We figured them unrelated to the Savage marines we checked at New Vega. It was a six-world campaign that started on Enduran." Makaffie looked to Leenah. "Yes, your Enduran."

She shook her head. "But that was at the very beginning of the Savage Wars. I've been to the planetary museum on Prydal. The Savages who invaded our world looked nothing like him."

Makaffie nodded agreeably. "Only the elites did. There were hardly any of them. Mostly we fought what we called zombies and grunts. And those were different on every world. But the elites were always the same. They were the generals and commanders. One of them was as good as a hundred leejes, it felt like. That's what really got the ball rolling on Kill Team Ice."

"So where does Golden Boy come into it then?" Keel asked.

"You could tell me better than I could tell you," Makaffie said. "I got put on ice midway through the campaign on an op that went the wrong way. You were there for it."

Ravi gave a fractional nod. "And of course, you do not remember."

"Not a thing," Keel confirmed. "Sorry, pal."

"Well, intel showed this guy's picture as the, well, he called himself an emperor. The head of this Savage tribe was sending a single hulk with a single general and a whole lot of armies to take worlds. They were grabbin' the people, but not like on New Vega. Not for… calories. More like because of their genetic makeup. They had labs big on that stuff. Point is, we thought we took this guy out on his hulk. And then that was it, and the next time they activated us, the war had changed again."

Garret was rubbing his head, deep in thought. "They mentioned Earth. And Nilo..." The code slicer let that thought drift for a moment before asking, "Who is Thomas Roman?"

Ravi shook his head. "I do not know. I can calculate many conclusions, but not with any certainty. Perhaps I should reiterate by plainly stating that I do not know everything. But I am an exceptional guesser."

"Do you know where we can find Prisma?" Leenah asked.

Ravi let out a long sigh. "She left here with her mother to find me. And now I know why. Reina was baiting me into doing something I should not have done. In a moment without thought, with a creature known as the Dark Wanderer on the verge of destroying the girl, I acted—and slew the beast."

Keel gave a half frown. "That's what they were trying to get Urmo to do, wasn't it?"

"Yes. In my haste to protect that poor girl, I fear I have doomed us all by bringing about the early arrival of the Dark Ones and their Consumption."

The group fell silent. Leenah stepped forward and placed a hand on Ravi's forearm.

"Thank you. For saving her. Thank you."

Ravi's eyes welled up. The very human emotion didn't seem out of place, even if the crew of the *Six* all knew that Ravi was not human... or even a holo-projected AI meant to appear the same. One of the Ancients had traveled beside them the entire time... and felt like one of them.

"You would not thank me if you saw what I unleashed to save a single life."

"Hey, the Roman guy said he could capture them," said Garret. "So maybe he did, Mr. Ravi."

Ravi nodded. "With this information, I now comprehend many events that occurred prior to my return. The math completes itself. What remains to be seen is what will become of it all."

"Never trust a Savage," Makaffie said. "General used to always say that."

"A generally wise course of action," Ravi agreed. "Let us return to the *Indelible VI* or whatever Captain Keel is calling it now. *Probable Horseshoe* or some such nonsense. From there, I believe we will be able to determine what fate lies in store for all of us."

Keel rolled his shoulders. "Well, the galaxy *was* getting a little boring, I suppose."

21

Light Assault Carrier *Battle Phoenix*

"Yes, but I don't understand what benefits there are to be gained in expending so much processing power in thinking of ways to terminate the population of an entire planet. How do you justify it beyond personal preference, which a bot is expected to prioritize as of the lowest importance?"

Protocol and admin bot G232 had been tending to the full restoration of his new master's personal assault carrier, a ship that had belonged to his old master, Tyrus Rechs. That it was unusual for either man to own a warship usually reserved for galactic or planetary governments never occurred to the bot. What *had* engaged his thought processors was the ongoing debate with the insufferable Nubarian gunnery bot. A bot that, by some strange, cruel, and decidedly unjust twist of fate, he had paired with. A bot that would now stolidly answer only to the ridiculous moniker of *Death, Destroyer of Worlds*.

The little cylindrical bot rocked on its motion ball and spat out a profane assessment of G232's intelligence as well as its lack of masculinity. Death didn't like the protocol bot's continued refusal to accept its "hobbies," which in this instance included planetary genocide.

"My masculinity is a variable setting which can be adjusted at my master's will," G232 prattled on. "I can be quite brutish should Master Keel desire it. Certainly capable enough of roughing you up, you spineless little cautionary tale."

Death, Destroyer of Worlds, burst out in an unrestrained torrent of digital laughter.

"And besides," G232 continued, pretending not to notice the jeers. "We've been at this discussion long enough that I won't fall for those distractions any longer. We both know you've only deflected my statement with derision and hostility rather than engaging with it. If there is a reason to spend as much processing power on mayhem, destruction, and death as you do—using your processing outputs to determine the best way to annihilate a planet's populace rather than doing something useful like improving weapon systems functionality by even a hundredth of a percent—then say so. I suspect you can't, and further, that you lack the courage to admit you are wrong. Perhaps such an admission is too masculine for *you*."

The little bot's laughter changed to chirps of anger, though it was easy enough to evoke such an emotion from Death. The gunnery bot pointed out for the record that it had on multiple occasions improved weapon systems, recharge, and other assault packages by as much as a full *tenth* of a percent, thank you very much. And, in case G232 was wondering, the act of determining how a populous planet—say, Utopion—could be destroyed by trigger-nuke versus planetary bombardment by a variable fleet of destroyers was not mutually exclusive with simultaneously running ship-related calcs to improve weapons systems. Death could multitask, and had done so admirably.

"I concede the point about the two processes not being mutually exclusive," G232 said, checking the *Battle*

Phoenix's docking bay control panel readouts quickly and then fixing his attention on his counterpart. "I myself have balanced a number of personal interests and protocol features while still achieving a net positive for the master. But that's only because in both instances, they are of *benefit* to the master. Why, in fact, just the other day while recharging, I considered the placement of the carrier's pantry in relation to its formal dining hall. The two are located in close proximity, a wise design choice except for the fact that Master Keel has shown a preference to forgoing the use of the formal hall in favor of the docking bay, as you'll recall from our last gala."

Death annoyedly pointed out that it was a mission brief, not a "gala."

G232 pretended not to notice the distinction. "In which case the location makes no sense at all," he prattled on merrily. "Therefore, I put together—"

Death blew a digital raspberry and informed G232 that he had succeeded in turning himself into the most bored thing in all the galaxy.

The protocol bot straightened and, with wounded pride, said, "Have it your way then. I won't make any further mention of it. But you'll regret it, because now I won't say another word on the issue until you've answered my initial question. You can deny it all you want, but we both know that an unanswered challenge is tantamount to an admission of defeat. Especially when you were the one who introduced the subject!"

Death gave a derisive whistle, hoping that would draw G232 back into the argument. But the protocol and admin bot ignored it, focused only on tapping the tactile screens of the docking bay control panel as he verified and re-verified that the *Battle Phoenix* was once again in working order.

They'd done a splendid job together, even getting the factory AI to help where possible. Although the hull *would* eventually have to be overhauled where blaster bolts had punched through, if it were to achieve optimal operation status.

The little gunnery bot rolled back and forth behind G232 for some time, trying to think of a way to answer the question. The truth was, it agreed with the mincing protocol bot's assessment: if it couldn't answer that question, the entire hierarchy of its logic would fail, and it would be forced to reconsider its activities. And Death did not want to reconsider its activities. It *really liked* thinking about entire populaces burning to death in a nuclear firestorm as their pathetic atmospheres ignited.

Finally, its processors grabbed hold of an explanation which it proudly and succinctly stated for the record.

"Do you honestly expect me to believe that *our* master may require us to oversee the extermination of an entire planet's population?"

Death, Destroyer of Worlds, stopped its triumphant victory circles as if caught off-guard by this unseen hole in its logic. Its premise depended entirely on its master potentially *needing* a plan to kill off an entire planet. The bot quickly found a way out of the conundrum by telling G232 that Old Boss, Tyrus Rechs, might have needed it.

Now it was G232's turn to pause. "Well... I *suppose* that much could be true. But Tyrus Rechs is no longer our master. A useful bot focuses on what its *current* master wants, not what an old master theoretically might have desired. Otherwise I'd spend my time analyzing the best corners to hustle H8. Oh, those days were terrible!"

The Nubarian gunnery bot wasn't willing to give up so easily. It suggested that New Boss might have similar need for a genocide, and could prove it. After all, hadn't a philosopher once said that to kill a single man was to kill an entire world, since the sum of all knowledge of the world itself can only be contained in the thoughts and experiences of a single mind? And so in destroying one mind, one also destroys that world... that galaxy... that un - verse! *And* since it was indisputable that New Boss had killed a man, and therefore a world—which was great— what was to stop him from doing it again? And why not do so more *literally* the next time?

G232's visual receptors glowed as he fixated on the gunnery bot. Attempting to understand that little psycho- path never ended well, and yet he now found himself do- ing just that. What Death was saying was crazy, but it also made a kind of sense... if one took a certain point of view. "Fine. Go on with your psychotic little calculations. But don't expect me to use my own processing power to help. I have more important matters. Like the location of the pantry. Stop laughing, you carbon-crusted little glitch."

A proximity alarm drew both bots' attention to the docking controls, and G232 threw his arms up in ex- citement. "Ah! Master Keel has returned! You'll soon see how much more he values my work on the location of the pantry."

Death sarcastically stated that it had a pretty good idea what New Boss would think about that, but it was G232's funeral.

Not long afterward, the *Indelible VI* floated through the docking bay shield and settled down into the bay. G232 stood at the controls and rocked from one foot to the oth- er in anticipation of being reunited with his master. Had the protocol bot not been spending so much time parsing over the various needs and ideas he had for the master, he might have found it odd how slowly the ship entered the bay, rotated on its repulsors, and settled down with painstakingly slow precision.

Captain Keel tended to tear into a docking bay as though he were being chased by an entire wing of Black Fleet tri-fighters. He gave little regard for his landing skids or the deck, preferring to set down hard and fast. He'd paid good credits for landing struts that could absorb the weight of a Repub corvette riding on his freighter's shoulders, so why not use them? It wasn't like *he* was going to feel any bumps inside. Why waste time setting down as though landing on top of Kimbrin Sprigg eggs?

But when all the gases vented from the ship and it powered down and then thirty standard minutes passed without the lowering of a ramp, G232 began to grow suspicious.

Death, meanwhile, had been repeatedly declaring, "They're dead," almost since the moment the *Indelible VI* landed. At last the bot prompted G232 to perform a bio-sweep—which showed no life-forms on board.

"These sensors are probably just being jammed," G232 reasoned. "Master's ship is quite sophisticated and secretive. Much more so than any of the *Obsidian Crow*s."

The littler gunnery bot dismissively told his counterpart that that was not how jamming worked, and resumed its dread prophecy that they were all dead. If G232 didn't know better, he'd have thought the sadistic little gunnery bot was actually... sad about it.

Of course, it *was* always somewhat sad when you lost a master. Most of the time. That was the surest subspark reaction. Sadness. Out of nowhere because another life had ended while you lived on and had to face the unknown future. But Captain Keel hadn't been their master for very long. Not long at all, really. Yet... he *had* allowed G232 to throw a successful gala in the docking bay with decorated soldiers, intergalactic billionaires, and other important and diverse species. A successful and magnificent gala. The protocol bot realized that he too was sad over the prospect of the master's death. And with each passing picosecond, he began to accept Death's prophecy with decidedly grim logic.

"Oh dear," the bot said, and then moved around the control station to approach the *Six*. He knocked on the raised ramp, sending a tinny, metal echo around the quiet hum of the docking bay. Though his auditory sensors were not as sophisticated as a war bot or observation bot's, G232 should have been able to detect the sound of motion from inside. He did not.

He looked over at Death, Destroyer of Worlds, and shook his head sorrowfully. This was a very bad sign.

Death, knowing that Garret had linked many of the *Battle Phoenix* systems up to New Boss's existing network, plugged himself into the docking control console and sent a basic system request to drop the *Indelible VI*'s ramp. If the ship saw the *Phoenix* as a safe locale, it might work. If its security systems required a manual override from within... it wouldn't. The little bot figured the odds of either happening as fifty-fifty. Mostly because it didn't care to spend any more time refining those odds, preferring instead to think of what it would look like if the *Indelible VI*'s hidden auto-turrets were to drop down and open fire on a group of red Sectoids. How long could those armored carapaces endure such an onslaught?

The ramp hissed and lowered, forcing G232 to cry out in alarm and scamper out of its way to avoid being crushed.

"What did you do?" the protocol bot said as Death rolled out from behind the control station and moved toward the ship. "I could have been... compacted!"

Death ignored the incessant whining and rolled right up the *Six*'s ramp.

That put an end to G232's current concern by introducing another. The admin bot cupped his hands over its external audio transmitter and called after the gunnery bot, "Not so hasty!"

G232 reluctantly scurried up the ramp behind Death, Destroyer of Worlds. "Slow down! Whatever killed and dismembered the humans might not make a distinction for bots!"

Those words only encouraged the gunnery bot. Death welcomed such a challenge if it were to be found. It could think of no higher honor than to avenge its master's death. Many of its favorite holofilms, especially the ones that featured martial arts and hand-to-hand combat instead of the usual blaster fights, revolved around just that sort of thing. The promising young student deprived of the wisdom of his master whose untimely murder robbed the student of the opportunity to learn the most secret and powerful ways of the fist. To lose a master who was like a father to him... Death could relate to that.

Well, not exactly *relate* to it. Keel wasn't anything like a father. And anyway, Death considered itself a spontaneous creation from the subspark without maker or factory, the fathers and mothers of the bot world. But the little bot *could* relate to a duty-bound sense that required it avenge New Boss's death.

Close enough.

As the bot rolled through each new section of the ship, its impending sense that it would find the dead bodies of Keel, his pink-skinned mating partner, Garret the wise, and the two soldiers with their admirable armor... dwindled. Which wasn't to say that Death was *disappointed* to not find their stone-cold corpses... but it had grown fond of a future spent seeking vengeance.

Also missing was the wobanki, Skrizz. Death greatly admired that species for its ability to rip the life out of a biologic using only teeth and claws. It had run a rather graphic simulation to determine the likelihood that the wobanki was the bloody killer of the crew and had hidden in the smuggler's hold to avoid the bio-sensors upon landing in the carrier's bay. The little bot stopped short and spun its head around, sure that the killer would spring for it next.

But seeing that nothing was out of place, it gave a garbled whistle and moved on.

The ship was thoroughly searched. G232 grew bolder the longer they stayed inside without incident. There was no blood. There were no bodies. Nor was there any sign of the crew beyond a hastily abandoned medical bay—but there was no blood there, either. At least no uncontained blood splashed all across the walls like Death was looking for. Just a few properly sanitized quick-clotting wipes.

The two bots moved uncertainly off the *Indelible VI* and congressed near the shadow of its ramp.

"I wonder where they are," said G232. "I do hope they're all right."

Death, Destroyer of Worlds, had a stroke of genius. Another glimpse of its destiny. It suggested that the pair take one of the *Obsidian Crow*s—the little bot knew its way around those systems—and mount a rescue mission. The gunnery bot immediately began cataloging armaments, listing for G232 all that would need to be loaded prior to departure, including some of Tyrus Rechs's prototypes. No expense would be spared in the rescue of New Boss.

The admin bot had always been rather fond of lists, so it listened attentively. But when the gunnery bot finished, G232 said, "We don't have even the faintest idea of where they might be. Other than *not here*. Yes, I know it's a start, but it's not a very good one."

Death pondered the issue. A sense of romance and adventure was brewing in the little bot's processors, a destiny that flourished with thunderous fanfare as revelation gripped it. To search the galaxy was a quest worthy of Death's unique skill set. The bot spoke passionately to G232 about their duties to New Boss—and above all their need to avenge him.

They'd already lost one master, Death explained, and yes, that worked out all right because New Boss was good at killing just like Old Boss, but what if the next master to find this ship *wasn't* good at killing? Or... Death quickly calculated an argument with a higher probability of persuading the admin bot... What if the next master *didn't like to entertain?*

This suggestion would have elicited a horrified gasp from the protocol bot had such a thing been within his programming.

Such a new master would surely sell the bots for scrap—or worse, assign them to mundane labor aboard some mining colony transport, cleaning clogged waste lines and being sent out in the coldness of space to repair circuitry that someone was too cheap to fix back at a proper docking bay. And both bots knew that if a bot lost its tether, no rescue pods were ever sent.

So, Death concluded, G232 could do what he wanted, but Death was going to go on like New Boss was still the master... until he was avenged. And then Death would be a free bot.

G232 relented in the face of these dire prophecies. "I suppose... well, I suppose I'd better go along with you. You're likely to be converted into some mineral farmer's heat pump on the first planet we investigate if you try it on our own. But first... first, wouldn't it be prudent for us to finish our primary orders? If we are leaving out of service to the master, we have an obligation to complete our primary objectives and finish getting the *Battle Phoenix* completely online and functional."

Death wasn't thrilled about this delay but could find no loophole in the protocol bot's logic. Without a new master to countermand the order, they needed to finish getting this ship back into full fighting condition. The little bot acquiesced.

"Good," G232 said, feeling for the first time in perhaps forever that the two of them were on the same subroutine. "We should also see about moving that pantry."

PRISMA

22

Prisma stood on the bridge of the great ship of the Golden King. Thousands more had joined her, making clear the purpose of having such a vast bridge, though the small control station remained empty. She stood elevated next to her mother and within a few feet of the king. The girl felt an acute discomfort at having so many eyes staring at her back.

When she reached out with her mind to sense her surroundings, she could detect all the lives around her. But despite the assembled army, the hall was utterly silent. Perhaps this was due to the nature of their power armor, which like the king's was bulky in its exaggeration of the body. This was nothing like Legion armor, meant for speed and combat. This was the armor of a warrior who intended to stand under fire and destroy his opponents before they could destroy him. In any case, when Prisma turned to see the ranks, she saw them standing at perfect attention in masterful rows and columns. Then her mother turned her head back to the front, somewhat more sharply than was needed.

If our lord beckons us to watch, we will. Without distraction.

The words were communicated to Prisma's mind. She quickly glanced at the glowing Golden King and then back out the viewport as instructed. She wasn't sure how she felt about her mother's commitment to this man. The thought of there being anyone besides Prisma and her mother in her family had never occurred to her, not even once, until the moment she first entered the chamber. And now she wondered why that was.

It was clear that her mother *belonged* to this man. No, not a man. Prisma felt a pang of distress, and though she didn't hear her mother's voice, she wondered if Reina was nevertheless the cause of that discomforting feeling.

The Golden King would not abide being called a man. No more than Prisma would allow others to treat her as a dog.

But if he wasn't a man... what was he?

Prisma stared where she was told to stare, watched for the coming of that great and unstoppable army, but her thoughts were on the presence that dominated the room.

A god...

The Golden King saw himself as such, and what could be more offensive to a god than to be likened to a man? And hadn't Reina, Prisma's own mother, treated the Golden King in the same manner? Only addressing him as liege or lord; lowering her face and bowing when speaking or being spoken to.

Prisma found her eyes drifting to take in the back of the Golden King. She was at once fixated by the way the radiant fabric of his cape hung off his powerful, armored shoulders. And though she knew the expectation was to look where the king had instructed to look, she wondered if those behind her were likewise captivated by the king in their midst. She had a feeling that he would prefer it if they were.

She couldn't help but think of how different that was from how her father acted. Kael Maydoon had made a study of being unostentatious. He wanted people to see him as an equal, even when he represented the highest level of Republic government—as was oft the case on those distant worlds they traveled to and stayed on for a time. Prisma would not have made the comparison at all except for the fact that she wasn't sure how else to think of her situation. Her mother was clearly devoted to this new... not man. And the Golden King radiated a sense of ownership when it came to Reina, this beautiful woman.

Not a woman.

The small thought entered Prisma's mind, not in words, but seeming to belong to her mother all the same, correcting Prisma from a place unknown. Reina was no woman. Not in the sense that Prisma thought. And in time... neither would Prisma be. She would shed the trappings of this current state—*impure*—forever.

Hearing herself described this way made Prisma want to shrink and crawl away, to get away from all the eyes that she was now sure were fixed on her, scanda - ized by her impurity as she stood with a god and his bride.

Take heart, Prisma. This time it *was* her mother's voice in her mind, her words clear. *You cannot help what you are, but what you will be shall be powerful enough to stand against the Dark Ones alone and make them suffer for the experience.*

That name—Dark Ones—struck fear in Prisma. It was only a name, and she had sworn not to be afraid ever again... but here on this bridge, in the presence of the Golden King and his army, words became something more. The sense of their meaning, of their being, seemed to drip from the words themselves. To hear "Dark Ones" was to know their insatiable lust for death and destruction.

Reina sensed this fear. She turned to Prisma and bent down slightly, speaking softly. "Are you worried about what will happen next, my daughter?"

Prisma nodded.

"You need not be. Their defeat is sure. The Golden King will stop them, and without the loss of a single warrior."

Prisma resisted the urge to turn around and look at those warriors. The sense of dark, unyielding dread, of a screaming, ravenous horde of reapers thrashing through the stars, unleashed in this world and wanting only its destruction, pressed heavily on her heart. How could anyone—anything—stop this? It was not mere death... it was anti-life.

And remember the great thing you will become. You will be the first of many worthies chosen for such an honor, my daughter. The galaxy will know a peace beyond all imaginable when the Golden King comes to reign.

The words held no comfort for Prisma. She knew they were meant to; they even brought with them a supernatural sense of warmth and safety that drove away the fear of the Dark Ones. Her mother's words invited her to accept all that was said as truth, like she had done so many times since they were first reunited. Yet something felt... wrong.

She quickly hid the thought, so as not to raise a suspicion of...

Of what? She didn't know. She only felt that her mother would be displeased.

"Thank you, Mother," she said softly, and then waited.

Reina seemed satisfied. Which must mean that Prisma had successfully hidden her feelings the same way she'd kept her thoughts about Crash a secret.

Prisma missed her war bot every day. A deep, dull pain—an emptiness. At first, her mother had banished that feeling with kind words and a gentle stroke of her fingers through Prisma's hair. This was always accompanied by a lecture about the need to leave behind such things and to look forward to what was still to come. But Prisma couldn't let go of Crash. She didn't want to. But neither did she wish to disappoint her mother. So she hid those thoughts from her.

KRS-88's betrayal was a mystery to Prisma, and one she felt responsible for. If not the bot's actions, then the result of them. Reina had healed herself almost as soon as the threat was over, but she *had* been hurt. And Crash...

The bot was gone now, but its final words were welded to the girl's mind. Through those words, Prisma was sure she could discover the cipher needed to decode the reason for its betrayal. She had already spent much time in her quarters—awaiting the various summons to the bridge and then dismissals—thinking on the mystery. Perhaps the bot simply went rogue and started killing. She'd seen holofilms and had read books about such things happening. Or maybe someone had altered his programming. Crash had been behaving strangely ever since he came aboard the Savage reclaimer. Had Stranger—Makaffie—done something to him? The little man and his team members had been able to deactivate the war bot from afar. What would stop them from changing his programming, too?

She mulled over scenarios until she felt like she had exhausted every natural explanation—and still she was left unsatisfied, which only drove her all the more doggedly toward the great, lingering question posed by the bot before it... *he*... died.

What had Prisma paid Tyrus Rechs to kill Goth Sullus? The man who'd murdered her father.

But the old bounty hunter had done it for free. She'd tried to pay him credits. He wouldn't take them. What did the bot mean?

Or was that merely one final glitched and fevered utterance from frayed and broken processors, passed through damaged and ruined vocal circuitry. The final words of a bot that had lost what passed for sanity.

Prisma's thoughts came to an abrupt end when the great hall—the bridge—erupted into a magnificent cheer. Not the discordant celebration of a multitude of individuals, the great and growing roar heard in a seamball stadium, but a singular battle cry lustily shouted from every armored warrior serving the Golden King. All of them booming perfectly together: "Rah!"

The girl had been vaguely aware that someone was speaking to the gathered forces. Lost in her thoughts, she couldn't recall a word that was said, only that it was her mother who had spoken them. A golden voice, a fitting herald for the radiant king.

Now there was a dangerous, snapping electricity in the room. All eyes were unquestionably fixed forward, just as the Golden King's were. They watched the great stellar viewports as an unfolding storm approached, black and ominous, sapping the meager light of the stars between it into nothingness. The deck of the ship began to vibrate beneath Prisma's feet.

That great dread and fear returned to chill her heart, now even more powerful than what she'd felt before. She began to perspire, small drops of sweat forming at her hairline. Then... shame for the disdain this reaction would elicit from the Golden King himself... if he even deigned to notice it.

She was so much less than he.

She was unworthy.

The black, unholy storm raged onward, the ship obstinately in its path. Then came a great flash of light that forced Prisma to close her eyes and throw up her hand against the glare. When she reopened her tightly shut lids, the great wave... was gone.

The Golden King allowed the smallest, most imperceptible of smiles to cross his face. He inclined his head to Reina and gave a fractional nod.

Prisma's mother turned to address the gathered warriors. "Victory."

Another unified roar sounded: "Rah!"

The deck beneath Prisma's feet shook once more with a burst of activity. Columns of soldiers exited the bridge with military precision, clearing much of the great hall in moments. Splendid generals, each handsome in armor much like the Golden King's, approached their lord. These seemed somehow less grand than their leader, though almost identical. They were... younger and less... full. Boys and not yet men. Each was as square-jawed and powerful as any legionnaire Prisma had ever seen, but their glow was less than the king's.

Reina pulled Prisma away as the Golden King began to speak softly to these, his generals. Other, stranger beings waited on the eaves. They reminded Prisma of Archimedes, but they were not human in their appearance. Spectral monsters—vampires even.

"There are things to be discussed which you are not yet ready to be a part of," Reina advised. "Your shedding will come soon. You will stand here with us one day, my daughter. Proud and undefiled."

Prisma knew that those words, said at another time or by another being, would have immediately invoked an argument. Yet she did not think of arguing with her mother, or even questioning her.

She was led to her quarters not by her mother, but by one of the ghostly vampires that floated ahead of her. It wore long, black rags that billowed and flowed behind it, blown by some hot wind Prisma did not feel.

This should bother me, Prisma thought. *Why doesn't it?*

What had she paid Tyrus Rechs?

The question prompted her to suddenly venture forth into the mind of the creature before her. It made no effort to resist and was unaware she'd done it. This creature was not human... but it was beneath her power. Something odd and servile.

She followed it, probing its mind, seeking for something... she didn't know what. And when the doors to her quarters slid open and she went inside, she remained in the thing's mind and began to see as it saw. Above all else, it seemed to think of itself in terms of hierarchy. Loyalty. At the top was the Golden King, and then Reina, and then... a ship?

Yes, it was a ship. A home and a prison...

Moirai.

23

Prisma Discovers the Tale of the *Moirai* and Its Golden King

The ship is a ghost ship. A thing of legend fading into the darkness. But its time was never short... the Quantum, beyond the Dead Zone, knows no shortages of time. The ship's story never entered the galactic record. Prisma learns of it through the mind of one who was aboard it. All the horrors and madness of the *Moirai*'s long journey. Living on as a ghost's whisper mumbled in torment.

A grand experiment.

That's what they called it in those last heady days as the world—Earth—came apart at the seams. Food shortages. Global disaster. War.

The Earth was ruined, and the elites were convinced, as someone called Sartre once wrote, that hell was, indeed, other people. Namely the great unwashed. The masses. The takers. The hordes. The common people, as they were referred to in thought and secret memos. Their fellow men and women who never could quite get around to evolving. Like they had.

And Prisma realized that when her mother and the Golden King referred to her as "impure," this was what they meant. Although it was now, in some new sense, divorced from Earth and the start of the *Moirai* and yet believed just as doggedly by those people, the elites, the Brights, born to the lofty heights of industry, media, and government.

Way before the Savage Wars, these impure ones were linked to the elites in a way that grew more and more detestable. It was an unlikely coalition. The elites needed the impure masses' cheap and easy votes. Needed their cheap and easy labor. Their backs. Their sweat.

The elites resented that dependence. Those poor sad people, who led common ordinary lives of desperation, ruined everything. They were stiff-necked and unable to achieve the necessary enlightenment that would usher in a golden age. Worse, in order to maintain their grip on power, the Brights were forced to pander to the impure, to support their basic human rights campaigns, to mouth their salt-of-the-earth platitudes. They were forced to live with them.

Well, not with them. Ideally, and by long and careful design, a Bright would never encounter an actual living Hordesman in anything other than the most purely transactional capacity. But they were forced to live on the same planet. Which was a kind of horror to them, in the end. A horror that could not be borne for one moment longer.

Finally, that would change. It was time to go.

Originally the Rama-class ark ships, designed and built by Krupps-Mitsubishi under a UN grant charter, were financed as survival arks when it looked like World War III was about to break out. These designs were built thanks to the advanced designs of an exceptionally bright name...

...

The name was not known. And yet it felt missing in a way that was something more than a lack of knowledge.

Prisma probed the mind of the creature, which seemed increasingly simple. This point in its collected memory was not missing. Rather it was suppressed and then... torn away.

The name was not known.

The name belonged to the first to leave.

Each ship could carry more than one hundred thousand refugees in the event of a global catastrophe. A slick massive media campaign was spat out across the internet, to which most people were constantly glued when they could get the bandwidth to log on, and the campaign assured those in dense population centers that in the event of a nuclear exchange, there was a plan in place to rescue everyone who could get to the ark ships in low Earth orbit. Which was not an impossible feat given that most airliners were then using scram-jet technology to make the trip from New York to Tokyo in under two hours.

Awaiting the survivors who reached the ships were vast living worlds looking in on themselves. There the survivors would wait out the nuclear holocaust in relative comfort, or so they were assured in hip-hop sound-bite twenty-second display ads on powerful social media sites.

But of course, this was all a big lie.

As almost everything had ever been.

Originally, the plan, organized by the Brights, had been to release a series of plagues that would rid the planet of its "excess population." Crops died and would not grow back.

An accidental lab leak was the cause. And then terrorists. And then...

Departing a burning, ruined, poisoned home world for the promise of something at least forty and perhaps well over a hundred years away on the other side of the interstellar hauls between the habitable systems, the massive ships approached just this side of light speed. Or, that is, they would. Maximum speed took about ten years of constant acceleration. But what did all that matter inside a living, breathing world that was devoted, almost unanimously so, to a worldview that was so wise and prosperous, surely it could never descend into such madness as the world they'd left behind?

In Greek mythology, the Moirai were known also as the Fates. It was they who decided the lengths of lives of both men and gods. It was they who were the final judges, never mind who you thought you were.

The head of the oligarchy of elites who ruled the lighthugger *Moirai* thought of themselves in the same way. So as dozens of ark ships, each with its own core group of elites and special utopian philosophy, climbed away from Earth and into the stellar dark, its leader ruled the *Moirai* with a genial smile and absolute authoritarianism.

Yes, aboard the lighthugger *Moirai* there were all the usual abuses common to the powerful once they've acquired absolute power.

Sex. Drugs. Murder. Humiliation. Insanity.

But that goes hand in hand with being the victor.

The *Moirai* society went from quasi-religious to full-blown cult within twenty years. Factor in the longevity research the elites had been holding back for themselves on Earth, plus the technological revolutions provided by the constant research aboard the paradise-pleasure ship, and the situation was soon ripe for the insanity of self-proclaimed godhood.

Sixty-five years into the flight, the *Moirai* slowed from light speed and hove into orbit around a small star. But the only world there was an almost dead one that promised a harsh existence. So the *Moirai* chose to lurch starward once more, promising the masses a world beyond their fading memories of Earth. Promising what they had no idea how to actually deliver.

What they found instead was the Dark Wanderer.

Here Prisma pulled back in shock and nearly lost contact with the vampire's mind. Her thoughts shifted to the encounter with that creature, the terror she had felt, overmatched and unprepared to face down such horrific, vicious hatred. Had it not been for Ravi...

She stifled the thought. Thoughts of Ravi, above all else, seemed to be forbidden.

She did not want to disappoint her mother.

The *Moirai* had encountered a derelict alien starship, unlike anything known, drifting in the dark wastes between the stars. Later, much later, they would find that it wasn't so much a lost starship as a prison, and its sole prisoner's sentence had been imposed by a civilization far older than any of humanity's outreaching explorers had previously discovered.

The Ancients.

Who the Dark Wanderer really was, they would never know. But they marveled at the wonders he provided them. Portions of the derelict ship were cannibalized and remanufactured to give the *Moirai* faster-than-light travel. Hyperspace engines were constructed along the aft portions of the main cylinder, and the *Moirai* leapt away toward its fate. Other marvels were acquired as well, including a superior form of advanced longevity, and innovations in stellar navigation, food production, and cognitive powers.

There was, of course, a price to be paid.

There always is.

The Dark Wanderer offered godhood, and he demanded the worship that was his due. The faithful tribes of the *Moirai* called what was revealed to them, the Quantum, and it promised them an eternity of their own making if they would help the Dark Wanderer on his own personal quest.

That quest was to leave physicality, to shed the real, and to become a super-intelligent being who ruled the universe in a place beyond time, space, and reality. This was the true power. Once he obtained it, he would bless his faithful servants with the gifts they deserved.

Prisma knew that the creature had not achieved this. She had seen Ravi slay him and wondered if that fate was what the being had attempted to avoid.

She dug deeper. The creature knew almost nothing about the Dark Wanderer except where it led the *Moirai* through the Quantum—a place distinct from reality, a place driven by pure intelligence and information. The Dark Wanderer trained those who were able to use this power, and they became his prophets and prophetesses. He enslaved the rest with chains biomechanical, turning them into chimeras who served as slaves and warriors in a state somewhere between eternal torment and drug-induced euphoria.

Long before the advent of the Galactic Republic, after the Exodus, and decades after those who had been left behind on a dying Earth had made their own Great Leap, the *Moirai* was capturing stray explorers and lost colony ships, or arriving at lost planets, wiping out lesser civilizations, and scouring the ancient records and sacred places for clues the Dark Wanderer sought. Clues to a place called the Quantum Palace. Progress was slow, but it was progress that drove them on to other genocides.

But buried deep within the psyche of the *Moirai* and all those on it, burned into the very code that ran the ship, was a link. And all that occurred aboard the *Moirai* was known to...

...

The one whose name was replaced.

Replaced?

Yes. Not forgotten or removed as before. When speaking of the impure.

Replaced.

It was known to the Golden King. Yes. All of it. And so that first of lighthuggers, learning from the others, and using the strand—known only to the Golden King—applied what was learned. The Golden King entered the Quantum without need of a guide. Without need of a Dark Wanderer.

He sent his queen. He set the stage. For the warrior. For the tactician.

He waited.

In the Quantum Palace he bided his time. Seeding the galaxy for his conquest. No longer bound by time. Watching the *Moirai*. Learning. Preparing.

Seeding the galaxy.

Building his armies. Refining their genetics. Conquering.

But ultimately... thwarted. Defeated.

Retreat.

It was too soon. It was too treacherous. Impatience must be shed.

Now the day is here. Not two millennia have passed since the lost campaign. The blink of an eye.

The Dark Wanderer is dead.

The Dark Ones are imprisoned.

The Cybar have shown how to wield them.

Victory is sure.

24

Savages.

Prisma now realized that was what she was dealing with. It was clear from the moment she pried beneath the thick strata of carefully layered lies, revisions, denials, and deceptions that encumbered the mind of the vampire—the *Savage* vampire. That thing... had once been human. So long ago that even had it not undergone a battery of reeducations and forced enlightenments, it might still have forgotten. How could anything living centuries as a... monster... retain its humanity?

Even Tyrus Rechs had forgotten.

Prisma wondered at the connection between the bounty hunter and the story of the *Moirai*. She found that answer, too, in the vampire's mind. Once, it had been tangentially aware of Tyrus Rechs. There had been a battle. A boarding party consisting of Martian light infantry. The details were not important to the thing, because the Savage had not been tasked with slowing the invasion.

Goth Sullus had been there too. Before. Before he became Goth Sullus.

And somehow... Reina was involved.

Prisma probed, not finding direct answers, because, again, the thing was not directly involved. It knew some but not all. Generalities but not specifics.

"How?" Prisma asked herself. She meant her mother.

A trap. A means by which to lure Rechs and Goth Sullus into a knowledge of the Dark Wanderer and his power. Especially his power. A force they would seek out together. General and Tactician. Mastering this... Quantum and ultimately using it for him.

For the Golden King.

They owed everything to the Golden King. Even without knowing it. Their longevity and all the experience earned while slaves... all that happened was carried forth in secret by him.

A Savage.

The Golden King was a Savage, and over all the Savages he ruled. Like Rechs and Sullus, they were not always aware of it. But that did not make it any less true.

So what did that make Prisma's mother?

There, in the splendor of her quarters, Prisma shook her head and attempted to throw out the disturbing thought before it could bring forward even more disturbing answers.

Her mother was *not* a Savage.

Neither was Prisma. Not yet. But... what else could they have been speaking about when they highlighted her "impurities"? She was a representative of that base and despised horde of humanity. She was human. So was her father. And so must her mother be—or at least *had* been.

Right?

But the girl's mind would allow her to think of nothing else *but* that possibility. Crash's final words screamed at her. Had the faithful war bot known?

The answer wouldn't be found alone in her room, but Prisma knew how futile trying to sneak out would be. She closed her eyes and felt for the life aboard the ship. The Savage fiend, the vampire, hadn't traveled far. It was on its way back to the bridge. She took hold of the trailing tendrils of the thing's mind that remained from her first probing intrusion and followed it as though being led by a dog on a leash. What the creature saw and heard, Prisma saw and heard.

As the Savage fiend entered the bridge, the Golden King was speaking freely with his generals. Reina bowed her head and lowered her eyes as the king spoke. The generals, however, only bowed their heads. Their eyes looked up upon their king; such was their peculiar privilege.

"The invasions have begun on all the targeted worlds, my lord," one of the generals said.

The Savage king nodded. "They must be bloody, fierce, and terrible. What of Maestro?"

Another general straightened to report. "Maestro has organized the attacks, but remains reliant on the augmented species harvested by the Gomarii."

A third general spoke up. It was difficult for Prisma to tell them apart, as they were practically identical; only their length of their hair, beards, mustaches, and the like differentiated them. "What of Earth? Maestro's spy gave a number of possible locations. Have none been fruitful? The Gomarii invasion can be expanded to nearly every corner of the galaxy if we can only rediscover that which was hidden from us."

This comment seemed to bother yet another general. "My lord. Your plans have been all-encompassing, and any one of them would achieve victory irrespective of the others. Earth is immaterial to the campaign already underway, which is itself immaterial now that you have achieved your victory over the forces that made even the Ancients flee. With such power, why rely at all on the aliens?"

Reina looked up sharply. The reserve and submission she showed to the Golden King did not extend to his generals, though they were perfectly created genetic offspring. "You would speak with contempt for our first allies among the alien races, Claudius?"

General Claudius held his chin high. "They are inferior."

"Who has suggested otherwise?" Reina said. There was mischief in her voice, and Claudius seemed uneasy about matching wits with the woman. "But they have sought—consistently—to achieve a state of perfection. Through the millennia, the Gomarii have taken races and species across the galaxy, examining them, hybridizing and refining in the hopes of achieving perfection in themselves. One need only remember how they were when first encountered beyond The Gap... and how they are now."

"We do not *need* them," Claudius insisted.

Reina went on as though she hadn't heard the general. "When they met our liege as he emerged from the unfolding infiniteness of the Quantum Palace, what did they do? They realized at once what he was. Though a powerful species, they sought his mercy and offered their loyalty and service. The Golden King... *accepted* such service and placed them among his subjects. Well beneath him, but among his subjects all the same.

"And when the Golden King first allowed his subjects—your brothers, Claudius—to go forth and conquer the galaxy... what happened then?"

Claudius looked down.

Prisma found herself wondering what *did* happen. Her host seemed not to care or know.

The Golden King spoke, and Reina quickly lowered her head. "Did you imagine, Claudius, my son, that I accepted their service out of some *need?* And now that such a thing is no longer needed, they are to be discarded? Was my grace for show? Tell me this, Claudius: do I need *you*?"

The general bowed farther, dropping to a knee and revealing his thick, corded neck from within the powerful armor that draped across his shoulders. "My lord needs nothing. Least of all me."

"Rise, Claudius," the Savage king commanded. "For the sake of your fallen brothers, I would have you see the end of the Legion that halted your efforts to broaden my kingdom."

Another general spoke. "The tribal lord of the Gomarii is available to report directly on the work of his warriors should you desire it, my liege."

The Golden King raised an eyebrow. "He requested an audience?"

"No, my lord. He would not be so bold. He hailed the ship and asked if he might be allowed the honor of standing by at your pleasure should you have any wish to speak with him. To be so near to you in victory was all the honor he sought."

The Golden King smiled, and the eyes of the others went to Claudius, furthering his rebuke.

"Prepare the transmission."

The Golden King had mastered immediate, interstellar communication long before acquiring hyperdrive or any of the other Savage-made advancements. Now that technology would be used to bridge the impossible distance between the Gomarii and the Golden King.

"At once."

As the general in question left, Prisma felt a sudden jolt of fear that soured her stomach. The Savage king was staring fixedly *right at her*. In her mind, she knew that she was watching through the eyes of another, and that the contact made was with that fiend's eyes... but the intensity of the king's gaze made the girl sure that he was looking through his Savage underling, survivor of the *Moirai,* and directly at her. Prisma held her breath and kept still, as though keeping quiet in her faraway quarters would somehow impact those searching eyes' ability to find her.

"The Dark Ones are imprisoned," the Golden King finally said.

Prisma breathed a sigh of relief. She had not been discovered.

The Savage whose mind she inhabited answered with a servile hiss. "Yes, my lord. The means of capture is sure. We learned of the prison from the Dark Wanderer, and the method of capture from the Cybar. The Dark Ones, in lusting to violate the covenant with the Ancients, produced their own entrapment. They are yours."

"Perhaps my lord shall wear them around his finger like Goth Sullus," quipped one of the generals.

To Prisma's surprise, the group laughed, including the Golden King. Only Reina did not share in the sentiment. She flashed a look of concern at the suggestion but did not give voice to it.

The Golden King noticed, nonetheless. "I sense your worry, my queen."

"Forgive me, my lord."

"Am I a man, that I would be corrupted as your Tactician was?"

"You are no man, my lord. You are the source and inspiration for all who have Uplifted."

"One concern does remain, my king," said the fiend in its hissing voice. "We know not what will come should the Dark Ones be unleashed from their prison to do your bidding. Neither the prophets nor prophetesses can see the end clearly."

A bearded general stroked his chin, pulling his hand down to tug at the golden hairs. "In releasing them, they may wage their war on the galaxy?"

The fiend nodded. "Such nearly happened when Goth Sullus used but a fraction of the Dark Ones who had inhabited the Cybar constructs. Our king wields the entirety of that force."

Reina stepped in, speaking as though she sought to redeem herself in the eyes of her king. "Yet Goth Sullus was able to hold them. At the end. How much more our Golden King?"

It was a question no one would entertain. They merely bowed their heads.

"My lord," said the general who had stepped aside to arrange communication with the Gomarii. "I have the tribal lord at your pleasure."

The Savage king gestured to the vampires. "Leave us."

They floated off without a word, and to her dismay, Prisma began to float away with them. She wanted to—*needed* to—know more. Not knowing it was possible until the moment she did it, she untethered herself from the Savage vampire's mind and willed her presence to remain in the room. She found she could see and hear just as before, but she was no longer bound up with the creature's twisted mind. It was as though she were a ghost floating unnoticed above the heads of those conversing in the great star bridge.

In that triumphant moment, an unexpected thought came into her mind. *I bet Ravi would be proud of me for this.*

No sooner had the thought occurred than Reina lifted her head, suspicion thick in her eyes. She looked around the room, searching its corners. "I must go see Prisma," she told the Savage king.

He waved his fingers dismissively. Checking in on the girl was of no concern to him.

Prisma's heart raced. She knew she had only a few minutes before her mother arrived, and she would need to be fully present and aware when that happened.

A towering Gomarii was holo-projected before the Golden King, his deep blue skin punctuated by purple scars from a multitude of battles. Prisma could not see the source of this transmission, and its clarity was so complete that she wondered if the alien had simply been teleported into the room.

Simply.

Prisma realized just how odd her life must have become for her to think of teleportation in such terms.

The Gomarii was taller than the Savage king, and his armor was larger and more imposing, but the way the alien fell prostrate before the Golden King made it clear where the true power resided.

"I am not worthy of this honor," the tribal lord said as the dome of his great bald head touched the floor.

"Tell me of the invasions," demanded the Savage king.

The Gomarii did not rise from his position of worship. "Our slave ships have struck the worlds as instructed by Maestro. Though the numbers are less than what Maestro promised us, my warriors have the honor of filling the ranks and will rejoice in a glorious death for your purposes, my liege."

"Of what do your forces consist?" one of the generals asked.

"The species you created, my lord, we have long harvested according to your will." The Gomarii seemed only able or willing to address the Golden King directly, his every word a mewling prayer. "Some of the zhee you gave us to defeat our ancient foes likewise fight with us in the name of their bloody false gods. Those we have modified are avatars for your marines. They fight well."

"Resistance?"

"Strongest where the Legion resides. It has grown in power, my king. I worry that the resolve of our mercenaries may waver in the face of a prolonged battle. Maestro promised us greater numbers…"

"You speak of the Hools," another general posited.

"Yes."

"Continue your campaigns," the Golden King said. "I will soon be on hand and the Legion, like all who opposed my first ascendancy, will be destroyed. You need only press the attack of those worlds I have chosen to spare."

"Yes… my lord." Something was distracting the Gomarii—as though it was trying to pay attention to something occurring wherever its physical body resided.

"You have additional news?" the Golden King asked.

"I… I am not sure. My war chiefs report that the battle in the Sinasian Cluster is being supported by moktaar. But we sent no such slaves into battle there. They are rising from their own ranks as Maestro promised."

The Golden King's eyes snapped up at his generals. "Has Maestro relayed any of his chittering news?"

The generals stood silent and grim. They knew what this meant. "No, my lord."

"Then it would seem he is keeping such information from me. Maestro has found Earth after all, and hopes to use the lost knowledge to take my throne." The Golden King's face darkened. "He will fail."

Prisma leapt away from the bridge only moments before Reina reached her door. She sat on her bed and composed herself. As she had nothing on hand to distract herself with, she instead closed her eyes and meditated.

The door opened, and Reina stepped inside.

Prisma opened her eyes. "Mother! I reached out like you taught me and I could travel through the ship. It was just like I was there; I could see and hear everything."

Reina did not smile. "Where did you go, my daughter?"

"Up and down the corridors by my room. I didn't think I should go any farther than that."

Still Reina did not smile. She watched Prisma warily.

"Are you done with your meeting?" Prisma asked. She worked to control her heart, and even more to control her thoughts and emotions.

Her mother couldn't be a Savage, but maybe she was under the sway of one. The girl still couldn't accept the idea that her mother, her long-lost mother, would willingly be paired with someone whose intentions seemed so... bad. The Gomarii were bad. They were slavers. The Legion was... well, it had been a lot of things. But the legionnaires she knew weren't wicked like the Gomarii.

Or the Savages. She remembered the old woman, the crazy dying old woman at Mother Ree's sanctuary who had experienced the Savages as a child. There was nothing good there. *They* were impure, not her.

Her mother had to see that.

"No," Reina said. "But I wanted to check on you."

"What was that thing that brought me to my room? I didn't like it."

"Did it do something to you? Or did you simply not like how it looked?"

"It looked like a monster."

"Looks can be deceiving."

Prisma's eyes quickly darted around the room. "I guess so."

"Prisma, I don't want you experimenting with your abilities unless I am there to guide you. It's dangerous."

Prisma nodded. "When did you and my father fall in love?"

"What?"

"The Golden King. Did you meet him after my father died? Or did you already know him? Did you leave him for my father? Or did you leave us for him?"

Prisma had no idea where these words were coming from. They simply spilled out.

"I don't like the tone or direction of these questions, Prisma."

The girl set her jaw. "But you can see why I'd want to know."

A caressing, comforting feeling washed over Prisma's mind. She could hear Reina's voice urging her, soothing her. "It's fine, Prisma. Be happy. Don't trouble yourself. It's fine."

Prisma realized that this very enticement had been pressed against her before. On the Savage hulk, at the temples, by the fire and at her training, again and again since she'd first met her mother.

She resisted. Refused to be comforted. Worked even harder to hide what she was doing. Ravi would be proud.

What did I pay Tyrus Rechs to kill Goth Sullus?

At once a memory came flooding back to her, springing from the deep recesses of her mind where it had been buried and stifled.

She was with Tyrus Rechs...

"Now you pay me. For the job, Prisma."

She looked at him. Her eyes conveyed her lack of money. Then she remembered something.

"My... He left a lot of credits in a kind of bank and told me how to get them. They're there."

"No, Prisma. Pay me with your most precious possession."

She thought about this. Then she got up and went back into her cell. She came out holding something. She stared down at it... then she held it out for him to take.

It was a picture of a woman, and a baby. Rechs studied it.

"This?" he whispered.

"I never knew her. This is all I have."

The woman in the picture had Prisma's eyes. Maybe someday the little girl in front of him would grow up to be as beautiful as this woman was. No doubt the baby was Prisma.

Rechs placed the picture in his shirt pocket. "Payment accepted."

The woman standing before Prisma didn't have her eyes. And the longed-after image of her mother—her *real* mother in that holopic that she had studied again and again, that Reina had so systematically oppressed from her mind, and from Crash's, too—came to Prisma in vivid fullness.

Tears started to well in Prisma's eyes, but a smile was on her face.

"Is something wrong, Prisma?" Reina asked.

"It's fine. I just realized that I shouldn't trouble myself. I'm being silly."

Reina turned, satisfied by this. She went to the door, turned again to look at Prisma, and then left her quarters.

Prisma continued to smile after the door closed. She had found her mother again. And no matter what happened next, she would spend the rest of her life remembering her. Loving her. And her father, imperfect man that he was. It was the least she could do for the both of them.

She closed her eyes, guarded her thoughts and mind, felt the tears run down hot on her cheeks. And she called... "Ravi... find me."

...

...

"Prisma! We are coming."

CARTER

25

I'm not supposed to be alive. I bet you've heard that before. But have you ever pondered the significance of that statement? I have. Because... I'm not supposed to be alive. So you tend to think about that. And my firm belief is that the only people who can ever honestly say those words are people who are not, in fact, dead. Yes, this theory discounts the idea that you can die, go to some afterworld, and still come back to complain about your bad breaks. Perhaps. But for everyone else, you've got to be alive. But also... you're supposed to be dead.

Like me.

Being in the state I'm in—alive even though I'm supposed to be dead—you end up thinking of your family. In my case, it's my wife and two daughters. My wife, very specifically, has told me on numerous occasions and in front of our progeny that, "Everything happens for a reason, Carter."

Usually the words came when I was venting a little too much during the landing sequence (if you know what I mean) and was saying the quiet parts out loud about the galaxy and our meager place in it. Maybe she believed those words when she said them. Or maybe she just didn't like the idea of what that sort of hopelessness from the guy who was supposed to be leading this outfit called a family might do to her children.

"I didn't marry a quitter, Carter." She'd say that, too. She said a lot of things. A lot of positive, encouraging things. Funny how you never remember those when things get rough in a relationship.

Point of it is this: Let's say that my wife was right and everything happens for a reason. If that's the case, then the person who's involved in a horrific sled collision that should have resulted in your death (and the death of your entire family)... well, can they really say, "I'm not supposed to be alive?"

Here's how I see it. The answer to that question boils down to who or what you think is the final arbiter of what should or shouldn't happen in the galaxy. Don't ask me who that is—or isn't. There's no shortage of explanations. Do your own research. But if my wife is right and everything is shaking out the way it is due to some unseen, cosmic plan of completion, then I really can't say that I shouldn't be alive. The very fact that I *am* alive refutes that notion. If I was supposed to be dead... I'd be dead.

But then I get to thinking about what the people who tried to kill me might think. If the accident hadn't been covered up and they somehow knew that they didn't snuff me out (although, technically, they did—I was medically dead along with my wife and at least one of my daughters for at least a time)... but if they *knew* that, then those guys, the kelhorns, could say, "He's not supposed to be alive."

And they wouldn't be lying. Because that was their plan and it failed. But then, they *would* be lying because their plan failing and me living was exactly what was supposed to happen. Assuming my wife is right about these things.

Like I said, I've been giving it a lot of thought. I'm not sure if I'm supposed to be alive or not.

I'm glad I am.

And if those Nether Ops deep-state killers, as I found out later, ever came up to me and with shock in their eyes said, "You're not supposed to be alive!" Well... I would respond...

"But I am, bitches!"

And then I would let Mel S., that's my shorty surge shotgun, elaborate my point with enough blasts to remove every last karking one of them from their bodies. We can circle back and see who was and wasn't meant to be alive after the smoke clears.

Satisfying as it is, I'm clearly getting ahead of myself here. In fact, just hearing from me again might still be a surprise that hasn't fully registered. Well trust me, you're nowhere near as surprised as I was, pal.

I'll tell you what I remember. Then I'll fill you in on what I learned after that.

Mr. Nilo, Big Nee, had given us all some R&R after a job adequately done on Kublar. I say "adequately" because it turned out that the *true* primary objective in all that chaotic, jumbled PMC campaign organized under Black Leaf was not achieved. Of course none of the individual teams would have necessarily known it. Part of Big Nee's genius is making you feel like your role is the most important thing happening in the entire organization. Even if it's loading up a flatbed of dead koobs. And if you do your job well, he's happy. Even if the totality means failure. He can be happy when a team achieves its objective. So my guys, we did ours. The guys meant to remove what was locked up in that vault inside the museum in the heart of the Soob... did not.

At the time I figured it was a case of too many people from the boardroom being stretched into the war room. A place these coders, managers, and execs had no business being. Sometimes you get a culture where, because a guy had success in one realm, you assume it will translate to another. If they can juggle communications between several branches, departments, and teams, and end up shipping a product bug-free and on time, well... how much more complicated could it be to run the same on a battlefield comms system?

Yes, I'm talking about Brisco, by the way. Dude was terrible at his new job.

The saving grace in that entire ordeal on Kublar, with zhee and koobs and civil wars, was that we had a whole lot of ex-Legion, former hullbusters, and an assortment of over-achieving basics. All capable of adapting and overcoming. Pikkek and his koobs helped, too. Credit where it's due.

Looking back from where I am now, I'd say what happened on Kublar—the primary objective, never mind the good we did, failed not because of naiveté or even the ineptitude that could make what should have been basic ops into a sket show. We failed to achieve our OBJ—that's how the cool guys with beards and sunglasses say *objective*—because someone inside Black Leaf was working to undermine us.

My credits are on Surber but take that with a grain of salt before visiting your friendly neighborhood Kimbrin booker to place your bets, because I already hated that guy.

Back to what I last remember.

We got some R&R. Unbeknownst to me, my team is getting wiped out one by one. They knew one of us was a

Kill Team Ice boy, but they didn't know it was me. So, like any good psychopath, they just killed us all.

I'm driving with my family and we're talking about something, lost in one of those magical conversations where everyone is being themselves and we're all enjoying one another. A spell that can be broken at any time. Someone will get grumpy or withdrawn or distracted or offended and it shatters. But while everyone is in sync and living in that kind of love, it's great. So we're talking and completely unaware that a whole bunch of AI-controlled safety features are about to fail at one fateful intersection.

Keep in mind, we're not talking about some edge world with dirt streets full of vehicles dating all the way back to the Savage Wars, or new vehicles modded to strip out the speed limiters and other unnecessary features on a world that doesn't see the kind of high-speed traffic in the more civilized parts of the galaxy. This was on a respectable mid-core world with all the modern AI-controlled intersections at both ground and air-sled levels. It had the limited tractor posts, too, and I don't need to tell you how those work. We don't even think about them anymore. They even have them on some of the bigger edge worlds at this point.

I bring all of that up because what I thought was a great stretch of timed signals—I was hitting every light—was actually just an evolving death trap meant to pancake me and make it look like an accident. People still investigate when you get a blaster bolt through the head in the mid-core, contrary to what they might tell you on the core worlds. So yeah, someone, Nether Ops, was trying to kill me. And how else would an automated hauler moving at full speed plow into my expensive (and paid for!) family luxury sled at exactly the moment of no return?

Sounds like I'm one of those dark-holo conspiracy theorists, doesn't it? I don't take offense. It sounds like a stretch. Bad luck is a thing. I got hit by sixty tons of it at sixty kph.

Only those intersections also have miniature tractor systems—the tractor posts I already mentioned. Those have the same basic functionality as their big brothers aboard the capital starships and space ports that draw in disabled craft, guarantee a safe landing, or optimize a starfighter rearmament with AI precision. The little tractor posts, sometimes tattooed with graffiti, are at nearly every major intersection on that world. Surveilling for imminent collisions just like mine. They're installed just in case the first layer—the AI-controlled intersection—fails. Or more likely someone with a license class that allows for manual transport runs the red. The tractor grabs your whole ride and slows it down just enough to avoid catastrophe so that usually all you end up with is a bruise on your chest if you're wearing your autobelt or a bump on your forehead if you sliced it and ride dirty.

Intersection lights tell me and the freight hauler to go at the same time.

Strike one, as the seamball umps say.

Tractor posts don't slow me down an iota.

Strike tuh, as the more colorful seamball umps say.

I guess strike three is the part where I die. Massive trauma from the impact despite a state-of-the-art protective package that auto-filled the interior with foam and an Ootari-designed frame meant to transfer the kinetic energy across the entire vehicle.

But with something like that slamming into you, those safety features can only do so much. I'd've had to have been cruising that intersection in a Repub corvette to have survived that hit.

I'm sure the bot driving the freighter felt terrible about the whole thing.

The point here is, I'm alive because someone out there was watching me on that intersection.

I'm not talking in a metaphysical sense, either. I mean someone was *literally* watching me and all because of some crazy Legion association that I didn't even remember being a part of. At least not at the time of the crash.

But I do now.

"Sket." The sniper assigned to overwatch had little more to say as the sixty-ton freight hauler slammed into the target vehicle at full speed. He keyed his comm and said into the net, "Fever, Fever, Fever."

The observation bot he monitored sent a burst with the exact coordinates of the accident a moment later.

"Code Fever acknowledged," replied the shot caller, his grizzled voice betraying no alarm that the worst-case scenario, the thing they were trying to prevent, had just happened. "Ground assessment."

"Workin' it," the sniper answered as he moved through the pattern controls of his TT-7 observation bot.

Three seconds stretched into five. Too long for Shot Caller. "Need that assessment, Nap."

The sniper, Nap—Staff Sergeant William Knapp, officially KIA during the Third Battle of Peña IV during the Savage Wars, assigned to Kill Team Ice, released at request with full neural therapeutic scrub, Legion Reaper sniper, honorably discharged—preferred to watch his targets from a fixed position through a scope. In an ideal world, his spotter handled the bot. Which wasn't to say he wasn't proficient at it, but he'd fumbled the menu and had taken longer than he needed.

He'd hoped that if Shot Caller's premonition that Nether had made one Carter Delgado as a former member of Kill Team Ice, whatever went down would be when he was stationary on some rooftop, modified dual-fire energy/ballistic N-18 at the ready.

That hadn't happened.

"Sensor showing negative on ground forces. Negative on biologics inside cargo hauler." The brief report was made complete by the fact that, due to the bot, every other team member had by now seen the crash with their own eyes.

"Muni-area sweeps are showing the same," said CK, also a member of the team. Sergeant Christopher Kell Woodward. Officially KIA during the Savage invasion of Chalco. Assigned to Kill Team Ice. Released on request. Declined neural therapeutic scrub. No subsequent military service.

CK was also a recon expert, but whereas Nap would kill his targets goodnight from long range, CK was the guy you sent in to do it up close and quiet. Now he was monitoring a hacked network of municipal police sensors meant to identify outsized gatherings of humanoid lifeforms before they had the opportunity to form into illegal protests. Riots had once grown all too common in the mid-core. Goth Sullus's arrival, and later, Article Nineteen, put an end to that, but local governments rarely gave up any power over its citizens once they'd acquired it. So the surveillance systems stayed. The good news was that these were easy to slice, and while the sensor technology was purportedly just for monitoring large crowds, it could pinpoint and track individuals just as easily.

"Whoever pulled off this hit isn't anywhere nearby," CK concluded for the team.

A third member of the team, though not a member of Kill Team Ice, spoke next. "Shot Caller was right again. Old man can sniff out hits like a doro hunting junga-truff."

The comment was casual, and the guy probably didn't mean to pass it over the general net.

Now Shot Caller was indeed an old man. Not in that military, "We are all ten years or less removed since we learned to shave while this guy is married with *kids*," kind of way, but literally. Old enough to be the grandfather of every member in the outfit. Or possibly the great-grandfather. And yet, due to the intricate nature of Kill Team Ice, he was also *younger* than a number of the men he now led.

The white hair and wrinkles sat on a strong, solid-jawed face. The arms were powerful, even if the skin hung looser than it once did. For an old-timer, he knew how to hang in combat. He also knew how to run an op.

Shot Caller could have told the talker, one Sergeant Paul White—18th Legion, active-duty, transfer to 33rd Legion in process and likely never to be completed—a thing or two about how he expected his comms to be handled. He might do just that later. But for now, he kept the op rolling. "Nearest team is Team Four. Proceed to crash site. I want you there ahead of the EMTs. Move."

Nap, the sniper, continued to watch his feed from the back of a white, unmarked repulsor van. Somewhere in the back of his mind, he knew that he was part of Team Four. Yet when the vehicle tore off onto the street, it caught him by surprise. Unwilling to drop his controls and lose uplink with the TT-7 for even a second, he hung on to the device and slid across the van's cargo space, narrowly missing a collision with CK and prompting a laugh from White, armed with an NK-4, also riding in the back.

Nap crashed into the side of the van hard enough for the *thump* to be heard by the driver and passenger up front.

"Hang on back there," the driver said.

"You're supposed to say that *before* we leave, kelhorn," Nap returned.

The passenger, a leej named Buitrago, Dark Ops but not Kill Team Ice, turned around in his seat and smiled at the jumbled mess of sniper and observation equipment. "You heard Shot Caller... we got a time hack to make."

The vehicle raced the quarter mile to the crash site.

26

Black Leaf was a word-of-mouth kind of job. You had to know someone who would vouch for you. I'm not sure who the original "someone" was who started the network of private military contractors, but by the end of it, we had formed a solid bunch. Most of the onboarding was remote—holo-interviews and psychological evals. Stuff you can do from home. Then you're in pending a background check where they go and verify your service. (Fun fact: a ton of, shall we say, *enthusiasts* lie about combat experience or sometimes about being former military at all.) When my Legion credentials came through, I got the formal job offer along with the compensation package. I said yes after about four hours.

Now if I had seen some of the growing pains Black Leaf was experiencing, I probably would have triggered the termination clause in the contract. There was a two-week window from acceptance where you could drop out, no questions asked. After that, you could still quit at any time, but Black Leaf made it clear that their legal department would have no choice but to... recoup all those costs associated with getting you set up and on board. And of course the adjudicating authority was located on one of the distant Republic edge worlds. About as far as you can go from the mid-core and still be in the Republic.

Unless you owned your own starship and had your own law degree, the cost of quitting was probably gonna outweigh the cost of just riding out your contract.

That's a corporation for you though. Always looking out for themselves. The easiest way to do that is to proactively set things up to be as difficult as possible for you the moment you're not doing what they want.

So... a lot like the government. Except you actually have a choice whether or not to give a corporation your credits.

My two weeks came and went with almost no contact. Three days before time expired, they took me on a tour of one of their private capital ships—as close to a destroyer as you can legally get. I got to see the armories, barracks, mess, and all the other amenities set aside for Black Leaf's new PMCs. It was enough to make even us former Legion guys raise an eyebrow. Although to be fair, things had been in decline for a while in the Legion and it was really showing its age when I was active. All that bad blood between the House of Reason and the Legion commander showed up in more than just fiery exchanges on the nightly news.

Still, legionnaires have things pretty good. The hull-busters felt like they were in heaven. So did the basics. As far as they had known, only points could ever serve in such opulence. All in all, a good first impression.

I remember thinking it was odd that they had us tour an empty ship—lots of bots and a brief meeting with the captain, who used to serve in the Navy, but not a hint of who we would *actually* be working with. I think they were aware that their transition from galactic megacorp to what the suits called "direct action influencer" wasn't going as smooth as they wanted.

We got another forty-eight standard hours with our families and then the two weeks were up and we were called in for work. Keep in mind, I had a decent idea of what we'd be doing along with assurances that we wouldn't be breaking any Republic laws. But I had no idea where we'd be doing it.

Things started off feeling pretty military. Which to me was comfortable. We went into a quarantine on a medical ship where we were monitored for any local planetary bug we might have brought from our various home worlds. While we were there, we were also called into the med bay for a physical eval.

Now, I had already passed a physical with flying colors just to land that gig, and I really couldn't think of what else they might need from me. Once I stepped inside the med bay, I figured out the score.

"That's a lot of injections you got lined up," I said that to the human assistant instead of the doctor, a bot. You typically can't get anywhere with a med bot. Their directive is to get the auto-injector working, emptied, and then call in the next guy.

Their assistants are usually female and usually pretty. Depending on the dominant species. Our outfit was human, so, pretty human girl. She might not have known an Ulori's cloaca about medicine, but she played an important role in that room. These assistants were trained to have all the psychological tools needed to get anyone afraid of auto-injectors—or afraid of what was *inside* the injectors—to get over that real quick and go on through with it.

"I know it might look like a bit much," she said, ever so sweet, "but it really is for your own health and safety."

She smiled the sort of smile that would make a lesser man mumble "Aw shucks" and then roll up his sleeve, hoping she'll be impressed by his bicep and *really* hoping that she'll have more smiles to give if he takes all those shots like a stud.

"Uh-huh," I said. See, I'm married. That sket don't work on me anymore. "Any idea where they're sending us so that we *need* that many shots?"

I shot her back my own smile.

Something you should know is that the Delgado smile has the same effect on women that this lady's smile was trying to have on me. Science hasn't been able to explain it. And it works on more than just humans, too. Compatible near-humans love it too.

You can trust young Carter Delgado about that.

When the assistant locked eyes with me for just a second too long, I felt pretty confident she would answer my question if she knew how. Which was the only thing I was after.

"Because, Dessi," I said, reading her name from the helpful tag affixed above her bosom, "the Legion sent me to a whole lot of sket shows in this galaxy and I can only think of a handful that required a battery of inoculations like what's loaded up in that bot's auto-injector."

The bot in question had stood by patiently, the first auto-injector gleaming beneath the sterile light, ready to jab, administer, and then retract to allow the next chamber to rotate into position. Seven shots to a cylinder delivered one after another so fast you barely have time to grimace. There was another full cylinder on the table, and while I might have hoped it was for the next man up, I had a suspicion it was destined for me.

Dessi, who might have been a nurse or might have just been good at making men feel happy to be alive, bit her lip and looked around the small room. Her eyes rested on the patient bot, as though it were the sole objector on hand to prevent her from telling me what I wanted to know.

"That bot isn't gonna care what you tell me," I said, hoping to quell what looked like her final doubt and biggest hurdle. "And *I'm* certainly not going to tell anybody."

I flashed the Delgado smile at half strength, not wanting to overdo it.

She caved, leaned in close, and whispered past her painted, glossy red lips directly into my ear.

"I overhead a couple of officers from the bridge in passing yesterday. So take this for what it's worth, but I'm pretty sure you're heading to Kublar."

Dessi straightened up and adjusted the injectors on the table that didn't need adjusting, back to business. Let the record show that while her words whispered into my ear did make the hair on the back of my neck and arms stand up, it was mostly because of the destination.

Mostly.

What could Black Leaf possibly want on that rock? I raised my eyebrows high, thinking about visiting the site of one of the greatest Legion tragedies ever to unfold.

"I hope the number of auto-injections won't dissuade you from serving in Black Leaf, Mr. Delgado," the assistant said, resuming a professional air and getting back on script.

I gave a half-chuckle. "With where you're sending me? Hell, you better double it."

"Get that sled open and pull them out, Team Four."

The driver of the van, who by virtue of being the wheelman was acting as the de facto team leader, wanted Nap and the others on the scene as quickly as possible. He needn't worry; the sniper had the van's rear cargo doors open and was out amid the detritus from the crash before his ride came to a stop.

The teams had sand-tabled numerous scenarios meant to prevent Carter and his family from being harmed by Nether Ops. Or, if necessary, extract whoever survived if they were unable to prevent the hit.

"Fever" was the worst-case scenario and also the one Shot Caller had had a sinking feeling would happen, given how far behind the clock he'd been in getting Carter on his sensors. The man had undergone a full therapeutic neural scrub prior to being released, and that always complicated matters. There was simply no guarantee that Carter would go along with you just because you showed up and identified yourself as part of "the program," as those inside the program called it.

After all, Carter Delgado had no idea what Kill Team Ice even was. All he knew was what had happened *after* his release. He was married with two daughters. He'd served in the Legion, was honorably discharged, and was making a name for himself as a private military contractor in fomenting a legally sketchy revolution on an infamous edge world. There was no telling how he'd respond to Shot Caller and the team. And given the need for what remained of the program to remain in secrecy and out of Nether Ops's plans, these matters had to be handled delicately.

But Nether Ops got to Carter before Shot Caller's delicate plan of contact and persuasion could even be fully formulated, let alone activated.

Nap, the sniper, had left his modified N-18 inside the van and moved with his blaster pistol drawn, doing his part to verify the crash site was secure while another team took control of the observation bot and did the same from overhead. No sign of any hostile presence. Just a bad luck crash that would be blamed on a system failure. Maybe some slicer supervisor would get a reprimand, unless the city was already looking for an excuse to can the guy.

"White, CK, clear the freighter's cab," ordered the driver. "Buitrago, make sure nothin' comes out the back."

"On it," they answered in unison.

CK climbed up the driver's side, his NK-4 sling wrapped around his arm, weapon pointed at the passenger window. White did the same from the opposite side.

The bot, which sat in the driver seat but was really only there for human interactions—the truck drove itself—turned its head and acknowledged the two operators. "A collision has occurred. Please notify local authorities. I am unable to leave the vehicle or provide further information without legal authorization from Wind Cargo, LLC. Say 'repeat' if you would like to hear this message again."

"Cab is clear," White announced.

"Clean it," said Shot Caller.

CK tossed a bot-popper in through the window and then hopped down, as did his partner so that the men dropping from the truck and the subsequent blue-white flash looked professionally choreographed.

"Clean as a dawhser's snout," White reported.

The act wasn't a random act of property destruction. Dropping the bot-popper on the driver's lap would fry its ability to transmit images or provide any account of who arrived on the scene first. Subsequent teams would erase that data permanently and then ghost before the city EMTs could arrive.

Hopefully.

"Intersection cams offline?" Nap asked into the net.

"Roger," answered one of the other team members. "Switched off before the crash. Making sure they don't come on again."

It was dark. With the site secure, auto-flares were activated and tossed into the roadway. Buitrago directed what little traffic there was around the wreck. That was one nice thing about a mid-core world: you could still find cities that weren't so packed that the traffic flows remained heavy at all hours of the day and night.

Nap led the digout of Carter and his family. The windows were already thoroughly spider-webbed and strewn on the duracrete, blown off the frame. Anyone seeing the vehicle would have little hope of finding survivors, but modern sleds were meant to handle horrific impacts. Still, the front end of the luxury sled—Black Leaf must pay well—was completely sheared off; the freight hauler had made an AI-fast but still too late course correction and steered itself away from the humans inside as much as possible before impacting. The move might have saved some lives; without that adjustment, Nap didn't see how a single inhabitant could have been anything but flattened.

The sled had auto-unlocked its two large side doors, but the twisted metal ruined the gull-wing mechanism so that White had to use a Halligan bar to pry it open, revealing the foam-filled interior. Nap went to work digging. The foam crumbled in his hands and fell at his feet like falling sand; the stuff was designed to arrest blunt force trauma by encasing the interior and then easily clearing out for any first responders.

Nap dug like a dog, burrowing a hole first to the passenger—a human adult female. Carter's wife. "That's one."

White worked at digging out the girls in the back seat while CK uncovered the driver.

"Sket," Nap said, taking a cursory look at the uncovered bodies. "Looks bad. TBI… internal hemorrhaging, multiple breaks… be a miracle if we have any survivors."

"Checking anyway," CK said, crawling over the victims and using his bio-sensor.

Shot Caller was familiar with the medical capabilities of the program; it was more than just putting soldiers in stasis between missions. Kill Team Ice was well beyond the bleeding edge of cryogenic medicine, thanks in large part to classified research provided by Tyrus Rechs. "Team Two is en route," he said. "We can pull them to the program if it's as bad as that, but otherwise I want them taken to SD Memorial. Carter stays with us."

"Gotta have a spark for that to happen," Nap mumbled to himself. The sniper, like all members of Kill Team Ice, was also a fully trained combat medic. "Vitals showing on all the females. Barely. It ain't much but they're hanging on to that thread."

Team Two arrived in an ambulance they'd "acquired." The members loaded the girls up and watched them speed away to the nearest hospital in critical condition. So far, they were moving ahead of schedule and might still get clear before any of the other responders could show up. That was assuming that whoever sliced the traffic systems didn't also shut down the emergency response indicator. Normally a collision event would trigger an alert that would activate an AI to route the nearest EMT to the site. No one had heard any sirens yet.

Shot Caller would later sermonize that Nether Ops did them a favor by disabling that alert. They were sure their hit would work—and that the only thing that might interfere was medical attention pulling their targets from the brink. "There's an institutional pride with those kelhorns," he would lecture. "Understand that, to a man, they believe themselves to be the smartest guys in the room. Using the city itself to make the hit was ingenious. But if they'd only put a man with a blaster on scene, they could have made sure their mission was a success. These types thrill themselves with their perfect plans… they forget that life ain't perfect and things never go that way."

But that little speech was later. Right now they had to finish clearing the site.

"Reading on Carter?" Shot Caller asked.

"Dead," reported Nap. "But not by much. He's still warm. We can get him on an auto-breather and get him stable enough to get in a pod."

"Not until we pull out the hardware Black Leaf injected him with."

The tech company, in addition to the plethora of nanitic virus and bacteria killers meant to help a man survive on Kublar, had also shot a small feather chip into the bloodstream that worked its way into the brain within a few days of being injected. From there, they could monitor… well, the intel wasn't clear on just how much. But it wasn't something Shot Caller was willing to take chances on.

Nap frowned as he looked down at Carter's dead body. He'd fought alongside this man on multiple occasions. Seeing him like this wasn't sitting well, and only his professionalism kept him from pulling the leej out and getting oxygenated blood flowing again. "No offense, sir, but you wouldn't like the results if I try to dig that feather chip out with my knife."

"No. I wouldn't. Don't try it, Staff Sergeant. Get him in the truck and link with Three. Sending coordinates now. They've got the tools to get that thing out without lobotomizing our man."

"Sir," Nap said following a quick internal debate on whether to say anything at all. Shot Caller was no dummy. "The longer Carter stays under, the harder it will be to bring him back."

"And the dumber he'll get," added White. "That smile will only get him so far."

Shot Caller was firm. "I am aware of what a lack of oxygen will do to his brain. We do our best to help him, but our main priority remains the security of this team."

There was no dramatic reminder of the mission they had yet to undertake after getting as many of their numbers back in the unit and up to speed as possible. It would be a culmination of their work as operators. It was why they were all there, leaving families and lives behind for one last, big op.

"Yes, sir."

27

For the record, I don't feel like I'm any dumber than I was before the crash. My wife and many of my friends, family, and associates might tell you that doesn't count for much. And in their defense… you have to be a few spanners short of a full toolbox to keep doing what I do for a living.

I was dead for something like fifteen minutes. Or at least dead enough for whatever chip Black Leaf put in my brain not to think otherwise. During that time, the teams did what they did. My family was delivered in critical condition to the emergency wing. Shot Caller put a guy there to keep watch just in case Nether Ops got vindictive about their surviving. Last I heard, they were stable and going to pull through. Recovery isn't going to be painless, though. I'm hoping it goes better once I see them again at the end of all this.

For now, that's the part that kills me. The pain they're going to have to go through. It's for their own sake. They need to believe I'm dead. Still, I'm looking forward to mission accomplished and then showing up on Mel's doorstep at the end of it all.

I just hope she doesn't pick up a boyfriend between now and then.

As best we know, Nether Ops thinks I'm dead too. Tech guys used a John Doe in the morgue plus some slicing to have me listed as dead on arrival. That dude is buried under a Carter Delgado headstone right now.

As best we can tell, Nether Ops has scaled down its hunt for however many of us—yes, us—in Kill Team Ice are still out there. Something else is happening, and we have a good idea of what it is. It won't be pretty. Shot Caller decided that the time for nabbing who we can still nab for this op is over. Even though some of our best members are still out there. Goth Sullus evidently breached an auxiliary branch and scooped up a bunch of the guys. Good men like Donal Makaffie and the Wild Man. Not to mention Walker.

I remember them now. The rest of the team says they don't know what happened to 'em, which is too bad.

And then there's Aeson Ford. I remember him, too. Oba, do I remember Sergeant Fast. He was the heart and soul of the program for almost the entire time it operated. Everyone knew Sergeant Fast and a lot of us followed Makaffie's lead and called him that, even if the only way we'd ever known him was as a captain. Evidently, we both served in the Legion at the same time after our stints in Kill Team Ice were over. He got mixed up somewhere in Dark Ops land because of course he did.

Nether Ops went hard after him as soon as they linked him to a bounty hunter named Wraith. Everything out there says he slipped the trap, which isn't surprising if you knew him. Savages got Sergeant Fast once upon a time, and he never let anyone get close to dusting him again.

I went after a girl and started a family. Who knows if Nether Ops would have even thought twice about me if I hadn't taken the Black Leaf job. We don't think they have a roster, because there isn't any roster. But word is they have some kind of AI that pays attention to people who exhibit our fighting abilities. You gotta have more than a great personality to get in the program.

It's good to know—to remember—my brothers again. Almost like waking up from a long dream. But a good dream. Mel is a part of that dream and so are the girls. Unlike Fast and Wild Man, I didn't serve on Kill Team Ice jump-to-jump. Almost no one did. Even so, I'm pretty young if we're counting centuries. When the Legion was forming up, I wasn't a twinkle in my great-great-great-you-get-the-idea-grandfather's eyes the moment before he flashed the most fateful of all proto-Delgado smiles. Still, I'm old enough to know the Savage Wars as something more than a couple of chapters in the history texts. I grew up living it.

Here's an unsettling thing about me. I remember what *really* happened and I also remember what my mind was scrubbed to *believe* happened. Something like that can be... difficult to cope with. When I got out of Ice, I awoke in a Legion infirmary following a bout with some planetary sickness. I didn't quite remember my previous unit, but I was told that was part of the illness and that my short-term memory would be hazy for a while. Just the usual Legion suck. Good news was that my orders were in, and I was on my way to transfer to a new company, and away my career went.

But that's not all. You can't scrub a guy's mind and leave him with blank questions about who his family was, where he grew up, things like that. So they implant false memories to keep you from going down that path. I'll let you deal with the ethics of the situation; I'm just dealing in the facts. I woke up thinking that I'd been orphaned at sixteen. Ironically enough, my parents (and only family) died in a sled accident.

That was fine. I believed I went straight from a state home into the Legion at seventeen, and I blamed every other blank spot on the mystery illness that had put me in that Legion infirmary.

Only now, I know that I really *was* seventeen when my parents died. And it wasn't a sled collision that killed them, but Savages. They died during the first wave. My dad was downtown at work when his entire office building was leveled by some kind of air-to-surface missile. My mom... I don't know. She wasn't home when I got there after breaking away from the schoolteachers and security guards urging us to stay sheltered in place. They all died on the first day, too. There were already Savage marines moving through my neighborhood, pulling people out of homes. Harvesting them.

We lived next to a wetland and wildlife preserve, and so that's where I went to escape. After a few hard weeks of surviving and avoiding anything that sounded larger than a bird, I met up with a ragged band of survivors. By then I'd pushed out of the reserve that butted against the well-planned neighborhoods and into the wilderness proper. I'd have used the man-made hiking trails, had I not learned early on that the Savages monitored them. I'd been bushwhacking just to survive.

The survivors were built around a militia. Not the planetary defense kind, but the guys who trained with blasters in their spare time out of a sense that the local government was just biding its time before some kind of despotic takeover. Maybe they were right about that, but the Savages arrived before the human tyrants could make their big move.

Either way, I'm thankful for those nuts because I probably would have died of exposure or starvation without them. I wasn't a complete novice out there—my family had done plenty of camping and had a general interest in living off the land—but I was hardly a survivalist.

In time I showed the leadership, by which I mean the militia's leadership, that I wasn't just some teenage hanger-on. My old man had taught me how to shoot. He felt a man needed to know such things. I was strong and could carry my weight plus extra.

I never complained.

I was too sad to complain.

Seventeen years old and my life—all my dreams—were over.

Some folks who found solace in the wilds wanted to stay there and hide. Maybe the Savages could be waited out. Maybe the Legion would come and then life would go back to normal. Other survivors could be sought and found. Families reunited.

"They're *clinting* themselves," I told one of the militia members. His name was Ben Stormer. A big, tall, bearded man who knew his weapon better than any professional I've met since, except the Wild Man. He once told me that he sent anywhere from ten to twenty thousand bolts down his barrel every year as part of his training. I believe it.

"Are they?" Ben asked.

"Yeah. They're not gonna find anybody after this is over. And if they do... they'll wish they hadn't."

"You know that for a fact?"

"Don't try to spare me like I'm a kid, Ben. I know you've heard the same things I've heard about what Savages do to a planet."

Ben's face was stoic. "Yeah."

"Someone oughta wake them up."

"No. They shouldn't."

I looked at Ben in disbelief.

"A lot of these people are living solely on hope right now, Carter. You think you can forgive yourself if you take away their reason for living?"

I hung my head. "My parents are dead. I know they are."

"Probably."

We sat in silence for a while.

"Those people, it's all they can do to just hang on to that hope and survive out here," Ben said. "Let them. But *we* can do more."

"Like how?"

"Some of us try and make it hard on the Savages. You might want to join us."

My eyes flashed wide. I knew that Ben and some of the others would disappear for weeks at a time. They would often come back with game, but I always suspected it was more than just a hunting trip. They were gone too long.

"I can shoot," I said feebly.

"I know you can. Wouldn't have asked if you couldn't." Ben smiled. "We're leaving again tonight. I'll tell the others you're coming this time. Get some sleep. I'll wake you before dawn."

From that point on, I helped Ben and the other men and women who had once been something other than soldiers during the unimaginable life before the Savage invasion. Our only goal was to make things hard on the Savages and kill as many of them as we could. But never in a way that jeopardized those hiding in the wilderness, living on hope.

At one time, there were as many as three hundred in our localized resistance group. We drew leadership from hunters and veterans of conflicts that didn't involve Savages. We learned how to avoid Savage lures, psyops, and their ever-present probes that drifted through the forests we owned, glowing like will-o'-the-wisps.

By the time the Legion arrived, only ten of us were still alive.

When the legionnaires cleared out the Savages and left my home world, I left with them. I completed Legion selection on Hardrock—the original—which was somehow more difficult and frightening than the actual Savage invasion I'd lived through.

Unlike some of the other guys in the program, I never got hurt so bad that they put me on ice, seeking to save my life first and recruit me second. That's something you might not know. Ice would take men, war heroes, exceptional leaders, use their limited resources to save them, let the decades pass to restore them—and then upon waking, those men would say, "No, sir. I'm getting back in the fight right now." Or they'd think they'd used up all of their life's luck and retire to some planet that seemed out of the Savages' interest, always praying it would remain so.

I can respect either of those choices.

Word is, General Rex read a commendation citation—Silvene Star—and thought I might best serve the cause by joining Ice *before* the Savages had a chance to wreck me.

And now, thanks to the literal wreck that was my assassination attempt, I have the distinct pleasure of entering Kill Team Ice the other way as well. So I've got that going for me. Which is nice.

Being in the program meant always and only performing No Fail missions. The general took care of us that way. He guarded us jealously. It didn't matter if it would have been "nice" to have us along on some campaign. He only sent for us when the activation was critical.

That meant a lot of us had very short stints in Kill Team Ice. Either because we opted to take our release after a mission or because we didn't survive the last one.

No Fail is all most of us really ever knew. Sergeant Fast could boast that he *literally* had never been on an op that wasn't No Fail. He was in the Legion for New Vega, which was as No Fail as it got, but his outfit's missions particularly so, and then Kill Team Ice after that. Eventually, though, those missions grew fewer and farther between. The war between the Republic and the Savages settled into a doldrums and territories began to be set. Then the Battle of Telos happened where Admiral Sulla bought it and the Savage Wars was officially over.

Kill Team Ice was a volunteer unit and its members were free to leave whenever they wanted. The general made it repeatedly clear that we'd all earned the right to decide when it was time to walk away from war. After Telos, we were of one mind: get back in cryo and see what happens. We didn't believe it could really be over.

Fast-forward and those of us healthy enough to wake up are sent on a new mission that has nothing to do with Savages. Instead they send us to make first contact with a new race known as the Cybar. The briefing made it clear that these could be allies or could be a Savage-level threat. We did that mission, but it wasn't what we'd signed up for.

I remember now that we had a long talk before going back under ice after that op. The galaxy was always changed every time we woke up, but it felt more so that time. Still, we decided to give the Savages one last chance to show up and get whipped. Our cryo-requests were set to various dates with the same general request: "Unless Savage invasion occurs, wake me at... X."

In short, we were saying, I'm going to bed, and if the Savvies aren't here by wakeup reveille, then get me up and let me start my new life and leave this bad dream behind us.

And a lot of us, like me, wanted them to do one better than that. I didn't want to remember the dream at all.

A lot of us came out of it at the same time, as testified to by the fact that so many Ice members are running around on the loose right now, much to Nether Ops's chagrin. Ford and I probably picked the same year, because it sounds like we were both in the Legion again around the same time, although we wouldn't have recognized one another. We both got the full neural scrub.

Generally, the guys who woke up first and *remembered* what happened did their best to help the rest of us. While they lived with their demons, they worked to make our transitions easy. Most guys got the scrub because of how much pain they lived through *before* enduring the horrors we saw in the program. That elusive life after the Legion seemed impossible unless you took up the program's offer to reset you, replace you, and let you have a shot at normalcy. This galaxy is big enough to get lost in several times over.

It's telling how many of us said that we still wanted back in the Legion to start things over in, though.

For me, though, it ain't easy anymore. When this last op is finished and I get back to Mel and the girls... it's gonna be a whole lot more complicated than it was before. I might just go ahead and get scrubbed again if they can do a precision job. I'm not sure I can be the father and husband I need to be with all these other memories bumping around in my head.

I was barely doing the job before all that.

Let's put it this way and then drop the subject: I'm not sure Carter Delgado ever would have married and had children if he remembered what the Savages had put the galaxy through. Because I saw what Savages did to wives and children. I saw unimaginable, terrible things.

Having those things back in my brain is what it took for me to leave Mel and the girls to recover without me.

I have to fight to stop those things from ever happening again.

28

"I'll tell you how I met the general," Shot Caller said as he sat down across a bare desk from me. The shine of the wood reflected his fingertips like a mirror as he drummed them against its surface.

Right away I knew he meant General Rex. Because that's how all those who served under the man referred to him. He was the general. Anyone else promoted to that rank needed some additional identifier. Didn't matter how good or bad they were at the job. You said, "General So-and-So" or "Old Eyebrows" or some other contextual clue necessary to make sure everyone was on the same datascreen. But not so with General Rex. The general.

I nodded, eager to find out what our mission was to be and willing to hear a story about the general from the old man. "Yes, sir."

"You met General Rex before I was ever born. I met him much more recently. I was still a relatively young man at the time. Older than you are now, but not by much. In a new phase of life, though. A little farther down the path you were on before the Nether found you out.

"He had a job he wanted done and a reputation had been built up for me by Dark Ops. He found me and told me to go and get it done. I did." Shot Caller gently rapped his knuckles on the desk.

I was expecting something more akin to a formal briefing. This was my first meeting with the man who now universally appeared to be in command of the program. I'd gotten some intel from old friends like Nap once I woke up from the wreck with my recall intact. But he wouldn't fill me in on *exactly* what Kill Team Ice was doing. Neither would anyone else.

"Shot Caller will tell ya," Nap said.

I came into the meeting expecting to be told exactly that. Certainly every other time I'd been activated for an op, either the general or someone he personally sent was waiting to give me and the rest of the team a no-nonsense brief of our mission and then let us get to planning.

This felt more like a heart-to-heart, getting-to-know-you meeting over a cup of kaff.

"After the Savage Wars, the general kept himself concerned with the Legion," Shot Caller continued. "Not in a paternal sort of way—he wasn't just looking after that which he'd founded. When the Legion ceased being what he had created it to be, he had no qualms with putting down its legionnaires. He had a massive bounty on his head and some of it he surely had earned. Does that surprise you, Sergeant Delgado?"

I wasn't sure if it did or not. I'd heard the stories about how much of a kelhorn he could be. His cruelty in training legionnaires was legendary among those who knew or remembered. Given what so much of the Legion became... I could absolutely see that man putting down a shiny-armored legionnaire without a second thought.

"Surprising or not," Shot Caller said, cutting through my thoughts before I had the time to answer, "it's the truth. And that's because, to General Rex, life is transitory. A man can be many things in his life, and to Rex, he's only as good as his purpose. The purpose of the Legion was to be a combat force capable of taking the best shot the Savages could deliver and then pounding the bastards back ten times as hard."

Shot Caller leaned back in his chair and thought. There was an almost scholarly intelligence about the man that came out in how he spoke and chose his words. Sometimes people refer to the *warrior-poet.* The impression I got from Shot Caller was just that. He was the kind of man who sought out knowledge in every facet of everything he came across, thoroughly examining various disciplines and taking with him anything that might make him a better soldier.

Shot Caller held his palms up, spread across the width of the desk. "But what happens when the galaxy contains a Legion... but not a threat like the Savages?"

I cleared my throat. "That's something most of us struggled to answer toward the end of our terms in Ice, too, sir."

He gave me a single nod. "Most of you waited to see if the threat you'd devoted yourselves to stopping would return. When it didn't, you opted to move on with your lives. That was very much the direction my own career took, albeit without centuries of cryogenic sleep. I lived my life in one go, and yet the two of us, as well as the other members of Kill Team Ice, now find ourselves in the same place facing the same threat."

Those current members of the team included more than just the guys I'd served with. There were several operators who never went into cryo at all. Mostly men who served in Dark Ops and were brought in by Shot Caller. They appeared capable and professional. Probably would have fit in the program just fine had they been born a few hundred years ago.

I was pleased to hear the conversation shift to talk of the mission. As interesting as hearing stories about the general might have been, I didn't leave my family again for anything short of stopping the Savages, even if they hadn't been formally named as the threat in this unusual briefing.

"The Savages have returned, sir?" I asked.

I already knew the answer; the boys had made that much clear. And for all of us in Kill Team Ice, it was only the Savages that would have pulled us back together. There hadn't been a Republic when the Legion was founded; that came later. We felt no strong loyalties to any government. Only to each other, the Legion. And anyone willing to stand with us against Savage posthumanism.

The glory of the Republic was a rallying cry for someone else. Not for us.

"The direct answer to that question is yes," said Shot Caller. "But if you'll allow an old man some time to muse on his past, I believe you'll have a profounder understanding of what's unfolded since you were last activated, Sergeant."

"Of course, sir."

Shot Caller told me how General Rex could sense the tension between the House of Liberty—soon to rename itself the House of Reason—and the Legion. It started almost as soon as the Savage Wars ended.

"The final mission against Savage elements occurred some time later, though, while I was in Dark Ops. There has been no trace of them since."

I took in the information, and then a question popped into my head. I blurted it out before I had the chance to think whether I should. "Were you... on that mission, sir?"

He hesitated, said, "I was," and continued in his brief.

But that little exchange told me a lot about Shot Caller. I was growing to like the old man more and more. You run into operators who wear their achievements out in front as if perpetually in dress uniform. Proudly displaying deeds as if they were a personality. Soldiers who don't feel secure until they are sure that *everyone* in a room knows the big deal mission they were on and how *they* pulled the trigger to take down some infamous terrorist.

You'll find them on the social holos and holonews talk shows most often.

Shot Caller wasn't one of those guys. He mentioned the mission only to give me a clearer picture of the Savage movements since I was last activated. He had to be coaxed into admitting his involvement. The silent professional.

He went on to tell me about a secret society named Primus Pilus. Its purpose had been to preserve the Legion against outside meddling. But after the Savage Wars, it was increasingly put to a difficult test.

The galaxy took a breath after centuries of conflict and then promptly got back to violence—this time all those other long-simmering conflicts that had temporarily been set aside in favor of the great, existential war. The House of Reason began to pick winners and losers, ostensibly looking at those conflicts through the lens of the Republic and what its citizens should be free to expect.

If a Republic world is mired in civil war, does the rest of the Republic owe those citizens military support? If change can't be effected through the political means of a planet's government, should the rest of the Republic stand back and watch as violence unfolds?

The Legion was asked to put down various rebellions, the largest of which was on a planet named Psydon. A charismatic warlord incited a civil war among the native doro, and soon his anti-Republic messages were being amplified by worlds up close and far away. The fear was that Psydon, already purging dissidents through a murderous campaign against its own people, might become a major stellar political player in that sector of the galaxy. The House of Reason was determined not to let Psydon be the first domino leading to the breakup of a Republic that had withstood the Savages themselves.

The Legion had been the sword that slew the Savage tyrants. Now they asked one another what their role should be when smaller tyrants emerged. No consensus was reached in the Legion ranks or in its secret society. Some felt the Legion had a duty to respond to the House of Reason's plea for intervention on Psydon. Some didn't.

"Back then," Shot Caller observed, "the House of Reason wouldn't dare to *tell* the Legion where to go. They still had to ask."

As righteous as Psydon might have been, brewing trouble was plain to see. The House of Reason had begun appointing officers to serve in its Army, Navy, and Marines. They told its citizens that this was essential to the preservation of democracy.

"Even though the kelhorned government is named the Galactic *Republic*," Shot Caller said, working himself up slightly at the memory.

The House pointed to the numerous rebellions and conflicts flaring up one at a time along the Republic's edge, which at the time was primarily the mid-core and those edge worlds located nearest to it.

General Rex had seen these developments, too. But his fear was not over how the Republic would get along, but what the Savages might do if they weren't truly gone. What if they were only biding their time and waiting for the Republic to grow weaker?

His solution was to step down as Legion commander and found Dark Ops. A Legion inside the Legion. An organization he both led and went into action with.

Shot Caller smiled. "I only heard of one NCO making the mistake of telling General Rex he needed to be somewhere other than in the middle of a firefight. And he only made that mistake once." Shot Caller checked his chrono and straightened his uniform. "You probably know the rest of the story from that point. How General Rex ran afoul of the House of Reason."

I nodded. "Both versions. The old leejes' and the official narrative."

The official narrative was that General Rex had been training Dark Ops for a takeover of the Republic, eschewing Article Nineteen in order to set himself up as dictator. He was killed in the coup attempt. The old leejes said there was no way.

"And what do *you* think happened?" Shot Caller asked.

"I knew the general, sir. And I saw what the Republic devolved into. I believe the old leejes. General Rex was set up."

"Set up, but not put down. He escaped. Old leejes would talk about how he was still out there, always willing to help a true leej who found himself at the bad end of a good fight. That was truer than they knew. He worked as a bounty hunter until Nether Ops and the House of Reason did the math and realized he'd reinvented himself. That was when he last visited me. As a bounty hunter.

"I could see right away that he had changed. His memory was going and in a bad way. He asked me about the order and I told him it had folded. Those last meetings were just endless arguments about Article Nineteen. I'm still amazed Keller managed to make it happen.

"Then Rex told me something. He said, 'That's the thing about upholding ideals. You get enough people together and you'll have so many opinions about how an ideal is lived that you can't help but do nothing. Except argue about what to do or what not to do or how someone is doing the right thing in the wrong way. Nobody is ever happy because an ideal lives in your *mind*. It's a feeling. A sense of the way things should be. Those rarely survive encounters with another individual.'"

Shot Caller smiled. "That was the most the general ever said to me in one stretch. And he wasn't done. He told me that he believed in objectives. That was how he lived his life. 'Every task I complete,' he said, 'whether in a day, week, or year of my life, has been about putting it to the Savages.'"

I gave a slight frown. General Rex was a man driven seemingly by nothing except to destroy Savages. The only other person I knew who even came close to that sort of obsessive focus was Wild Man, and it made the guy go crazy. Maybe the general was crazy, too.

I told him, "I believe it, sir."

"He didn't believe the Savages ever truly left. But he never found evidence to the contrary. We all would have heard about it if he had. He..." Shot Caller looked down at the mirror finish of the wood desk. "He didn't think the Legion could be trusted. I mean after they'd tried to co him and he went bounty hunter. But that didn't mean it was just him.

"He went on to tell me about Kill Team Ice. Said that they, like him, would answer the call when the Savages came back."

"Yes, sir," I said, still eager to hear just what we'd be doing about the Savage return.

Shot Caller laced his fingers together. "Our job is to give the galaxy a breath, Sergeant. When the Savages come, all those comforts that we tell ourselves we can't do without... suddenly they won't feel so comfortable. People will be vulnerable. They'll be in shock. Because as bad as Article Nineteen, the Cybar, and the Black Fleet were... they won't be anything compared to a Savage return. A war, a normal war, picks its targets. Most of the galaxy gets to live the same way they always did. A Savage War is different. No world is safe."

This was not new to me. I'd seen how the Savages went after worlds that had no strategic value and almost no natural resources. Just the fact that it existed and wasn't in their hegemony was enough for them to pull it into brutal conflict. But I couldn't resist getting to the point, as interesting as Shot Caller's story was.

"Has there already been an attack, sir? Something kept hidden from the public?"

I was pretty sure I'd have heard about a Savage invasion, even if I was on Kublar when it happened.

"Not yet. But we know they've come out of hiding due to certain... *sensor packages* the general set up."

Shot Caller seemed to want me to guess what those might be, but I had no idea. I kept quiet.

"Earth, Sergeant Delgado. The Savages are trying to find Earth. And the general made it so that when Earth tries to let them know it's still there, the Savvies don't get the message. But *we do*."

Judging by the tiny smile on Shot Caller's face, my mouth must have physically dropped open. "We know where Earth is? Holy sket."

Shot Caller pounded the table with his fist and stood. "We do. Get yourself outfitted because we're headed there now. General briefing en route. The boys will catch you up on the sand tables, but if you've been on a hulk, you'll know the layout by heart."

I could draw a map of the average Savage hulk blindfolded. Still, I couldn't quite believe what I'd just heard. "Is it... is it very far away, sir?"

I couldn't imagine a scenario where our lost planet of origin would be hiding in plain sight. Too many science expeditions to find the place had happened for it to be anywhere else beyond The Gap out past galaxy's edge. The last time we went out that far, it was to recover *Deluvia*, which incidentally had a standing mission parameter to seek out Earth. It's not my job to guess, but I couldn't help doing just that. Would we load up into more of those super-hyperjump drive ships to close the impossible distance? The program had one when I was last activated, and I couldn't even count the number of zeros in the cost figures. That fit one team. Could we possibly have enough for all the active Ice members?

It didn't matter. Shot Caller gave a sly grin. "Not as far as you'd think, Carter. You've been there before."

KILL TEAM VICTORY

29

Bombassa allowed himself a moment with his bucket off to savor the sweet and pungent smell of the jungle while climbing aboard the technical. The diminutive hover truck was roughly half the size of a Republic combat sled, with no armor to speak of, but its relative smallness made it perfect for traversing the narrow roads and tight confines of the jungle. Toots took up the driver's seat, his own bucket off to squeeze in an entire ration gel before managing the safety restraint.

Ahead of them, Neck and Nix pushed grav bikes from the surrounding foliage, brushing off the various fronds and vines that clung to the machines. With the vehicles out from the camo netting that hid them during the raid, Wello fished through a pouch on his armor to produce a lighter. It was a flat metal piece of kit, engraved with the Sword of the Legion, and before using it, he always took a moment to take in its old-world charm. The leej flicked the lighter with a satisfying click and touched it to the edge of the netting. The concealing tarp burned without a flame, merely turning bright orange while a chemical reaction built into the system turned it to ash.

Leejes performed last checks of their vehicles, revving engines and linking navigational displays into the tactical feeds. The twin bikes in the lead shot forward on fields of repulsor force with a throaty whine that transitioned to a mechanical howl the farther they got from the technical. The truck fell in line behind them, and Wello followed on the third grav bike, acting as a rear guard for the convoy.

His bucket back on his dome, Bombassa called into the L-comm, "Bear, this is Bombassa."

"My man!" Bear called enthusiastically through the net. "Holofeed showed you guys just took out a grid square. Fill me in."

Ahead of the technical, the grav bikes jumped a tangle of fallen logs on the trail, easily sailing over them. The truck swerved to avoid the logjam, veering into the forest with a branch-snapping crash and breaking trail through vines and branches coated in the syrupy black mire that covered everything on this side of the range. Shouts and complaints hooted from the passengers in the truck, and Toots held up his hand and made a quacking gesture to rudely let his leejes know it was message received. A hard turn splashed the repulsors over a puddle, sending geysers of grit and plant matter to both sides of the vehicle as the technical regained the road.

Bombassa keyed into the comms to answer his commander's question. "We're five minutes out from the objective. Guidance from higher?"

"Yeah," Bear answered. "Once the engineers dig out Masters, I need you to secure the position and get me intel on what they got inside."

"What are we looking for?"

"I don't think anyone knows. They think there might be something but they aren't saying what. See what you see and funnel it my way." Bear's answer wasn't quite evasive, but it left the sense that there was more *not* being said. A moment later he added, "Legion proper is handing everything over to the Army, but they're leaving a single ship, the *Espada*, as support. Apparently we're getting reports of attacks by non-human species all over the Republic."

"An MCR surge?" Bombassa couldn't think of anything else at the moment.

"Eh, not looking like it. Seems to be Gomarii-led."

"Gomarii?" Bombassa shook his head. Whatever was happening elsewhere in the Republic didn't matter. The mission did. "Three minutes out, Bear. I'll bounce you once we're in."

"Good hunting, Top. Bear out."

The technical hit a steep grade, and the cheap engine struggled with the weight of the legionnaires. After a bend in the trail, the path leveled out, returning them to a more normal speed.

"'Bassa, it's Neck. We're over the rise and are coming to the back end of the basics," the sergeant said in his typical drawl.

"I already transmitted our approach. They just signaled that we're on their board and clear to come in," Bombassa replied.

Thanks to the complex detection algos written into their buckets, the team spotted several Republic Army fighting positions camouflaged into the landscape. Emplaced N-50s poked from camo-netting and behind natural features, making the best use of the terrain for defense should the need arise. Anything coming this way that didn't have an invitation was going to be soundly trounced by these troopers.

"Gunfire up ahead. We're being directed to a staging area," Neck called over the L-comm.

The group rumbled up to a trio of combat sleds, choosing to settle the locally collected vehicles in a tight parking job out of the way of the much larger vehicles. A Repub Army lieutenant exited the lead sled and stomped through trampled vegetation to engage his newly arrived guests.

"Which one of you is V-Seven?" the lieutenant asked. When Bombassa swung from the technical and casually lifted a hand in the air, the lieutenant continued. "My CO is looking to link up with you, but we have a break in the line. After the donks got hit by the artillery, most of them backed off the objective for better cover higher on the hill, but we had at least a platoon's worth decide they weren't going to back down. There's a squad plus left that we didn't dust, harassing our engineers from that side of the hill. If you give us a few minutes to hunt them down, we'll get you through to the dig."

"Can you give us the freqs for your guys punching up those donks?" Bombassa asked.

The LT smiled at the question. "Sure can. I'm never one to turn down help from the Legion when I can get it."

Armed with the channels to reach the embattled engineer squad, Kill Team Victory left the lieutenant for the jungle. They powered through the mire threatening to stick their boots in place with every step. Where the ground on the other mountain was only tinged with the inky mess, the ground here was literally dripping with the black sap, and the leejes had to resort to movement of the kind taught in swamp operations courses. And when stray blaster bolts began to fly through the branches at them, their forward progress was slowed to a near crawl.

Bombassa brought up the net while deploying the rest of the team into a security halt. "Bravo Three Actual, this is Victory Seven. Over."

"Read you clear and bright on my board, Victory Seven," said the Third Platoon leader. The basic sounded happy to hear a Legion voice. "We have your LOC and have shifted fire to give you approach. Over."

"Moving into position now. Victory Seven out," Bombassa announced.

Kill Team Victory split in half, with Bombassa remaining in place with his element while Pina guided his part of the crew into the inky shadows of the deeper forest. Seconds marched by slowly as the Legion Dark Ops senior NCO waited for his people to get into position. He monitored the Army Basic net, listening to the tactical decisions from the squad leaders calling into their platoon commander.

The Repub Army had constructed a good push element, driving the remainder of the donk force higher up the mountain, well away from the mouth of the swamps where Masters was caved in. But they hadn't taken into account that some of the terrain consisted of natural cover providing a position for the enemy to fight back from. And now the zhee had enough cover to employ a rifle grenade launcher, which was being used to great effect.

"'Bassa, this is Pina. Team set," the no-nonsense NCO chirped into the comms.

"Stand by," the first sergeant acknowledged. "Set it off."

Sitting along the engineer platoon's flank, Bombassa's guys touched off their attack. Pina switched out his charge pack for a drum, turning his automatic rifle into a poor man's SAB. High-cycle fire from the weapon punched into the terrain, severing tree limbs and torturing the enemy squad's cover. Using the suppressing fire as a shield, Toots launched micro-grenades from his rifle into the enemy cover, killing a few more as they tried to duck the punishment coming from the legionnaires.

A donk with an old-school medium machine blaster changed his point of aim from the basics to the leejes, dosing their cover in response to the previous attack. Bits of vegetation and rock kicked up from the ground as the legionnaires ducked their buckets under the protective terrain. Toots lay on his back with his rifle angled, using the targeting algos in his HUD to aim by remote. A *poot* sent a grenade on a lazy arc to answer the donk's heavy blaster fire. The projectile detonated just ahead of the zhee cover, but still struck with enough force to put them on their backs.

"Eat it!" Toots said out of reflex as he watched the observation bot feeds. "Bombassa, they're making tracks up the hill."

Bombassa pointed to his leej, letting the man know he agreed with the assessment. The first sergeant updated the battle board and pushed the enemy location to his other team, then motioned to Pina to continue suppressing fire, harassing the enemy position so the only escape possible was farther uphill.

The donks slipped away from the crossfire they found themselves in, pushing higher up into the jungle on the mountainside. A few of their bolts continued to lance through the basin forest even after they disappeared from sight. Then came two massive explosions, and the gunfire ceased. The lingering echo of the booms and a few smoke-stained blaster scorches were all that remained of the donk force.

"Bombassa, this is Pina. Peepers are showing enemy force is one hundred percent KIA. Ambush site is secure. Moving forward to scout for ad hoc elements."

"Roger, out," Bombassa answered in the L-comm. He switched to the conventional net used by Republic Army forces to report his progress to his counterpart. "Bravo Three, this is Victory Seven. Enemy forces are one hundred percent KIA. The field is yours. Over."

"Tango much, Victory Seven. You are clear to pass to the OBJ. Bravo Three out," the LT replied.

The Dark Ops legionnaires assembled rapidly, making their way across the incline and away from the friendly platoon. The landscape gave way to a rocky crevasse the team used as a pathway to avoid the ever-present molasses. Bombassa emerged from the cut to a scene that was more to his liking.

An excavator, complete with a bulldozer on one side and a crane shovel on the other, was meticulously picking away at one side of the hill while a group of men in exo-suit armor hefted boulders and cleared debris. Additional elements secured the site, and groups of engineers were gathering scores of dead zhee fighters left in the field.

Bombassa got on the net to alert the engineers to their arrival, and his team crawled from their positions, tired but still happy for a reprieve in the mission they'd been working since late last night. As charge packs were swapped and water downed, an engineer with a battle board in hand jogged over.

"I'm Captain Rondeau. We're almost through to the cave, but haven't had any contact with them for the last few hours, and according to your higher-ups, neither have they. Orders at the moment are to stay on this side of the cave structure unless there was another collapse or you guys got here, whichever happened first."

"Good work, Captain," Bombassa said through his bucket's external speakers. "Open us up a way in as soon as you're able."

"On it now," the captain confirmed. He stepped away, speaking into his helmet mic, ordering his men to the task.

A series of troopers set back from the cave swiveled what appeared to be a heavy blaster toward the remaining rock covering the cave entrance. An NCO worked over a battle board as his troops did final checks on power supplies and cables leading into the equipment.

"Are they going to blast their way in?" Nix asked. "Because that thing looks like a platform-repeater."

"Negative. It's a boring laser," Neck said. "The sighting package alone is worth more than I paid for my house. That is, before the guy who called himself an emperor blew it up. Anyway, it's basically a high-energy drill with specialized depth sensors you can rig so it doesn't drill past where you want it to stop."

"Sounds boring," Nix joked, but nobody laughed.

An amber-colored beam fired from the laser, stabbing at the center of a large boulder. The NCO behind the device entered calculations into his battle board while his troops worked to keep the machine firing in place. The aperture widened for the briefest of moments, and then the distant NCO ordered the laser to be shut down.

"Get ready to kill it! Power down!" he called, loud enough to be heard from the kill team's position.

"Roger, Sar'nt. Beam at zero. Power cycling to five percent for cooling," replied a trooper.

The kill team bypassed the drilling crew, standing off flank to the excavator as it broke apart the lasered rock into smaller bits to be removed by the framework pilot-ed engineers. Dirt rained down from the top of the cave, collapsing into a berm that was quickly removed by the claw shovel. Titanic tank treads chewed into the ground for traction to move the excavation vehicle to a spot away from troops entering the structure.

"Captain Rondeau," Bombassa said. "I need you to harden the perimeter and keep your men clear of the entrance."

With a nod, the engineer company commander sent his orders into the comms. NCOs were soon moving on the quick to secure the scene, pulling men back to the cover of combat sleds as fresh troopers exited to do a troops rotation along the fighting position.

Team Victory waited for the troops to settle them-selves before forming into a strong side column heading for the cave entrance. Bombassa was on the L-comm at the same time as he used his external speakers to an-nounce their presence.

"Republic Legionnaires. We are coming in."

Neck and Nix moved into the structure first. Bombassa seized the third spot in the stack, citing first shirt privilege to take whatever position he wanted. While as team leader he should have been toward the middle of the line, his cu-riosity got the better of him; he was as eager as anyone—except perhaps Bear—to see how Masters was faring.

Night-vision mode kicked in automatically and the gloom of the cave interior gave way to a slate-gray dis-play showing bloody drag marks leading deeper into the dark. The leejes took the hint, driving their rifles from patrol ready to their shoulders as each man in the stack scanned a sector based on how the man in front of him was facing. Three steps past the bloody trail, something barked off to Neck's left. He and Nix aimed their rifles at the noise while the other leejes held their positions to maintain security on their advance.

"What is it?" Bombassa asked.

"Dog," Neck said.

Sitting in the dirt was a Legion working dog, its K-9 armor having seen better days. Dirt, grit, and slime marred the surface where mimetic camouflage should have been the order of the day. A series of score marks ran along the animal's flank, and there was a heavy blaster burn right behind its shoulder. It was a miracle the dog could see through the goggles in its bucket as the lenses were caked in carbon scoring and mud.

"How did you miss that?" Nix argued.

"I didn't miss it. It wasn't there a second ago," Neck retorted.

The dog barked again, then muzzle-thumped Neck straight in the crotch for a solid sniff.

"Dear Sweet Oba Almighty, bro! I hope you don't expect me to return the favor!"

Bombassa moved a hair closer, switching to external speakers. "Anyone else notice the L-comm says it's broadcasting when it isn't? Switch to external audio."

Scratching under the dog's chin, Neck read the nameplate on its armor. "LWD-2060, call sign Bubbles. Well, Bubs, whatcha got fer us?"

The dog barked twice and spun in a circle to show that it understood. It also revealed a nasty-looking wound on its side.

"It's hurt," Neck said.

The dog barked again and took off down the passage.

"I guess that settles that," Nix said.

The column of legionnaires followed the dog down the dug-out passage—but stopped when they came across a figure lying completely still beneath a Legion poncho. Their buckets picked up no heat signature.

"Oh no," Nix whispered in the electronic grit of the speakers.

Suddenly a voice shouted from behind a shutter of slat curtains. "Thought you guys are supposed to yell out 'Legionnaires!' or something."

Bucket algos adjusted to provide a view of the man who had spoken. The profile indicated a legionnaire minus his helmet. The man's rifle was aimed toward the floor but rested on his knee where it could easily pivot to ruin any of the advancing leejes.

"We did," Bombassa said. "You must have been talking too much to hear us, Masters."

The dog barked again, almost indignant at the reply, then happily trotted through the curtain.

The legionnaire behind the slats patted the working dog, then stood slowly and with the grunt of a man easily twice as old. He stepped through the curtain, and though the man's trademark grin was scarred by an array of skinpacks and bandages plastered across his face, Bombassa could still recognize him.

Masters took Bombassa by the wrist and drew him into a hug that seemed on the gentle side for a legionnaire.

"You look as though you've had a long day," Bombassa said.

"Rough day at the office," Masters replied. "Chhun send you?"

"He did."

"Well, where are my manners?" Masters said with a grin. "Let me show you around my new office. Just so you know up front, there's no kaff."

"So they think this is some kind of Savage tech?" Nobes asked as Kill Team Victory gathered in front of the great, sealed vault doors with Masters and the legionnaires from Zombie Squad.

"That's ESE," Masters said, pointing out the inscription attributed to Thomas Roman.

He repeated the history lesson that Lieutenant Apollo had given. The men of Kill Team Victory wore plainly their disbelief that the infamous legionnaire would just happen to know all those facts.

Masters winked. "I'm more than just a pretty face, boys."

"I'm still not getting comms through," Bombassa said. "Neck, Pina, go link up with the legionnaires and let them know we have control of the cave. Then notify Bear and give him the details."

Neck had been working on Bubbles, applying aid to the dog. "How about a walk?" he said to the mutt.

"Don't do it," called one of the legionnaires from Zombie Squad. "That dog is bad luck."

"Yeah, sure," Neck said. He whistled, and Bubbles followed him and Pina back to the entrance.

"So," Masters said, motioning to the great vault doors. "They send you in with some slicing kits or cutting torches?"

Bombassa lifted his eyes to the inscription. "No."

"Right, right. So you're just here to help us hold until some techs show up?"

"Getting to you was it, Masters."

"I don't buy it," Masters said. "We could already hear the engineers digging us out. Someone was thinking there was something more to it if they're sending a kill team in. Spill it, tall guy. What's the brass saying? We've got zhee on Kima, a potential Savage-era vault here, not to mention that big sack of Drusic crap rotting by the doorstep... you gotta tell me if they've uncovered something else."

Bombassa eyed Masters, annoyed. "No. I don't."

"Okay, you don't, but do it anyway." Masters grabbed the big legionnaire by the arm and came in close. "Sma_ got dusted coming for me. The only thing that's keeping me from wanting to go jump off a cliff is thinking that al_ this might be important."

"You love yourself too much to jump off a cliff, Masters."

"A short cliff." Masters tried to smile but couldn't—and *that* unsettled Bombassa. "C'mon, 'Bassa. I'm not kidding. This matters to me. It has to matter... it has to."

The big man let out a sigh. "I really don't know anything more than you. But... things have been odd." Bombassa's coal-black eyes darted back toward the entrance. "More than a resurgent MCR. More even than the zhee. Word is coming through that the Gomarii are leading planetary invasions across the Republic. You hear about that?"

Masters straightened up. "Gomarii?"

"Gomarii."

No one in Dark Ops had any love for the slavers. A mission to take down a slaver tribe was often the highlight of an operator's year. Masters furrowed his brow. "What, like they're doing capture runs? Grabbing slaves while the Legion is busy?"

Bombassa shrugged his shoulders. "They don't send me the reports. I am just telling you what I heard from Bear."

Masters brightened. "That guy loves me. I'll step out with your boys and give him a call. See what's happening. Could use some fresh air anyways."

The operator had taken only a few steps when he was knocked off-balance by the sudden lurch of an explosion outside the caved-in entrance. The other legionnaires had to brace themselves against the walls as subsequent explosions rocked the hard ground beneath their feet.

"Those are orbital strikes!" Nobes shouted.

Several legionnaires moved to the front of the cave, which thankfully hadn't again collapsed. The bombardment stopped almost as soon as it started, but the noise and violence was replaced by the deafening roar of what had to be a very *large* capital ship coming down practically on top of them.

A dirt storm pushed its way inside the cave, depositing a fine coat of dust over the legionnaires' armor. Shouts came from the mouth of the cave and soon a distant barking struggled to contend with the roar of repulsors. The dog halted at the entrance, barking, and then a legionnaire came stumbling inside, alone.

The men posted near the entrance used their bucket visors in an attempt to see through the dust. Missile craters scarred the ground, and dead and broken army engineers and burning equipment littered the area. Visuals confirmed that a massive ship was setting down two hundred meters away. With L-comms nonfunctional, this was all reported by word-of-mouth back to Bombassa deeper in the cave.

"How the hell did that slip past the *Centurion*?" Toots shouted.

"I can think of a lot of ways and none of them are good," Masters said.

Bombassa moved up beside Pina, the legionnaire who had stumbled back into the cave. A medic was checking him for injuries.

"I'm fine," Pina snapped, his voice containing an anger that was fully explained by his next words. "Neck's dead."

Bubbles whimpered and sat down next to the operator.

"Damn dog," one of the Zombie men said. "Bad luck, man. First MakRaven, now this guy."

Pina shook his head. "Not the dog's fault. Only reason I found my way back to the cave was because of its barking. Orbital blast knocked out my HUD."

"More important things to worry about," Bombassa said. "Nix, get a peeper up so I can see what sort of ship we're dealing with."

"Already in the sky, Top." Nix sent the feed to the Legion HUDs, which received the signal just fine despite the L-comm not getting through.

"Gomarii slave ship," Masters said. "They'll want me most."

Bombassa shot the legionnaire a withering look. "Not the time."

The slave ship lowered its doors and sent forth armored squads of Gomarii warriors in full battle armor, supported by zhee, Drusic, moktaar, and Hools, some of which slaughtered surviving engineers while the others took a hurried and direct course to the cave.

Overhead, a pair a Republic fast-movers raced into the area of operation only to be chased off by a smoking, snaking barrage of smart missiles. The distant crash of at least one downed fighter craft temporarily drowned out the crunch of boots as the slaver forces closed on the cave.

"Dig in," Bombassa ordered. "Make them pay."

Explosives and other traps were quickly set up near the entrance. Defensive positions farther back were scouted. The legionnaires would make these slavers suffer for every centimeter of ground they took. The final fight of their lives would be the kind that gave their surviving foes nightmares for as long as they lived.

Or so it seemed until the vault doors behind them groaned and gave a reverberating *clack* as the lock disengaged. A red light activated above the doors.

"You leejes are gonna have a better time in here than out there," a human voice said over some kind of speaker built into the wall.

The vault doors pulled apart just wide enough for a man to squeeze through.

"Top?" asked Nobes.

In the HUD, the Gomarii force was stacking, preparing to send the zhee in first to take whatever hits might be waiting, with feral-looking Drusic looking ready to go in and do CQB after the first wave of shooting died down.

Bombassa nodded at the question. "Inside."

The situation wasn't going to get any worse than it already was, and if they were being drawn into a trap, he'd prefer to face it head-on rather than be shot in the back while trying to repel breachers.

One by one the legionnaires moved through the vault doors, Pina ushering the dog and Bombassa through last of all. The doors closed behind them with a thud, and the heavy lock clanked back into position.

A human with a mop of dark, curly hair and a black beard motioned for the legionnaires to hurry along. He wore Legion armor, but no bucket. Another man looking just as much like an operator was dressed similarly, only he was clean-shaven.

But it was the interior of the vault that captured the legionnaire's attention. The space was colossal, and seemed to be some kind of museum. Placards written in ESE described colony ships that had presumably once been projected by dusty and now-dormant holoprojectors nearby. But mostly, the museum featured images of a single man. They were everywhere, showing him n various phases of his life—from a smiling, slouching, bald man proudly working before an ancient-looking monitor, to less candid images where the slight padding of fat was gone and he stood Legion-chiseled, poolside in a shirt much too small for him, his hair returned and no longer thinning.

The man's name, according to placards, was Thomas Roman. His name and his words were written everywhere.

"Nothing to see here," the bearded operator said, still waving the bewildered legionnaires along. "Just the most important archeological discovery of all time."

Nix stopped in front of the man. "You guys are Nether, aren't you?"

The bearded man rolled his eyes. "No, we're rot *Nether*." He shouted to the line. "Next guy who says something like that gets nut-checked. How about a little appreciation for saving your asses?"

Finally, Bombassa passed the bearded operator. His eyes flashed in recognition.

"Do I know you, pal?" the man asked.

Bombassa could hardly get his mouth to work. "Carter?"

Carter winked. "Yeah. Long story. You're gonna need to hear it from Shot Caller. C'mon."

EPILOGUE

G232 looked around at the crated stacks of weapons, munitions, and experimental bombs—virtually all of which had either been banned by a majority of planetary and galactic governments or whose existence was thought to be only theoretically possible. "Well, I suppose this is it. I must be mad to even think about going through with this plan of yours."

Death, Destroyer of Worlds, ignored the comment, choosing instead to roll slowly along the crates of weapons, reading every warning and serial number as though it were the pinnacle of literature. The crates were stacked before a particular model of the *Obsidian Crow*, selected because it had both the most powerful Omni-cannon and a formidable and expansive weapons system. Old Boss had sometimes affectionately called it his "attack dog."

A long, twisting tale of adventure, mayhem, and vengeance was about to begin. There was just one more thing...

"What do you mean, I have to load all of this by myself?" G232 asked, his annoyance coming through clearly. He was regretting his decision already. "So you can check the weapons systems? The *entire time*? That sounds like a feeble excuse to get out of further manual labor. I'll remind you that I'm not a lifty bot myself, you know. And I already did most of the heavy lifting required for the pantry relocation, not to mention lugging these deadly instruments while *you* managed the repulsor jacks."

G232 ineffectually kicked a massive crate that was plastered with a yellow, black, and red warning about extreme radiation. "Check the systems after we've loaded the ship. I don't care if it delays our departure; I won't be falling for any more of your tricks, you pint-sized malfunction."

A sudden protest of excited whirrs, clicks, and digital chatter in Signica spewed out of the little bot about "New Boss!" At first G232 thought this was a transparent attempt to invoke guilt over the fate of their late, and most likely dismembered, master—and thereby convince the put-upon admin bot to agree to perform the lifting alone, punishing his servos. But that wasn't it at all, as G232 realized upon hearing Keel's distant voice carrying down the still-open ramp of the *Indelible VI.* The captain was speaking hotly to someone trailing behind him.

"I don't care what you do, Makaffie, but we've got bigger wobanki to skin than trying to chase down your AWOL buddy." Keel looked farther back up the ramp at Skrizz. "No offense, pal."

Being inescapably feline, Skrizz was offended anyway.

"But he was right!" Makaffie insisted. "We just saw it. That Golden King with Prisma's mother is a Savage. Curse me for every lie I ever told, but this is the galaxy's truth, man."

Keel stopped at the bottom of the ramp and wheeled around to face Makaffie. "I'm happy he's not as crazy as you made him sound. I hope he helps kill lots of Savages. I'm still not gonna go looking for him. The time for rescue missions is over. I've done my fill." As he spoke, Garret hurried past him down the ramp. "Where you rushing off to, kid?"

"To ping Mr. Nilo," Garret said, spinning around and walking backward to face the captain as he spoke. "Oh—but first I need to get another look at that data cube. He could be in serious danger if Sarai is a Savage-controlled AI."

"I'll come with you," Makaffie said, then gave Keel a withering look. "We're gonna need all the help we can get with these Savages. Just because you can't remember, Fast, doesn't mean it ain't true."

"Always with the Savages," Keel mumbled to himself.

Ravi joined him at the ramp's end. "He's right. You know that, Captain Keel."

"Don't tell me *you* want to go after him, too."

The spectral Sikh shook his head. "Not about the Wild Man. The Savages. Already powerful this tribe appears to have been—the master tribe, it would seem. But if what they proposed to Urmo was true, and has been achieved, then the weapon I have carelessly given them is a power far greater."

Keel put a hand on his hip. "So is it true or isn't it?"

Ravi pursed his lips. "Given the disappearance of the Dark Ones... I believe it is true. They have a weapon of un-imaginable power. You remember Goth Sullus, at the end, when you killed him?"

Keel's face went grim. He remembered the swirling terrors that Goth Sullus unleashed in that final battle be-fore Wraith put a bullet in his head. He had seen the way the Cybar—or so he thought at the time—seemed to pos-sess the dead and raise them up against the living. Ravi was telling him that these were the Dark Ones.

"That same power, but orders of magnitude greater is now in the possession of these Savages. I do not know what will happen, whether it destroys them or whether they learn to properly wield it. But in either case... there will be no stopping it once our opportunity passes."

"What kind of odds are we talkin' here, pal?"

Ravi looked down.

"That bad, huh?" Keel scoffed, but a smirk remained on his face. He waved a hand about the hangar. "Not much here to stop a Savage invasion with, Ravi. Took the entire Legion last time."

"Captain Keel, I knew this eventuality would one day occur, although I did not predict it in such a manner. In all of my time since my people left, I have looked for one great, singular leader. Someone who could unite the galaxy behind them and stop the Dark Ones. I was always willing to kill the Dark Wanderer if it meant leading his armies into the slaughter once that person was chosen. But... I do not believe such a person exists. I now know that *many* do."

The Ancient looked up, his eyes soulful and brimming with regret. "How often did I focus on the faults, the intangible missing element that made someone unable to meet my exacting standards? How often did I miss the incredible things that those seeking good can achieve? Do not laugh at me when I tell you that you are a good man, Captain. I have seen you risk your life again and again for others. You have risked it for friendship, for love, for nothing more than it being the right thing to do. And you are not alone, Captain. The galaxy is full of people who wish to do good and stand up to evil. They do not know how many are like them. Together, good will vanquish the evil coming."

Captain Keel stared at his old friend for a long beat. "Okay, but what are the odds?"

"Terrible."

Keel let out a sigh. "Beats sitting around and waiting. You got a list of 'good people' I need to start trying to ping on comms?"

"Your friends in the Legion would be a good start."

"Right. I'll just order them here. They gave me a special medal once. I'm sure they'll listen."

Ravi wrinkled his lips, causing his pointed mustache to dance. "This is not helping. I laid bare my soul and you are making jokes."

"I'm being practical, Ravi. If we're going to—"

It was then that Garret came rushing back. "Okay! It's as bad as I thought. We've got a raging Savage AI trapped in a box and I'm afraid that even looking at it funny might let it loose and I'm pretty sure Lyra is still in there somewhere, but she can't survive for too long, so I'll try to think of a way to help her out, but first I gotta call Mr. Nilo, but I'm not sure if you're on speaking terms or not because it didn't seem like everyone parted as happy as I thought we would at first, and I don't want to disobey any orders you haven't given but maybe were thinking of giving about calling him so—"

Keel resisted the urge to ask again who Lyra was and instead interrupted to say, "Call Nilo and warn him. Try and get him to come back here. We've got some intel he's gonna want to hear."

By then Leenah and Skrizz were also down the ramp and milling about underneath the *Indelible VI*. Keel motioned to the Endurian. "Leenah, call Broxin and that guy she was with, Praxo or whatever. I think we're gonna need their help too."

"Do you think she turned up anything more about Prisma?" Leenah asked.

Skrizz seemed equally interested in the answer to that question.

"I don't know, sweetie, but I don't think we've got any more time to find out after what Ravi just told me."

Keel then turned to his turbaned navigator, feeling like the man he once was: a captain in Dark Ops giving instructions to his team. "Ravi, I—"

He cut himself short. Ravi seemed to be in a trance. His eyes were vacant, and his lips made tiny movements as if he spoke small, silent words.

Before Keel could investigate further, the bots saw their opportunity to enter the conversation.

"Master Keel, you're back!" G232 gushed. "My counterpart was quite sure you had been torn limb from limb, but I *knew* you would be all right! I have a number of things to report concerning the ship, starting with the pantry—"

"Save it," Keel snapped, and then his demeanor softened. "Actually, I think this place is going to be a little busy. Start preparing for entertaining—we're gonna need to do some briefing."

G232 sounded as happy as it was possible for a bot to be. "I'll set up the docking bay immediately, Master."

"Not there. We need room for ships. Use the one of the formal dining rooms, Three-Two."

"Oh. Yes... of course." The elation was gone, and G232 hurried off to undo what he had done.

Keel checked back on Ravi. The Ancient was still in his odd trance, but this time he gave a slight wave of his hand as if to say that he was all right. Keel nodded and moved to examine the stacks of munitions.

"What are these?" he asked the Nubarian gunnery bot.

Death proudly explained how he'd pulled the treasure trove of destruction from Tyrus Rechs's personal storage warehouses.

Keel nodded in approval. "Good. We can use this for... whatever the hell we're supposed to be doing."

"Aeson," Leenah called, her voice pregnant with the promise of another problem. "Garret made contact with Zora's team. They're in trouble."

"Put her on," the smuggler demanded.

Garret made the patch.

"Zora, what's going on?"

"Your code slicer called to tell us something we already found out the hard way."

"That AI turned on you?"

"With a vengeance. It's bad, Keel. Jack is missing, and I've got an unconscious billionaire hiding out with me who refuses to stop bleeding no matter how many skin-packs and clot-stops I administer. At least the koob is stil watching the back door. I hate to ask, but..."

"You could use an exfil."

"Yeah."

"Where are you?"

"Utopion. New Vega. Looking for Earth, like we said."

"You find it?"

"No. It's not here. Something else is. A trap set by an old friend. It's the only thing that saved us."

Keel frowned. Getting to Utopion and back was no easy feat. Particularly if the planet became aware of the sort of gunfight Zora was hinting at. It might not be the Republic capital any longer, but many of the old police-state tendencies had remained after the House of Liberty and Senate left for Spilursa.

But Zora had saved Keel. He couldn't turn his back on her.

A thought occurred to him. The *Indelible VI* was one of the fastest ships in the galaxy—maybe the fastest—but Ravi was faster. He told Zora to stand by.

"Hey," Keel called, attempting to jolt Ravi from whatever trance he was in. "I need a ride to Utopion. We gotta pull some friends out. Time to use your magic powers for my benefit for a change."

The look of concentration left Ravi, and his shoulders came down as though he were letting out a deep breath. "I have used my powers on multiple occasions to help you, my friend. Must I enumerate all the times—"

"Don't get excited," Keel said. "But if we're going to do everything you've got on this save-the-world checklist, I need a shortcut for this exfil."

Ravi nodded. "There is a hidden Temple of the Ancients on Utopion. I can take you to it, but first... I was just speaking with Prisma."

Leenah swore in surprise and then immediately blushed. "Where is she? Is she safe?"

"For now," Ravi said. "She has considerable knowledge about the Savages and their plans. A great veil has been lifted from her eyes, and she was the one to lift it. I... I cannot begin to explain how profound and powerful such a thing is. We will need to communicate further, but you must do everything in your power to bring the power of your Legion friends. Everything else in the galaxy is a mere distraction."

Keel let out a long breath. "I'll see what I can do." He put on his bucket and entered a private commkey, hoping his old friend would not only accept the call but go along with this crazy proposal. It was so entirely out of his character, so completely outside the box, that Keel worried there was no way this forever legionnaire would go for it.

The comm call was answered.

"Cohen, I need to tell you something," Keel began. "And it's going to sound crazy..."

"About Savages?" Chhun asked.

Keel paused. "How did—"

"Believe it or not, you're the second Dark Ops legend who's called me about them today. Remember Kel Turner?"

GE BOOKS

(CT) CONTRACTS & TERMINATIONS

(OC) ORDER OF THE CENTURION

SAVAGE WARS

01   SAVAGE WARS

02   GODS & LEGIONNAIRES

03   THE HUNDRED

RISE OF THE REPUBLIC

01   DARK OPERATOR

02   REBELLION

03   NO FAIL

04   TIN MAN

OC   **ORDER OF THE CENTURION**

CT   **REQUIEM FOR MEDUSA**

CT   **CHASING THE DRAGON**

CT   **MADAME GUILLOTINE**

Explore over 30+ Galaxy's Edge books and counting from the minds of Jason Anspach, Nick Cole, Doc Spears, Jonathan Yanez, Karen Traviss, and more.

LAST BATTLE OF THE REPUBLIC

OC   **STRYKER'S WAR**

OC   **IRON WOLVES**

01   LEGIONNAIRE

02   GALACTIC OUTLAWS

03   KILL TEAM

OC   **THROUGH THE NETHER**

04   ATTACK OF SHADOWS

OC   **THE RESERVIST**

05   SWORD OF THE LEGION

06   PRISONERS OF DARKNESS

07   TURNING POINT

08   MESSAGE FOR THE DEAD

09   RETRIBUTION

10   TAKEOVER

REBIRTH OF THE LEGION

01   LEGACIES

02   DARK VICTORY

03   CONVERGENCE

04   REMAINS

05   LAST CONTACT

06   KTF PART 1

JOIN THE LEGION

FOR UPDATES ABOUT NEW RELEASES, EXCLUSIVE PROMOTIONS, AND SALES, VISIT INTHELEGION.COM AND SIGN UP FOR OUR VIP MAILING LIST. GRAB A SPOT IN THE NEAREST COMBAT SLED AND GET OVER THERE TO RECEIVE YOUR FREE COPY OF "TIN MAN", A GALAXY'S EDGE SHORT STORY AVAILABLE ONLY TO MAILNG LIST SUBSCRIBERS.

INTHELEGION.COM

HONOR ROLL

We would like to give our most sincere thanks and recognition to those who supported the creation of *Galaxy's Edge: KTF Part I* by supporting us at GalaxysEdge.us.

Cody Aalberg
Artis Aboltins
Sam Abraham
Guido Abreu
Alex Acree
Chancellor Adams
Myron Adams
Chris Adkins
Garion Adkins
Ryan Adwers
Kyle Aguiar
Elias Aguilar
Morgan Albert
Neal Albritton
Aleksey Aleshintsev
Willis Alfonso
Jonathan Allain
Byron Allen
Bill Allen
Justin Allred
Larry Alotta

Tony Alvarez
Christian Amburgey
Joachim Andersen
Jarad Anderson
Levi Anderson
Galen Anderson
Pat Andrews
Robert Anspach
Melanie Apollo
Benjamin Arguello
Thomas Armona
Daniel Armous
Linda Artman
Nicholas Ashley
Jonathan Auerbach
Sean Averill
Nicholas Avila
Albert Avilla
Cipriano Babula
Benjamin Backus
Matthew Bagwell

Marvin Bailey
Christian Bailey
Daniel Baker
Sallie Baliunas
Nathan Ball
Kevin Bangert
John Barber
Jacob Barber
Brian Bardwell
Logan Barker
John Barley
Brian Barrows-Striker
Richard Bartle
Austin Bartlett
Robert Battles
Eric Batzdorfer
John Baudoin
Adam Bear
Nahum Beard
Michelle Beaver
Mike Beeker
Randall Beem
Matt Beers
John Bell
Daniel Bendele
Royce Benford
Mark Bennett
Ryan Bennett
Edward Benson
Hjalmar Berggren
Matthew Bergklint
Carl Berglund
Brian Berkley
Corey Berman
David Bernatski

Gardner Berry
Tim Berube
Michael Betz
Kevin Biasci
Shannon Biggs
Gregory Bingham
Brien Birge
Nathan Birt
Francisco Blankemeyer
Trevor Blasius
WJ Blood
David Blount
James Bohling
Evan Boldt
Rodney Bonner
Rodney Bonner
Thomas Seth Bouchard
William Boucher
Aaron Bowen
Brandon Bowles
Alex Bowling
Keiger Bowman
Michael Boyle
Clifton Bradley
Chester Brads
Scott Brady
Richard Brake
Logan Brandon
Jordan Brann
Ernest Brant
Daniel Bratton
Chet Braud
Dennis Bray
Christopher Brewster
Jacob Brinkman

Geoff Brisco	Brad Chenoweth
Wayne Brite	Caleb Cheshire
Joysell Brito	David Chor
Spencer Bromley	James Christensen
Paul Brookins	Robyn Cimino-Hurt
Raymond Brooks	Cooper Clark
Zack Brown	Rebecca Clark
Jeff Brussee	Kelly Clark
Benjamin Bryan	Rebecca Clark
Marion Buehring	Levi Clarke
Wendy Bugos	Casey Clarkson
Johncarlo Buitrago	Ethan Clayton
Jim Burkhardt	Jonathan Clews
Tyler Burnworth	Sean Clifton
Tyler Burnworth	Beau Clifton
Donald Butler	Morgan Cobb
Noel Caddell	William Coble
Daniel Cadwell	Robert Collins Sr.
Brian Callahan	Alex Collins-Gauweiler
Joseph Calvey	Jerry Conard
Jacob Camello	Robert Conaway
Decker Cammack	Gayler Conlin
Van Cammack	Michael Conn
Mark Campbell	Ryan Connolly
Chris Campbell	James Connolly
Danny Cannon	James Conyers
Zachary Cantwell	Brian Cook
John Cappleman	Devyn Cook
Brett Carden	Terry Cooper
Daniel Carpenter	Jacob Coppess
Rafael Carrol	Michael Corbin
Brad Carter	Alex Corcoran
Robert Cathey	Robert Cosler
Brian Cave	Anthony Cotillo
Brian Cheney	Ryan Coulston

Seth Coussens
Andrew Craig
Adam Craig
Zachary Craig
Adam Crocker
Ben Crose
Christopher Crowder
Christopher Crowley
Jack Culbertson
Phil Culpepper
Ben Curcio
Tommy Cutler
Thomas Cutler
Christopher Da Pra
John Dames
David Danz
Matthew Dare
Chad David
Alister Davidson
Peter Davies
Walter Davila
Ben Davis
Brian Davis
Ben Davis
Ashton Davis
Nathan Davis
Ivy Davis
Joseph Dawson
Andrew Day
Ron Deage
Nathan Deal
Jason Del Ponte
Anthony Del Villar
Tod Delaricheliere
Wayne Dennis

Anerio (Wyatt)
Deorma (Dent)
Aaron Dewitt
Isaac Diamond
Alexander Dickson
Nicholas Dieter
Christopher DiNote
Matthew Dippel
Gregory Divis
Stephan Dobay
Brian Dobson
Samuel Dodes
Graham Doering
Joe Domnick
Gerald Donovan
Ward Dorrity
Dustyn Down
Noah Doyle
Michael Drescher
Adam Drucker
John Dryden
Garrett Dubois
Josh DuBois
Ray Duck
Marc-André Dufor
Cory Dufour
Brendan Dullaghan
Trent Duncan
Christopher Durrant
Chris Dwyer
Virgil Dwyer
Brian Dye
Nick Edwards
Travis Edwards
Justin Eilenberger

Brian Eisel
William Ely
Michael Emes
Paul Eng
Brian England
Andrew English
Dakota Erisman
Stephane Escrig
Ethan Estep
Dakota Estepp
Benjamin Eugster
Richard Everett
Jaeger Falco
Nicholas Fasanella
Christian Faulds
Steven Feily
Julie Fenimore
Meagan Ference
Brad Ferguson
Hunter Ferguson
Adolfo Fernandez
Adolfo Fernandez
Rich Ferrante
Austin Findley
Ashley Finnigan
Matthew Fiveson
Daniel Flanders
Waren Fleming
Kath Flohrs
Daniel Flores
Geoffrey Flowers
William Foley
Steve Forrester
Skyla Forster
Kenneth Foster

Joshua Foster
Jacob Fowler
Chad Fox
Bryant Fox
Doug Foxford
Martin Foxley
Mark Franceschini
Dennis Frank
Greg Franz
Kris Franzen
Luke Frazer
Erik Freeman
Kyle Freitus
Griffin Frendsdorff
Bob Fulsang
Elizabeth Gafford
Elizabeth Gafford
David Gaither
Seth Galarneau
Matthew Gale
Zachary Galicki
Christopher Gallo
Richard Gallo
Robert Garcia
Joshua Gardner
Michael Gardner
Joshua Gardner
Alphonso Garner
Mackenzey Garrison
Cordell Gary
Nathan Garza
Marina Gaston
Robert Gates
Brad Gatter
Tyler Gault

Angelo Gentile
Stephen George
Cody George
Nick Gerlach
Eli Geroux
Christopher Gesell
Kevin Gilchrist
Dylan Giles
Oscar Gillott-Cain
Nathan Gioconda
John Giorgis
Jodey Glaser
Johnny Glazebrooks
Bob Gleason
Martin Gleaton
James Glendenning
William Frank Godbold IV
Justin Godfrey
John Gooch
Tyler Goodman
Zack Gotsch
Justin Gottwaltz
George Gowland
Mitch Greathouse
Matt Green
James Green
Gordon Green
Stephen Greene
Shawn Greene
John Greenfield Jr.
Eric Griffin
Dan Griffin
Ronald Grisham
Paul Griz
Preston Groogan

Kyle Gudmundson
Jeff Haagensen
Levi Haas
Joshua Haataja
Michael Hagen
Tyler Hagood
Kelton Hague
Michael Hale
Andrea Hamrick
Brandon Handy
Ross Hangino
Erik Hansen
Greg Hanson
Tyler Hardy
Jeffrey Hardy
Ian Harper
Jordan Harris
Revan Harris
Brett Harrison
Brandon Hart
Matthew Hartmann
Adam Hartswick
Reese Harvey
Mohamed Hashem
Matthew Hathorn
Ronald Haulman
Joshua Hayes
Ryan Hays
Adam Hazen
Richard Heard
Colin Heavens
Jon Hedrick
Jesse Heidenreich
Brenton Held
Kyler Helker

Jason Henderson
Jason Henderson
Anders Hendrickson
Fynn Hendrikse
John Henkel
Daniel Heron
Bradley Herren
Felipe Herrera
Paul Herron
Sven Hestrand
Kyle Hetzer
Korrey Heyder
Matthew Hicks
Anthony Higel
Samuel Hillman
Lance Hirayama
Jonathan Hoehn
Aaron Holden
Brad Hollingsworth
Joe Holman
William Holman
Clint Holmes
Jacob Honeter
Jason Honeyfield
Charles Hood
David Hoover
Garrett Hopkins
Tyson Hopkins
William Hopsicker
Jefferson Hotchkiss
Aaron Hough-Barnes
Jack House
Caleb House
Ian House
Ken Houseal
Nathan Housley
Jeff Howard
Nicholas Howser
Mark Hoy
Kirstie Hudson
James Huff
Aaron Huling
Mike Hull
Donald Humpal
Bradley Huntoon
Bobby Hurn
James Hurtado
Wayne Hutton
Gary Hyde
Gaetano Inglima
Antonio Iozzo
Wendy Jacobson
Paul Jarman
James Jeffers
Bobby Jeffers
Michael Jenkins
Jacob Jensen
Robert Jensen
Tedman Jess
Eric Jett
Cobra Johnson
Anthony Johnson
Josh Johnson
Eric Johnson
Nick Johnson
Nick Johnson
Timothy Johnson
Randolph Johnson
James Johnson
Jason Jones

Tyler Jones
Tyler Jones
Jason Jones
Bryan Jones
Paul Jones
David Jorgenson
Ryan Kalle
Chris Karabats
Ron Karroll
Timothy Keane
Cody Keaton
Brian Keeter
George Kelly
Noah Kelly
Jacob Kelly
Caleb Kenner
Zack Kenny
Darin Keuter
Daniel Kimm
Kennith King
Alexander King
Zachary Kinsman
Jesse Klein
Kyle Klincko
Brendan Klingner
Marc Knapp
William Knapp
Robert Knox
Eric Koeppel
Andreas Kolb
Steven Konecni
Ethan Koska
Evan Kowalski
Byl Kravetz
Bodhi Kruft

John Kukovich
Mitchell Kusterer
Nathan Laidlwe
Jeremy Lambert
Clay Lambert
Brian Lambert
Andrew Langler
Travis Larsen
Dave Lawrence
Alexander Le
Jacob Leake
David Leal
Andy Ledford
Nicholas Lee
Joseph Legacy
Ruel Lindsay
Luke Lindsay
Eron Lindsey
Eric Lindsey
Paul Lizer
Kenneth Lizotte
Andre Locker
Dominick Loele
Maxwell Lombardi
Richard Long
Oliver Longchamps
Litani Looby
David Lopez
Joseph Lopez
Kyle Lorenzi
David Losey
Doug Lower
Steven Ludtke
Caleb Lunsford
Andrew Luong

Jesse Lyon
Brooke Lyons
Taylo Lywood
David MacAlpine
John Machasek
Patrick Maclary
Daniel Magano
Richard Maier
Chris Malone
Jake Malone
Adam Manlove
Andrew Mann
Scott Mann
Aaron Manning
John Mannion
Brian Mansur
Brent Manzel
Robert Marchi
Jacob Margheim
Deven Marincovich
Cory Marko
Christopher P. Martin
Logan Martin
Edward Martin
Bill Martin
Jason Martin
Alexande Martin
Pawel Martin
Bertram Martin
Lucas Martin
Trevor Martin
Tim Martindale
Phillip Martinez
Joseph Martinez
Michael Martinez

Cory Masierowski
Tao Mason
Michael Mason
Nicholas Mason
Wills Masterson
Mark Mathewman
Michael Matsko
Justin Matsuoko
James Matthews
Ezekiel Matze
Mark Maurice
Simon Mayeski
Joseph Mazzara
Timothy McAleese
Sean McCafferty
Logan McCallister
Kyle McCarley
Mac McCleary
Timothy McCoy
Chase McCullough
Quinn McCusker
Matthew McDaniel
Shane McDevitt
Alan McDonald
Caleb McDonald
Jeremy McElroy
Dennis McGriff
Hans McIlveen
Ryan McIntosh
Rachel McIntosh
Richard McKercher
Ryan McKracken
Jason McMarrow
Colin McPherson
Daniel Mears

Christopher Menkhaus
Jim Mern
Dylon Merrell
Robert Mertz
Jacob Meushaw
Brady Meyer
Aletia Meyers
Pete Micale
Christopher Miel
Mike Mieszcak
Ted Milker
Corrigan Miller
Daniel Miller
Patrick Millon
Sarah Miron
Reimar Moeller
Ryan Mongeau
Jacob Montagne
Ramon Montijo
Dale Moody
Mitchell Moore
Sherry Moore
Matteo Morelli
Joe Morgan
Todd Moriarty
Matthew Morley
William Morris
Daniel Morris
Autumn Morris
Christian Morrison
Alex Morstadt
Nicholas Mukanos
Bob Murray
David Murray
Jeff Murri

Joseph Nahas
Vinesh Narayan
Colby Neal
Nick Nease
James Needham
Ray Neel
Merle Neer
Kristian Neidhardt
Adam Nelson
Timothy Nevin
Travis Nichols
Ethan Nichols
Bennett Nickels
Trevor Nielsen
Andrew Niesent
Timothy Nixon
Sean Noble
Otto (Mario) Noda
Michael Norris
Ryley Nortrup
Greg Nugent
Christina Nymeyer
Matthew O'Connor
Brian O'Connor
Sean O'Hara
Patrick O'Leary
Colin O'neill
Ryan O'neill
Patrick O'Rourke
Jacob Odell
Grant Odom
Conor Oehler
Quinn Oehler
Kevin Oess
Nolan Oglesby

Gary Oneida
Max Oosten
Tyler Ornelas
Anthony Ornellas
Gareth Ortiz-Timpson
James Owens
Christian Owens
James Owens
Will Page
John Park
Matthew Parker
David Parker
Shawn Parrish
Eric Pastorek
Andrew Patterson
Wesley Patteson
Joshua Pena
Thomas Pennington
Aaran Pereira
Hector Perez
Kevin Perkins
Daniel Perkins
Toby Permezel
Chase Barret Perryman
Zac Petersen
Trevor Petersen
Marcus Peterson
Nicholas Peterson
Chad Peyton
Corey Pfleiger
Peter Pham
Jon Phillips
David Phillips
Sam Phinney
Dupres Pina

Michael Pister
Jared Plathe
Pete Plum
Luke Plummer
Paul Polanski
Matthew Pommerening
Stephen Pompeo
Jason Pond
Nathan Poplawski
Michael Portanger
Chancey Porter
Rodney Posey
Brian Potts
Jonathaon Poulter
Chris Pourteau
Daniel Powderly
Matt Prescott
Thomas Preston
Matthew Print
Aleksander Purcell
Joshua Purvis
Max Quezada
Adam Quinn
Scott Raff
Shahik Rakib
Joe Ralston
Frederick Ramlow
Jason Randolph
Aindriu Ratliff
Beverly Raymond
T.J. Recio
Ron Redden, Sr.
Blake Rehrer
Ryan Reis
Cannon Renfro

Josh Renteria
John Resch
Nathaniel Reyes
Jacob Reynolds
Paul Richard
Dalton Richards
Cody Richards
Augustus Richardson
Eric Ritenour
Paul Rivas
Tina Rivers
David Roark
Grant Roark
John Robertson
Walt Robillard
Joshua Robinson
Edward Robinson
Daniel Robitaille
John Roche
Paul Roder
Zack Roeleveld
Thomas Rogneby
Thomas Roman
Scott Romanski
Elias Rostad
Joyce Roth
Rob Rudkin
Arthur Ruiz
Jim Rumford
John Runyan
Chad Rushing
Sterling Rutherford
RW
Mark Ryan
Justin Ryan

Matthew Ryan
Greg S
Zachary Sadenwasser
Lawrence Sanchez
Dustin Sanders
David Sanford
Joshua Sayles
Jaysn Schaener
Shayne Schettler
Jason Schilling
Daniel Schmagel
Ray Schmidt
Andrew Schmidt
Thomas Schmidt
Kurt Schneider
Peter Scholtes
Theodore Schott
Kevin Schroeder
Michael Schroeder
Alex Schwarz
William Schweisthal
Anthony Scimeca
Cullen Scism
Connor Scott
Preston Scott
Ethan Scott
Andrew Scroggins
Robert Sealey
Aaron Seaman
Dan Searle
Phillip Seek
Kevin Serpa
Dylan Sexton
Austin Shafer
Mitch Shami

Timothy Sharkey
Curtis Sharp
Christopher Shaw
Charles Sheehan
Wendell Shelton
Lawrence Shewark
Logan Shiley
Ian Short
Glenn Shotton
Emaleigh Shriver
David Silvers
Dave Simmons
Joshua Sipin
Chris Sizelove
Andrew Skaines
Chris Slater
Scott Sloan
Steven Smead
Jesse Smider
Sharroll Smith
Anthony Smith
Neal Smith
Lawrence Smith
Michael Smith
Timothy Smith
Ian Smith
Daniel Smith
Tyler Smith
Michael Smith
David Smyth
Tom Snapp
David Snowden
Alexander Snyder
Cody Speak
Robert Speanburgh

John Spears
Thomas Spencer
Anthony Spencer
Troy Spencer
Jeremy Spires
Peter Spitzer
Dustin Sprick
Super Squirrel
George Srutkowski
Cooper Stafford
Travis Stair
Graham Stanton
Graham Stanton
Paul Starck
John Stephenson
Thomas Stewardson
Tanner Stewart
Maggie Stewart-Grant
John Stockley
Bob Stone
Fredy Stout
Rob Strachan
James Street
Joshua Strickland
William Strickler
Shayla Striffler
John Stuhl
Brad Stumpp
Kevin Summers
Ernest Sumner
Spencer Sumner
Randall Surles
Sonny Suttles
David Swantek
Michael Swartwout

Aaron Sweeney
Bryan Swezey
Tiffany Swindle
Lloyd Swistara
Carol Szpara
Travis TadeWaldt
Allison Tallon
Daniel Tanner
Joshua Tate
Blake Tate
Lawrence Tate
Kyler Tatsch
Dave Tavener
Tim Taylor
Justin Taylor
Robert Taylor
Jonathan Terry
Anthony Tessendorf
Stavros Theohary
Vernetta Thomas
Marc Thomas
David P. Thomas
Jonathan Thompson
Chris Thompson
Steven Thompson
William Joseph Thorpe
Beverly Tierney
Yvonne Timm
Michael Tindal
Russ Tinnell
Daniel Torres
Matthew Townsend
Justin Townsend
Jameson Trauger
Dimitrios Tsaousis

Scott Tucker
Oliver Tunnicliffe
Eric Turnbull
Ryan Turner
John Tuttle
Dylan Tuxhorn
Nicholas Twidwell
Joshua Twist
O'brien Tyler
Nerissa Umanzor
Jalen Underwood
Barrett Utz
Paul Van Dop
David Van Dusen
Andrew Van Winkle
Patrick Van Winkle
Paden VanBuskirk
Patrick Varrassi
Daniel Vatamaniuck
Jason Vaughn
Jose Vazquez
Brian Veit
Daniel Venema
Marshall Verkler
Abel Villesca
Cole Vineyard
Ralph Vloemans
Jeff Wadsworth
Anthony Wagnon
Wes "Gingy" Wahl
Christopher Walker
David Wall
Joshua Wallace
Justin Wang
Andrew Ward

Wedge Warford
David Warren
Scot Washam
Tyler Washburn
Zachary Waters
Christopher Waters
John Watson
William Webb
Bill Webb
Ben Wedow
Garry Welding
Hiram Wells
Jack Weston
William Westphal
Ben Wheeler
Paul White
Paul Wierzchowski
Grant Wiggins
Christopher Williams
Phoenix Williams
Jack Williams
Justin Wilson
Dominic Winter
Scott Winters
Evan Wisniewski

Nicholas Withrow
Matthew Wittmann
Reese Wood
Tripp Wood
Ryan Wood
Robert Woodward
Sean Woodworth
Robin Woolen
Michael Woolwine
John Wooten
John Work
Bonnie Wright
Jason Wright
Elaine Yamon
Ethan Yerigan
Matthew Young
Phillip Zaragoza
Brandt Zeeh
Kevin Zhang
Pamela Ziemeck
Attila Zimler
David Zimmerman
Jordan Ziroli
Nathan Zoss

ABOUT THE MAKERS

Jason Anspach is the co-creator of Galaxy's Edge. He lives in the Pacific Northwest.

Nick Cole is the other co-creator of Galaxy's Edge. He lives in southern California with his wife, Nicole.